ALL AMERICAN BOY

AN AMERICAN BOY

ALL AMERICAN BOY

A Novel

William J. Mann

OPEN ROAD

INTEGRATED MEDIA
NEW YORK

Portions of this work first appeared, in slightly different versions, in the following anthologies:
His 2: Brilliant New Gay Fiction (eds. Robert Drake and Terry Wolverton),
Boston: Faber and Faber, 1997.
Shadows of Love (ed. Charles Jurrist), Boston: Alyson Publications, 1988.
Shadows of the Night (ed. Greg Herren), New York: Harrington Park Press, 2004.
Sons of Darkness (eds. Michael Rowe and Thomas S. Roche), San Francisco: Cleis Press, 1996.

ISBN: 978-1-5040-8768-1

This edition published in 2023 by Open Road Integrated Media, Inc.
180 Maiden Lane
New York, NY 10038
www.openroadmedia.com

For Tim

ALL AMERICAN BOY

1

BROWN'S MILL

His hands, as Wally remembers them, were like the gnarled, twisted fruit left behind on the trees when the apple-pickers were through.

Not like the hands of the boys he's watching now: soft hands, smooth, cupping each other's hard pink butts. They don't know Wally can see them. They think they're hidden among the trees, but Wally knows where to look, how to spy secrets in the shadows. He watches as the boys kiss, as they unbutton each other's shirts. He watches their faces, their tongues. But it's their *hands* that fascinate him most: hands so unlike the ones he remembers from this place, hands that remain forever twisted, forever beautiful, in his mind.

As a boy, Wally had loved this orchard, the sweet fragrance of the cider, the hard tartness of the apples. He remembers the way the juice would spit in his face when he took his first bite, how Zandy would laugh, apple juice dripping from Wally's chin. Here, in the shadows of the apple trees, they would make love, Zandy's gnarled hands splayed against Wally's smooth young skin.

So it is still a place of sex, Wally thinks as he spies on the boys. They're exquisite. Nothing about them reminds Wally of the boys of the city, the ones who have traipsed through his bedroom these last few years, hard-edged children with ambition and presumption. So unlike these boys here, making love in the woods. These are simple boys, the milk under the cream, boys who will remain in Brown's Mill all their lives, indifferent to the flash and lure of the city. Wally might have been like them, had it not been for Zandy.

His breath is steaming the window. The show is almost over now: one of the boys drops to his knees and fills his mouth with cock. It doesn't take long. The standing boy ejaculates, the other swallows, and then they both stumble out from the bushes. Wally watches as they mount their respective bicycles and pedal off in opposite directions. Somewhere in the orchard a crow lets out a long and scandalized cry.

Wally rolls down his window and takes time to breathe. The autumn air is sharp in his nostrils, sharp and cold, sharp and clear, sharp and blue, very blue, the hard blue of a cloudless sky. He looks out into the orchard. By now its apples have been packed into crates and shipped into stores, baked into pies and dropped into lunch bags. All gone, except for the few twisted ones left behind on the branches, tiny deformed babies that cling desperately to the cold limbs, ugly stepchildren who have aged too quickly, abandoned by their beautiful brethren, picked over and left to rot.

Would you come home, Walter? Please?

It's time to go. He didn't come back to Brown's Mill to spy on boys making love in the woods. He came here because his mother had asked him to. That she would make the request remains surprising enough. The fact that Wally agreed, however, is by far the bigger surprise.

Given what had happened.

Here, in the orchard.

All those years ago.

"Would you come home, Walter? I—I don't know what's happening to me."

They hadn't spoken in four years. Hadn't *seen* each other in over a decade, since Wally left Brown's Mill for college in the city. His mother's call had cut through a rare lazy Tuesday morning free of auditions or casting calls. Wally had had hopes of sleeping in, of taking the day off, but the shriek of the telephone shot through his morning at a little past eight. He'd been awake, but in that dreamy place between night and day, between oblivion and consciousness, sporting an impressive morning bone and contemplating vaguely what to do about it. That's when the shrill ring of the phone shattered his mood. And his morning. And the rest of his day.

"Please, Walter? I don't know what else to do."

He closed his eyes. "Are you still seeing Doctor Fitzgerald?"

"No, no, no, he died, Walter. Years ago."

"Then you need to find a new doctor, Mom. I can't do anything for you."

"But, Walter, I—I think I may be losing my mind."

Wally resisted the temptation to tell his mother that that had already occurred many years ago. How else to explain everything she'd done—or *hadn't* done?

"Please, Walter?"

He finally lied and told her he'd come, just so he could get her off the phone and out of his life, but his hard-on was gone and the morning already felt different. He threw off the sheets and got out of bed.

That's when he got the second call. From Officer Sebastian Garafolo of the Brown's Mill police department.

Egg salad in his walrus mustache. That's the image the voice brought back after so many years. Egg salad in his mustache, and on the collar of his blue shirt, and his breath was reeking when Wally walked into the station and admitted that yes, he'd had sex with Alexander Reefy in the orchard.

"How long has this been going on?"

"Since I was thirteen," Wally said, and then, without any hesitation, without any compunction, signed his name to the complaint.

"I'm looking for your cousin Kyle. Do you know where he is?"

Over the phone, Garafolo's voice sounded exactly the same as it had twenty years ago. Wally imagined he was sitting at the exact same desk, still eating egg salad and wearing the same stained blue shirt.

"Why would I know where Kyle is?" Wally could feel the irritation tighten his throat. First his mother's call. Now this even more egregious reminder of a past he tried to forget. "I haven't seen Kyle in years. Why would you call *me*?"

"Well, your mother reported him missing."

"My mother?"

"He was living with her. You didn't know that?"

"No."

There was no reclaiming the day now. Wally might just as well have gone back to bed after Officer Garafolo and his smelly egg salad breath had been thrust back into his life. But he pulled on his sweatpants, intending to take a run in the park. Yet by the time he got down to the street, it had started to rain.

Once past the orchard hills, the road winds its way back down into the town. From here Wally can see the brownstone spire of St. John the Baptist, the red brick of the old factories, the swampy blackness of Dogtown. On a sweltering summer day a little over three decades ago, Wally was born down there, almost killing his mother in the process. Nineteen hours, she was in labor with him. Finally they had to knock her out and cut her open. The neighbors clucked that she was too old to have a baby, too frail. She should never have tried it. Remember what happened to her sister, they said. Those Gunderson girls weren't built for babies.

Wally drives into town. He knows these streets, these alleyways, crosshatching through the meadow and ending at the river. He knows the big white houses on top of the hill and he knows the shacks down in Dogtown, where the river floods every spring. He knows the places where kids hide so their parents won't catch them smoking pot or drinking Jack Daniels or sucking boys' cocks. He knows who walks these streets, who comes out by day and who by night. Brown's Mill hasn't changed. He can see that all too clearly. The world changes but Brown's Mill goes on, always the same, no matter the factories closing or the scandals of an All American Boy.

Wally Day, I know what you done, Kyle had taunted him. *I know it was you that sent that perv to jail.*

Yes, he had known, and so had the whole town. But Wally knew a few things, too. When Wally lived in Brown's Mill, back in another time, he knew everything there was to know. He would listen to his mother on the telephone sharing stories with the ladies from the church. He knew about the long, drawn-out saga of Gladys Millstein, who broke up the fifteen-year marriage of Ted and Jeanette McCarthy. He knew all about poor Dicky Trout, the TV repairman, who was turning into an alcoholic in front of their very eyes. He knew about Mr. Rogers, the guy at the bank in the pinstriped suit who cooked the books for old Mayor Winslow for so long, then opened up a bookie joint in the back of Floyd's Barber Shop.

For his entire sixteen years in this town, Wally knew all of its secrets. He'd listen to the clerks at the A&P, to the waitresses at Henry's Diner, to the old men on the steps of the post office who lamented the loss of the great factories even before Wally was born, rotting old husks of iron and brick that lined the swamps of Dogtown. Wally listened, and he watched. Watched old Mr. Smoke steal a pack of cigarettes at South End News. Watched Ann Marie Adorno make out with Phillip Stueckel in the choir loft, her big pimply tits heaving. Watched Freddie Piatrowski's father beat off in his basement to a greasy pile of *Penthouse* magazines. Watched Miss Aletha take off her wig when she thought she was alone. Watched, listened, without ever being seen, without ever being heard.

"You're not really going back there, are you?"

His friend Cheri had been unbelieving.

"My mother is a wreck," he told her. "This time she may really be going over the edge."

"So what are you going to do, have her committed?"

He laughed. "Maybe."

"What about—?"

"What about what?"

"Him."

"Zandy?"

Cheri nodded.

Wally sighed. "I don't even know if he's still alive."

He loves Cheri. Had he been straight—yeah, yeah, Cheri would say, she's heard that a million times. But it's true. Since Ned's death, Cheri's been the closest person in the world to him. They met on Wally's first day in the city seventeen years ago, when both were still bright-eyed teenagers, convinced they'd be famous by the time they were twenty. It was Wally's very first casting call, and he and Cheri both won small parts in the chorus of an off-Broadway revue that was supposed to be a smash but ended after six nights. Still, therein was born a friendship that has endured, and which Wally credits with keeping him alive.

So of course he told Cheri about Zandy. He told her about the sex in the orchard and the confession to Officer Garafolo. He told her how he'd rewarded the first man who'd ever loved him with a stretch in jail, and how that memory has dragged behind him for two decades, a broken slab of concrete tied around his neck.

"You want to see him," Cheri said. "That's why you're going home. It's not your mother."

Wally laughed. "No, it's my mother. Underneath it all, it's always my mother."

So they went dancing, a little dose of gaiety to hold Wally over during his journey back to the past. One too many cosmopolitans, with Wally waking up this morning with a headache and a major case of dry mouth. But it was worth it: to dance, to cruise, to laugh. How long had it been?

"Why don't we do this more often?" Cheri asked him.

"All right. Every Tuesday night then."

"I have psych drama class Tuesday nights."

"So Thursday nights then. No wait. I bowl on Thursday night."

"Well, it can't be Wednesday, either," Cheri said, "because I'm starting Pilates."

Wally just laughed and lifted her into the air. John Travolta and Karen Lynn Gorney in *Saturday Night Fever*.

The movie that had made Wally gay.

On the corner of Pearl and Washington streets, he passes the Piatrowski house. From their name on the mailbox, Wally deduces the family still lives there. Mr. and Mrs. and probably still Helen, too—but Freddie's sure to have moved on by now, married probably, divorced most likely, with a handful of kids. The big yellow Victorian still gives Wally the jitters. In an upper room lived Freddie's big-faced retarded sister Helen, who was always screaming. When Wally was very young and Freddie was his best friend, he sometimes slept over at the Piatrowskis, lying awake and listening to Helen scream. Her family would go on as if nothing were out of the ordinary, but Helen's screams unnerved Wally for weeks—for all of his childhood, in fact, he thinks now. Even in his own bed back at home, he'd be convinced he could hear her still.

That's Brown's Mill in his memory: Helen Piatrowski's screams bouncing off the brownstone of St. John the Baptist Church, echoing down Main Street through the abandoned factories into the streets of Dogtown, and finally to the little cul-de-sac where Wally grew up, in a ranch with an American flag out front and an unused basketball hoop growing rustier with each passing year over the garage.

He turns off the ignition in the driveway and looks up at his childhood home

It's the same. Even the trees and shrubs look the same, as if his mother had kept them trimmed back to what they were decades ago, frozen in time, like this entire town.

He sees a hand pull back the curtains of the large picture window. It flutters for a moment and then the curtains fall still.

Once, in another time, another world, Wally had loved his mother more than anything else in his life. He loved how soft she was, how blond, how without makeup she had no eyebrows or eyelashes, so fair was her color. "Dear Angel," the fellas had written across their pictures in her high school yearbook, which Wally had loved to peruse, looking at all the faces. "Dear Angel," the fellas had written. "Don't forget about me."

She would later tell him which ones had gone off to die in the war.

I think I may be losing my mind.

Wally takes a breath and opens his car door.

His mother had never reacted to the scandal he'd caused with Alexander Reefy. Never. His father had hit him, knocked him across the room—but Mom had never said a word, not even when the papers were full of it, not even when the other boys began taunting him, not even when Wally ran away from home and refused to leave the refuge of Miss Aletha's house. Not once had Mom spoken of it, not then, nor at any time since.

She knows nothing of my life, Wally thinks as he walks slowly up to the door. *Nothing.*

Please, Walter. Would you come home?

She opens the door and looks up at him with those round blue eyes of hers. They haven't changed. Big and round and blue. Penciled eyebrows arch across her pale powdered forehead.

"Hello, Mom."

"Oh, Walter, Walter, thank you for coming."

The house smells exactly the same as he remembers it. Perfume. Powder. Soap. A lady smell. That's why his father always hated it here, why he was never home longer than he had to be. Dad blamed Mom for making their son gay. Wally knew this for a fact, even if he had never heard his father utter those words.

"How many years it's been, Walter."

Does she expect an embrace? Wally doesn't offer one.

"You look well, Mom," he tells her.

"You, too, Walter. So handsome. The spitting image of your father."

She's wrong: he's blond, as Scandinavian as she is, blond and fair and blue-eyed. His father was dark, black Irish, black as night. But Wally makes no objection. He just strides past his mother into the living room. On a card table sits a half-finished jigsaw puzzle of the Taj Mahal.

He turns and looks back at his mother. "So why is Officer Garafolo calling me looking for Kyle?"

"Oh, Walter, Walter, he keeps coming by here, harassing me, asking me all sorts of questions—"

"Is that why you called me? Why you said you thought you were losing your mind?"

She touches her forehead with her fingertips. "I said that? About my mind?"

He glares at her. "What's going on, Mother? Was Kyle in some sort of trouble?"

"Oh, he was always in trouble. You know that. He was a bad boy. He wasn't like you, Walter. You were the good boy and he was the bad one. That's what your poor Aunt Bernadette always said. You know that."

"No, I don't, Mom. I don't remember anything about Brown's Mill and really don't care to."

His eye catches the framed photograph on the wall over the telephone set. The three of them. Mom, Dad, Wally. Wally is eight. He wears one of those big wide striped ties from the seventies. His father is in his navy uniform. Somber, angry, imperious, unsmiling.

Yes, the spitting image.

You were the good boy, Walter.

"It's really upsetting the way that policeman keeps coming by here," his mother is saying. "I'm at my wit's end about it. All the questions. I don't know what to do."

I lived here once. Wally has to repeat the thought to himself as he looks around the place. *I lived here. In this house. For sixteen years.*

Here, in this very room, he watched *Land of the Lost* and *Josie and the Pussycats* every Saturday morning, reeling from a sugar buzz of Lucky Charms. Over there in the dining room he ate his mother's turkey loaf and "Swedish goulash"—a mishmash of hamburger and Franco-American spaghetti that he'd loved so well. And in the bathroom, from the time he was twelve, he masturbated looking at pictures of bodybuilders in the ads in the back of Superman comic books.

"Are you still in there, Wally?"

His father would bang his fist against the door. Wally twitches a little, remembering.

"Jesus Christ, hurry up! What do you do in there anyway?"

Ah, but his father would find out. Once, when the door wasn't locked, Dad had caught him. He said nothing. He just grabbed the comic book from Wally's hand, glared down at it, and tore it up savagely, leaving the pieces on the floor.

"You can stay here, Wally," his mother is telling him. "Your room is still—"

"The same?" He laughs, looking over at her as she wrings her hands. "No, thank you, Mom. I've made other arrangements."

She looks hurt, but just for a moment. She's too caught up with losing her mind to spare much time for him. And wasn't that always the way?

"I need your help, Walter. *Please.*"

He sighs. "I can't give you the kind of help you need, Mom. You need a professional."

"Just one small favor, Wally. That's all I ask."

He studies her face. It, too, is the same. She's seventy-three, but she could easily pass for twenty years younger. Her blond hair has faded to gray, yet her eyes are still fluorescent blue, her skin still creamy and smooth. Only her hands have aged: wrinkled and spotted, with the veins raised and purple.

She implores him now with those hands. "One favor, Wally."

He looks at her. "What's going on, Mother?"

"I need your help."

"What kind of help?"

"I need you to get rid of a crate for me."

He blinks. "A crate?"

"Yes. Take it down to the swamp in Dogtown. It's too heavy for me to move. But I need to get rid of it as soon as possible."

Wally leans in close, studying her eyes.

"Will you do it for me, Walter? Please?"

"Why should I do anything for you, Mother?" he whispers, only inches now from her face. "What did you ever do for me?"

"Please, Walter. Please."

He backs off. "Where is it? This crate?"

"In the basement, Walter. Behind the furnace."

In Wally's last show, some moth-eaten musical touring upstate New York, he met an old woman. She was about his mother's age, fair and pretty like her too. Her name was Cora, and she'd been in show business since the days of vaudeville, tap-dancing behind Al Jolson and Eddie Cantor at the age of eight. Now the poor old thing was always forgetting her lines, and the director, fed up, was going to drop her. All she had were three simple sentences in a scene where she played a bag lady, but they always came out wrong, and in reverse order. So Wally cooked up a plan: he wrote her lines down on his shirt with a black permanent marker so she could read them. It meant he had to keep his back to the audience and never got to show his face, but Cora got to keep the job, and she was tremendously grateful.

One night, after the show, they sat in a coffee shop, still in their makeup and costumes. "Do you have someone special in your life?" Cora asked him.

Wally considered the question. "I have some good friends."

"But no special one among them?"

He hesitated. "I did. But he died."

Cora smiled. "What was his name?"

"Ned. His name was Ned."

"And was he your first love?"

"No," he admitted. "But close to it."

"And there's been no one since?"

Wally thought of the boys who'd paraded through his bedroom in the years since Ned had died. Boys only a few years older than he had been when he'd sent Alexander Reefy to jail.

"No," he told Cora. "No one since."

"But the world is a large place, Wally. There are others out there."

"Yes. But none like him."

"Of course not like him," Cora said. "Never like him."

In that short conversation, Cora had learned more about him than his mother had in his whole lifetime.

Heading down the staircase into the basement, Wally realizes that while Brown's Mill may not have changed, while his mother might not have changed, one important thing had. Once Wally had known all of Brown's Mill's secrets. He knew what was hidden where, which bodies might be found in whatever closet.

But no more.

Wally lifts the lid of his mother's crate and looks inside.

2

THE BASEMENT

Until she killed him, he'd been a moody sort with yellow hair buzzed close to his head and a wicked little smile that dared her to do it. And so, one day, she did. It was a bright, sunny autumn day, with orange maple leaves twirling through the air, and he was asleep on the couch. She had just finished working in the garden, turning the mulch for the winter, and she carried the iron rake in with her, raising it up and smashing it down into his face, aiming for his temple, while he slept.

Regina Day is a good woman. Everyone in Brown's Mill would agree to that. So much tragedy in her life: her mother, her sister, her husband, her son. Yet every Sunday, there she is, attending services at St. Peter's Lutheran church at the south end of Main Street. She's always giving generously whenever those adorable little Puerto Rican children come around from Dogtown, ringing her bell, collecting for the heart fund or the leukemia drives. And everybody in town gets a Christmas card from Regina, even that scandalous Gladys Carroll and the disgraced former Mayor Winslow.

Yes, Regina Day is a good woman. It's just that one day she'd had enough, and so she killed the boy. She was surprised by how easy it was to decide to do it. Never in her life had she made a decision so easily. She usually fretted and worried and hemmed and hawed. But this time it was a snap.

Even the killing was easy. The only difficult part was the cleaning up afterward. He'd gushed a great deal of blood, and an Oriental vase that had been her grandmother's had shattered when his arms flailed out and over the sides of the couch. Mopping and sweeping was what took a long time, and dragging the boy's body downstairs into the basement and stuffing it into the crate was especially arduous. Regina was an old woman, after all, seventy-three this year, with arthritis in her legs, and the boy had weighed at least a hundred and fifty pounds.

But once it was done, she sat down at her kitchen table and had a cup of orange tea and some graham crackers. Once her breath returned, she dialed the number for the police.

"Hello? Is this the Brown's Mill police department? Yes, this is Regina Day. May I speak with Officer Garafolo? Oh, yes, hello, how are you? I'm fine. No, no, it's not anything like that. I just—well, I want to report a missing person." Pause. "My nephew. Kyle Francis Day. He was in the navy. I think he's gone AWOL."

"Mother!" Walter calls up the stairs. "There's nothing in this crate but a bunch of old linens!"

Regina stands at the top of the basement stairs looking down.

"No, no, Walter, don't look inside—"

Her son has appeared at the bottom of the stairs glaring up at her. "Why in God's name would you want to sink a crateful of linens into the swamp?"

"Oh, dear, oh, dear," Regina says, gripping hold of the banister and starting down the stairs. Her arthritis twinges but she keeps going. She brushes past her son to hurry round the furnace and peer down into the opened crate.

Linens.

She begins moving them aside, digging underneath. The crate is filled with musty old linens. And has been for fifteen years.

Regina closes the lid and sits down on top of the crate.

"Mom," Walter says, and dare she think it? Is there a small hint of compassion in his voice? "What did you *think* was in that crate?"

"I—I'm not sure."

"Are you on any medications that might be—?"

"No. Well, for my arthritis. But I've taken those for years."

She lifts her eyes up at him. Yes, he does look like Robert. *Exactly* like Robert, so tall and handsome when she met him, resplendent in his uniform.

Would you come back to my room with me? Robert had breathed in her ear. *Before I head off to face certain death in the jungles of the Mekong?*

Oh, how Robert had dazzled her. He was younger than she was, and far more handsome than she deserved. In that moment, Regina had felt not like herself, but like her sister Rocky, who all the boys had fancied. Rocky—who was never afraid, who was always taking risks—

"Mom."

She looks up at her son.

"Does this have anything to do with Kyle?"

Kyle.

Dear God, I'm afraid I'm losing my mind . . .

"Mom," Walter says again

It happened before. Why not again?

"*Mother!* Do you have any idea where Kyle went?"

Not in the crate. Why had she thought he was in the crate?

I buried him. I remember now. In the back yard. The shovel . . . Yes, I took the shovel and I dug. Beside the poplar trees . . .

"He was a bad boy, Walter," she says finally. "Such a bad one. He got into so much trouble as a boy. You remember, don't you? You were a good boy, Walter, but he was bad."

"Stop saying that."

"Oh, but you *were* good, Walter. You—"

"You know what I did, Mother!" Her son is raising his voice now. "Stop saying I was a good boy!"

I dug a grave in the backyard. That's where he is. I'm sure that's where he is.

"You all wanted to make me out to be a good boy, but I wasn't." Walter is looking at her with hard, glassy eyes. "You know what I did, even if you won't talk about it."

"It was Kyle who was bad, Walter. Don't you remember when he stole that money from Father Carson? Oh, how ashamed poor Bernadette was. And then he got into that fistfight with his teacher. Remember, Walter? How embarrassing it was for the family?"

Walter laughs. "*That's* what embarrassed the family, Mother? Nothing else?"

Beside the poplar trees.

"A bad boy, Walter. That's what Kyle was. A very bad boy."

Already at ten Kyle was bad. Sitting beside his parents as Walter received his certificate from Sister Angela, Kyle had squirmed and made noises with his hands. "Farting noises," he'd called them, and though Bernadette had shushed him, it was to no avail. Sister went on singing Walter's praises, commending his perfect attendance and straight As, but Kyle would not be silenced. Regina felt a spitball land in her hair. Out of the corner of her eye, she saw Bernadette take the boy by the arm out of the room to spank him, but Kyle managed to wriggle out of her grip and run away, disrupting the whole ceremony.

Such a bad boy.

If only he had never come back.

"I'm sure your father will be very proud," Regina told Walter that day, shutting out Kyle's cries from her ears. She told her son to hold up his certificate so that she could take a photograph and send it to Robert on the aircraft carrier. Somewhere down here in the basement she still has the photos from that day, probably in one of those moldy boxes stacked against the far wall. But it doesn't matter where they are: she can see them clearly in her mind. Walter was wearing his Boy Scout uniform that day, and he was beaming, a big ear-to-ear grin, holding up the school certificate that proclaimed him a straight-A student. Regina had snapped a dozen photographs, sending them all to Robert. And when he got them, she was certain, her husband had passed them around to all of his men, boasting, "This is my son. My son Walter, the future admiral."

"Walter's a faggot! Walter's a faggot!"

Kyle was shouting from the back of the hall. His mother had finally caught him and was spanking him, but it made no difference. Still he shouted, still he tried to ruin Walter's moment.

"Mom," Walter is saying. "Come upstairs."

She stands but doesn't follow. The basement smells damp and musty. It's been years since she's been through all these boxes. So many of them are Robert's things. She has no idea what he might have been holding onto. After he left the service there were things he told her never to look at, never to open or ask questions about. So she never did. Boxes stamped USN have mildewed down here ever since he died.

"You ought to have your father's things," she tells her son.

"I don't want his things."

"Then *your* things, Walter. I still have all your things here. All your toys, your comic books, your school papers—"

"I have everything I need, Mom."

"But look, Walter. Do you remember?"

She bends down and retrieves from the cobwebs a plastic model of Frankenstein's monster. She holds it out to Walter, who takes it from her and looks down at it in his hands.

"I had them all," he says. "Frankenstein, the Wolfman, the Phantom of the Opera." He lifts his eyes to look over at Regina. "I glued them all together and then painted them."

"Oh, yes, Walter. How you loved your models."

"Dad said it was like playing with dolls."

Regina just makes a little sound in her throat.

"Don't you remember, Mom? How he said it was a sissy hobby? If I wanted to build models, why not of ships? Or airplanes?"

"You had a Dracula model, too. It must be here somewhere—"

"He brought me home a kit for an aircraft carrier. Do you remember that, Mom? When I never built it, he got so pissed he went into my room and broke my Wolfman model into bits, right in front of my eyes."

She finds the Dracula model and hands it over to Walter. He doesn't take it. He just stands there looking at her.

"You never said anything," her son tells her. "He did what he wanted. You never said a word."

"You were a good boy, Walter," she says. "You were a very good boy."

And he was. Straight As from first grade until ninth. Cub Scout, Boy Scout, Eagle Scout. Everyone said Walter Day would go far in life. That he'd make his parents proud.

Not like Kyle Day. Oh, no, not like him at all. Kyle Day shamed his parents. That's what sent poor Albert, Robert's brother, to an early grave, and why poor Bernadette, Albert's wife, took to drink. It was all Kyle's fault. He was a bad, bad boy.

That's why I did what I did, Regina tells herself. He was bad. To the core.

I buried him in the backyard. That's where he is. Out by the poplar trees.

"His car is still in the garage," Walter says, after they've gone upstairs.

"Yes," Regina agrees. "It's still there."

Her son sighs. "Wherever he went, somebody else was apparently driving." Walter gazes out at the car through the door between the kitchen and the garage. "Looks like the car meant a lot to him, the way it's been rebuilt and all."

"Oh, yes, it did," Regina says, looking at the car darkly. "He was always out there, working on it, polishing it."

It's a shined-up, repainted 1979 red and gold Trans Am. The interior is all-new black leather. Regina remembers when he had it installed, how he was out there all day, cursing, spitting, drinking beer.

"Odd that he'd leave it behind," Walter says.

"Yes. I suppose it is."

He's looking at her. "Why was he living here?"

"He had no where else after your Aunt Bernadette died."

"How long was he here?"

"This last time, maybe three weeks. But he'd been using this as his base for the past few years."

Walter sighs, walking into the living room. He passes by her jigsaw puzzle, moves a few pieces around with his fingers, then gives up. He sits down on the couch. Regina is watching him carefully. There had been blood on the couch. Can he smell it? Does he notice anything? Regina had washed the cushions as best as she could, then turned them over to hide any lingering stains.

She sits in a chair opposite her son. "How long can you stay, Walter?"

"Just a day or so."

"Are you sure you won't stay here?"

"No, thank you."

"You'll stay with—her?"

He nods. "Yes. I'll stay with Miss Aletha. I called her this morning."

She isn't really a her, Regina thinks. *She used to be called Howard Greer and the men always used to pick on him.*

"Before you go, Walter," Regina asks, sitting forward in her chair, "maybe I could ask you to do another favor for me."

He narrows his eyes at her. Once again he reminds her of Robert. "What's that?" he asks, not quite generously.

"I want to get some soil. I want to build a rock garden."

"Mom, it's October."

"Yes, well, I want the soil ready for the spring. I want you to just make a little mound of earth, out in back by the poplar trees."

The grave is shallow. Anyone can find it. Dogs will dig him up . . .

"Mom, these favors—"

"Please, Walter."

He leans back into the cushions on the couch. "Have you been getting confused like this a lot? Have you seen your doctor?"

"I told you. Doctor Fitzgerald died—"

"Then you need to see another doctor."

"All that's wrong with me is a little arthritis."

"You told me you thought you were losing your mind."

"I said that?"

He stands, seeming angry with her. She follows him with her eyes. Oh, but he is the exact likeness of Robert. He even walks the same way.

"Will you get the soil for me, Walter? Please?"

* * *

Did she ever love him? Of course she did. What a silly question. He was her son. A bright-eyed boy with so much imagination. He was like Rocky in that way. Oh, Walter would have loved his aunt, and Rocky would have loved him. Before Mama died, Rocky would put on little shows in the parlor, giving Regina songs to sing and parts to play. It's clear where Walter got his imagination. When he was a boy, he would make up stories and act them out in the backyard. He'd watch that vampire soap opera on television when he'd get home from school and then afterward run around the yard with a blanket, using it as a cape, biting imaginary girls on the neck. Sometimes Grace Daley would call from next door and say she'd been watching him talk to himself, suggesting that maybe he ought to see a psychiatrist. "Oh, he just has an active imagination," Regina would tell her. "He's just like my sister."

In fact, Bernadette had often wished Kyle was as creative as Walter. "All Kyle's interested in is fighting and soldiers," Bernadette had confided to her. "He scares me, Regina. He really does."

Give me the money, you crazy old cunt.

"He was a bad boy," Regina murmurs. "A very bad boy."

Kyle had had a girlfriend. Her name was Luz. Just a girl of eighteen, far too young for Kyle. After all, Kyle was Walter's age; they would have been in the same class at school if Kyle hadn't been held back in third grade, to Bernadette's undying shame. Kyle was more than *thirty* when he started seeing Luz, and Regina was simply horrified. He would bring the girl to Regina's house and he'd kiss her right here on this couch. Oh, but it was horrible to watch. From the hallway Regina would spy on them kissing and she'd cry. She'd just cry and cry and cry. Luz was a good girl. Regina knew that from the start—and it was because of Luz that Regina did what she did.

Luz Maria Carmelita Sanchez Vargas was her name. Almond eyes, black hair, beauty mark. She'd won a beauty contest at school in Puerto Rico, and Regina could see why. They became friends, Luz and Regina, with the girl seeming to like the older woman as much as Regina liked her. They'd sit together at the kitchen table while Kyle was out, Luz helping Regina with her puzzles. She was very good at them. And they'd talk, and drink orange tea, and laugh. It had been so long since Regina had laughed.

And, oh! How the police have hounded poor Luz. "They have been asking me all sorts of questions," Luz told her yesterday, near tears. "They said I had to know *something*. But I don't, Mrs. Day! *You* believe me, don't you?"

"Yes, of course, dear."

Every day since Kyle was reported missing, Luz has visited Regina. They don't talk much about him. They talk about other things, like the weather, and school, and how proud Luz had been to win that beauty contest. Luz makes Regina smile, and she's started helping her around the house, too. One day, the girl had spotted Regina wheeling her little cart of groceries and saw how difficult it was for Regina to lift the bags from it.

"Let me help you," Luz insisted.

"Oh, thank you, dear. Arthritis, you know."

Now, every week, Luz takes her grocery shopping and helps her clean around the house, vacuuming, dusting, scouring the sink. Regina watches the girl work as if mesmerized.

"Here," Regina said yesterday, when the girl had finished vacuuming. "Let me give you something." She opened her purse and pulled out a twenty-dollar bill.

"Oh, no," Luz objected. "Please, no."

"But can't I give you *anything* for your help, Luz?"

"No, no, no, Mrs. Day," Luz said. "I like helping you."

"Bless you, dear," Regina said, and snapped shut her black patent-leather purse. On its surface, Regina saw the reflection of her face.

"Mother."

Her eyes flutter back to her son.

"I think you need to see a doctor," he's saying.

Yes, there's compassion in his voice. Regina is sure of it.

"It's difficult for me to get around," she protests. It's true. She'd never learned to drive. Rocky died in a car crash. Regina can't imagine ever being behind the wheel of a car.

Walter sighs. "Make an appointment and I'll take you tomorrow."

She blinks.

"Will you do it?"

"All right, Walter."

He turns to leave.

"But the soil, Walter—"

He looks back at her.

"Will you get the soil?"

"Why am I doing *any* of this?" he suddenly shouts. "Why the fuck did I come back here?"

Regina takes a step backward, startled by his outburst. Yes, like Robert. So much like Robert.

"Because I needed your help, Walter," she says in a tiny voice. "You came because I needed your help."

"No, Mother. That's *not* why I came. Do you know why I finally agreed to come back to Brown's Mill? Any clue?"

She says nothing.

"Because I want to find Zandy."

Regina makes that sound in her throat again.

"You know who I mean, Mother." He says the name deliberately. "*Alexander Reefy.*"

She looks away.

"*He's* the reason I came back here, Mother. Not you. I want to find Zandy and apologize to him for sending him to jail."

Once, she'd been a girl who thought maybe, just maybe, she might become a famous singer. She and Rocky both. What did the Andrews Sisters have on the Gunderson Sisters? Regina and Rocky were both pretty enough and talented enough. "Voices as sweet as birdsong," the *Brown's Mill Reminder* had declared after their gig at the VFW hall. So they ran off to the city to become famous. Eventually, Aunt Selma sent Uncle Axel to reclaim them in his old Ford pickup truck, but for a while, there had been the stage, and the microphone, and all those servicemen applauding, hooting, whistling with their pinkies between their teeth.

She looks up at her son.

"The soil, Walter. Please will you get the soil?"

3

BEYOND THE RAINBOW

On the soundtrack: Judy Garland is singing "Somewhere Over the Rainbow."
On the screen: a door slowly opens, wiping away blacks and whites to reveal
bright primary Technicolors. Fade in on a rock garden, green leaves and orange
marigolds, and a little boy in a bright red shirt playing with shiny Matchbox cars
in the dirt.

"I'll get you, my pretty," Wally cackles, doing an awfully good Margaret
Hamilton for a seven-year-old boy. He drives a miniature Corvette straight into
a dump truck and cackles again.

The Wizard of Oz was on TV three nights before, and Wally's become
completely obsessed. He draws pictures of melted witches and asks his teacher
questions like, "What did the winged monkeys do with the melted witch-goop?"
He imagines that they used it to mold the witch back to life. After all, once the
witch was gone, the movie had become far less exciting, so Wally has mapped
out an elaborate sequel in his head. The Witch returns from the dead to capture
the Scarecrow and the Tin Man. Glinda gets tossed in the dungeon, and Dorothy
has to return to save the day. In his mother's rock garden, Wally plays all the
characters, using his Matchbox cars to enact the story because his father won't
let him play with dolls.

Sitting in the dirt, Wally decides he wants to be Dorothy. He wants all those
things that happened to her to happen to him. He wants a cyclone to pick him up
and drop him down in the middle of flowers and thatched cottages and round-
faced Munchkins. He wants to meet a pink lady in a flying bubble who wears
sparkling dresses. He wants to melt the Witch. And he wants to see the Emerald
City, most of all.

Lighting cue: sunny sky begins to darken. Heavy, black-rimmed clouds roll
in as if on fast-motion. Wally looks up, suddenly fearful, wide-eyed. He starts to
run, then stops, remembering his Matchbox cars. He scoops them up and darts
off toward his house, just as a thunderclap reverberates on the soundtrack. The
wind shrieks, the rain begins to pound.

Cut to: a gleaming kitchen with orange wallpaper and avocado green appli-
ances. "Take your shoes off if they're wet, Walter," a voice says. Close-up of
Wally's mother, a tired, attractive blond woman in her forties, standing at an
ironing board. She has large turquoise curlers in her hair.

"Are we having a cyclone?" Wally asks.

"No, I think just a thunderstorm," his mother replies, as if she's disappointed.

"Mommy," Wally suddenly announces. "I want to be a witch for Halloween."

"A witch?"

"Yes. And not a witch with a mask. I want to be a witch with a pointed hat and a long clay nose that you make for me."

"I don't know, Walter."

"Please?"

The thunder gets louder.

"Please, Mommy?"

"We'll see, Walter. Go to your room now and get ready for supper."

Fade to: a boy's room. There's a desk, a globe, and a poster of the Partridge Family on the wall. The door opens. Wally enters.

He jumps up onto his bed. He's listening to the roars of the thunder and feeling just a little bit afraid. What if a cyclone *did* pick up his house—tearing it from its cellar, ripping it out of the ground as if it were a weed, exposing a gaping, obscene hole in their half-acre lot in their quiet little cul-de-sac? What then? Mommy's gone outside; Wally can hear the regular squeaks of the clothesline as she pulls his shirts and underpants in from the rain. What if the cyclone picks up the house while he's in here alone? The thought terrifies. Suddenly Wally doesn't want to go to Oz. (On the soundtrack, the loudest boom yet.) He thinks of Dorothy in the Witch's Castle, and puts his pillow over his head.

Judy Garland's face suddenly fills the screen. "If I ever go looking for my heart's desire again," she says, "I won't look any farther than my own backyard."

Wally had lifted his face to his mother as he lay on the floor watching the final credits roll. His mother sat across the room, at a little table, putting together a jigsaw puzzle of the *Last Supper*.

"What does 'heart's desire' mean?" the boy asked.

His mother hadn't answered him for several seconds. "I don't know, Walter," she finally said. "I suppose it means something you want but you can't have."

Now Wally sits here on his bed listening to the thunder and thinking about Dorothy and her heart's desire. Whatever it is—and he isn't quite sure—Dorothy learned that it had been in her own backyard all along. He thinks of the stretch of lawn out behind his house. There wasn't much to his backyard, just his mother's rock garden and the three-foot-tall poplar trees his father had planted the last time he was home. Is that where it is, his heart's desire?

Last night, he'd slept over Freddie Piatrowski's house, developing a terrible case of homesickness. He had really been convinced that he wanted to stay the night, lugging over his sleeping bag and sixteen issues of *Action Comics*, but when it got dark and Freddie's sister Helen kept screaming upstairs, Wally started having second thoughts. Looking out the window, he saw his reflection in the dark glass, but he imagined instead he was seeing his mother's face, the way Dorothy had seen Auntie Em in the crystal ball. "I'm here in Oz, Mommy! I'm locked up in Mrs. Piatrowski's castle, and I'm trying to get home to you! Oh, Mommy, the hourglass is getting low!"

Close-up of a crystal ball: inside, Wally's mother is standing in the rain, hair pasted down around her face. A few clothespins are clasped between her teeth as she pulls in the drenched Fruit of the Looms from the line.

"But Mommy *said* I could be a witch."

"No, no, Walter, I didn't say yes." His mother's hands are fluttering. "I just said, 'We'll see.'"

Their lives have changed overnight. Wally's father, Captain Robert Eugene Day, has come home. Whether Wally's mother was expecting him, Wally doesn't know—but Wally certainly wasn't.

"No son of mine is going to be a *witch* for Halloween," Captain Day says.

"But that's what I *want* to be!"

"What you want isn't always what you get, son." His father considers the subject closed. "You'll need to learn that sooner or later."

The boy stands in the middle of the living room looking at his father, who sits in the big La-Z-Boy that no one ever uses while he's gone. But Captain Day doesn't return his son's gaze. He opens the *Brown's Mill Reminder* and begins to read.

Ever since he can remember, Wally has thought his father was very handsome. Wally likes how square his father's face is, how dark and shiny is his hair. And his uniform: it's shiny, too, with all those gold buttons and medals. Wally especially loves his father's hat. Inside there's a shiny satin lining that Wally loves to touch and place against his face. They have lots of photos of him wearing his father's hat.

"There he is," his father will say when he sees the photos. "My son, the future admiral!"

But it's not a navy hat that he wants to wear for Halloween. It's a tall black pointed witch's hat he desires, and Wally heads down the hallway to sulk in his room.

"You can go as the Scarecrow if you want," his father calls after him. "Or the Lion. We can get you a Lion's costume."

"I don't want to be the Lion."

"Well, those are your choices. Pick one of those or don't go trick-or-treating."

Wally stops walking. "Okay, I won't go."

To him, his answer is not sass. His father gave him a choice, and Wally merely chose the least objectionable option offered.

Captain Day, however, hears it differently. He looks up suddenly, throws down his newspaper, and leaps out of his chair in a terrible, violent flash. In seconds Wally's small arm is twisted behind his back and his father is spanking him hard, ten times on his baby butt.

Wally cries for his mother, but she is nowhere to be seen.

Iris-in on hands, kneading soil, sifting out stones through the fingers. Open to reveal Wally's mother, in her rock garden, planting chrysanthemums. She's wearing a kerchief as she kneels in the dirt. It's a bright, sunny day, and she's humming. Camera pulls back to reveal Wally not far away, playing with his Matchbox cars at the perimeter of the garden.

"Be careful when you play in here that you don't dig up the mums, Wally," his mother says. He makes a sound in his throat in acknowledgment.

Panorama of the yard: young, tender trees held up by wooden posts and white ribbon. A few blue lawn chairs are scattered near the patio, and a picnic table is topped by a slightly crooked red umbrella with white fringe. The back of the house hasn't been completely painted yet; much of it is still bare wood. The half that's finished is painted green: primary green, like kindergarten crayons. It's a ranch-style house, one floor and an attached garage that's still under construction. A blue rubber hose is coiled like a long, beneficent snake beneath the kitchen windows. Similar houses line the cul-de-sac, their half-acre lots evenly drawn, connecting to each other, dotted here and there by newly planted shrubs. Nobody has much grass, but lots of grass seed.

Wally's getting bored with the Matchboxes. He trots over to watch his mother plant flowers. He loves her rock garden. She's taught him the names of all her flowers. Mostly marigolds, but she has others, too, depending on the season: daffodils and narcissi, petunias and portulaca, pansies and petunias, sweet williams and Johnny-jump-ups. She's putting in some late-blooming mums, hoping to keep as much color in the garden before frost.

"Can I plant one?"

"All right, Walter."

"Show me how."

She digs a small hole in the soil with her hand and places the tender young plant inside. "Press the soil firmly around the stem," she says. "A flower needs a strong base from which to grow."

Wally reaches over for a mum, gently pulling it from the box of four Mom had bought at Grant's. He shakes its roots free from those of its siblings.

"Mommy," he asks as he pats down the earth around the plant, "who do you love more, me or Daddy?"

"Oh, Walter, what a thing to ask."

"I like it better when he's not here."

"That's not very nice."

"I don't want to be a Lion, Mommy."

She puts her hand over his, covering it. Wally looks down at her hand. Her blue veins stand up prominently and her wedding band is worn dull. Her chipped pink nails are caked with soil.

"Your Daddy just wants you to grow up to be big and strong like he is," she tells him.

"But I'm not like him, Mommy." Wally turns his eyes up to her. "I'm like *you*."

Cut to black.

* * *

He loves his mother more than anything in the world. More than *The Wizard of Oz*. More than his Matchboxes. More than Peter on *The Brady Bunch*. More even than Freddie Piatrowski, who Wally had announced in kindergarten as the person he would someday marry.

"Boys don't marry boys," his teacher had chided him, while the rest of class laughed. Wally's cheeks burned.

"You'll see," his father is telling him. "They're all going to laugh at you."

They're in the living room. His father is watching Wally's mother fit him in his costume.

"Then you'll say I was right. When they laugh at you, you'll wish you had listened to me."

"Hold still, Walter."

His mother is measuring the black cloth around the boy's waist, marking it with a safety pin. Wally looks down at the back of her blond head and feels his love for her just bursting out of his chest.

His mother is making him a witch's costume.

"But what about the hat?" Wally asks. "How are we going to make the hat?"

His mother gets up from her knees. Her joints crack and she winces a little from the pain. She opens the closet in the living room and withdraws a box.

"What's inside, Mommy?"

She removes the lid and lifts out a cardboard cone. It's white and has no brim, but Wally can see the possibilities.

"I had it made at the craft shop," his mother tells him. "We'll have to paint it black and add some cardboard around the bottom to make it look like a witch's hat."

Wally beams, placing the cone on his head.

"It's a dunce cap," his father says, finally looking over. "You'll see, Wally. They're all going to laugh at you."

One time, when Wally was staying with Aunt Selma and Uncle Axel, he'd fallen out of a tree. He hated staying with them. Uncle Axel told him scary stories and dribbled tobacco juice down his chin, so Wally had climbed up into the tree to get away. But on his way back down, he'd lost his footing and fallen flat on his stomach, knocking out his wind. Flapping his arms wildly, Wally tried to gulp air into his lungs, but it felt as if he were drowning. Uncle Axel just stood there, laughing at the sight of Wally flailing about, wheezing and turning blue. So hard did the old man laugh that afterward he got hiccups, for which he cursed the boy.

Wally hates being laughed at.

Another time, in one of those bizarre, unexplainable hysterias that suddenly take over children, Wally's entire class had decided to taunt him with "*Wally Gator, he's a swinging alligator in the swamp!*" Friends one day, tormenters the next. They ganged up around him in the schoolyard and sang at him as if the inane cartoon lyrics were curses. "*See ya later, Wally Gator!*"

And then they laughed.

"I don't care," Wally says, standing in his room, looking at himself in the mirror with his black witch's hat on the top of his head. His mother had done a very good job putting it together. "I don't care if they laugh."

But he does. He cares a lot.

They're all going to laugh at you.

He pulls the witch's hat off his head.

See ya later, Wally Gator!

"I don't want to go as a witch," he tells his parents.

His mother frowns. "Oh, Walter, but it took forever to make the costume—"

"But I can't wear it! They'll laugh at me!"

"That's right, they *will* laugh," his father says, suddenly looming in. "Which is precisely why you *will* wear it. You're going to have to learn to live with your choices."

"No, please! Don't make me!"

"You're behaving like a child," Captain Day snaps.

"He *is* a child, Robert," his mother says softly.

Wally sees the look his father gives to his mother. It's a bad look. There have been a lot of bad looks since his father has come home. Wally worries that the bad looks mean he'll soon be sent to stay with Aunt Selma and Uncle Axel again. That always happens when the bad looks start, and Wally hates staying with Aunt Selma and Uncle Axel.

So he doesn't complain again about his costume. He just sits in the back of his father's Buick Le Sabre with his hands clasped in front of him in the lap of his black dress. The putty nose on his face feels cold.

No one laughs. There are some stares, some curious smiles. But no one laughs when they walk into the auditorium.

"Captain Day, how honored we are to have you here," Sister Angela says.

"Welcome home, Robbie," says Mr. Piatrowski, clapping his father on the back.

Wally looks off past him. Freddie is dressed as Cornelius from *Planet of the Apes*. It's a plastic ape mask and a flimsy costume that Wally had seen on sale at Grant's. It's totally boring. It doesn't even have real ape hair.

His cousin Kyle is worse. Kyle's supposed to be a vampire but all he's wearing is a black cape and plastic fangs in his mouth. Everything else about him looks the same as always: red Scooby Doo shirt and blue frayed corduroys.

Some lady is bending down at Wally now, touching the tip of his long cold nose with her finger. "And what's Walter dressed as? A *witch*?"

"No, no, no," his father says. "He's a warlock. Aren't you, Wally?"

The boy looks from the lady to his father and then back to the lady again. She's wearing blue glasses and bright red lipstick and is smiling crazily.

"No," Wally says. "I'm a witch."

His father laughs. "Well, that's what a warlock is. A boy witch." He nudges Wally past the lady's prying eyes.

"You've embarrassed me in front of the whole town wearing that outfit," his father seethes. "Take off the hat."

"You wanted me to wear it."

"Take off the hat!"

"No," Wally says.

His father's lips go white. "Do what I say." He makes a grab for the hat.

"No," Wally says, ducking. "Mommy made it for me." He looks to her for help, but his mother is nowhere around.

His father is so white it looks as if his face will burst. "Give me the hat or take a spanking!"

Wally stands his ground. "I'll take the spanking."

His father's eyes nearly explode out of his head. His lips draw tight against his teeth and he makes a move toward Wally. But he stops himself. Just in time, too, because Wally's teacher, Sister Marita Claire, has come up behind him, and she's beaming.

"What a *creative* costume, Captain Day," she says. "I understand your wife made it."

"Yes," Wally's father says, his eyes still on his son. "She's very handy with a needle and thread, isn't she?"

"And for a boy to come as a witch. How very clever."

"Yes," Captain Day says. "Clever."

So that's how they'll manage it, Wally realizes. He's a clever boy with clever ideas. He manages to slip away from his father, his eyes searching for his mother. He finds her sitting by herself surrounded by empty rows of folding metal chairs.

"The awards will be given in a little while," she tells her son, holding her purse tightly in her lap. "I wanted to get a good seat."

"Can I sit here with you?"

"If you want, Walter." She seems to think of something. "But ask your father first, though."

Wally pays her directive no mind. "Mom," he asks, "do you think I'm a clever boy?"

"Why, of course, Walter. You always get good marks in all your subjects."

"No, I mean, do you think I'm *clever*? Like, clever in—you know, like how I do things?"

She's looking at him, clearly not sure how to respond. Before she has a chance to think of something to say, Wally feels a tug on his witch's dress.

It's his cousin Kyle, the so-called vampire.

"How come you're wearing a girl's costume?" Kyle asks.

"It's not a girl's costume," Wally tells him, wishing he'd just go away and leave him and his mother alone.

"Yes, it is," Kyle says, arms akimbo. "Witches are *girls*."

"I don't care. My mother made it for me."

He looks back at her for help but she's turned her gaze back toward the empty stage. Wally knows his mother used to perform on stages. She was a singer once, a long time ago, before she married his father. Once in a while he'll hear her sing around the house. She has a beautiful voice. Wally loves to hear his mother sing.

"You must really be a girl, Wally," Kyle taunts, his teeth like a donkey's when he laughs. "That must be why you're wearing a dress."

"Go away," Wally tells his cousin. "Or else I'll tell your mother."

Kyle just hoots and wanders off to find someone else to terrorize.

Wally slides in next to his mother and looks up at her. She gives him a little smile as she takes his hand in hers. Wally closes his eyes and remembers the last time he heard his mother sing.

"My little baby loves short'nin', short'nin', my little baby loves short'nin' bread."

Wally had watched her transfixed, as she sang herself silly, making a cake. It wasn't like his mother to sing and smile so much.

"Why are you making a cake?" he asked her. "It's nobody's birthday."

She'd covered her mouth with her hand. "No. It's for something else." She tried to look serious but the smile kept tricking the corners of her lips. "Your grandmother died, Walter. I'm making a cake for the get-together after the funeral."

Wally thought it was odd that his mother was smiling and singing when Gramma Day had just died. When his father came home from the ship, all solemn and serious, Wally's mother had quit her singing. She walked with him behind the dead lady's coffin with a very sad look on her face, but Wally had the feeling she still wanted to laugh, maybe even break out into song. She hadn't wanted Wally to attend the funeral, telling Wally's father that the boy was too young. But Captain Day insisted his son be there to watch his grandmother lowered into the ground.

Wally was glad to go. He loved coffins and the people in them. On *Dark Shadows* an old lady died and they laid her out in her coffin right there in the living room. She even opened her eyes and sat up, scaring everyone on the show. But as hard as Wally willed his grandmother to move, she remained still and waxy lying there in the funeral parlor.

I wonder what she looks like now, Wally thinks, sitting there holding his mother's hand, imagining the maggots and worms eating through Gramma Day's face.

"And the winner for the second grade's Most Creative Costume goes to our always imaginative Wally Day!"

Sister Marita Claire leads the applause. Everyone turns around in their chairs to find the little witch. Wally doesn't dare look up at his father. He just slides out of his seat and hurries down the row of folding chairs, his heart beating in his ears. He trips over his long black dress as he climbs up the steps to the stage, but quickly catches himself. He accepts his award from Sister: a small carved pumpkin with candy corn inside.

"I think it's marvelous that Wally came as a witch," Sister Marita Claire says into the microphone. "How very, very clever!"

Wally feels as if he might break down and cry, so much attention is suddenly thrust upon him. He seems to float back to his seat rather than walk, lost in the sound of the applause.

"He's a good boy, Robbie," a man tells Wally's father afterward. "Even in that girl's costume, he's still got your charm."

"A smart boy," another says. "Everyone says that about Walter. Smart and clever."

"Clever," his father repeats.

"He's going to go far, Robbie."

"That boy's going to make you proud."

"Congratulations, Wally," his Aunt Bernadette says, leading a tearful Kyle out of the auditorium by the arm. But she doesn't mean it. She's angry because Kyle never wins anything. He brings home Cs and Ds and his teachers all ask him why he isn't as smart as his cousin Wally.

"Will you stay for more cider?" Sister Angela asks.

"No, thank you," says Wally's father. "We have to be heading home."

"You must be so proud of Wally's creativity."

His father smiles.

"And might I add, Captain Day, how proud everyone in Brown's Mill is of your service to this country. At a time when so many are out in the streets protesting and shouting, your bravery and patriotism are inspirations to us all."

No one speaks on the ride back home. Wally just sits in the backseat with his pumpkin in his lap.

In the morning his father is gone.

"He got a call," his mother explains, ironing shirts. "He was needed back on the ship."

"So he won't be coming back for a while?"

"Not for a while."

Wally smiles. But his mother doesn't keep eye contact with him. She just concentrates on her ironing.

Pretty soon, though, she starts to sing, low and sweet.

"*My little baby loves short'nin', short'nin'. . .*"

Wally joins in. "*My little baby loves short'nin' bread.*"

Fade in on a boy, a few years older. He's in the basement, stacking comic books on a shelf. Each one is carefully bagged in plastic, labeled with issue date and number. On a lower shelf he notices a box. He bends down.

On the soundtrack: "If happy little bluebirds fly . . ."

He stares down at the box.

"Beyond the rainbow . . ."
He lifts the lid.
"Why oh why . . ."
It's a pointed witch's hat.
"Can't I?"
Fade to black.

4

TOUCH ONE

The phone rings like a witch at the window in the middle of the night and a little girl picks it up to learn that her mother has died.

"She's gone," she hears, and her aunt, on the phone downstairs, starts to cry.

Regina gently hangs up the extension so that her aunt will not hear. She turns to her sister, sitting in bed with the covers pulled up to her chin, and asks, "What would you do if Mama died?"

"I'd drink iodine," comes the unhesitating reply.

"Me, too," Regina says, and she means it.

A month before, Regina and Rocky and their mother had made boiled potatoes and succotash for supper. The girls had mixed the lima beans and corn together with their fingers, imagining the bowl of raw vegetables to be a treasure chest of emeralds and diamonds. Mama was peeling the potatoes over the sink.

"Do the potatoes have eyes, Mama?" Rocky asked.

"Yes, they do."

"Can they see us?"

"If you believe they can."

"I believe." Rocky looked at Regina. "Do you?"

"If you do, Rocky, I do, too."

"Rochelle," their mother said, "set the plates out. Regina, you put out the cups."

The girls opened the cupboard. The door stuck. Both of them had to pull together to get it to pop open. The plates were chipped. Mama had tried to paint the chips white so they wouldn't be noticed, but now the paint was almost gone. Rocky took out three plates and set them symmetrically around the table. Regina took out four cups.

"You forgot Papa's plate," Regina told her sister.

"He doesn't eat here anymore," Rocky insisted.

Their mother didn't turn. She continued peeling the potatoes over the sink. "Put out a cup for your father, Rochelle," she said. "If he comes in, I want a place set for him."

Regina smiled, pleased. Rocky put a cup out for her father, but her lips were pressed together so tightly they turned white.

* * *

The play unfolds itself. Regina and Rocky are sitting on the edge of the bed, hand-in-hand, waiting. They can hear the clock ticking. One second, two seconds, three, four. Above them a solitary light bulb burns from the ceiling.

Their aunt climbs the stairs with two lace handkerchiefs, newly pressed. She opens the door to their room and her eyes are red from crying.

"The angels have come," she says, "and carried your Mama home."

The little girls cry on cue. Their aunt kneels before them, bringing their heads to her breast. Then she hands them the lace handkerchiefs.

"Will my Papa come?" Regina asks.

"I don't know," her aunt replies.

"He'll come home now," Regina says.

"No, he won't," Rocky spits. "He'll never come home."

"You have us," the aunt says. "Me and Uncle Axel and Mormor . . ."

Regina doesn't say anything. She keeps her head pressed against her aunt's breast. Her tears are starting to sting her cheeks.

"I'm going to have a baby," their mother had told them after dinner.

"A baby?"

"A baby?"

"Yes," she said, without smiling. "Would you like a little brother?"

"Yes, Mama!" Regina put her hand on her mother's belly. "Is he in there now?"

"He is," her mother answered.

"I can't feel him."

"That's because he's still very small."

"What will we name him?" Rocky asked.

"How about Peter?"

"That's Papa's name."

"Yes. Do you think he'd like that?"

Regina leaned against her mother. "But what if it's a girl?"

"Then we wouldn't name her Peter, now would we?"

"Would we name her after you?" Regina asked.

"Maybe. We could do that."

Regina nodded. "I want a girl."

Mormor lived across town in an old white house covered in ivy. When she wasn't working at her diner on Main Street, she would be in her living room listening to *Stella Dallas* on the radio. A few days after they learned about the baby, Regina and Rocky went with their mother to see Mormor. Mama was being very quiet, and she'd scolded them on the way over, something she didn't often do.

"Behave at your grandmother's, please," she said. "Don't get her upset. Just be good girls."

Mormor meant mother's mother in Swedish. When Mama was a girl, she had lived in the big old house on Oak Avenue with Mormor and Aunt Selma. That was back in the days when they all had just come over from Sweden to live in Brown's Mill. Regina didn't remember anyone ever talking about a man named *Morfar*, or mother's father. It was always just Mormor.

To Regina, Mormor seemed enormous. She was tall and wide and had two silver balls of hair on her head, one on top of the other. There were only a few teeth left in her mouth, so she never smiled. Mormor had arthritis in her legs, so she didn't walk around much. She just sat in her chair listening to the radio. If anyone asked her about her legs, which sometimes swelled to the size of tree stumps, she would say they had gotten so bad from all the years she had to stand waiting on customers at Britta's Lunch. Everybody used to go to Britta's for Mormor's Swedish meatballs and grilled sardine sandwiches. Mama has shown them where it was, in the place where Henry's Diner now stood, and told them how she used to work in the kitchen when she was little, peeling apples from the local orchards for Mormor's pies.

"Now, please, girls," Mama said when they got to Mormor's house. "Stay outside and be good. Promise?"

Regina and Rocky promised. They were glad to not go inside. They much preferred Mormor's yard to the dusty echoes of her big house. Mormor had tall oak trees, knotting into each other as they crosshatched the sky, and birdhouses of all shapes and sizes, and beautiful roses growing on a trellis. Regina especially loved the roses. They were big and full, red and pink and yellow. It smelled so wonderful near the rose trellis. It smelled almost as nice as Mama's dressing table at home, with her powders and puffs and old perfume bottles.

But Mormor's voice had drifted across the afternoon. "How could you let this happen?" Their grandmother's words were deep and thick and angry in her guttural Swedish accent. "You foolish, foolish girl. As if the two you already have aren't enough to feed and clothe!"

The girls said nothing to each other. They just stood in front of the rose trellis, smelling the beautiful flowers.

"Listen to the hum," Regina whispered.

The girls drew closer to the trellis. Behind the vines, dozens of bees droned their monotonous song. A few flew out, and the girls jumped back.

"I wish I had one of those roses to put in my hair," Regina said, and she reached in, pricking her hand on the thorns. She pulled back in pain, shaking the trellis, and a dozen bees swarmed angrily out at her.

"That's God punishing you, Gina," Rocky lectured her crying sister. "You almost killed Mormor's roses."

"I just wanted one."

Rocky shook her head. "It's just like the robins, Regina. You touch one, you kill them all."

At the mention of the robins, Regina started to cry harder. For several seconds Rocky just stood there, watching her. Finally she put her arms around her sister and held her close, kissing the blood off her fingers.

* * *

"You've got to call an ambulance," Mama whispered in the night. "I've hurt myself."

Regina stood in the doorway. Her mother was on the floor, next to her bed, its linens draped over the side, as if she'd tugged on them, trying to get up. Now she held her knees to her chest, and she had blood on her hands.

Regina had awakened to the sound of her mother calling her name in the dark, the way Regina used to call to her, when she was very little and woke up from a bad dream. She had the feeling her mother had been calling for a long time.

"Just pick up the phone and tell the operator to send an ambulance," Mama told her. "Can you do that? Just give her our address."

"What's wrong, Mama?"

"I've hurt myself. Please do it now, Regina. Go quickly."

Mama made a little gesture with her head, a little toss of her chin in the direction of the stairs. The sweat on her face and the blood on her hands glistened in the moonlight. Regina turned and ran.

She could hear her heart pounding in her ears. She tripped at the bottom of the stairs. She picked up the phone and held it to her ear.

"Is this the operator?"

She spoke directly over the mouthpiece, trying to be clear.

"Can you help my mother?"

Regina gave the address, and the operator made her repeat it. Then she replaced the phone on its hook and sat down on the floor, waiting for the ambulance. She pulled her knees up to her chest and held them, just as she knew Mama was doing upstairs. She thought about waking Rocky, but she didn't want to go back upstairs. She would sit on the cold wood floor and wait.

The house was very quiet. The buzz of the electricity filled Regina's ears, and she wondered why it made that noise even when everything was turned off. And she thought she heard a bird, trapped in the kitchen, but then the sound was gone.

She heard the sirens a long way off, and suddenly they were at the door, bright lights shining through the windows, illuminating the dark house. Men in white were banging against the glass. She opened the door and said calmly, "My mother's upstairs. She's hurt herself."

The men in white ran up the stairs, and Regina followed, a small, slow figure trailing behind them.

"Get a stretcher," one man called, and Regina looked past him, into Mama's room. Mama had fallen over on to her side, and Regina could see more blood under her now. Rocky had walked out of the bedroom, rubbing her eyes. A man led her downstairs. Regina walked over and sat by her mother.

"Mama?"

Her mother's face was against the floor. Her eyes were closed.

"Mama, I did like you said."

They came in with the stretcher.

"Where's your father, little girl?" one of the men asked her.

"We don't have one."

"How about grandparents?"

"A grandmother."

"Why don't you go down and call her?"

"Will my mother be all right?"

They lifted her up on to the stretcher. Blood dripped to the floor. "Don't look, honey," the man said. "Go downstairs and call your grandma."

It was only after they left, when Regina started to clean the room, that she found the wire and the bloody bundle. That's when Mormor got there with Aunt Selma and ordered her to her room.

"I'll take them for a few days," Aunt Selma is saying, "but Axel isn't good with children, you know that, Mother. Especially not *girls*."

Mormor sits at the head of the table, with the radio on a stand next to her. She raises her hand to silence Aunt Selma as she listens to the end of Stella Dallas's travails this week.

"Mother, please, Axel is very upset. We can't afford—"

Regina and Rocky stare at their plates. They are pretending not to hear. Regina cannot eat the roast beef on her plate. It is too runny, too red.

"Eat your meat, Regina," Mormor says in her heavy accent.

"Mother—"

"Selma, you'll do what is required," Mormor says, cutting her off. "Your sister is dead. And I'm an old woman with arthritis in my legs."

Aunt Selma makes a face. "I just want to know where *he* is. He does have *some* responsibilities in this. *Two* of them, to be exact."

Mormor holds up her hand again, listening to the opening theme of the next serial.

"I'm not hungry," Regina whispers.

"Eat your meat, Regina," Mormor says, turning to her, "or else you'll end up with arthritis, too."

Last spring a robin had built a nest in the wisteria that grew along their house just outside the back door. Every morning Regina, Rocky, and their mother would watch the robin bringing straw and twigs, fashioning together a safe little bed, hidden among the ivy. One day they stood on a stool and peeked into the leaves to see two tiny blue eggs in the nest.

"The baby robins are inside those eggs," their mother told them. "But we mustn't touch them or else the mother will fly away and leave them all alone."

Regina was very disturbed by this. "But then they'd die, Mama. Who would bring them worms?"

"No one, Regina. So we must never touch them."

One day the baby birds hatched and Regina could hear their constant chirping all day long. The mother flew in and out of the leaves.

Regina and Rocky stood on the stool looking in at the babies, their beaks open, tiny heads turned up. Somewhere in the bushes the mother bird screeched.

"Come on, Gina," Rocky said, "we're making the mother afraid."

But Regina wasn't listening. She reached in and cupped one of the babies in her hand.

Rocky screamed and pushed her sister from the stool. "You can't touch them!" The baby bird fell, fluttered for a moment on the ground, and then was still. Regina began to cry.

"Gina touched them!" Rocky screamed to her mother. "She touched the baby birds!" Their mother stood in the doorway and her eyes filled with tears.

"Come into the house, girls. There's nothing we can do now."

The mother bird flew in once and then she was gone. She didn't come back to the nest. The remaining baby cried all through the day. Finally Mama went out and brought the nest inside. They fed the baby apple juice with an eyedropper. They put it in a warm spot in the kitchen. During the night Regina could hear it chirping, sometimes frantic, sometimes irregular. In the morning the bird was dead in its nest.

"But I only touched one," Regina said between sobs. "Why did the mother leave *this* one?"

Mama didn't know what to say. Rocky looked at her sister, choking with hatred, and explained what seemed to her to be absolutely common sense:

"You touch one, you kill them all."

Mama bundled the baby bird in a cloth and took it outside. She was crying, too.

Now they are back at Mormor's house by the roses. The roses smell beautiful, and the bees are dancing around the vines, humming a more varied tune today, up and down and swirling through the air. Regina and Rocky are looking into the roses, not speaking.

Regina is thinking about the weak little gesture Mama had made with her head, when she told her to run for help. She's thought about that a lot. It bothers her more than the blood. It was the last thing Mama ever did.

A long time passes.

Regina says, "I want to kill these roses."

"Yes," says Rocky, "I do, too."

They grab the flowers in their fists, squashing them and pulling their heads from the vine. Petals flutter to the ground like snowflakes. Rocky grinds them into the dirt with her heel. Regina continues to pull at the vine, ripping the roses and their leaves, mindless of the thorns and her bloody hands. The bees dive angrily at them. The girls simply swat them away, intent on their work. They keep pulling and ripping at the flowers until every last one of them is gone. A blanket of crushed petals lies at their feet.

They see Mormor leaning on her cane in the doorway, looking at what they've done. They see her mouth open into a large, angry O. Regina doesn't care. She hears her grandmother shouting at them, ordering them inside to account for their behavior, telling them what bad girls they are. Regina runs. She doesn't think. She just keeps running. She runs out of the yard and down the street. She runs past St. Peter's Lutheran Church, where Mama used to take them. She runs onto Main Street and then right through the busy intersection of Washington Avenue, a bus driver leaning on his horn at her. Right past Henry's Diner she runs, right past the town hall, past the Palace movie theater and St. John the Baptist Roman Catholic Church, which has always scared her with its black-robed priests and heavy smells of incense. Into the tall grass of Devil's Hopyard she runs, where she finally collapses, her legs feeling as if they'll snap right off.

Only then does she turn to see that Rocky was behind her the whole way. They roll into each other's arms and cry for a long, long time.

Aunt Selma doesn't go to the funeral. She stays home to watch her sister's girls.

"Sit here and eat your oatmeal," she tells them. She is dressed all in black. "I don't want you to move from those chairs. I want to say good-bye to your Mama. They're going to drive her by here after the church. I'm going to watch from the front door."

"Can we watch, too, Aunt Selma?" Rocky asks.

"No. I don't want you to remember your Mama in a hearse."

They don't know what a hearse is. Aunt Selma goes to the front door. They sit and drink their milk. It is a quiet morning, except for the birds chirping outside. The girls do not talk. Rochelle starts to hum. Regina fidgets.

"I have to go to the bathroom," Regina says softly.

"Aunt Selma said we can't move from these chairs."

"I have to go to the bathroom," Regina says again.

She stands up. Rocky resumes her humming. Regina slips softly upstairs.

From a bedroom window she watches the black cars drive slowly down the street. There are three of them, and she knows Mama must be in one. They come up from Main Street and turn onto Oak Avenue. They pass in front of the house and wind back the way they came. She thinks she sees Mormor sitting in one of the cars. She doesn't know for sure. She doesn't know where they're taking Mama. She doesn't know why the black cars came by the house. She doesn't know where she and Rocky are going to sleep tonight.

All she knows is: you touch one, you kill them all.

5

GHOST MANAGEMENT

Wally drives along the river into Dogtown, where the stench of sewage and swamp water hangs so heavy in the air he can taste it on his tongue, like soot after a fire.

"Don't go down there," his mother used to warn him, wringing her hands. "It's bad down there. *Bad.*"

And bad it was. Behind the crumbling factories the old tenant housing remained, rowhouses built by factory owners for their immigrant workers at the turn of the last century. Irish, then Swedes, then Poles and Jews, finally Italians and Puerto Ricans. The houses of Dogtown were built over swamps, where skunk cabbage grew plentiful and tall, where velvety cat-o'-nine-tails enticed children to wade across the muddy, stinking water that licked the edges of the tenements. "Don't go down there," Wally's mother had pleaded, but although he continued to listen intently to every conversation dropped in line at Grant's department store, he had long since stopped listening to her.

"It's got to be Alzheimer's," he tells Cheri on his cell phone. "That's the only way to explain her behavior. It's bizarre, even for her."

"So what are you going to do?"

"She has no one else." Wally sighs. "I've got to get her in to see a doctor."

"You okay managing all these ghosts?"

"I don't believe in ghosts." He makes a left turn. "I've got to go, babe. I'm almost there."

"Okay, Wally. Good luck."

He hits END. Ahead of him is the house he seeks: the place where he once sought refuge, a place without which he believes he wouldn't be here today. He'd be over in Eagle Hill Cemetery, in the plot next to his father, "pushing up daisies," as Miss Aletha liked to say.

He parks the car on the street and heads up the walk. Her rosebushes still show some buds, even this late in the season. The leaves are a deep purple.

"Can I help you?"

Wally looks up. A boy is sitting on the front steps, his short hair dyed bright orange and his eyes thick with mascara.

"I'm looking for Missy."

"And you are. . . ?"

Wally stands over him. The boy can't be more than fifteen, sixteen. Acne reddens his chin, but he's cute. Large brown eyes, seriously pouty lips, surprisingly broad and powerful shoulders for so slight a frame.

36

"The name's Wally Day."

The boy's lips twist into a grin. "Oh, yeah, the actor. Missy said you were coming."

"Do you live here?"

"Yeah. Missy's been feeding me like a stray cat and I won't go away." He stands. "I'm Dee."

They shake.

"I'm going to be an actor, too."

Wally smirks. "It's my duty to advise you to consider a career that doesn't require as much effort or discipline. Like maybe rocket science or brain surgery."

The boy ignores him. "Can you help me get me a part in something? I don't care what it is. TV show. Play. Even a commercial."

Wally looks past him toward Missy's front door. "Sure, kid. I'll give Geffen a call for you."

"Don't think I don't know sarcasm."

"Is Missy here?"

Dee nods over his shoulder. "She's never anywhere else."

Wally raps on the door.

"Just go on in," Dee says. "She's too deaf to hear you knock."

Miss Aletha saved Wally's life. She gave him refuge, shelter, a way out. She got a dentist to cap his tooth after his father had broken it. She found a shrink for him to spill his guts out to in twice-weekly sessions. She even paid for a tutor to help with his studies after school became unbearable and Wally started skipping classes.

He's going to go far, that Wally Day, his teachers had once said.

But at the time it didn't seem he'd get much farther than Dogtown.

"Wally," Miss Aletha says, her arms outstretched, welcoming him home.

How old she's gotten. How unlike his memories. But it's her, just the same: Miss Aletha, who saved his life, who set him right, whose roses every year still win first place in the Brown's Mill Flower Show, despite the clucking of the biddies in the big white houses on Eagle Hill. Every year on her birthday, Wally sends a card and she always remembers him with a Christmas gift—but they haven't seen each other now in many, many years. After Wally first moved to the city, Miss Aletha would come and visit. Once she came to one of his parties and gotten high with his friends. Wally has an image of her: holding a banana as a microphone and lipsynching Cyndi Lauper's "Girls Just Wanna Have Fun." Everyone had loved Miss Aletha.

"Missy." Wally pulls her close and looks down into her soft blue eyes. How strange it feels to be so much taller than she is. Miss Aletha had always seemed so big. She's shrunk, withered down into a little old lady.

A teakettle whistles. "Join me?" she asks.

Wally nods. Her kitchen, unlike herself, is exactly as he remembers: cluttered and odoriferous, with a tanginess underneath, as if something in the refrigerator has gone bad. But it's not an unpleasant smell: rather, it's the candied scent of overripe fruit or the tempting promise of old wine.

She pours some tea. Wally sits at the table overlooking the swampy backyard. Along the trellis outside shiver a few roses, a deep red-purple.

"You always did manage to keep them blooming all year," he says.

"Eh?"

"Your roses," he says, louder. "Still in bloom."

"Yes," she says, settling the teacup in front of him. "But tonight there will be a frost."

"Will you bring them inside?"

"I can't save them all," she says, taking the seat opposite him.

Wally smirks. "Oh, I don't know about that. Who's the monkey on your front porch?"

"His name is Donald. He's sixteen. You can fill in the rest, I'm sure."

"Kicked out of his house when his parents found out he was gay."

She nods. "Fundamentalists. They took him to a faith healer."

"I see it did the trick."

"The world has changed, I hear," Missy says. "But not Brown's Mill."

One of her cats rubs against Wally's ankles. He reaches down to stroke it.

"Your call came as quite a surprise," she says softly, finding his eyes.

"I'm sure it did."

"You've seen your mother?"

Wally sighs. "Yeah. She's not right. Not that she ever was, but—"

"There's been a lot of talk, Wally, ever since that boy disappeared."

Wally shakes his head. "Kyle isn't a boy, Missy. He's my age, a navy SEAL or whatever he is. And he hasn't disappeared. He's hightailed it out of town. Maybe he didn't want to be shipped off to Kosovo or wherever. I don't know why the police are making such a mystery out of it."

"Well, I guess Uncle Sam doesn't like it when one of his boys takes off without letting him know where he's going."

"Kyle's always been a fuck-up. But I don't want to talk about him."

Miss Aletha smiles. "I know who you *do* want to talk about."

How long has this been going on?

Since I was thirteen.

"I'm going to see him," Wally tells her. "If he's still alive."

"He's alive." Her old eyes hold his. "But you don't know if he wants to see you."

"No. I don't."

She reaches across the table to take his hand. "Have you been seeing anyone? Anyone special?"

Wally looks back out the window, at the purple rose on the vine.

"Still no one," Miss Aletha says, reading his mind. "No one since Ned."

"Who would want me?" Wally asks. "I'm an *old man* in gay years, Missy. Long gone is the boy you knew. Once you pass thirty, you're old meat. Who adopts the old hound at the pound? Everybody wants a puppy."

Miss Aletha gives him a stern look. Even with her thousands of wrinkles, it is still the same look she used to give him all those years ago, a look that said: "You are being foolish but I love you anyway." Wally receives that look for what it is, and he smiles.

Once she had been a drag queen on the stages of the city, feted and celebrated and revered. But she had come back here, to Brown's Mill, where she had been born a boy, with the name of Howard Greer. "We're not so different," she once told Wally. "We were both born here in this place. We both did things people said were bad. You're no different from me, Wally Day. I know who you are. I may be thirty years older, but there's no difference between you and me."

Ah, but there was. Maybe they had both been boys who did bad things, but Missy had never really been a boy. At twelve, she took a pair of garden shears and snipped off the head of her penis. After spending three weeks in a hospital, her parents committed her to Windcliff Sanitarium over in Mayville, a place where doctors did horrible things to her—like strapping her to a table and sending electric shocks through her frail little mutilated body. She lived in constant terror of more of those shocks until one night she ran away and hitchhiked a ride to the city. Within a few weeks she was performing on stage at a backalley dive that was forever being raided by the police. *Come see Miss Aletha—the amazing, the amusing, the astounding—you'll swear she's Eartha Kitt! Marilyn Monroe! Ethel Merman! Sophie Tucker!*

But Miss Aletha didn't care about all that. "What's so great about being astounding?" she'd laugh, years later. All she'd ever wanted was to be a lady who grew roses and entered them in contests. And so that's what she became. She returned to Brown's Mill and bought a house in Dogtown. The job she'd started with those garden shears was finally completed some twenty years later, with more professional tools, and with much more satisfactory results.

"Missy," Wally says, taking her hand and pressing it to his lips, "it feels good to be here."

She smiles. "I'm glad."

"I didn't know how I'd feel."

She nods. "It's been a long time, Wally."

"Too long."

"So what will you do? Put your mother in a home?"

"I don't know. Maybe. What other options do I have?"

"You could get to know her."

"Oh, please. You know the whole story, Missy. Tell me honestly that you think there's anything more that can be done."

She shrugs.

"You see? You can't. The only thing left to do now in our long, sorry saga will be to bury her out beside my father when she dies. Then it'll all be over. I'll sell the house, pocket the cash—"

"Is he the one who sent Zandy to jail?"

They look up, startled. Dee has come inside. He stands in front of them with his arms crossed against his chest. He wears enormous baggy jeans that threaten to slide right off his narrow hips.

"What did he say?" Miss Aletha asks, adjusting the hearing aid hidden under her wig. "I just know it was something fresh."

"It's all right, Missy," Wally tells her. "He didn't say anything that wasn't true." He levels his eyes at the boy. "Do you know Zandy, Dee?"

"Yeah." The kid's studying him with his mascara eyes. "I've met him."

"How is he?"

"Old. And sick. And his breath reeks."

Wally looks across the table at Miss Aletha. "His health . . ."

She lets out a long sigh. "He's gotten to be very reclusive. When he realized the drugs weren't working, he just kind of closed himself off from most people."

"Are you going to go see him?" Dee asks.

"Yeah." Wally looks out the window again. The wind is kicking up and the sun is starting to set. He hates these short autumn days.

"You want me to take you there?" the boy asks.

Miss Aletha tries to wave him away. "Donald, go watch television or play your ridiculous rap music."

Wally smiles. "Actually, I might like the company."

"Yeah," Dee agrees. "If it were me, I sure as hell wouldn't want to go all by myself to face somebody whose life I ruined."

"Now, scat, you!" Miss Aletha shouts.

"He's only stating the obvious, Missy."

She frowns. "You've got to stop blaming yourself, Wally. Zandy knew what he was doing. You were too young. I told him that."

"But I sent him to prison."

She stands and walks back over to the stove for the tea kettle. She refills Wally's cup as Dee sits on the linoleum floor, staring up at them with his knees pulled up to his chest.

"He survived prison," Missy says. "Prison wasn't what was so bad. It was afterward. Things started happening here in Brown's Mill after you left, Wally. Some of us tried to put together a community center. Zandy was part of that. And we got a political group going. Do you know we got a civil rights bill passed in this state?"

Wally nods.

"We did some good things. But then ten, twelve years ago somebody came along, some do-gooder from the gay rights alliance or whatever they call it up in the state capital, and he says that it's not such a good idea to have a convicted child molester playing such a public role in such a small town. Bad for the image, you know. What would the media do if they got ahold of it? The *community*, he said. Think of the *community*. So Zandy dropped out."

Wally's quiet, watching the day get colder outside the window. The temperature is dropping: the purple roses shiver on their vine, and gray clouds are moving in to obscure the sharpness of the blue sky.

"I bring him over his mail sometime," Dee says. "He can't make it to his PO box anymore. So I bring him whatever comes in, like *The Advocate* or *Out* magazine. He keeps up on everything. I told him how I took my boyfriend to my junior prom last year, and he just loved it. Thought it was really awesome."

Wally lifts his eyebrows, looking over at Miss Aletha. "What do you mean, Brown's Mill hasn't changed? Can you imagine me going to my prom with some guy in matching tuxedos?"

"That's what we had," Dee agrees. "White tie and tails. Top hats, too. Zandy wanted to know all the details, see all the pictures."

"It's what he always predicted," Wally says, feeling a smile stretch across his face. "He said someday things were going to be easy. Someday we wouldn't have to hide."

"Hide?" Dee echoes. "I've never hidden in my life and I'm not planning on doing it, ever. Even when I make it as an actor. I'm going to be out as queer right from the start. I'll never have to worry about being outed because I'll always be out."

Wally's looking at him, this strange, orange-haired man-child, but he's thinking of Zandy, hearing his words. "He was the first to tell me stories," Wally says dreamily. "Stories about places like Greenwich Village, and the Castro, and P'town . . . They were like fairy tales. That's how I thought of them." He laughs. "He told me we were going to change the world."

"He was a leftover hippie," Miss Aletha says. It's just a statement. Nothing else.

Wally looks at her. "I use the stuff he taught me every day. Do you know that?"

Miss Aletha is quiet. Dee listens to every word.

"He taught me so much," Wally whispers.

And he thinks of Zandy's hands, scarred and twisted, the hands of a laborer, the hands of a *man*, on his fourteen-year-old boy's body.

"You tell him that," Missy says, "when you see him."

Alexander Reefy was the man who first touched Wally's trembling skin. He is the man whose hands live on so strongly in Wally's memory, hands that first caressed the pink buds of his nipples, hands that stroked his hair and gripped his innocent butt. There, among the shadows of the orchard, lit only by an autumn moon, he did things to Wally's body that made him shake, that made him cry, that made the boy love him. Things he shouldn't have done, maybe, things that were wrong—but things Wally has never forgotten, things that have remained a part of him. Zandy's hands. Big hands. Rough hands. And then his breath, hot against Wally's face.

"Why do you want to see him again?" Dee asks as he shows Wally upstairs to his room. It's the same one Wally had as a boy, when he stayed here with Miss Aletha for those few months, the months that saved his life.

"I don't know. Think it's a bad idea?"

The boy looks over at him. "You want my opinion? Are you really asking for my opinion?"

"Sure."

The boy grins. *He's actually adorable*, Wally realizes. Underneath the dyed hair and mascara and attitude, he's soft and cute, like the boys Wally remembers from the pages of *Tiger Beat* magazine, stashed under his covers and read by flashlight after he'd gone to bed. The boys he had crushes on: David Cassidy. Bobby Sherman. Jack Wild. And especially Christopher Knight—Peter from *The Brady Bunch*.

"Yeah," Dee's saying, "I think you should see him. Otherwise you'll always regret it when he dies."

"He's that sick, huh?"

"Man, he's nasty."

Wally unzips his backpack. He'd only brought one change of clothes. But he's going to need more now that he's promised to take his mother to the doctor.

"Hey, Dee, is Grant's department store still open?"

"Grant's? Never heard of it. What do you need?"

"Just a couple sweatshirts, maybe some socks and underwear."

"You could go to the mall."

"There's a mall in Brown's Mill?"

"Well, it's in Mayville, but it's only about fifteen minutes away on Route 16. They've got a Gap and an Abercrombie there." He grins. "What kind of underwear you want?"

"Whatever's on sale."

"Oh, come on. Boxers or briefs?"

Wally laughs. The boy's jeans are so loose his own choice in undergarments is evident. Boxers. Tommy Hilfiger.

"Today it's briefs," Wally says. "Calvin Klein."

Dee smiles. "You are *so* gay."

"Yup. Last time I checked."

"Gay guys your age *always* wear Calvins. And you all go to the gym."

Wally smirks. "So what makes you such an expert on us old-timers?"

"I've been around." Dee smiles. "I actually *like* older men."

Wally laughs. "Well, such noblesse oblige."

Most of his life, Wally had been the boy. Even with Ned, who had been just a year older, but who had been so much wiser, so much smarter than Wally. Not book wise, not so that it would show on any standardized test. Wally was the brain but Ned was the smarts, and that kept Wally the bright-eyed boy all through the sixteen years they were together. Sixteen years. As long as Dee has been on this earth.

It's odd being the older man. He'd watch the boys he tricked with, their faces unlined as they slept, their easy bounce out of bed in the morning, their quickness to laugh, to presume, to believe. When had he stopped being like them? Wally's sense of himself remains colored by his life as the kid at the bar, the one for whom the older guys were always buying drinks. "Watch," Wally would say to Ned, sidling up to a stool. "See how fast I get a beer bought for me." Such a cocky little child he was, filled with all the arrogance that comes with having a claim on the future.

"No, I mean it," Dee is saying. "I can't stand how some young guys talk about older guys." He positions himself against the dresser, leaning back just far enough so that his shirt rides up, exposing a glimpse of his flat, smooth stomach. "You know. How they call them old queens. Piano rats. Fossils. *Trolls.*"

Oh, the kid's good, Wally thinks, watching him. Just by putting the terms out there he establishes their positions relative to each other. Dee's gotten accustomed to having the same power Wally remembers having himself. A power that brings rewards. A power that reveals itself now in the way the boy plays idly with the few strands of hair that grow up from the waistband of his underwear toward his navel.

"Not that they'd say it about *you*," he tells Wally coyly, throwing in a compliment for good measure. He reaches forward to slap his palm against Wally's chest. "Nice body. Guess you have to stay buff, being an actor, huh?"

Wally feels himself blush, even as he remains acutely aware of the kid's machinations. "Yeah," he says. "Never know when I'm gonna get the call asking to take over from Arnold in the *Terminator* franchise."

"There's that sarcasm again," Dee says. "I'm not sure it's all that becoming on you."

"I'll work on it."

"So can I go clothes shopping with you?" Dee asks. "I *love* going clothes shopping."

"If you like." Wally sets his razor and shaving cream on the bureau. "You can show me how modern Brown's Mill has become."

"Modern? Brown's Mill? You say those words in the same sentence?"

"Hey, I saw an Internet cafe on Main Street when I came through."

"Yeah, it's got two computers." Dee flops down on the bed. "And still on dial-up. You have no idea how much I want out of this town."

The same words, the same room. *I've got to get out of this town. That's the only answer. I've got to get out.*

"I really *am* a good actor, you know," Dee is telling him. "I did Molière in my sophomore year."

Wally stands over the kid, looking down at him. Dee's shirt is pushed up higher now to expose even more flesh. "Well, then," Wally says, "Shakespeare in the Park can't be too far away."

Dee grins. "You know, I think it's cool for older guys to have sex with younger guys."

Wally can't think of a quick retort.

"I mean, about you and Zandy. I don't think it was nasty or anything."

"Gee, thanks, Dee."

"I had sex with a guy when I was eleven."

"That's not cool, Dee. I don't know who it was, or any of the circumstances, but at eleven there's no way you could have known what you were really getting into."

"Like you could at thirteen?"

"I'm not saying I did."

"So then you think you did the right thing in sending Zandy to jail."

Wally feels himself getting angry at the kid. "Look, I need to make a few calls on my cell phone, okay? You get lost for a while, and I'll find you when I'm going shopping."

"All right." Dee hops up off the bed. "Can I get a pair of jeans? I'll pay you back later, I promise."

"Get out of here."

Wally closes the door. He leans against it, closing his eyes.

They would meet here, in Dogtown. Strange folk lived down here on the river-banks, the kind who drove rusty old VW vans and smoked pot and wore patchwork-covered bell-bottom jeans. Every house seemed to have a big old dog tied to a post in the front yard, digging holes all through the lawn and going spastic whenever anyone walked by. Hence the name: Dogtown.

"Don't go down there," Wally's mother warned, but he turned a brazen shoulder to her pleas, hopping on his bicycle and pedaling as fast as he could from his quiet little cul-de-sac down Washington Avenue and into the swamps of Dogtown. There he would sit and listen to Zandy's tales of the world beyond Brown's Mill, and let him touch his body with those rough and beautiful hands.

But a little more than a year later he would give his statement to the police that caused Zandy to be arrested and sent to jail.

He gave it willingly. To say otherwise now would be a lie. His parents did not coerce him. Wally walked briskly into the police station ahead of his father, and even spelled Zandy's name for Officer Garafolo, who sat behind his desk, egg salad in his bushy black mustache. Wally had just turned fifteen years old.

"And now I'm back," he whispers to himself.

Back here, in Dogtown, in Missy's house.

There's a light rap on his door. Wally opens it. It's Missy.

"Donald's smitten," she says, coming into the room. "Oh, he won't admit it, but I can tell. I can always tell."

"He's smitten into thinking he's found somebody to buy him stuff."

"You know, Wally, the city may have saved your life but it's also turned you into a cynic."

He laughs. "Oh, it's the city that did it? Not the fact that I had a father who beat me, a mother who didn't care, and on top of all that, I lost my lover to a plague that by rights should have claimed me instead?"

Miss Aletha grasps hold of the bedpost. "My, you *are* worked up."

"It's coming back here. I should have known."

"It was good you came."

Wally doesn't answer.

"You had to come back sooner or later," Missy says, approaching him. "You just couldn't go through the rest of your life with all this hanging in your closet."

"Why not?" He strides over to the window, looking out over the factories toward the orchard and the town beyond it. "What more is there for me to do here? Oh, sure, I can take my mother to the doctor. What a *good* son I am. I can go apologize to Zandy for ruining his life. As if that will make any of it better for him."

"It might." She walks up behind him, placing a hand on his back. "One never knows what effect the most seemingly inconsequential action might have. I went to see my father in the hospital when he was dying of cancer and it ended up changing my life."

"Why? Because you resolved all your history?"

She twinkles. "No. Because his nurse was this handsome young man by the name of Bertrand and he asked me out on a date."

Wally laughs. Missy and Bertrand went on to be lovers for twenty-seven years.

"So you see?" she says to him. "You never know what might happen."

"When I first left Brown's Mill," Wally says, closing his eyes for a moment, "I dreamed of coming back here. I had it all planned out in my mind. I'd come back, the most famous actor in the world. A hit Broadway show, or a big movie, or a TV series. I'd come back and they'd line up along Main Street to get my autograph."

"Donald was very impressed when I told him you were an actor."

Wally laughs bitterly. "An actor. Yeah, right. My biggest moment was playing a psycho killer chasing Susan Lucci on a forgotten Lifetime television movie from the late eighties. Tell me how impressive that is."

"You've done some very good work, Wally. I've *seen* you. On film and on stage. Don't be trivializing your career."

He shakes his head. "It's just that if I was going to *make it*, Missy, I mean really make it like I always dreamed, it would've happened by now. I have to accept that."

"I don't think you have to accept anything of the sort." She grips his chin and turns his face toward her. "What has gotten you so fatalistic?"

He tries to smile. "I guess I'm just having a little trouble managing all my ghosts."

"I know, baby. So I'll give you a hand. We'll get them all in line."

He smiles down at her. She's the only thing good about this place. The only truly decent, unblemished part of his past.

He reaches his arm around her and pulls her in close as they look out over the orchards and the rooftops of the town.

6

DOGTOWN

"Would you like Kyle's car?" Regina asks the girl. "I can't imagine what else I'm going to do with it."

Luz looks over at the old woman. "His car? I can't take his car, Mrs. Day. He'd be very angry."

"Oh, I'm sure you'd take good care of it. Here are his keys. Really, Luz, what's an old woman like me going to do with a car like that?"

They're standing in the doorway leading from the kitchen into the garage. They're looking at Kyle's red and gold Trans Am. It had been his pride and joy. For months he had worked rebuilding the engine. Grease and oil and smudgy handprints had made their way all through Regina's kitchen. Kyle would drink beer while he was working on the car, and his friends would come over. They'd be very loud, cursing and laughing and belching. Regina would watch them from the window, hiding behind the curtain, saying nothing, not wanting to be seen.

Luz is studying her face. "You don't think Kyle's coming back, do you?"

Regina puts her fingers to her lips. "No, I don't think he is, dear. I think he's gone for good."

Gone for good.

And it's good he's gone.

His body lies in a shallow grave out in the backyard, near the poplar trees. *Yes, of course, that's where it is. I remember now how I dragged his body by his arms from the living room through the kitchen and then out the back door. I dragged him across the grass and dug a grave. That's where his body is. Out in the backyard.*

Regina wonders if it has started to decompose. She doesn't like the idea of rotting bodies. Rocky had been so disgusted by the thought of decomposition that she'd made Regina promise that, if she died first, Regina would have her cremated. Of course, when Rocky *did* die first, Regina broke her promise. Aunt Selma was against the idea. She said cremation was barbaric and un-Christian. Now Regina wakes up sometimes from a cold dark sleep with images of Rocky's skeleton decaying in the ground.

I'm sorry, Rocky, I'm so very sorry.

She watches Luz drive off in Kyle's car and lets out a long sigh. She's glad it's out of the garage.

"He was nothing like my son," she says, speaking to no one.

She often talks to herself when she's alone. She has whole conversations out loud, monologues that go on for hours. She doesn't think it odd or crazy; it's just something she's always done.

"Walter was always polite," she says. "He was a good boy. That's how I raised him. All his teachers said he was a good boy."

She pulls the curtains closed against the picture window in the living room. She snaps on a lamp and takes comfort from the warm yellow electric light.

"My son never called me names. He never said bad things to me. He never made me give him money. He never got drunk. He was considerate, thoughtful. He never put his feet up on the coffee-table or left smudge prints all through the kitchen."

On the wall hangs a picture from many years ago. Regina walks across the room to stand in front of it.

There are three people in the photograph. That's her, in the middle, wearing her favorite dress, yellow with blue polka dots. It makes her look so gay, so happy—so much like Rocky. Next to her is her husband, resplendent in his navy uniform. Robert was a captain. He took shrapnel in Vietnam. He was a hero. A great man. Between them is their son, Walter, with his lips parted to reveal his two missing front teeth. Regina thinks he was in third grade.

"He was a good boy," she says. "He never took drugs. He never yelled. He never stole any money from me. He was a good son. That's how I raised him. To be a good boy."

Her face darkens.

"And he certainly never hurt a girl the way Kyle hurt Luz."

Luz.

So pretty. Such lovely almond eyes.

This morning, Regina had been transfixed as she watched the girl vacuum under the bed. Luz was bending over, exposing her cleavage above her blue-and-red striped tube top. Regina sat watching her, rolling a twenty-dollar bill very tightly between her fingers. Then she stood, her joints creaking, and slipped the money right down between the girl's breasts.

Luz made a small sound. She straightened up, removing the offending object from her cleavage. She switched off the vacuum cleaner and turned with an expression of surprise to Regina.

"No, Mrs. Day. I told you. I *like* helping you."

Regina tilted her head at her. "*Please.*"

Luz closed her eyes then opened them again. "Oh, Mrs. Day," she said.

Such a good girl.

And so pretty. All the boys must like her. She's almost as pretty as Rocky was, and oh, how the boys had liked Rocky.

But boys can do bad things to girls they like.

"Oh, Luz, poor, poor Luz," Regina says in the backseat of the cab.

"What's that lady?" the cab driver asks.

"Oh, nothing." Regina smiles. "I'm just talking to myself, I suppose. I do that a lot. Guess I'm getting old."

"Ah, age has nothing to do with it. I talk to myself all the time, and I'm not even fifty yet."

Regina laughs. "Do you have any children?"

"Oh, sure."

"Any daughters?"

"I got three daughters. Eight, twelve, and fourteen."

"Oh, how lucky you are."

"Yeah, well, I'd have liked a son. At least one boy."

"I have a son," Regina tells him.

The cabdriver drops her off where she requested.

"You sure you're gonna be all right here, lady?" he asks her. "You want me to wait for you?"

"Oh, no, thank you very much. I'm fine. I'm here to visit a friend."

He just shrugs, takes her money, wishes her a good day and drives off.

Regina watches him zip down River Road back toward Main Street. She knows people are afraid of Dogtown. She used to be, too. She grew up hearing all sorts of things about the bad people here. But Luz lives here, and Luz is her friend.

Like the daughter she never had.

How much Regina always wanted a daughter! Not that her son wasn't a good boy. He was. But Regina always wished she'd had a little girl to dress up pretty, to put bows in her hair, to name after her mother. Elsa Christina. What a pretty name. That was Regina's dream: to have a daughter and name her after her mother.

She walks up the steps to Luz's house. The red and gold Trans Am is parked in the driveway. A little fuzzy elephant dangles from the rearview mirror. That's new. Luz must have put it there. She was always putting nice touches on things. From inside the house Regina can smell the frying of beans. She knocks.

A dog begins to bark inside.

"Get the door, Jorge," comes a man's voice.

The door is opened by a little boy.

"Hello," Regina says, "I'm looking for Luz."

The child says nothing, just looks up at her with a strange little face. Luz comes up behind him.

"Mrs. Day!"

"Hello, Luz."

"What are you doing here?"

She seems anxious, glancing quickly behind her, then returning her eyes to Regina.

"You left without taking this." Regina holds up the tightly rolled twenty. "I found it on the table."

"Oh, Mrs. Day—" Luz looks over her shoulder again. "Wait one minute, please."

She shuts the door. Regina stares at it blankly. She hears shuffling inside the house, the sound of footsteps, the dog barking wildly for a moment. Then the door opens again and Luz is shaking her head.

"Mrs. Day," she says, "you came all the way down here to give me money?"

"I want you to have it for helping me."

"Oh, Mrs. Day, I don't want to—"

"And I wanted to see where you lived, too. I wanted to meet your family."

Luz looks back inside the house again. She lets out a sigh, then nods, stepping aside so that Regina can enter. They're in a little hallway, with paint peeling off the wall. The smell of beans is heavy. Regina follows Luz and the little boy through another room, stepping over a ripped bag of pretzels on the floor, with several of them ground into the green shag carpet. A thin gray-haired man is stretched out on a couch watching *Wheel of Fortune*. Beside him sits a Great Dane that growls when Regina enters. The volume on the television is very loud.

"Turn that down," Luz says, but the man ignores her. "I said, *turn it down!*"

The old man grunts, aiming the remote control at the TV. The volume subsides.

"This is my friend," Luz tells him. "Mrs. Day. You know, Kyle's aunt."

The man eyes her and laughs. Regina sees the look that Luz gives him. The old man just returns his gaze to the television set.

"This is my grandfather," Luz says. "My father is at work."

In the kitchen the beans in the frying pan are starting to splatter, pop. Luz hurries over to the stove to lower the blue flame, and the bubbles in the beans die down. Now that Luz and Regina are in the kitchen, the old man turns the volume of *Wheel of Fortune* back up. "*I'd like to buy a vowel, please, Pat.*" Luz just shakes her head.

Regina sits down at the aluminum kitchen table. She glances around the room, from the paint-peeling walls to the cracked ceiling to the mousetraps beside the stove. Luz sighs, leaning against the sink. "Yes," she says, "it is terrible."

Regina looks at her friend. "You're not happy here, are you, Luz?"

"I hate it. I hate Brown's Mill. My father promised it would be nice here. Right by the river, just like our home in Puerto Rico, he said. But in Puerto Rico the river was clean enough to drink from. Here it is dark and gray, coming through those rotting factories."

The little boy, Jorge, has tottered into the room. He clings to Luz's legs, staring his odd brown eyes over at Regina.

"This is my brother, Jorge," Luz says.

"Hello, Jorge," Regina says, reaching out her hand.

"He is retarded," Luz tells her. "He is afraid of people."

But the little boy takes Regina's hand nonetheless. The old woman smiles.

Luz walks over to the stove and stirs the beans in the pot. "Kyle always promised me we would leave Brown's Mill. When he got out of the service, we would move away."

"Well, I'd miss you if you left, Luz," Regina says, still shaking the little boy's hand, making him laugh.

"This town is dead," Luz says. "Look at the buildings. Hunched down and bitter, facing not the sky but the earth."

"Luz wants to *go*," Jorge tells Regina suddenly.

"Go where?" Regina asks.

"Just *go*," Jorge says.

Regina sighs, gently removing her hand from Jorge's and looking once more around the kitchen. No curtains at the window, no bright yellow curtains as there were in Regina's own kitchen. The linoleum floor is dull and scuffed, not shiny the way Regina keeps hers. There's a puddle of water collecting under the refrigerator. It gives off a bad smell, not the clean scent of lemon Lysol that Regina's used to.

Luz slides some beans from the pan onto a plate for Jorge. He sits at the table and eats with his hands. His sister sits down now too, between Jorge and Regina.

"When I was a girl," Regina tells her, "I wanted to go, too. My sister and I actually ran away to the city. We sang at clubs. The Gunderson Sisters."

"Yes, you've told me, Mrs. Day. I love picturing you as a singer."

Regina grins. She feels her cheeks push up into her face.

"Yes. I was a *singer*."

"I'll bet you have a beautiful voice."

"Oh, not anymore. Now it's old and dry. But then . . ." She laughs a little. "Maybe then it was all right. We sang at a place called Heck's. At night sometimes, right before I fall asleep, I can still hear the soldiers cheering and whistling . . ."

"Soldiers?"

"It was during the war. The audience was always mostly soldiers and sailors. They were so appreciative of us, because you know . . . they were all going to leave there and . . . well, you know, they might not come back . . ."

Luz rests her chin in her hands, her elbows propped against the table. "So why did you return to Brown's Mill? Why ever would you come back *here*?"

Regina stops smiling. "Well, my sister, she . . . she got sick for a while. We had to come home."

"Did she get better?"

"Oh, yes, she got better."

"So why did you stay here then? Why didn't you go back to the city after she got well?"

"Oh, well, so many things . . ."

Luz sits forward suddenly in her chair. "Mrs. Day, if I leave Brown's Mill, I'm not ever coming back."

Regina's taken by surprise. She doesn't respond.

"If I leave, I'm going to become a model in the city. I'm going to become a famous model."

Regina tries to smile. "Well, you're certainly beautiful enough. You won that beauty contest, after all."

"And I want you to know, Mrs. Day, that no matter what, I always liked our talks. I always did, no matter what."

Regina looks at her oddly. "Are you planning to *go*, Luz?"

The girl glances over at Jorge. "I *would* go, but I can't leave him. That is the problem." She seems near tears. "They don't understand Jorge."

There comes a shout from the other room. A loud, hoarse shout, then nothing.

"What is it?" Luz stands abruptly, calling in to her grandfather. "What is wrong?"

The dog has started barking again. Luz hurries out of the kitchen.

"*I'd like to try to solve the puzzle, Pat.*"

"Oh, no!" Luz calls from the other room.

"Luz!" Regina stands now too. "What is it?"

The girl suddenly rushes back into the kitchen. Her face is white. Regina watches as she snatches the phone from the wall and presses some buttons. She shouts in Spanish, then changes to English.

"Please! You must send someone! My grandfather! I need an ambulance!"

Regina looks over at Jorge, who just keeps on eating his beans.

Regina Day is a small woman, with a square face and fair complexion and compelling blue eyes. Crystal blue, as crystal as the glassware displayed throughout her house. Her features are what were once called *handsome* in a woman, and even the ravages of more than seven decades have not completely erased her handsomeness. She walks now with a slight stoop, and she winces occasionally from a sharp pinch of arthritis, mostly in her legs. But she still stands slightly taller than Luz, who is no more than five-foot-two.

She holds Luz in her arms as they watch the old man carried out of the house on a stretcher. They pack him into the ambulance and drive off, red lights flashing, the siren wailing. The setting sun casts long blue shadows of bare twisted trees across the street. The wind picks up. Bitter cold.

"You were supposed to watch him." Luz's father is a tall, dark, scary man with deep-set black eyes. Regina is terrified of him. He looks like every man who has ever scared her in her life. He glares down at them and shakes his finger at the girl in Regina's arms. "He was an old man. He's had heart attacks before. You know that!"

"All he was doing was sitting on the couch," Luz says, defending herself. Regina feels the girl's body stiffen.

The father yells at her in alternating languages. "You should have seen it coming!" Then something in Spanish. "You should have called a doctor!"

He spits on the ground and turns to walk away.

"Don't go, Papa!" Luz calls after him. "Come back and I will make dinner!"

"No, Luz, don't," Regina says, holding the girl back.

Her father just keeps walking.

"Papa wants to drink," Jorge says, watching him entranced.

Luz pulls out of Regina's arms and slaps her brother across the face. "Don't say that," she scolds.

The boy doesn't cry. He just keeps staring after his father.

"Come stay with me tonight, Luz," Regina offers.

"I can't. I have to watch Jorge."

"Bring the boy. It will be delightful to have you both."

Luz looks at her. "My father will be angry."

"Yes," Regina says, looking after the man. He turns a corner and disappears. "I imagine he will."

"But we'll come," the girl says, suddenly defiant. "What do you think, Jorge? Should we go spend the night with Mrs. Day?"

The boy nods.

Regina beams.

How pretty Luz is. Pretty like Rocky.

Strong like Rocky, too.

"We don't have to stay here," Rocky had told her, one night in the dark. Papa was in the other room, blaring his radio, smashing bottles against the wall. "We can get out of here anytime we want," Rocky said.

"But how?" Regina couldn't imagine leaving.

"We can *run away*, Regina. You've seen it in the movies. We can climb out our window at night and run away."

"But where would we go?"

Rocky was looking at her swollen lip in the mirror. It was all purple and black, like a fat nightcrawler. "He'd never find us," she said, her eyes in the mirror. "We'd go to the city. No one would ever find us there."

Luz packs a small bag for herself and Jorge. Regina watches her, jubilant. They climb into Kyle's Trans Am, Jorge sitting on Regina's lap in the passenger seat.

"Is he too heavy for you?" Luz asks.

"Oh, no, not at all. He's just right."

Luz smiles as she starts the engine. "I've never seen him take to anyone the way he's taken to you. Usually he is afraid. Shy."

Regina lets the child kiss her powdered cheek.

Luz backs the car out of the driveway. A heavy blue darkness settles over Dogtown. The wind howls.

This is the bad part of town. That's what Regina had always heard all of her life. Mormor said the dirty Eye-talians threw garbage in the street down here. Uncle Axel said whores did their business in the old factory tenements. Robert said pinko commie hippies burned the flag in public.

And this is where Walter came—

"Walter."

She sees him. There, ahead of them in the street.

A boy on a bicycle, pedaling as fast as his little legs can take him. Walter. Little Walter. And he's crying.

She turns. But he's not so little anymore. He's a man now, looking so much like Robert, standing there in Howard Greer's driveway, opening the passenger's door on his car to let a boy with orange hair slide inside.

Regina leans down to whisper into Jorge's ear. "Do you see that young man there? The one in the driveway of that house?"

Jorge follows the direction of her finger but says nothing.

"That's my son," Regina tells him.

"Really, Mrs. Day?" Luz asks, overhearing. "Is that really your son?"

"Yes. That's Walter."

"What is your son doing in Brown's Mill? I thought he had moved to the city."

"He's come back."

Luz makes a little laugh. "And he lives here in *this* neighborhood?"

"There's nothing shameful about Dogtown, Luz," Regina insists. "I used to think there was, but I was wrong."

They pass onto Main Street, leaving the swamps behind.

"But I was wrong," Regina repeats.

7

ALL AMERICAN BOY

It's the summer of tall ships, fifes and drums, and flags flapping from every house—and Wally Day has just been named this year's All American Boy.

"Can you turn this way a little? Yeah, that's it. Say cheese!"

The photographer from the *Brown's Mill Reminder* snaps his camera, Wally blinking from the flash. Around his shoulder his father's arm feels heavy and damp. The temperature outside is steadily ratcheting up into the nineties but Captain Day is nonetheless in full uniform, and Wally's in a long-sleeved shirt with a clip-on blue necktie. After all, it's not every day that one is named All American Boy by the American Legion.

"You must be very proud of your son," the photographer says.

Captain Day's face glows as brightly as his buttons. "You bet I am."

"How's it feel to be asked to lead the Fourth of July parade, Wally?" the photographer asks, snapping another shot.

"It feels great," Wally says.

His eyes move over to the kitchen, where his mother is watching from the doorway. She wasn't asked to be in the picture. Wally feels bad about that but says nothing. She doesn't seem to mind.

"Is that it then?" Captain Day asks.

"I think so," the photographer tells him. "Until the parade."

"Don't you want a picture of the certificate?" Captain Day lifts the piece of paper that officially names Wally the town's All American Boy. "*For excellence in academic achievement and extraordinary devotion to community and nation,*" he reads.

"Good idea," the photographer says, snapping a picture of Wally's father holding the certificate. "You know what they say about the apple not falling far from the tree."

Captain Day beams.

Wally feels as if he'll pass out from the heat. "May I take the tie off now?"

"Go ahead," the photographer tells him, being escorted to the door by Captain Day. "We'll have you on the front page of next week's paper, Wally."

The boy unclips his tie, popping open the shirt button that's been cutting off his windpipe.

"We'll put this in our scrapbook," his mother says, finally coming out of the kitchen. She lifts the certificate from the table to gaze at it. Wally can see his name written in calligraphy beneath stark black letters that read ALL AMERICAN BOY.

"Scrapbook?" his father barks, returning to the room and startling his wife. "We'll do no such thing. We'll frame it! Hang it on the wall! This is the *American Legion*, for God's sake, Regina. We're not going to hide it away in a scrapbook."

Wally blushes. His father takes the certificate from her and hands it to his son. Looking down at it, Wally feels his face burn.

"May I change my clothes now and go over to Freddie's?" he asks.

His father tousles his hair. "Of course, Wally."

The boy carries the certificate to his room and stuffs it into the top drawer of his dresser. He hopes his father doesn't have it framed. It's not that Wally isn't proud of it. He is. He just doesn't want to have to look at it.

He changes out of his starched shirt and wool pants. His skin feels clammy. He pulls on a pair of plaid shorts and a T-shirt.

He's late. He told Josephine he'd be at her house by noon.

"I'm going to Freddie's," he says, coming back into the living room.

"Another softball game?" his father asks.

"Yup."

"Okay, son. Hit a homer for me!"

"Will do!"

The screen door slams behind him.

Of course, there's no softball game. There's *never* a softball game when Wally tells his father there is.

Instead, he's heading to see Josephine Leopold, who's eighty-seven years old, and who, in her day, had been a great actress. She had trod the boards, as she put it, with all of the greats: Mrs. Fiske, Mrs. Campbell, and all three of the Barrymores.

"But mostly Miss Le Gallienne," Josephine told him.

"Who's she?"

Josephine's rheumy yellow eyes had narrowed in outrage. "Why, Eva Le Gallienne was the greatest actress ever in American theater! Don't start with me about Kit Cornell! Or Helen Hayes. *Hah!* Miss Le Gallienne had more talent in her pinky finger than any of the rest of them had in their whole bodies!"

Wally smiles as he pedals his bike down Washington Avenue, thinking of her. Josephine's become this *presence* to him, this big, colorful, commanding presence that fills up his mind. When he's with her, it's like she takes up all the space, sucks the air out of the room. When he thinks about her, he's got no room left to think about anything else, no room for any other foolish little inconsequential thoughts that might—

"Hey, watch it, kid!"

He has to slam on his brakes to stop his bike from zooming right out into traffic. The light's changed to red at the busy Washington and Fisk Drive intersection. He waits impatiently. A Camaro full of teenagers rolls up next to him.

The kids are all singing along with the radio: *Life is a rock—but the radio rolled me—got to turn it up looooouder—so my DJ told me* . . .

One of the girls looks over at Wally on his bike. He recognizes her from the grade ahead of him in school. She smiles at him. He blushes, turning away.

The light changes and he makes a dash across the street, quickly zigzagging down Gate Road. It's ten after twelve. Josephine doesn't like to be kept waiting. He rides straight through a game of soft-ball some boys are playing in the street in front of her house.

"If you want to succeed as an actor," she calls from the front door, "it's best to be on time for auditions."

She fills up the entire door frame. She's a tall woman, at least six feet, with broad shoulders and short red hair. Wally figures she must dye it that color. It's red almost the color of a fire engine.

"I'm sorry, Josephine. There was some guy at my house taking pictures."

"Pictures?"

"Yeah. I was named All American Boy."

She grunts, stepping aside so he can enter the house. "And what does that mean?"

Wally sighs. "That I get good grades, I guess. And I'm president of my class." He pauses. "And I'm patriotic."

"How do they know that? Are you out there waving a flag for some bicentennial pep rally?"

"No."

"What a useless honor," she sniffs. "What will you ever do with it? How can it ever help you?"

He shrugs.

"I assume your father was very pleased," she says, folding her arms over her chest. She's wearing a long red housecoat, fastened at the throat with a safety pin.

"I guess it *is* kind of stupid," Wally says.

"Who would want to be All American anything? If I'd had my way I'd be living in Paris. This country had its chance in the 1930s. We might have become a nation with a conscience, with values, ideals. But instead what do we do? We hound men to death for their political beliefs. Our highest elected official is forced out of office for criminality. The land of the free. Hah! I've never heard of anything so absurd."

Wally sits down on her sofa, looking up at her. "I'm going to have to lead the Fourth of July parade on Saturday."

"You poor child." She places a hand over her heart, feigning weakness. "How will you *ever* get through it?"

"The photographer said I'll be on the front page of the paper."

She shudders. "It must have been *quite* the morning at your house."

Wally smiles. "It was. My father put on his naval uniform and everything."

"And he let you leave all that flag-waving so you could come here and study to be an actor?"

Wally sighs. "He doesn't know that I'm here."

She glares down at him. "You're playing baseball or something silly like that."

"Yeah." Outside he can hear the whoops and shouts of the boys playing softball in the street.

It's been three months. Three glorious months since he met her. For his final grade in his civics class, Wally had chosen to write an essay about Josephine. His assignment had been to write about someone interesting, someone who's had an interesting career or done interesting things with their life. Quite naturally, Wally's teacher assumed he would choose his father, but instead the boy selected old Josephine Leopold, the retired actress and eccentric recluse who people whispered was a Communist. Wally had long heard the stories about her. She lived in the house where she'd been born some eight decades earlier, before starting out on a career that took her from Brown's Mill to Broadway to Paris and finally all the way to Moscow.

"Well, I admit she's interesting," Wally's teacher had said. "But she wasn't a star, Wally, not really."

Yet Wally would not be dissuaded. The old woman had arched a suspicious eyebrow at him when he came knocking, but she'd let him in, and they ended up talking for hours. She showed Wally programs with her name heading the cast lists at theaters as far-flung as Des Moines and Syracuse and Pittsburgh and Kansas City. She showed him photographs: she and Miss Le Gallienne, she and Lionel Barrymore, she and Lord Olivier.

"And you were born here, in Brown's Mill, just like me," he said, in awe.

"That I was."

"But you left, and you became a star."

She smiled, clearly relishing Wally's admiration. She told her stories and he listened raptly. He got an A on his report, and when he returned to show Josephine his grade, he confided to her his secret dream, something he'd never told anyone else.

He wanted to be an actor.

"The theater is a great calling, but one not easily understood by those who do not hear it," Josephine told him. "And neither is it an easy path, my young friend. A life in the theater is not an easy path, nor should it be."

"I want it," he told her. "I want it more than anything."

Now that he's being taught by her, now that he's been taking instruction these last several weeks, he wants it even more.

"All right now," she's saying. "Did you study your lines?"

Wally nods.

"Fucking out, man, fuckin' out!" The high-pitched voice of one of the boys in the street comes through the window.

Josephine shudders, moving over to pull the window down with a bang.

"Now," she says, turning back to Wally, "move into character." She assumes her position in the middle of the parlor, drawing herself up to her full height. Her chin juts forward. "You are Alice and I'm the Red Queen."

Wally stands in front of her and imagines himself as Alice in Wonderland. There was no discussion about him playing a girl's role. Wally had understood it was irrelevant. This is the theater, and he is an *actor*. He can play *anything*.

"Alice is facing left," Josephine instructs. "She has been running from the Pack of Cards, but now she slows down wearily and comes to a stop."

Wally pantomimes the action. It is important to convey the weariness Alice feels. It's central to the scene. He huffs a little, hangs his head, but is careful not to overdo it. Josephine had scolded him yesterday for doing that.

"Presently, from the left," Josephine says, the stage directions still memorized from decades before, "come the *thump, thump, thump* of footsteps." She makes the sounds with her feet. "Enter the Red Queen."

She draws herself up even taller, her red housecoat lifting to reveal wrinkled, flaking, bare feet beneath.

"Where do you come from and where are you going?" Josephine's voice is high and shrill. "Look up, speak nicely, and don't twiddle your fingers."

Wally attends to all of these directions as best he can. "You see," he says, his throat dry, "I've lost my way."

"I don't see what you mean by your way, all the ways here belong to me—but why did you come out here at all? Curtsy while you're thinking what to say. It saves time."

Wally does. "I'll try it when I go home the next time I'm a little late for dinner."

"No, no, no!" Josephine calls. "You dolt!"

Wally's confused. That's not the next line. Then he realizes she's no longer the Red Queen. She's Josephine again and she's scolding him.

"That should be said as an *aside!*" She storms across the room, fuming. "Didn't you read the script at all? You're talking to the *audience*, not to me! It was Miss Le Gallienne's brilliant insertion of wry humor! Oh, Wally, if you failed to see the line as an aside, I'm afraid you'll never become a good actor."

"Give me another chance."

"Why should I?"

He's momentarily unsure of his answer.

"Because . . . because . . . somebody must have given you another chance once. You got out of here. You left Brown's Mill and became a great actress. You couldn't have done it all on the first try."

She narrows her old weak eyes at him. "Your father wants you to be a military man."

"Please give me another chance."

From somewhere in her house a clock chimes once. The shades are drawn against the bright day and the temperature in the room is stifling. Wally realizes he's sweating. Yet even with the window closed he can still hear the boys playing softball.

"He's safe, man! *Safe!*"

"I did Chekhov in Moscow," Josephine is saying dreamily. "It was the greatest night of my life. *Uncle Vanya*. I played Sonya." She laughs. "It was a long, long way from here."

Wally listens.

"Do you realize what an honor it was for me to do Chekhov for the Moscow Art Theater? I can still hear the applause from that night. The roses thrown at my feet. The reviews were glowing—"

"What did they say?"

"'A bright star from the heavens,' they called me. They said I *was* Sonya. They didn't know, didn't care, that I was a tailor's daughter from Brown's Mill, a tall, gangly, homely boy-girl who never finished the seventh grade. They just knew that, standing there, on that stage so far away from here, I was Sonya. That I was a bright star from the heavens doing Chekhov at the Moscow Art Theater!"

She stands there in the middle of the parlor, consumed by the memory.

"These sad autumn roses," she says suddenly, a voice different from her own. "Winter will be here soon and they will all be gone. Perhaps then, Uncle Vanya and I can get back to work."

Her eyes search out something Wally can't see.

"And in the long evenings," she says, "we can sit together and do our work, Uncle Vanya and I. Work will save us. We'll live through a long, long line of days, endless evenings . . . and God will take pity on us, and you and I, Uncle, darling Uncle, shall see life bright, beautiful, fine, we shall be happy and look back tenderly with a smile on these misfortunes we have now—and we shall rest."

She kneels down with some difficulty, her knees creaking, lowering her head now to gaze at an invisible photograph she holds in her hands.

"We shall rest! We shall hear the angels, we shall see the whole sky all diamonds, we shall see how all earthly evil, all our sufferings, are drowned in the mercy that will fill the whole world. And our life will grow peaceful, tender, sweet as a caress. I believe, I do believe . . . Poor, dear Uncle Vanya, in your life you haven't known what joy was . . ."

Large tears drip down off her face. Wally can almost hear them as they hit the carpet.

"But wait, Uncle Vanya, wait . . . We shall rest . . . We shall rest . . . We shall rest . . ."

She is still. She doesn't move.

Wally applauds. The sound of his little boy hands clapping echoes in the dark old house.

Josephine says nothing. She remains fixed in position, kneeling on the floor.

"Bravo!" Wally calls. "Encore, encore!"

Then slowly, softly, gently, she falls over onto her side.

"Josephine?"

"You're out, man, you're fucking out," comes the high-pitched voice of one of the boys in the street.

* * *

Ever since he played St. Joseph in his fifth grade Christmas play, Wally has wanted to be an actor. His lines had been enunciated loudly and clearly, and he'd taken three curtain calls—and afterward, in the cafeteria for punch and cookies, he'd overheard the parents saying to each other, "That Wally Day is going to go far."

Go far. It's a phrase he often repeats to himself, holds close to his heart.

He likes to believe those parents meant he had great acting ability, that his St. Joseph was the best they'd ever seen, that someday they were certain he'd be one of the greats, the star of *The Wally Day Show* on CBS on Saturday night. Now he studies his mother's soap operas whenever his father is away, watching how the actors move, how they deliver their lines, how they dress. They're all so handsome. They're what Wally wants to be: sturdy and handsome, a real All American Actor.

"Josephine?"

It takes him several minutes to realize that she's dead.

He tries to take her pulse but he doesn't know how to do it. He grips her wrist but feels nothing. He pushes his head in toward her chest to listen for her heart. Her body rolls over onto her back.

He sits back on his knees in horror.

She's dead.

Josephine is dead.

"You're going to go far," said Sister Angela, the principal of St. John the Baptist elementary school, after St. Joseph had made his last curtain call. "Yes, indeed, Walter Day. You are going to go *very* far."

Josephine is dead.

"And Dad will find out I wasn't playing softball," Wally whispers into the dark.

He stands, looking down at Josephine's body. He feels cold and dizzy. He wants to scream but knows he'd better not.

She's not dead, he tells himself. *She'll open her eyes. She'll make a sound. She'll be all right.*

"Josephine?"

Her eyes are still halfway open.

"Josephine, please be alive."

He leans down over her, looking closely into her face.

No, she's dead. She's really dead.

I've got to go.

Go far.

"Go to second! Go to second!"

In the bushes, Wally steels himself. The boys in the street had seen him arrive. They'd seen him go into Josephine's house. They could tell the police that someone had been there just before she died. But he didn't know these boys. They weren't in his class. He recognized none of them. Had any of them recognized him?

He can think of nothing but getting his bike and sneaking out through Josephine's backyard. He feels no grief, no sadness, no sympathy—just fear. He just wants to get away from the house, away from the body. He wants to get back home before his father can find out he lied about playing softball with Freddie.

That's when he spots his cousin Kyle with the boys.

"No," Wally whispers to himself.

Kyle had almost ruined his portrayal of St. Joseph. He had sat there in the audience and hooted, "Hey, look, St. Joseph's wearing Keds!" Wally's sneakers had been showing from under his robes. The audience had laughed, and oh, how Wally hates being laughed at it. He almost forgot his next line. But he recovered, as Josephine would say. He recovered and went on.

My bike, he thinks. *Please, just let me get my bike.*

It's lying in the grass beside the walkway to Josephine's front porch. If he can make a run for it, grab its handlebars, and dive back into the bushes, there's a chance he won't be seen. There's a possibility even Kyle's eagle eye will miss him. It's now or never. He can't wait any longer. Someone might come by and find Josephine dead inside.

She's dead! Josephine is dead!

Wally runs.

"He's safe! He's safe!"

He takes hold of his bike and trips, falling face down in the grass.

"No way, Baronowski, he's safe! He's fuckin' safe!"

The blood is pounding in Wally's ears. He gets up and runs with his bike into Josephine's backyard. He's skinned his knee and it stings but he hops onto the bike anyway and pedals the hell out of there, all the way across town, barely stopping for traffic, until he's home.

"Benjamin Franklin was not only a statesman but also a scientist, coming up with a new theory on the nature of electricity," John Davidson says, perky and dimpled on the television set.

Wally's always thought that John Davidson was very handsome, but of course he's never told anyone that. Boys weren't supposed to know who was handsome and who was not. But tonight John Davidson's dimples aren't really getting much thought anyway. "Thanks for watching," the baby-faced actor is saying. "This has been another Bicentennial minute."

Drums roll and flags unfurl. Wally's mother sits knitting on the couch, her eyeglasses having slipped down toward the brim of her nose.

"I'm going to bed," Wally tells her.

"You don't want to watch *Welcome Back, Rotter*?"

"No, I'm tired."

His father is stretched out in his La-Z-Boy. "Pooped from the game, huh? Who ended up winning?"

"We did."

"Attaboy."

He starts down the hall.

Josephine is dead.

And I left her there.

It's the only thing he's been able to think about all day.

Why didn't I call an ambulance? I can't believe I didn't call an ambulance. What if she needed help? What if she would've lived if I hadn't panicked and run off?

I killed her. I killed Josephine.

She's still there the next day, on the floor in the parlor, in the exact same position he left her. Wally's not sure what he expected to see, but somehow it surprises him that she's still there, in the same position.

Of course she is, he tells himself. *She's dead, and dead people don't move.*

There's no smell. He expected there would be a smell, especially with it being so hot outside. Ninety-three today. But there's no odor. Her house still smells the way it always has, like Lemon Pledge and mothballs.

No one had seen him come into the house this time. He'd left his bike in the Dairy Queen parking lot on Washington Street and snuck through backyards to get here. He came in through Josephine's back door. It was unlocked. The whole house is unlocked. Anybody could rob her blind.

But she's dead. Josephine is dead.

"I'm sorry, Josephine," he says, looking down at her.

He doesn't want to have to call anyone. This is what he wants: for someone just to come by and find her, like the mailman. Or some door-to-door salesman. That way Wally will never have to be associated with it. He'll never have to admit to his father that he wasn't playing softball with Freddie, that he was over here playing Alice in Wonderland with a crazy old Communist lady.

But Josephine didn't get much mail. And no one came to see her except Wally. She could lie here for weeks. Months!

Maybe I could make an anonymous call to the police. Yeah, I should do that. Just call them and hang up after—

But the police have ways of tracing phone calls. He's seen them do it on *Kojak*.

"Someone's *got* to find her," Wally wails, looking back down at the corpse. It doesn't seem like Josephine. It just seems like a body. A mannequin from Grant's department store.

"I'm sorry, Josephine," he whispers. "Really I am."

That night he stares out his window in the direction of her house. Next door he can see Mr. and Mrs. Daley fighting in an upstairs room. He can tell they're fighting by their silhouettes, the way they jerk back and forth. He can hear the sounds of their television lilting through the night, a tinny sitcom.

And underneath, as ever, he can hear Helen Piatrowski scream.

He knows this town. He knows the stories they tell, the secrets they keep. But they don't know his. Beyond the houses of his street rise the hills, where the orchards run deep and dark, and somewhere behind them is Josephine's house. Wally tries to picture the vibrant woman he'd known, the dazzling, all-consuming presence who had filled up all his waking thoughts. But he can't—he can't visualize her, as hard as he tries. All he can see is the body on the floor, staring up at the ceiling, in its frayed old housecoat, a final costume for the Red Queen.

"And leading the way is Brown's Mill's All American Boy—Walter Day!"

The crowd applauds.

The announcer leans forward into his microphone. "And next to him is his father, Captain Robert Day, one of our local hometown heroes who was wounded in Vietnam and remains a proud leader in our nation's fighting forces!"

More applause. Somebody from the crowd shouts out, "Way to go, Robbie!"

Trumpets sound and a drumroll kicks the parade off under bright blue skies. Wally and his father walk in front of the mayor and the town councilmen, waving to the crowd assembled on both sides of Main Street. An honor guard bearing an American flag and an original thirteen-colonies stars-and-stripes walk alongside of them.

All these faces. Waving, smiling, laughing. Wally stares into their eyes. Everyone looking at him.

And across town, Josephine is rotting on her living room floor.

Yesterday he had finally been struck by the smell. Thick and mangy. Fruity. For the past three days, he's snuck through the backyards to peek inside her house, just to see if the body was still there. And it always was. In the same place. The same position.

Josephine is lying dead on her floor. And only he knows. Only he.

"This way, Wally!" It's the photographer from the *Brown's Mill Reminder*. "Give me a big grin for the front page."

Wally waves and smiles. His cheeks are starting to hurt.

"Hey, Wally!"

A girl from his class. Her bright smiling face.

But in her place Wally sees Josephine, rotting on the floor.

"This is what it's going to be like, Wally," his father tells him as they march down Main Street, past St. John the Baptist Church and the Palace Theater. "People applauding, people looking to you to set an example. I've known this since the age of five, when my father first came home from the Big War and he took me with him to a victory parade. People need heroes, Wally. And the Days have a long history of providing them."

"Hey, Wally!"

It's Freddie Piatrowski and Michael Marino. They shout over to him. He waves.

And neither is it an easy path, my young friend. A life in the theater is not an easy path, nor should it be.

Josephine's dead. He can smell her. Even out here on Main Street, blocks away from her house, he knows her corpse is reeking. The day is wicked hot.

"Walter! Robert!"

It's his mother, on the sidelines, jumping up, trying to snap their picture. Wally gives her a little wave but his father is turned the other way, smiling toward the other side of the street. Then they're past her, and Wally watches out of the corner of his eye as his mother is pushed back by the policeman guarding the route.

Josephine's dead.

Wally's stomach roils. The hot sun bears down upon them.

"Hooray!" some kids shout up ahead. "Hooray for the USA!"

Captain Day beams, giving them the "thumbs-up" sign.

The land of the free. Hah! I've never heard of anything so absurd.

"This is it, Wally," his father says, as the photographs keep snapping, the applause keeps sounding. "This is what your life is going to be."

Wally looks from side to side, waving, trying hard to keep the smile on his face. Sweat rolls down his face and he has to fight the nausea that's bubbling up again in his gut.

Josephine's dead.

Josephine's dead.

Josephine's dead.

He sees her in the faces of the crowd, sees her wherever he looks.

"Hey, Wally!"

Josephine's dead.

"Hey, Wally!"

Josephine—

He can't hold it any longer.

He bolts from the parade to the side of the road and pukes into the gutter. Two little girls waving their tiny American flags scream as Wally's chunky vomit splatters onto their patent-leather shoes. Wally holds his gut as he retches again. The crowd pulls away in disgust.

His father is mortified. He stands over Wally with his mouth open.

"What are you doing?" he demands. "What are you *doing*?"

Wally retches with a dry heave.

Captain Day hurries away from him, back into the parade. Wally staggers away from the crowd, wiping his face. The little girls are still screaming.

And Josephine is dead on her floor, left there by an All American Boy.

His father ships out the next day. That's the way it goes. Wally never knows when he's leaving, and they never say good-bye. He just wakes up to find his father gone.

"Are you feeling better, Walter?" his mother asks as he stumbles into the kitchen, rubbing his eyes. "Heatstroke can be awful."

Josephine's dead.

"Your father left these for you," his mother tells him, indicating a stack of brochures on the table, promoting the state's military academy. Even though Wally's only entering seventh grade in the fall, his father likes to plan ahead.

Wally says nothing, just shakes some Lucky Charms into a bowl. He looks down at the kitchen table. Beside the brochures for the military academy sits the *Brown's Mill Reminder*. There, on the front page, is a photograph of Wally and his father waving in the parade.

And underneath the story, another headline:

ACTRESS FOUND DEAD AT HOME.

"Oh," Wally says, dropping the cereal box to the floor.

"What is it, Walter?" his mother asks.

Wally has picked up the newspaper and is reading it.

Josephine Leopold, 87, retired stage actress, was found dead on her floor yesterday afternoon by a concerned neighbor who had noticed a smell . . .

"Oh, yes, the article," his mother says, beaming. "Don't you both look so handsome?"

Her death appeared due to natural causes. The coroner estimated she had been dead for two or three days.

Five days, Wally thinks. *Dead for five days.*

"I'm going to clip it out and send it to your father. He'll be so proud."

Wally sets the paper down on the table and looks over at his mother.

"Mom," he says.

"Yes, Walter?"

He hesitates for just a second, then says it. "I want to be an actor."

She blinks at him, confused.

"I want to go to acting school."

"Oh, Walter."

"Could I? Could I take acting classes?"

She begins to tremble. "Walter, please—"

"I want to be an actor, Mom. That's what I've decided. Okay?"

His mother lifts her hands into the air, waving them back and forth as if to ward off some kind of attack. "Walter, those brochures please—your father wants you to go the academy—"

"I don't want to! Please! You've got to help me! Please, Mom!"

"Walter, your father—"

"Like you wanted to be a singer. Please help me, Mom! You went off to the city and became a singer!"

"No!" She's close to crying. "That was silly, Walter! Silly and stupid!"

"It wasn't!"

"Yes, it was! Stupid, stupid, stupid!" She's covering her ears as if she doesn't want to hear what she's saying. "It was stupid and so is this!"

"I want to be an actor! Help me, Mom, please! You could help me if you wanted to! Please, Mother, help me! It's my *dream!*"

His mother breaks down into tears and runs from the room. He hears the door to her bedroom slam shut.

He stands there for several minutes looking down at the newspaper.

Miss Leopold left Brown's Mill at age 16 to go on the stage with the company of Minnie Maddern Fiske . . .

Walter is the son of Captain Robert Day.

He walks down the hall to his room.

I left her there to rot, he thinks, staring into his mirror. Behind him his certificate is reflected hanging on the wall in a frame.

He walks over, removes it from its hook, and slips out the certificate from the back of the frame.

All American Boy.

Leaves his teacher to rot on the floor.

He crumples the certificate in his hand, then flushes it down the toilet.

From his mother's room he can hear her sobs. They are deep and guttural, wracking her body, louder and more terrible than he has ever heard them before. He doesn't go in to try to console her. There's nothing he can do for her.

And nothing she can do for him, either.

Nothing at all.

8

SINGING FOR THEIR SUPPER

In the backseat of the car, the soldier has his hands up Rocky's blouse. From the front seat, Regina can hear the soft pop of her sister's bra strap being unhooked. Her eyes dart over to meet those of the fellow sitting next to her. He is coming closer. He actually licks his lips. Regina makes a little sound, her body tensing. She knows he wants to do the same thing to her that his friend is doing to Rocky.

"No, Buzz," comes her sister's voice from the backseat. "Leave Regina alone."

The man pauses in his approach.

"Regina isn't that kind of girl," Rocky says.

It's as if Rocky can read her mind. It's always been that way between them.

"Not that kind of girl, eh?" Buzz says, laughing, cocking an eye at Regina.

She just twiddles a button on her blouse, not looking at him. *It's not that*, she wants to tell him. *It's just . . . no man would want me. Not now. No man.*

Behind them they can hear Rocky's sloppy kisses with Buzz's friend.

"But you *are*, huh, Rocky?" Buzz asks. "You *are* that kind of girl."

"Yeah," Rocky says, and her voice has that sadness to it that only Regina can hear. "But not Regina. So just leave her alone."

The club manager is named Mr. Heck. His slogan is "Heck sure runs a heckuva club." He's tall and wiry and has a gold tooth that glitters in the light, and he always wears a puff of red silk in the front pocket of his pinstriped suit.

"So long as you're both older than eighteen, I don't care," he says.

"We are," Rocky lies. "I'm nineteen and my sister is twenty."

He looks them both up and down. "Don't look it to me."

Rocky cups her breasts in both hands and practically shoves them in Mr. Heck's face. "You ever seen melons like this on somebody under eighteen?"

The manager's gold tooth sparkles. "Awright, awright, just be here at nine o'clock and I'll put you on."

"Thirty dollars?"

"I said twenty-five."

Rocky glowers in at him. "How can you split twenty-five between two girls? Make it an even thirty. Two tens, two fives, so we can each take our share."

Heck frowns. "You gonna show some cleavage?"

"Of *course*," Rocky says, cupping her breasts again and pushing them in close together.

Regina sees that look in Mr. Heck's eyes, the kind of look men always get when Rocky makes up her mind to go after them. "Okay," Mr. Heck says, staring. "Thirty. Just don't be late."

At night, even here in the city, Regina still dreams about Papa. She dreams about him all night long, but in the morning, she can't remember the details of her dreams, which is a good thing, Rocky tells her. In fact, Regina can hardly remember anything about her life before she and Rocky came to the city, even though it's only been a month. Brown's Mill is a vague, obscure memory. It's as if the city, their new home, with all its bleating taxicabs and towering buildings and flashing neon had just rushed right in and filled up her brain, obliterating everything else that had been in there.

Except, of course, when she dreams.

"We're okay," Rocky says into the telephone. "Really, Aunt Selma, we're fine."

Regina watches as her sister talks to their aunt. They're standing on the street, using a pay phone, and all sorts of crazy street people are walking past them, singing songs, talking to themselves, trying to beg a couple of nickels.

"No, I am *not* telling you where we are so that Uncle Axel can come down to get us," Rocky says. "We're *fine*."

Rocky makes a face, moving her lips to mock Aunt Selma's scolding voice on the other end of the phone. Regina laughs and covers her mouth with her hand.

"I've gotta go now, Aunt Selma. I've run out of coins. I just wanted to let you know we're okay. We'll send you lots of money when we become famous. See ya!"

She hangs up the phone.

Regina grabs her sister's arm as they walk down the street, past all the night-clubs and theater marquees. Pert Kelton in *Lady Behave*. Patty Pope in *Slightly Married*. Mary Martin in *One Touch of Venus*.

"Do you think we'll really become famous?" Regina asks.

"Sure we will," Rocky says.

"Famous like the Andrews Sisters?"

"Even more."

"*Even more*," Regina breathes.

They had run away on the night of Regina's fifteenth birthday, just about a month ago, and already they're getting famous. Mr. Heck put them on the regular bill after they did their tryout and the soldiers started asking when "the little ladies" would be coming back. "Okay, so Friday nights at nine," Mr. Heck told them. "Don't be late."

"Thirty-five dollars," Rocky insisted.

"*What?* Who d'you think you are, Maxene and Laverne?"

"You paid us thirty to try us out, now you've gotta pay thirty-five to keep us."

"Go on, get outta here!"

Rocky pulled down her blouse to expose more cleavage. "And what will you have when your GIs start calling for *these* little ladies?"

"I'm telling you, sister, you better show a lotta tit," Mr. Heck warned.

"Rocky," Regina said, after the manager had disappeared, "I wish you wouldn't do that."

"You want to sing, Gina?"

"Yes."

"You want to stay in the city?"

"Of course."

"Then you'd better get used to showing some tit, too."

Regina had blushed deeply. But it was true: she *did* want to sing. Ever since they were little, the girls have loved to sing. Mama taught them little ditties like *"My little baby loves shortnin', shortnin', my little baby loves shortnin' bread."* When Regina was ten and Rocky was nine, Aunt Selma brought them to sing at the Lutheran Church holiday party and everyone had said they had voices so sweet that they had made the Lord very happy. *"Yes, Jesus loves me, yes, Jesus loves me, yes, Jesus loves me, the Bible tells me so . . ."*

And then they'd sung it in Swedish: *"Ja, Jesus älskar, ja, Jesus älskar . . ."*

"Get up, Regina. Get up now."

It's black. Utter darkness.

They're back in their room at Papa's house.

Regina's having a dream.

"Why?" Her voice sounds strange to her ears, as if she's underwater. "Rocky, what's wrong?"

"We're leaving," her sister tells her. "I've packed your bag. We're getting out of here."

Regina looks at herself. She's not in bed. How long has she been lying here on the floor, curled up into a little ball?

"Where's Papa?"

"He's asleep," Rocky tells her. "Come on."

"Are we going to Aunt Selma's and Uncle Axel's?" Many times before, they'd gone there at times like this, hiking down the long dirt road that led to the farms south of town.

"No," Rocky says, and her voice is hard. "We're leaving Brown's Mill. Forever."

"Forever?"

"You want to be a singer, don't you? You want to be as famous as Dinah Shore, don't you?"

"Now the rain's a-fallin', hear the train a-callin'. . . " Regina sings.

"Come on, get up."

Their father is sleeping like a bear on the couch. Earlier there had been a birthday party. *Her own*, Regina thinks, but she can't quite remember. Papa had been drinking, and she has an image of a birthday cake smashed on the floor, but she can't be sure. Now he lies there stretched ungainly across the couch.

"Don't look, Gina. I want you to forget him. Promise me you'll forget him."

"No man will want me now," Regina says, almost not even sure why she says it.

"I said, *forget him*, Gina! *Forget him!*"

Where had Rocky gotten train tickets? And when? Regina doesn't know. The night is cold and their breath clouds up in front of their faces. On the platform, Regina starts to sing again.

"*Hear that lonesome whistle, blowin' cross the trestle . . .*"

"*My Mama done tol' me,*" sing the Gunderson Sisters, "*whoo-ee, whoo-ee . . .*"

"Swing it, sister!"

"*. . . there's blues in the night . . .*"

The soldiers applaud. Hank and Buzz are out front, whistling with their fingers in their mouths. Regina and Rocky take their bows, with Rocky making sure she leans way over so her cleavage is exposed, dark and deep.

It's time for a break. They wipe off their brows backstage, then sit with the boys at their table. "Hey," says Hank, shaking his finger at Rocky, "Heck's gonna have your ass if he sees you drinking scotch."

"Who says he hasn't already had her ass?" Buzz cracks.

Rocky throws her drink at him and snaps her fingers at the waitress to order another. Buzz looks crestfallen at his wet uniform but Hank thinks it's hilarious, cracking up, slapping his thigh.

"Here," Regina says, offering Buzz her napkin.

"Thanks, Gina," he says quietly.

"I've got Heck eating out of my hand," Rocky tells them, taking a sip of her newly freshened drink. "I just talked him into giving us forty dollars a pop."

"Next stop, a recording contract from RCA Victor," says Hank.

"I'm working on it," Rocky says. "Believe me, I'm working on it."

Buzz has returned Regina's napkin to her lap. He lets his hand remain on her knee under the table. She tenses up but doesn't move. Somehow Rocky can tell what he's doing. Regina sees the cold glare come into her sister's eyes.

"Leave her *alone*, Buzz. I've *told* you. You want something worse than a drink thrown at you?"

Regina feels his hand withdraw.

"Hank and me are going out for a walk," Rocky says, standing with her soldier beau. "You behave, Buzz, you hear me?"

"Rocky, it's so cold outside," Regina says, reaching up to place her hand on her sister's arm.

"We'll be in his car," Rocky tells her.

Buzz snorts.

Regina watches them go, shouldering through the crowd toward the door.

Later, Regina would tell Aunt Selma, "We were almost famous." Her aunt would just snort. "Really, we *were*," Regina insisted. "We were getting more famous every day."

Aunt Selma glowered at her. "Why did you run away from your father, Regina?"

The question was absurd. Regina couldn't believe her aunt would ask a question so absurd.

"Because we wanted to be *famous*," she said. "We wanted to be *singers*. And we would have been, too, if—"

If. If what? If what happened to Rocky had never happened? Would they really have gone on to become famous, the way Rocky had predicted? Would they have become world-renowned singers like the Andrews Sisters, or Dinah Shore, or Peggy Lee, or Rosemary Clooney?

"*Don't sit under the apple tree with anyone else but me,*" the girls had sung, "*with anyone else but me, with anyone else but me . . .*"

At night, for the rest of her life, Regina would close her eyes and hear the soldiers cheering for them. The hoots, the hollers, the whistles. She'd remember the lights shining up into their eyes, the pretty dresses they wore, the corsages made out of gardenias that the soldiers gave them. She'd remember the exhilarating taste of scotch whenever she'd sneak a sip of Rocky's drink.

"What happened to Hank and Buzz?" she would ask Rocky, much later, when the cheering was gone, the pretty dresses a memory, the corsages withered and brown.

"Why are you bringing them up? Are you trying to taunt me, Gina?"

"No, Rocky. Of course I'm not."

Rocky just stared out the window. "Hank got killed in the war. I don't know about Buzz. He probably got his arms blown off like that guy in *The Best Years of Our Lives.*"

"Oh, don't say that, Rocky."

But that's how Regina would always think thereafter of the handsome, redhaired soldier who'd wanted to kiss her so bad: mutilated, armless, his limbs blown off for daring to touch Regina's skin.

"Gina, you've got to help me. I'm hurt."

It's Rocky's voice. Regina wakes to see her sister standing over her.

"What is it, Rocky? What's wrong?"

"I don't know. I'm bleeding."

"Did you cut yourself?"

"No. I'm bleeding *down there.*"

Regina reaches over and flicks on her lamp. She gasps. Rocky is standing there naked in front of her, a trickle of blood running down the inside of her leg.

"Oh, my God, Rocky!"

Rocky is crying. "I think I'm losing my baby."

"Tour baby?"

"You've got to go down the hall and call Aunt Selma. I don't want to lose my baby."

"Your baby? Rocky, what baby?"

"Please, Regina! Call her and ask her what I should do."

Rocky's crying like a little girl. But that's what she is, Regina suddenly thinks. A scared little fourteen-year-old girl with breasts prematurely large and a taste for scotch. Regina wants to wrap her arms around her baby sister and tell her it will all be okay.

But she's never done anything like that before. Rocky's always been the one to take care of things, and now Rocky is crying. And bleeding.

"Go call Aunt Selma," Rocky tells her again.

"She'll make us come back to Brown's Mill."

"No, she won't. And if she does, it'll just be for a short while. Please, Regina, hurry! I don't want to lose my baby!"

So Regina runs. She runs down the hall and places the call to Brown's Mill.

The next day Uncle Axel is outside their rooming house in his battered old pickup truck stinking of cow manure, waiting to take them home.

"Tonight we have a special surprise," Mr. Heck had said—when was it? Just two nights before? Just two nights before it all ended, the whole mad crazy adventure of the Gunderson Sisters in the city.

The hoots of the crowd died down. "Miss Regina Gunderson is stepping out," Mr. Heck said, "just this one time, as a solo. Join me in welcoming the quiet sister, ladies and gentlemen. *Regina Gunderson!*"

"Go ahead, Gina," Rocky urged her backstage, as the applause reached a roar. "Go on. Listen to them. They love you!"

"I can't. I can't do a solo. Why are you making me? I can't sing without you."

"Of course you can. I do it all the time. Go on, Gina. Show 'em what you've got."

Regina had never known such fear. Two days later, all this will be just a memory, a moment in time, as she rattles home in Uncle Axel's smelly old truck, squished in between him and Rocky, who sniffles all the way back to Brown's Mill. Why couldn't Rocky have been stronger? Why couldn't she have found someone else to help her so they might have stayed in the city? Regina had always thought Rocky was so strong, that she wasn't scared of anything. But a little trickle of blood and she was terrified. And so they had to go home.

Regina stepped out onto the stage.

"Way to go, baby!" The soldiers whistled, hooted.

She placed her lips close to the microphone.

She began to sing.

"*I guess I'll have . . .*"

Her voice was shaky and off key. She stopped, cleared her throat, and began again. The band restarted with her.

"*I guess I'll have to dream the rest . . .*"

Her voice became fuller, richer, more confident as she went on. The crowd cheered. Buzz winked up at her, lifting his beer to her in salute.

"*If you can't remember the things that you said, the night that my shoulder held your sleepy head . . .*"

Yes, standing there, she was sure of it: she *would* be famous. Famous like Dinah Shore.

More famous even.

"If you believe that parting's best . . ."

The crowd was on its feet.

"I guess I'll have to dream the rest."

9

BRINGING THE DIRT

"Over there, Walter. Put it over there."

He and Dee each have two bags of top soil hoisted over their shoulders. Wally notices the muscles of the boy's arms, straining against his torn white ribbed tank top as he jostles the bags to keep them from slipping. *Strong little monkey*, Wally thinks. Meanwhile his mother, even more anxious than before, is directing them to a spot in the backyard beside the poplar trees. She tells them to dump the soil there.

"Here?" Dee asks, grunting under the weight of the bags.

"Yes," she says. "Next year, I'll have a rock garden again."

The boy lets first one bag, then another, fall to the ground.

Wally's mother is stepping all over the place. "Oh, wait," she says. "No. Over here more." She is getting flustered. "No. I mean here."

Dee sighs and lifts the bags back into his arms. Again Wally notices the sinews of the boy's back.

"Actually," Wally's mother says, reconsidering yet again, "I think . . . I'm not sure . . . further over here. It's over here more."

"Goddamn it, Mother," Wally growls. "Make up your mind."

She's studying the ground carefully, as if she's looking for something. The grass is sparse and gray here, old earth already hardening for winter.

"I'm sure it was here," she's mumbling to herself.

"It was *right here*, Mother," Wally tells her, the impatience chipping away at his voice. "Your rock garden. It was right here until you stopped tending to it and let the grass grow over it. Crabgrass crowded out whatever was left. Daffodils and tulips kept pushing up anyway but you had me cut them down with the lawnmower." He glares at her. "*Remember?*"

He throws his bags of soil at her feet. He's pissed at her for making him do this ridiculous errand. Pissed at her for being so crazy. Pissed at her for giving up on her rock garden all those years ago. But most of all he's pissed at her for making him cut down those plucky flowers that kept on rising through the grass, determined to bloom even if she had stopped tending to them, stopped caring about them, indifferent to their future.

I'm not like him, Mommy. I'm like you.

Watching from a distance away are a dark-haired, wide-eyed girl who clutches her little retarded brother in front of her. Kyle's girlfriend. Barely out of high school by the look of her. Wally didn't ask why she was still hanging around. He didn't want to get dragged into any more of his mother's life than he already had.

Dee's opening up the bags of dirt with his hands. "Where do you want it, Mrs. Day?" he asks.

"Oh, spread it out, all over this area," she says, near tears, wringing her hands. "Just cover this *entire* area heavy with soil."

Wally stares over at her. "Mother, this isn't for any rock garden, is it?"

"Oh, Walter, I almost forgot. There's one more favor I need."

"What now?"

"Your Uncle Axel. He's dying. Would you take me by the hospital so I can say good-bye?"

Wally's momentarily speechless. "Mother," he finally says, "you really *have* lost all sense, haven't you? I have no desire to go see that goddamn son of a—"

"*Here?*" Dee is calling, dragging in the last bag of dirt.

"Oh, yes, dear, right there." Wally's mother smiles. "What a nice young man, he is, Walter. Is he a friend of yours from the city?"

Wally can't even frame his words. He strides away from his mother and over to Dee. "Just dump the dirt," he says. "Spread it out and then let's get the hell out of here. I don't know what she's going to start asking me next."

He hadn't come home to see his mother.

She's irrelevant to his life now. Completely irrelevant. There's nothing left to work out with her. He rarely even thought of her anymore. She had forfeited any place in his life a long time ago—that day when he was eleven years old, in fact, when he'd asked her for help and she had refused him—and Wally was long past grieving over the fact.

Like you wanted to be a singer. Please help me, Mom! Please!

No, he hadn't returned to Brown's Mill because of his mother. Why would he do that?

He'd come back to see Zandy, to make it right.

"So were you in love with him?" Dee asks him, when they're done with the dirt. "Alexander Reefy?"

They're eating cheeseburgers and french fries at the Big Boy restaurant on Main Street. The fries are piping hot, straight from the fryer, and Dee burns the roof of his mouth eating too fast.

"*In* love?" Wally considers the idea. "I don't know. But I loved him. I know that much. In fact, that's the only thing that's entirely clear to me." He looks over at the boy wolfing down the fries. "You eat as if you haven't had a meal in a week."

"I've seen that girl before," Dee tells him. Wally has to shake his head at the way the kid's mind jumps around . . .

"What girl?" Wally asks.

"That Puerto Rican girl at your mother's. Luz something."

"Yeah?"

Dee nods, biting into his burger. A big drop of grease seeps out onto his plate. "Yeah, she was a senior when I was a freshman. She got expelled for selling crack."

"Well, now I understand what she and Kyle had in common."

"She was one of those bad girls. You know, tough. Hard."

Wally shrugs. "She looked sweet to me. But you never know."

"I saw her yesterday at the drugstore having this huge fight with some guy. She was swearing and spitting and everything."

"What did this guy look like?"

"Just a guy."

"Like how old?"

"I don't know. *Old.*" Dee looks up at Wally and grins. "Maybe your age."

"Brat," Wally says. "Was he white? Puerto Rican?"

"White."

"Did it seem like he was her boyfriend?"

"I dunno. She was just mad. Really mad." He looks over at Wally. "Why do you want to know?"

"Actually, I don't," Wally says.

Dee finishes his burger. "When I was a kid," he says, taking a sip of Coke through his straw, "my mom used to bring me here to the Big Boy every Thursday."

"Oh, yeah?"

Dee nods. "It would be after the prayer meetings at the church. We'd get the hot fudge brownie sundae. It was the fucking best sundae you'd ever want to get, man. Really moist cake with like *scalding* hot fudge and truly excellent mint-chocolate-chip ice cream. Fuckin' orgasmic." He sneers. "But then my step-father found out and put an end to our little Thursday night visits."

"Why was that?"

"It wasn't Christian. It was indulgent."

"So the fundies don't like hot fudge sundaes either? What *do* they like?"

"Jesus. They like Jesus."

Wally laughs. He watches the boy as he pours ketchup on the last of the fries. Dee's spiked up his orange hair, exposing his brown roots in little clusters. At least he washed off the mascara, for which Wally is grateful. The hair, the three pendants around the neck, and the six chains hooked to his belt loop are already drawing enough attention.

"Do you miss them at all?" Wally asks. "Your family?"

Dee shrugs. "My mom sometimes. But she's too weird now. Has been ever since she married Leo. I miss my brother Jed. He's only nine. No, wait, he's ten now." He bites into his cheeseburger. "Poor kid. I can only imagine what they're doing to him."

"When did you tell them you were gay?"

Dee makes a face. "I don't use terms like gay. Gay is so your generation. I'm queer. Or, actually, *nonheterosexual.*"

Wally smiles, restraining himself from sarcasm. "Okay, then when did you tell them you were nonheterosexual?"

"Like I *had* to tell them? Just look at me."

"Point taken," Wally says.

"When I bleached my hair the first time, my stepfather just knew. It was like, okay, so the kid's a faggot. Next stop: Faith Healers Inc."

"So who was this guy you had sex with at eleven?"

"Some teenager in my neighborhood. A basketball player at school. He was very hot. I know you think I had no idea what I was doing, but I *wanted* him. You can believe it or not, but it's true. I went after him. I got him to wrestle me in his backyard and then we started fooling around."

Wally doesn't like the fact that story turns him on. *The kid was eleven, for God's sake*, he thinks. *At least I'd hit puberty when I started with Zandy.*

But it was the same, wasn't it? Wally had gone after Zandy, like Dee had gone after the basketball player. It wasn't the other way around. Wally had rung Zandy's doorbell and—

"It was no big deal," Dee's saying.

Wally looks at him. "Of *course* it was a big deal. Whether you initiated it or not, the kid should've—"

Dee's grinning. "Should've *what*? Said no?"

"How old was he?"

"I think seventeen."

"Yeah, he should've said no. He should've known better."

Wally hates that he wants to ask what the basketball player looked like, hates that he wants to know what they did. Sucking? Fucking? What did Dee mean by "fooling around"?

"I figured everything out early," Dee says. He's got ketchup on his chin but doesn't seem aware of it.

"Everything?" Wally asks.

"Well, *nearly* everything. I watched *The Real World*. I knew I was the queer kid. So what?"

"Wipe your chin," Wally says finally.

The boy obeys. They sit there quietly for a while, Wally trying to erase the image of Dee and the basketball player wrestling around in the grass from his mind.

"So what's your favorite movie?" Dee asks.

"*The Wizard of Oz.*"

The boy smirks. "Like I said. You're casebook gay."

"Well, then, I'll go you one even further. *Saturday Night Fever.*"

Dee laughs. "I never even saw that. Seems so lame."

"Lots of gay code. It sent me over the edge when I was your age."

"I guess that's how I felt about *Beautiful Thing*. You seen that?"

Wally nods. "Two boys in love."

"It changed my life."

"And nothing coded about it. All right there, out in the open."

Dee takes the last fry, then pauses with it halfway to his mouth. "You want it?"

"You take it," Wally says. "You can handle the carbs better than I can."

The boy happily chomps away. "So is your mother a total freak show?"

Wally shrugs. "Yeah. I guess she is."

"What was up with that dirt?"

"Who knows?" Wally doesn't want to talk about his mother. He changes the subject. "But what about *your* parents? Don't you have *any* contact with them?"

Dee shakes his head. "Nope. Not since Leo hit me. All communication goes through my state caseworker."

"Who placed you with Miss Aletha."

"Yeah, she's a certified foster parent."

Wally smiles. Missy had found her calling. Roses and runaways.

"So fuck my family," Dee is saying. "Just because we share some chromosomes doesn't mean I have any obligation to them." He pauses. "Except maybe Jed. Someday, when I'm old enough, I'm going back to rescue him."

"And you have gay friends?" Wally asks. "Peers?"

"Well, some. Nobody here in Brown's Mill, but there's a Gay-Straight Alliance over in Mayville, and Missy takes me."

Wally rests his chin on his hand and leans in to look at the boy. "Is that where you met your boyfriend?"

"I don't have a boyfriend," Dee says, almost defensively.

"Then who's the guy you took to your junior prom?"

"Oh, him. Well, that's over now. He graduated."

"How long did you date?"

"I dunno." Dee seems uncomfortable with the topic. "Not long."

"How long is not long?"

"About nine days." He rolls his eyes. "I think we just wanted to say we went to the prom together. Kind of, to make a statement."

Wally laughs.

"So what do you say?" Dee asks, after sucking down the last of his Coke and making that sound with his straw against the bottom of the glass. "You want to go back to Missy's and fool around?"

Wally pulls back in his seat but keeps his eyes on the kid. "What makes you think I'd do that?"

"You find me attractive, don't you?"

The power thing again. The kid assumes that just because he's sixteen and lean and nubile he's irresistible. Well, Wally won't give him the satisfaction. "I suppose so," he says, half-shrugging. "Not really my type though."

"Oh, come on. Like it's every day you get a sixteen-year-old propositioning you. And not only that, you've got permission from his guardian. You know Missy wants it to happen. So why not? Won't it be a great story for your big-city gym-boy friends?"

Wally narrows his eyes at him. "So is this cocky wiseass persona just a way of occupying the time until you grow up?"

Dee's right back at him, not losing a beat. "Possibly. And maybe your obvious fascination with me is simply your own regret for not being more *like* me when you were my age."

They sit staring at each other, neither blinking, until the waitress comes by and clears off their plates.

I *watched* The Real World. I *knew I was the queer kid.*

How had Wally known?

It had been from the boys in his class at St. John the Baptist that Wally first heard about Alexander Reefy, the strange, bearded man who lived in a little red brick house behind the boarded-up factories in Dogtown. He was a homo. That meant he liked men. Alexander Reefy liked men the way most guys liked girls. He did *sexual* stuff with other men, like touching their dicks and kissing them right on the lips. And everybody knew it, because he always kept his front porch light glowing, which was a sign that he was free and available. Wally's classmates had all the facts. The story had been passed down from the older kids: Alexander Reefy left his front porch light on so that men would know to come by. *Just watch,* Wally's friends insisted: men went in and out of that house all the time. The light would go off for the duration, then flick back on after the guy had left.

That front porch light became an obsession for Wally. A light on a house he had never seen, owned by a man whose face he had never glimpsed, but whose name conjured up images that consumed his thoughts and his dreams.

Alexander Reefy.

It was a cold November morning, and Wally and Freddie Piatrowski and Michael Marino had decided to skip class. Eighth grade was a waste of time, merely treading water before high school. Freddie had cigarettes and a stash of his father's porno magazines in his backpack. Sitting behind one of the abandoned factories, Wally smoked a Camel, though he hated the taste. But as he looked through the magazines Freddie passed to him, he realized he hated the big fleshy knockers of the women even more.

"Hey," Wally suggested all at once. "Let's go find Alexander Reefy."

"You mean the homo?" Michael Marino asked.

"Yeah. You know, the one with the front porch light you told me about."

Freddie made a face. "What're we going to do when we find him?"

"I don't know. Let's just see if we can get him to come outside."

The boys shrugged, putting away the cigarettes and magazines and creeping through the marsh, stinking of bad water and rusting iron. Michael knew exactly which house was Alexander Reefy's. "Look," he said. "His light's on."

And that it was: a soft, golden light, burning through the morning fog. Wally couldn't take his eyes off it.

"Well, are you coming?" Michael insisted. "It was your idea, Wally."

"Yeah," Wally breathed. "I'm coming."

They approached like warriors, but there was no plan beyond getting there. No words were spoken. Freddie picked up a stone and threw it at the window. The other two followed suit. The tiny pings of the stones against the glass were the only sounds along the street.

He emerged finally, awakened by the stones: sleepy-eyed and disheveled, not shouting as the boys had expected. From his lair he crept dizzily, not stealthily or threateningly. "Hey, what the—?" he asked, rubbing his eyes, and Wally tried desperately to get a glimpse.

But Freddie barked: "Run!" So they ran, turning on their heels and plunging back through the swampy field, foul-smelling mud soaking into their shoes as they tripped over rusting casements of the old factory and dove into the darkness within.

But this Wally saw: Alexander Reefy, shirtless, a mat of mysterious black fur on his chest, in checkered pajama bottoms, standing on the steps of his house under the dull golden glow of his front porch light, and he was smiling.

"Hey, peace and love, you little hooligans," he said, and then he went back to bed.

They drive down Main Street. It's become a shadow of what Wally remembers from his childhood, its life sapped by the Wal-Mart out on Washington Avenue that sprung up about six years ago. Once dozens of shops lined Main Street, from South End News at one terminus, where Wally had bought every issue of *Action Comics* for nine straight years, to Schafer's Shoes at the other, where Wally's father had worked after whatever had happened to end his navy career. Now South End News is a parking lot, Schafer's Shoes a Spanish grocery, and Big Boy squats in place of what used to be Henry's Diner. NO LOITERING signs are posted everywhere, a futile attempt to ward off the homeless and mentally ill.

Wally turns into the cemetery near Devil's Hopyard and shuts off the ignition.

"What are we gonna do here?" Dee asks. "Make out?"

Wally ignores him and gets out of the car. He starts trudging through the tall, yellow grass that reaches up past his ankles. He hears Dee follow him. The sun has come out and the gravestones cast long, late-day shadows. It's been a long time since Wally has been here. He's never even seen what he paid for, years ago, when he learned from Miss Aletha that no stone had ever been erected.

"So who are you coming to see?" Dee asks, catching up with him.

"My teacher," Wally says.

"From Brown's Mill High?"

"No." He spots the stone. Pink marble. Wally smiles. She would have liked that.

They stand over it, looking down.

JOSEPHINE LEOPOLD
1889–1976
A BRIGHT STAR FROM THE HEAVENS

"Who was she?" Dee asks.

"My first acting teacher. And a great star. You ought to know about her if you want to be an actor. She trod the boards with Minnie Maddern Fiske and Eva Le Gallienne."

"She did what with who?"

Wally just stares down at the stone.

It had been the least he could do. It hadn't come cheap, and Ned had grumbled a bit at the expense, but he understood. Wally couldn't live with the fact that she lay here without any stone, without any marker. Without any proof that she had been here, that she had lived, that she had mattered to a frightened, confused boy.

Wally looks up. Dee has wandered off through the grass, scanning the stones, mumbling to himself. He's an odd one, Wally thinks. One moment so brash and arrogant, the next naïve and ingenuous. *I wasn't so different from you,* he thinks, watching him move through the cemetery. Okay, so he didn't have Gay-Straight Alliances and a boyfriend to take to his prom. But not so different. Not really.

Dee has stopped walking and stands several yards away, looking down into the grass.

Wally walks up behind him. "See somebody you know?"

"Yeah," Dee says.

Wally glances down at the flat stone at the boy's feet. Nearly obscured with grass, it reads:

DONALD KYRWINSKI, SENIOR
1960–1991

"It's my father."

"Oh."

"I was only like eight or something when he died. But he was cool. At least I think he was."

"Well, if you remember him as cool, then he probably was."

Dee grunts. "Who knows if he'd have turned into a prick when I got older? But sometimes I think what it might have been like if he hadn't died and my mom had never married Leo and never turned into a religious nutcase."

Wally places his hand on the boy's shoulder. "What did he die from?"

"A heart attack."

"He was only thirty-one," Wally says, realizing that's younger than he is now.

"Yeah, it was like this big tragedy, everybody crying, nobody believing it." Dee shrugs. "My mom didn't let me go to the funeral. So it's all kind of a vague blur to me."

The boy starts to trudge off through the grass back toward the car. Wally looks once more back down at the stone, then turns to follow him.

"Hey," Dee says, slowing down as his eyes spot something.

"Don't stop," Wally says. He knows what the boy sees.

"But isn't that your mother's name?"

Wally sighs. He had no intention of paying any respects. He had come here for Josephine. No one else.

But he looks down anyway.

And there's his father's name, etched starkly into the blue granite, just his name and his dates beside it. ROBERT DAY. 1934–1987. That's all. Elsewhere in the cemetery, Wally knows, stands the great black marble stone of his grandparents, with his grandfather's naval rank boldly, proudly inscribed. But nothing for Wally's father. Just his name and his dates. As if he'd been nothing more than a common laborer. Or a shoe store salesman, which he was, at the end.

And beside him, even more chillingly, is Wally's mother's name, her death date just waiting to be carved.

They head back to Miss Aletha's. The swamps of Dogtown are particularly rank this evening, foul and tart. But Miss Aletha is cooking something good in the kitchen, some kind of gingerbread cake, and that takes care of that. Wally sinks down deep in an overstuffed armchair, transfixed by the flames in Missy's fireplace.

"So when are we gonna do it?" Dee asks, coming around at his side.

"Do what?"

"Get naked. Your body parts and mine."

Wally laughs. "Isn't it past your bedtime?"

"Fuck off. You think treating me like a kid is funny. But you're just making yourself look like an idiot."

The boy flops down onto the couch, flicking the TV on with the remote control, settling on some stupid reality thing. Wally hates those shows. Dumb-ass twentysomethings doing whatever it takes for their fifteen minutes and a fistful of spending money. Not to mention using up all the airtime and taking jobs away from real actors.

He sneaks a peek at Dee on the couch. He's stretching, showing off his torso again, all those sinewy young muscles, no body fat. Wally looks away. Had it been this way for Zandy too? Had he looked at Wally with the same mix of repulsion and attraction that Wally feels for Dee?

"I'm going up to my room," he announces. Dee just grunts in reply.

Wally heads upstairs. He undresses, lies down on his bed, staring up at the ceiling. The first time Zandy fucked him, he remembers, he cried. There was so much pain—pain as he had never known, before or since. Not even his father's blows had hurt so bad. Zandy encircled him around the waist and lifted Wally up off his feet, holding him in front of him, pushing his dick deep up inside him, causing the boy to squirm, to writhe, to cry like a little baby.

He was fourteen.

And then afterward, they built a fire, in an open section of the old factory, where the roof had caved in. There was a pool of oily black water beside them, where Zandy rinsed off the Vaseline from his hands. Wally sat in front of the fire, feeling his sphincter still contracting, feeling as if he needed to shit, to piss, to pass out. And Zandy came up behind him, wrapped his big arms around the frail, shaking boy, holding him tight, kissing his neck.

In that moment, Wally loved him more than anyone else in the whole world.

Alexander Reefy was not a handsome man. His nose was too long and his eyes too small. And his hands, of course, were rough and gnarled, hit too many times with a hammer, scarred from too many cuts with a saw. But they were a man's hands, nothing so pristine as Wally's father's hands, hands of a naval officer, soft and manicured. Zandy was a bear, a big old lumberjack, whose scent was strong, whose embrace was solid. Wally can still smell him, taste him sometimes, when he closes his eyes, imagining his face pressed against Zandy's chest, falling asleep on his furry, silken pectorals, listening to his heart. Zandy would caress his hair, whispering in his ear: "It's gonna be okay, babe. Trust me. It's gonna be okay."

Wally never knew exactly how old Zandy was. Not quite thirty when they started, Wally thinks. Younger than he is now. The thought staggers. To Wally, Zandy had seemed much, much older than he was, but he also seemed ageless, like a genie or an elf out of Tolkien. And what did Wally care how old Zandy was anyway? Or even what he looked like? Zandy was a *man*—a man with a penis and a chest like a bear, a man who recognized the urgency within him, and affirmed it.

Zandy taught Wally the things his father should have: why he had to shower more frequently now that he was sprouting hair, how to wash his dick to keep it clean, how to lather up and shave the pesky little whiskers that showed up on his chin. He taught Wally that the feelings he'd been having were no cause for concern. "It's a natural thing," he said, "and don't you ever let anyone tell you otherwise."

It was twenty years ago. No, even more than that. Twenty-one, twenty-two ... a time before *The Real World*, before Gay-Straight Alliances, before Ellen on *Newsweek*, before there were any Wills or Graces. What Zandy was suggesting to Wally was a radical thing, a subversive act. "It's perfectly natural, your gayness," he told Wally. "*It's the way God made you.*"

Of course, there was more that Zandy taught: how to give pleasure and how to receive it, the best way to handle a man's dick, the best way to show your partner what turned you on.

But Wally never sucked Zandy's dick. He offered his own, and gave him his ass, but never could he bring himself to place his lips around the older man's penis. Wally was fascinated by it, and often couldn't take his eyes from it: but to put it in his mouth seemed vile somehow—*dirty*—and Wally just could never do it. Zandy didn't insist. He never pressured Wally to do anything that he didn't want to do.

Except, of course, he had.

"You had no consent to give," the judge said to Wally. "You didn't know what consent even meant."

He had said nothing then. The time for spilling out the truth had ended the moment he signed his name to the complaint and handed it back to Sergeant Garafolo.

"Hey."

Wally jumps. A voice in his ear.

He sits up in bed. Had he fallen asleep? Was he dreaming?

"Hey," the voice in the dark whispers again. "It's just me."

A shiver of moonlight reveals Dee in bed beside him.

"What the fuck?"

"Make love to me," the boy says, his voice urgent. "Make love to me, Wally."

The kid's naked. Wally can see that now, as the sheet falls away, the moonlight exposing Dee's arms, his smooth, hollow chest.

"What, are you *crazy*? Get out of here."

A fragrance of soap reaches Wally's nostrils. The boy leans forward, tries to kiss Wally on the lips. Wally pushes him back.

Dee grimaces. "Am I that bad looking?"

"You're sixteen."

"Yeah. Age of consent in this state."

"I don't care. Get out of here. Find a boy your own age to get your rocks off with."

"Why? Are you suddenly against older guys and younger guys doing it?"

Wally is getting furious. "Yes! Yes, I am!"

The boy sneers. "So you are saying what you and Zandy did was wrong."

Wally doesn't reply.

Dee pounces, gathering force. "You *don't* think it was wrong. If you did, you wouldn't be going back to apologize to him. It was *you* who did the wrong thing by sending him to jail!"

Wally feels as if he might explode. "Get out of my bed."

Dee slides out, his long boydick swinging between his legs. Wally notices a tattoo of a rose on his abdomen.

"Well, at least I've learned one thing," the boy says.

Wally sighs. "What's that?"

"You *do* find me attractive."

Wally's suddenly aware that his cock is spearheading his white briefs. He whips the sheet back up to cover himself.

Dee grins. "'Night, Wally," he says, and shuts the door behind him.

* * *

But he can't sleep. Wally throws the sheet aside, gets up, pulls on a pair of sweats. He heads downstairs to find Miss Aletha sitting at the kitchen table.

"That foster kid of yours . . ." he says.

She smiles. "Have some cake. You went to bed before I could slice you a piece." It's gingerbread and banana. Wally takes a bite. It's good. Everything she makes is good.

"I told you Donald was smitten," Missy says.

"Well, I just had to kick him out of my bed."

"Such willpower."

"Why does everyone assume it's such an act of will not to sleep with a teen-ager? He's skinny. He's got acne on his chin. His hair looks like a Halloween pumpkin."

Miss Aletha laughs. "You were just like him."

Wally grins in response. "Yeah, I suppose I did turn into a real derelict there for a while, didn't I? At least I didn't dye my hair."

"You were always a good boy, Wally."

"Please. You sound like my mother."

"Is she as confused as you feared?"

"More. She asked me to take her to see Uncle Axel."

"Not that *monster* you would stay with when you were little?"

"The very same. She wants to say good-bye to him. He's dying."

Miss Aletha clears off his empty plate from the table and sets it in the sink.

Wally sighs. "I still can't believe I came back here, that I'm dealing with bull-shit like bringing dirt for her rock garden and taking her to see Uncle Axel."

Missy comes up behind him and strokes his hair. "Sometimes we have to go back. Sometimes the past just doesn't stay where you want it to."

He closes his eyes and enjoys the feel of her hand in his hair. "My father," he says.

"What about your father?"

"He's the one I should be seeing. He's the one. He's what really fucked me up."

Miss Aletha sits back down beside him.

"Something bad happened to my father," Wally says. "I thought of that again when I saw his stone in the cemetery and his naval rank wasn't inscribed there. I never knew what happened. I don't think my mother did, either. One day he just came home for good, never to return to his ship, and he was miserable."

"He couldn't have been a very happy man to do the things he did."

"It must have been money-related. He must have been embezzling or some-thing like that. They don't care about sex scandals in the military. Unless it's a *gay* scandal, of course." He laughs. "Hey, maybe good old Dad was taking it up the butt out there on the ship. After all, they were gone months at a time. It would explain why he was so fixated on his faggot son."

"I suspect your father's unhappiness went back a long time before that . . ."

"All I know is he was miserable after it happened. Not that he was such a prince before that, but after he came home for good, he was nasty. He drank a lot. Bullied my mother. Hit me whenever he felt like it."

He lets go of her hand and gets to his feet, walking over to the window. He looks out at the dark silhouette of the abandoned factory next door, standing forlorn in the swamp.

"You know, my grandfather was in the navy, too. I was supposed to follow. I imagine my father felt a lot of pressure when he was a kid and so he then put pressure on me. And so it goes."

Missy has risen, too, walking up behind him. She slips her arms around his waist and rests her cheek against his back.

"My parents had expectations of me, too," she tells him. "They expected me to be a *boy*. At least you made good on that much."

Wally manages a smile. "Guess everyone is pressured one way or another."

"It's how we respond that counts. Bertrand used to say, 'I yam what I yam, and whatever I'm meant to be, that's how I'll turnip.' Get it? *Yam? Turnip?*"

"That Bertrand had a way with words," Wally says, smiling harder now.

"He sure did. Now *his* father was a great showman. He was with Barnum and Bailey for years. He expected Bertrand would follow, but poor Bertrand could never even get a rabbit out of a hat, though he was always trying. Remember all his magic tricks?"

"I remember."

"So we all have pressures. We all have expectations to either live up to or say 'no thanks' to." She sighs. "Like your mother. She must have had her own pressures, too."

Wally shrugs. "If she did, I don't know about them. All I really know about my mother's life is that she went off to the city to become a singer before she married my father, but she failed."

"She must carry around a great deal of disappointment then."

"Yeah. She must." He laughs bitterly. "Both of them, disappointed and miserable, and the result is me." He thinks of Dee. "Ah, the legacy we inherit."

"Maybe that's why you came back," Miss Aletha whispers. "To put an end to that legacy."

Wally turns around to look at her.

"You can do it. I know you can. You can put an end to it if you want to."

Their eyes hold.

"Make the choice, Wally. When does the cycle end? When does it finally end?"

And suddenly he's crying. She takes him in her arms, as she's done so many times, stroking his hair, shedding not one tear for herself, though both of them know she has just as much right to cry.

10

THE PURSE

Last night, Luz's grandfather died. Her father is blaming Luz, smashing empty whiskey bottles around the apartment and making Jorge cry. So their one-night sleepover at Regina's has quickly turned into two nights, and maybe more.

Maybe forever, Regina thinks.

"Did you think my son was handsome, Luz, when he came in after my doctor's appointment this afternoon?" she asks.

The girl looks at her but doesn't offer her usual smile. "He's very handsome, Mrs. Day," Luz says, though Regina thinks there isn't much enthusiasm in her voice.

Sitting at the small table in the living room, Regina dithers with a few pieces of her still-unfinished jigsaw of the Taj Mahal. Luz's uncertainty disturbs her. Walter had asked the girl some questions that Luz hadn't seemed to like. Oh, how much Regina was hoping that Walter and Luz would become friends. Wouldn't it be nice if all of them could live here together, happy and gay?

From the kitchen comes a bolt of energy, a tiny whirlwind spinning through the dining area into the living room, like that character from the cartoons Walter used to watch, the Tasmanian devil. It's Jorge, his cheeks and fingers covered with peanut butter. He's laughing about something, one of those invisible little experiences that only he can see or hear. Regina smiles. She enjoys having young people around. Young, happy, vibrant people filling up her house with happy words and big smiles.

Not the way it was with him. Not like Kyle.

Regina's hand pauses as she is about to fit a piece into her puzzle.

Kyle.

He's not buried in the yard.

The thought had come to Regina when they were all out there with the dirt. He wasn't there—of course not, because she put his body in the shed. That's what she did with it. Wrapped him in that old tarp and stuffed him in the shed.

"Walter," she had asked, "might I ask you one more favor?"

He wasn't listening to her. He was going on about her medications, which ones the doctor had given her, pinning up a list to the corkboard beside the telephone. "You've got to remember to take these," he was saying. "Can you do that, Mother?"

"I can help her," Luz had said, coming into the kitchen. "I can help her remember."

Walter looked at her. Regina saw the look. It wasn't a good look. It was dark. "How long are you expecting to stay here?" Walter asked the girl.

She stood her ground beside him, so small, barely coming up to his chin. "Just until I can find a job," she told Walter.

"Luz is such a help to me around the house," Regina offered.

Walter hadn't taken his eyes off the girl. "Who were you with at the drugstore the other day, Luz? Who was the guy you were fighting with?"

Regina had seen her lips purse tightly as Luz kept her eyes locked on Walter. "I wasn't at the drugstore," she said.

"And no word from Kyle?" Walter asked, without missing a beat.

"None," Luz replied, also without faltering.

Of course there had been no word from Kyle. He's in the shed, surely decomposing by now, starting to rot. He's in there crumpled beside some moldy bags of Hollytone, a big, dried, bloody gash in the side of his head.

"Missa Day."

Regina blinks, lifting her eyes from her puzzle. Jorge is on the floor, looking through the comic books she had bought for him yesterday. *Archie's Joke Book. Richie Rich.* He's pointing at something in one of them. She has to strain her eyes to see.

"It's the Taj Mahal," she says, smiling. "How very smart you are, Jorge. You've recognized it from my puzzle."

The boy gives her a wide peanut-butter grin.

How much like Walter he is, sitting there with his comic books. Walter had prized his comics, inserting each issue into a plastic bag and carefully ordering it into his boxed collection, which he kept downstairs on shelves.

"Don't you want your comic books, Walter?" Regina had asked, following her son to the door as he prepared to leave.

He grunted. "You ought to find a collector who'll buy them from you, Mother. You could make some money for yourself."

"Oh, Walter, I could never do that. They're yours."

His eyes narrowed at her. "She knows where Kyle is," he said, nodding toward Luz in the living room. "She's in cahoots with him."

"Oh, no, Walter, she doesn't know. She's glad he's gone. He was terrible to her, just terrible."

Her son sighed. "Well, I suppose for now it's good you have someone to help you remember to take your medication. Just be careful, Mother. Keep your eyes open."

He turned, his hand on the doorknob.

"One more favor, Walter?"

He looked back at her strangely.

"I was hoping you could board up the shed out back. You know, where we keep the rakes and the lawnmower."

"Board it up?"

Regina eyed him intently. Her heart was pounding a little bit faster. "Yes. Board it up. You don't need to go inside. Just nail some boards over the door."

Walter made a face in confusion. "But *why*?"

Regina twirled a button on her blouse. "Well, because, well—there are skunks that come around and get inside . . ."

"So just put a lock on the door. You don't need to board the thing up."

"No, I want it boarded. Sealed shut. I've taken all the rakes and the mower out already. You can put those in the basement. I want the shed secured so no one is tempted to try to get inside. A child could get trapped in there, Walter. He could die if he got trapped in there!"

"I'll do it for you, Mrs. Day," Luz had offered softly, coming up behind her. She turned to the girl. "You *will*, Luz?"

"Yes."

Walter eyed the girl.

"If your son can't do it for you," she said, "I will."

Regina saw the way Luz stood her ground, facing Walter. He just shook his head and left, saying nothing more, pulling the door shut behind him a little harder than was necessary.

Robert used to do the very same thing.

"You're a good girl, Luz," Regina tells her now, looking up from her puzzle into Luz's soft dark eyes. "A very good girl."

She can live here for as long as she wants. I can make dinner for her and Jorge, the way I used to make dinner for Rocky. I'll make dinner and lunch and break-fast, and we'll go to the movies, we'll take drives, we'll plant marigolds in my rock garden in the spring . . .

She wakes in the morning to sunlight filling her room. She bounds out of bed with an energy she had forgotten she could muster. "Yes, marigolds in the spring," Regina says out loud. "I'll make a pretty garden again, the way I used to."

It's grocery day. Sitting in front of her mirror, she thinks maybe she'll wear a little lipstick to the market. Just a little touch of pink. Why not? She puckers up and rolls it on.

In the living room, she checks that the money for the groceries is in her purse. Yes, it's there, just as they gave it to her at the bank. A roll of hundreds and twenties.

"It's all done, Mrs. Day," Luz says, startling her just a bit, coming up behind her. "I boarded the shed all up, just like you asked."

"Oh, Luz, thank you so much."

"But Mrs. Day, you know you *didn't* take out all the rakes as you said. I looked inside, just to make sure, and there were still several—"

"You looked *inside* the shed?"

"Yes. I took the rakes out and put them in the garage—"

"What did you see in the shed? Did you see anything in there?"

Luz looks at her with blank eyes. "Nothing. Other than the rakes and a few old bags, there was nothing in there at all."

"Nothing at all?"

"Nothing, Mrs. Day."

Regina just stares at her.

"Anyway, it's all boarded over now, just as you wanted."

Regina feels as if she might fall over. She grips the table next to her.

Where is he? Where *is* he?

I put him in the crate. Yes, that's where he is. Downstairs in the basement. The crate . . .

No, Walter opened that crate. He wasn't there.

Not buried in the backyard either. Not in the shed . . .

Regina feels the house beginning to spin.

I think I may be losing my mind.

"Mrs. Day?" Luz leans in close to look her directly in the eyes. "Are you ready to go to the grocery store?"

Regina doesn't answer, just stares into the girl's eyes.

"You can't do anything right," Robert is telling her.

He doesn't like how she's dressed, and they're going out. Something important. A fund-raiser. That's what it is. A fundraiser for the Republican candidate for— oh, dear, what is he running for? What is his name? Robert hates it when she forgets important things like this.

"You'd forget your head if it wasn't attached to your shoulders, and sometimes I wonder even about that."

"I'm sorry, Robert."

"I asked you to get your hair done differently for tonight. And to wear something gay. You always dress so dowdily." He huffed. "And for God's sake, wear some makeup, *please*. When you don't wear makeup you look like a ghost. You have no eyebrows, no eyelashes. Use a little mascara for a change, Regina. All the other men have wives who dress to impress. Make me proud to have you along."

"I'll use a little eye shadow, Robert."

"And please, above all, don't attempt any small talk. You're no good at it. Just smile and nod. Answer questions if you're asked but don't offer anything on your own. You always end up making me embarrassed when you try to talk."

"Yes, Robert."

"If you must say anything, talk about Wally. About his grades in school or something like that. Talk about Wally. Don't talk about yourself. Especially not that insipid story of you and your sister singing in the city."

"Mrs. Day?"

Regina blinks.

It's Luz standing in front of her.

"Yes, dear?"

"Are you ready to go?"

There's a chill of winter in the air. Luz is wearing her usual blue jeans and white lacy blouse, covered only with a thin black leather jacket.

"It's rather nippy," says Regina. "Let me get my sweater before we go."

She heads down the hall. Hanging on a hook behind her bedroom door she finds her sweater. She pauses before slipping it on. Through the crack of the door she can see Luz in the living room, but the girl cannot see her. Regina watches. She enjoys watching Luz in little moments of the day like this, when she's unaware that she's being watched. She likes how pure Luz looks in those moments, how sweet, how good. Sometimes Luz will be combing her hair, or plucking her eyebrows, or picking out something from between her teeth. Regina finds it soothing to watch her. She could watch her all day long. Right now Luz is flaring her nostrils, filling her lungs with the air of Regina's house. It's sweet air, slightly cool and moist, cinnamon and mothballs and Lemon Pledge.

Regina watches as Luz looks around the room. The drapes, as usual, are drawn. Mormor's old lace doilies decorate polished mahogany tables. Blue crystal bowls, brought over from Sweden, harbor ancient pink candies. On the mantel, a gold clock with Roman numerals ticks hard under its glass—the only sound in the house at the moment, except for Regina's own heartbeat, high in her ears.

She watches, mesmerized, as Luz's eyes chance upon Regina's purse on the table. It's open, just as Regina had left it. Even from here, Regina can see the thick roll of bills, their color almost glowing from the yawning mouth of the purse. She watches as Luz stands there, looking down at the purse.

There is a pause, a sudden cessation of all sound, a pause even the tick of the clock on the mantel seems to honor. Regina watches in utter silence, holding her breath. Luz's gaze remains fixated on the purse, the money glowing from inside.

And then, almost too fast for Regina even to see, the girl's hand darts out and into the purse. But then she freezes, stopped apparently by seeing the reflection of her face in the black patent-leather purse.

She gasps and withdraws her hand.

Regina moves out from behind the door.

"Here we are," she says, coming around the corner, a white wool sweater draped over her shoulders. "This should be enough, don't you think?"

"What?"

"It's chilly, but not that cold."

"I—" Luz stammers. "No. Not that cold."

"Before you know it, it'll be winter." Regina smiles. Her eyes settle on the purse. "Oh, there it is," she says. She picks it up, inspects the roll of cash inside, then snaps it shut. "Shall we go?"

Luz takes a breath and smiles. "Yes, we'd better," she says, "before it gets too dark."

* * *

She would be happy here. Wouldn't she? I could make it nice for her and Jorge. I could cook for them, sew for them, tell bedtime stories to Jorge, the way I once told them to Walter . . .

"Mother, tell me the one about Jack and the giant again."

That had been Walter's favorite. Oh, she had invented all sorts of things, adding to the old fable every time she told it. Jack grew another beanstalk after chopping down the first and this time he took his little sister Rocky up with him, and they met the giant's wife, who was not mean at all, but a lovely lady, just oversized, and she had all these magical fairy princesses living with her . . .

Jorge would love that story. Regina was excited to tell it to him. Maybe tonight.

Yes, they'll be happy here. Regina's *certain* of it.

Luz will never want to go.

Ahead of them the grocery store is very bright: yellow windows embedded into a gray, overcast day. Regina discovers her sweater is not, after all, enough to keep her warm, so Luz insists she wear her leather jacket. The old woman laughs as she tremulously slides her arm down one sleeve, then the other, zippers jingling. "My, my," she says, more to herself than to Luz.

Orange leaves, caught in a new wind, scamper after them as they walk.

Inside the store, Jorge runs ahead to the candy aisle. Under the bright lights, Regina fills the carriage as Luz pushes. "I just need enough to keep us going for another week," Regina says. Eggs. Skim milk. Toilet paper. Polident. Swanson's frozen dinners. Orange tea. Graham crackers. She says hello to a few people who recognize her. One red-haired woman with whiskers on her chin asks if she's heard anything from Kyle.

"No," says Regina, "not a thing." And they exchange rueful smiles.

At the checkout line, Regina hands Luz the roll of money that was in her purse, then takes Jorge by the hand to go sit on the bench in the front of the store. Her ankles hurt if she stands too long waiting in line.

"Gum?" Jorge asks, indicating the gumball machines.

"Oh. Of course, dear." Regina unsnaps her purse, scrounges around at the bottom for some change, and hands Jorge a few quarters and dimes. He scampers off.

From her spot on the bench, Regina watches as the clerk, a teenaged girl with acne, rings up $37.27. She watches as Luz pulls two hundred-dollar bills from the roll. Regina's certain that's what it was: two hundreds. Not two twenties but two hundreds. She may have arthritis in her legs, but her eyesight is perfect. The doctor had confirmed it yesterday. She sees very clearly as Luz gingerly folds one of the hundreds into her palm, and hands the other one to the clerk.

"Don't you have anything smaller?" the girl with the acne asks.

"What?"

The clerk licks her lips. "Something smaller. Like two twenties, maybe?"

"Oh," Luz says, and Regina can see the girl's fingers are trembling. "Okay." She reaches into her pocket and pulls out the roll again, peeling off two twenties this time. "Here you go."

Regina watches as the second hundred-dollar bill is also crumbled into Luz's sweaty palm. There are two of them in there now. Regina's certain of it. The clerk gives Luz the change from the two twenties. Luz thrusts it all down into the pocket of her jeans.

She'll be happy living here, won't she?

No, she'll want to leave. Go to the city. That's what she'll want.

That's what Rocky wanted.

What I wanted.

Luz carries the bag of groceries over to Regina, the paper crunching against her breasts. Regina tilts her head and smiles up at her.

"Thank you, Luz," she says.

"Come on, Jorge," Luz calls, and her voice sounds different.

They walk home through a flurry of furious leaves.

In the kitchen, Regina makes a pot of tea while Luz puts the groceries away.

"Luz, dear," she says quietly, just as the kettle begins to whistle in a long, high screech.

"Yes?"

"You forgot to give me my change."

Outside the wind whoops against the side of the house.

"Oh." Luz's breath comes out in a stutter. "I'm sorry." She fumbles in her pocket and pulls out the roll of bills, along with two crumpled ones and some coins. She plunks it all down onto the table. A penny, very shiny, rolls to the floor. Luz stoops and picks it up.

Regina holds out her old knotted hand. Luz places the penny in her palm. "Thank you, dear." The old woman picks up the roll of money and returns it uncounted to her purse.

She's not unaware of how shaky Luz seems.

"I need to pay the man for the wood, you know," Regina tells her. "He's coming by with a delivery next week."

"The . . . wood?"

"Oh, yes. My wood-burning stove in the basement." Regina smiles. "I love that old stove in the wintertime. My husband built a grate into the living room so we could bring the heat from the basement up here. It helps keep costs down in the winter. Electric heat can be so expensive all by itself."

Luz nods.

"Yes," Regina muses, opening her eyes. "Pretty soon I'll have to load up the stove and set it blazing again."

Luz pushes her hand into her pocket. Regina watches the girl's fingers make a pattern in the denim as they clutch what's inside.

"Mrs. Day, I—I'm going to go lie down. I have a headache."

"Oh, you poor dear. May I get you some tea?"

"No, thank you. I'll just go lie down."

"You poor child," Regina says again. "You do that. Maybe take a little nap. You look positively deathly."

Luz doesn't come out of her room for the rest of the day. Regina sits on the couch in her darkened living room, staring up at the family portrait from so long ago. She can hear Jorge outside, laughing and talking to himself.

"All of the Days were bad. Except for Robert and my son. All of the rest were bad, especially Kyle."

Right here. Right on this couch.

This is where she killed him.

"Bad stock. Oh, so very bad. What could I do but do what I did?"

But where is he? Where is his body?

Why can't I remember?

It was like this once before, when she couldn't make her mind work, when thoughts escaped her, when parts of her life slipped out from her grasp. She was living with Rocky and she couldn't remember how she'd hurt herself, how all the blood got on the floor. She rambled on about vampires and strange men who touched her in the night, but no one believed her, and next Regina knew she was in that place, that horrible place where she saw Howard Greer in the day room dressed as a girl. She had screamed when she saw that, screamed her lungs out.

I'm afraid I might be losing my mind, she had told Walter.

If it happened before, why not again?

Regina covers her face with her hands and starts to cry.

"And now Luz will go," she whimpers. "She doesn't want to stay here. She took the money so she can go to the city. That's what she wants, to go to the city, like Rocky did." She removes her hands and stares back up at the portrait. "Like *you* did, Walter. She'll go to the city like you did and I'll never see her again. Never!"

She's staring up into Walter's eight-year-old eyes.

"Why couldn't you have been a girl?" she asks. "If I had had a daughter instead of a son, nothing bad would have happened."

She stands, drying her eyes with her sleeve. She walks over to her puzzle table. She's almost done with it. It's taken her two weeks. She'll finish it tonight, perhaps. She'll put it all together and gaze down at the complete Taj Mahal, then break it apart, putting all the pieces back in their box. Then she'll start another.

But the Taj Mahal lies in pieces scattered across the table and on the floor below. All her work, broken apart.

She hears a snicker behind her. She turns.

It's Jorge. Dirty-faced, shoes untied.

"Jorge! Did you do this?"

He nods.

She stoops, retrieving the pieces from the floor.

"Well, then you're just going to have to help me put it back together." Her knees crack as she stands back up, placing the puzzle pieces on the table. Jorge instantly takes them and finds how they fit, assembling a whole section in seconds.

Regina smiles. "You're good at puzzles, Jorge."

She sits down on the chair and the boy crawls up into her lap.

"So *very* good at puzzles," she says.

He kisses her cheek. His breath still smells like peanut butter.

"Jorge," she says.

The boy's simple brown eyes look into hers.

"How would you like to help me solve another puzzle?"

He nods.

"There's a treasure hidden in this house and I need you to help me find it. Can you do it, Jorge? Can you find the treasure hidden in this house?"

Jorge's eyes gleam.

11

THE CORD OF LOVE

The phone is cradled between his chin and shoulder.

Ringing . . .

He's wearing just a silky green polyester shirt.

Ringing . . .

He's jacking his cock in his fist, lubed with Vaseline, watching himself in the mirror.

"Hello?"

"I want to fuck you."

"What?"

"I want to fuck you."

Pause.

"Who is this?"

"Or you can fuck me . . ."

Dial tone.

Fuck them when they won't talk. Why don't they swear at me? Why don't they tell me to go fuck myself? I want to hear these boys say fuck.

Wally's flipping through the phone book, his oily fingers staining the pages. Who's the sexy guy on Oak Avenue with the black Corvette? Jimmy something. Jimmy Genovese. Yeah, Genovese. He runs his finger down the page until he finds the number. His cock is still fucking his fist, trembling to come off. He presses Jimmy Genovese's number. The tones made by the push buttons on the phone have come to excite him. So do the rings before anyone picks up.

But no one answers. His cock can't take anymore. He shoots anticlimactic cum on the mirror. He lies back exhausted.

Wally watches as his cum runs down the glass. White water separates from the thicker goo. He stands finally and wipes it off with Kleenex.

Fuck them when they won't talk.

Outside his father is mowing the grass in the front yard. It's been several weeks now since he came home for good. Something happened on the ship. Wally doesn't know what exactly, but his father gets drunk a lot now, and shouts at the television set all the time, cursing President Carter and the goddamn A-rabs.

"What happened?" Wally has asked his mother. "Something happened, didn't it?"

"He's just not going back to the ship for a while."

"You mean he's home for good?"

"For a while, Walter."

Something happened. Something bad.

But something good, too: There was no more talk about Wally joining the navy.

He sits on the front step now and watches the yellow sweat roll off his father's back. Some of the neighborhood boys are throwing a football in the street. It's Sunday.

His father cuts the mower. He leaves it stranded in the middle of the yard and walks over to Wally, mopping his forehead with his T-shirt. His body is hard and toned, with a patch of gray hair curling between his flat, defined pectorals. Several brown moles above his father's right nipple form a little crescent pattern. Wally has come to notice these things, things he never paid much attention to before.

"Why are you inside on such a nice day?" his father asks.

"I'm outside now."

"Take over cutting the grass. I need a drink." His father presses his hand to his sweaty chest then puts his fingers to his mouth. "Too much salt. We eat too much salt. Your mother puts salt in everything."

Wally waits until his father has gone inside before heading out to the lawnmower. He starts it up, but it quickly chokes on the grass, then sputters and dies.

"Turn it over," his father calls from the front steps, drinking a glass of lemonade. It's probably spiked with vodka. "Pull out the grass that's caught."

Wally hesitates. He's afraid that the machine will kick back into gear, severing his hand. But he obeys. He flips the lawnmower over and begins pulling out clumps of grass in his hands. He sneezes once, twice, then three times.

His father has come up behind him. "What's the matter?"

"I'm allergic to grass," Wally tells him.

"You're not allergic to grass."

"Mom took me to the doctor. He said I was."

"Aw, go on, get out of here." His father shoves him aside to reclaim the lawnmower. Wally looks up to see the boys in the street are laughing at him.

And worse.

They're laughing at his father.

Something happened. Something bad.

High school changes everything. Once, Wally had many friends. Freddie and Michael and Philip and Steve. The teachers all liked him. He was going to *go far*. a straight-A student, a golden boy.

Not anymore. Now Wally's sullen and quiet and the teachers yell at him for never raising his hand in class. And in the entire school, he has just one friend, a geeky Jewish kid named David Schnur. His old friends from grade school went on to become cool, especially Freddie Piatrowski, who's on the junior varsity basketball team and has a girlfriend. Those two things alone are enough to make you cool. Wally has no such résumé.

But in the last three weeks, things have gotten even worse—ever since he and David went to see *Saturday Night Fever* at Cine 2 out on north Washington, the boxy little movie house that opened after the Palace Theater closed down. They each paid their three dollars and seventy-five cents and found two seats way in back, settling in to watch the kid from *Welcome Back, Kotter*. They had no idea of what was to come, any clue of the power the movie might wield. Yet from its very first frame it ensnared Wally: John Travolta strutting down a Brooklyn street to a throbbing Bee Gees soundtrack. The way he walked, the way he moved, the way he was dressed, the way he looked from side to side. The movie *did something* to Wally. Something weird. While David sat there shoving handful after handful of buttery popcorn into his mouth, Wally sat transfixed in the dark, unable to take his eyes from the screen.

The images burned themselves into his brain: Travolta in his black briefs shouting "Attica! Attica!" Travolta in those tight polyester pants. Travolta in the backseat getting a blow job. It didn't matter that the blow job was from Donna Pescow. What took hold of Wally's mind was the fact that all Travolta's mean, tough friends were *watching* him get it—mean, tough, handsome guys who said "fuck this" and "fuck that" and wore beautiful, shiny, tight-fitting clothes, topped off with gold jewelry and hairspray. Wally could practically smell their cologne through the screen. Something about the combination—the tough and the mean with the beautiful and the sweet—did something to Wally. Something weird.

He hasn't been able to get the movie off his mind since.

Since seeing the film, Wally has started styling his hair with a blow-dryer, something his father makes a lot of grumbling about. Extra electricity. Besides, it's girly. But Wally wants his hair to look like Travolta's, feathered back and shiny.

"Would ya just watch the hair?" he's said to David in a bad imitation of Travolta's Brooklyn accent. "Ya know, I spend a long time on my hair."

Last week, Wally pressured his mother to take him to Grant's to buy him some clothes. Usually she only bought him clothes in late summer, before school started. But even though it was spring now and school had only a few months left before summer vacation, Wally insisted he needed new pants, because none of the ones he had fit him right anymore. His mother acquiesced, not wanting Wally to make a fuss in front of his father. So down they trooped to Grant's, where Wally picked out the tightest, stretchiest, shiniest pair of burgundy slacks he could find, and threw in a silky green shirt with a yellow floral pattern as well. His mother was a little reluctant about the shirt, thinking his father wouldn't like the additional expense, but in the end she went along with it. Wally was thrilled by his new outfit. Trying the clothes on, his heart was thudding in his chest. He couldn't wait to wear them to school.

"Hey, John Revolting," Freddie Piatrowski teased, but somehow the taunt didn't bother Wally. He liked being John Travolta. He liked wearing the clothes. They felt good on his body. They excited him.

That's when he started making the phone calls.

* * *

His father's still snarling over the sputtering lawn mower when Wally walks off. He cuts through the group of boys in the street, ignoring their laughter. He should've taken his bike, but he has no idea where he's going, no plan. He's just walking. He heads down the cul-de-sac out onto Washington Avenue. Before long he's getting close to Main Street.

He knows it's wrong. Obscene phone callers—he's read about them in "Dear Abby"—are sick. Weirdos. And now he's one of them. But he can't help himself. He'll see a guy he thinks is sexy and then he just *has* to call him. He has to tell him he wants to fuck him. Then they'll say "fuck you" back and it will make Wally shoot.

At least that's how it usually works. Sometimes they just hang up. Wally hates it when that happens.

He used to worry that the police could track these calls, but not anymore. The old cop shows had made it look so easy. But *Starsky and Hutch* is far more realistic. You have to be on the phone for a long time before they can trace you, and your phone had to be rigged up with some gizmo from the police department. If Wally got them talking quick, got them to say *fuck*, he could hang up before no more than two or three minutes had elapsed. No one would ever catch him.

"Hello, Wally."

He looks up. He's been walking quite a while, all the way down Washington and crossing over to Main Street. He realizes he's passing by St. John the Baptist Church, next door to the school where Wally once attended, before his father was home all the time, before Wally lost all his friends, before he was an obscene phone caller and was still an All American boy.

"How have you been, Wally?"

At first he can't see anyone. The voice makes him uneasy, like it's God talking to him. But then he sees the priest standing in the doorway of the church, surrounded by little old ladies. It's Father Carson, and he's looking straight over at him. Wally gives him a small wave.

Wally was baptized in this church. In grade school, his class would troop next door for Mass on every First Friday and whatever holy day popped up in the calendar. But now the church seems an alien place to him, a place of shadows and whispers. Wally was a Catholic only when his father was home from the ship; when his father was away, his mother would take him to the Lutheran church. Now there is no church at all. Since he's been home, Wally's father has made no effort to get up on Sunday morning and head off to Mass.

"Wally," the priest is calling, "would you come over here a moment?"

Father Carson's a young man, no more than thirty-five, with wavy brown hair and green eyes. He's kind of like Travolta's older brother in *Fever*, but more handsome. He's saying good-bye to very small Italian ladies in black dresses who are coming out of Mass. Wally heads over slowly, watching as the priest makes the sign of the cross over one of the ladies' Rosary beads.

"It's been a while since I've seen you," Father Carson says, turning his full attention now to the boy. "How is your father?"

"He's fine."

"Tell him we miss him at Mass."

"I will."

"And how are you?"

Wally shrugs. "Okay."

"How's school going?"

"Okay."

Father Carson makes a sympathetic face. "I guess you'll be leaving Brown's Mill soon, going off to the military academy."

Wally's not sure why the priest is talking to him. Has there been talk? Have his high school teachers reported back to the nuns at St. John's? *What's happened to Wally Day? You said he was such a good boy.*

Wally looks up into Father Carson's face. The priest smiles at him. His eyes are set very deeply into his face.

"Wally," Father Carson says, "anytime you wish to talk, about anything, you're welcome to call me."

The boy makes a little sound. "Why should I need to talk to you?"

"I'm not sure. But if you want to talk, I'm here." The priest puts his hands on Wally's shoulders. "Sometimes you just want somebody to talk to, somebody you can trust."

Wally likes the feel of the priest's hands on his shoulders. He feels a tingling in his shoulders that goes all the way down his arms and his spine. He looks down at Father Carson's black pants. They're tight and very shiny. Wally feels his cock stir in his jeans. He wishes he could fall to his knees and bury his face in the somber black cloth of the priest's crotch.

Wally pulls away, hurrying down the street.

"Please call me," Father Carson says after him. "Please call me if you need to."

Three days after seeing *Saturday Night Fever*, Wally made his first obscene telephone call.

"You want to suck my cock?" he breathed into the phone.

"Who is this?"

"You want to suck my cock?"

Click. Dial tone.

Wally frantically pushed the buttons again. Freddie Piatrowski picked up the phone, irritated now.

"Or I can suck yours," Wally offered, disguising his voice.

"Who the fuck is this?"

He said fuck! Wally pumps his cock hard and fast in his fist, lubed with Vaseline.

"I *said*," Freddie growls, "who the fuck *is* this, faggot? I'll beat your fucking head in, you fucking faggot."

"Ohhhh!" Wally shouts, shooting a cannonball of spunk onto his mirror. He slams down the phone.

He said fuck. Oh, man, he said fuck!

That fuckin' faggot, we'll beat his fuckin' ass, huh, Tony? We'll beat his fuckin' ass.

Some of these chicks think if I fuck 'em, I gotta dance with 'em.

Travolta was always saying "fuck." In one scene, he said, "Fuck the future," but Fusco told him no, that you can't fuck the future. "The future fucks you," Fusco said. "It catches up with you and it fucks you if you aren't prepared for it!"

Wally had turned to David Schnur in the cafeteria a week later and asked, "What do you think he meant, that the future fucks you?"

"I dunno."

"You think it means that if you don't know what's coming, it can fuck you up for life? Keep you trapped? Keep you from ever being happy?"

"I don't know what you're talking about, Wally," David said, eating his Cheetos.

"Don't you ever think about it? Don't you ever have dreams about it?"

"About what?"

"*Saturday Night Fever.*"

"No," David told him, unwrapping his Ring Ding.

"Well, you're a fuckin' liar."

"Why should I dream about it?"

"Because you're a faggot."

"I am *not*," David protested.

"Don't lie to me," Wally said. "I could tell by the way you were looking at those guys on the screen. You wanted to have sex with John Travolta. And Joseph Cali. And the other guys. Admit it."

"Fuck you, Wally!" David tossed his Ring Ding at him. It bounced off of Wally's shoulder and rolled across the floor.

"Oh, lookit the little girlfriends having a spat!" Freddie Piatrowski shouted from the next table. "Whatsa matter, girls?"

Wally let it drop. David acted sulky for a while but eventually forgot about it, and they went on being friends.

"Hey, queerhead!"

Wally looks up. He's wandered over to the playground behind the church, and now some boys playing basketball have started taunting him. He pays them no mind. He just watches them through the fence. He likes the way their shorts inch up their asses when they shoot the ball. He stuffs his hands down deep into his pockets and rubs his cock through his jeans.

"Faggot, want to suck my cock?"

One boy approaches the chain-link fence and pulls down his shorts. He sticks his cock through the fence at Wally. It's very small and pink. It hangs through the fence like the trunk of a tiny sick elephant at the zoo. It disgusts him.

He returns home.

His father is asleep in his chair. His shirt is still off. He smells of grass and sweat. His chest rattles as he sleeps.

Wally finds his mother in the kitchen ironing. "Shh," she says. "Your father's asleep."

"I can see that."

"Where did you go? Did you quarrel with him again?"

Wally doesn't answer. He opens the refrigerator and takes a gulp of milk straight from the container. When he closes the door his mother is looking at him reprovingly.

"*What?*" he asks, daring her to say something.

Anything.

But she just goes back to her ironing.

He thinks of the phone and starts to breathe in quick little gasps.

He walks into his parents' room and takes the phone, its long cord trailing behind, twisting sinuously down the hallway.

"Why are you taking the phone in your room again?" his mother asks.

He ignores her, locking the door behind him, the phone cord pulled through the space at the bottom.

He unbuttons his jeans and lets them fall to the floor. From his closet he removes the polyester pants his mother bought him at Grant's. He pulls them onto his legs, snapping and zipping up the front. How tight they are. How smooth and shiny. He admires himself in the mirror. He moves his hand around to his butt, reveling in the tightness of the fabric across his cheeks. His cock goes rock hard.

"Fuck man," he whispers. "Fuckin' ass."

Lying facedown on his bed, he rubs his cock against the mattress, imagining John Travolta and his tough, Italian friends getting blow jobs as they wore pants like these, Donna Pescow on her knees in the backseat servicing them all. He rolls over and reaches under his bed for his jar of Vaseline. It's almost empty, with lots of finger valleys and pubic hairs. He unzips his pants and pulls out his cock. He begins sliding his fist up and down the shaft.

Maybe the Corvette guy is home.

The push button tones make his cock jump in his hand.

Ringing . . .

His eyes stare straight into the mirror.

Ringing . . .

"Hello?"

"I want—"

"What are you doing in there?" It's his father now, rapping at the door.

"*Hello?*" the guy on the phone demands.

Wally whispers. "I want to suck your cock."

"Speak up. I can't hear you."

"What are you doing in there with the phone?" his father shouts.

Wally cups his hand over the mouthpiece. "*I want to suck your cock!*"

"Who are you talking to?"

"Who is speaking?"

"Answer me! Who is on the phone?"

"*Who is this?*"

Wally slams the phone down. Damn them both! Damn them both to hell!

"I'm talking to David," he shouts. "It's about homework."

His father grumbles as he moves away from the door.

Wally presses the numbers again.

"*Hello!*" The Corvette guy is clearly pissed off.

"I want to suck your cock."

"You want to do *what?*"

"I want to suck your cock!"

Pause. "Who is this?"

"Would you like that?" Wally's voice is breathy and he's pumping his cock harder.

"No." Dial tone.

Wally slams down the receiver. *Why didn't he just say* fuck?

He hesitates. He needs to climax.

He pulls out the soiled phone book and flips through the pages until he finds the exact number he's looking for.

Push tones. Oh, God . . .

Ringing . . .

He pumps his cock, watching his reflection in the mirror.

Ringing . . .

"Answer the phone," he mutters.

Ringing . . .

Oh for God's sake, hurry up and answer the fucking phone!

"Hello?"

His throat is tight.

"Hello?"

"I want to fuck you."

"Excuse me?"

"I . . . I want you to fuck me."

"Oh." There is a long pause.

"Would you like that?" Wally asks.

"Would you?"

Oh, shit, he's talking. Wally can feel his cock getting ready to burst.

"Do you have the right number?" the voice asks him.

"Yeah."

"Do you realize you're talking to Father Carson?"

"Yeah." Wally imagines those deep eyes and those tight black pants. He imagines the priest's hands bearing down on his shoulders, snapping his bones, tearing his cartilage.

"I see."

He needs to climax. He pumps his cock so hard it actually hurts a little.

"Why don't you tell me who this is?"

Why can't I come? I want to shoot so I can fucking hang up.

"Why don't you tell me why you want me to fuck you?"

Jesus fuck he said it he said fuck and I'm coming I'm fucking coming! Fucking priest, he said fuck!

The cum shoots hard and splatters against the mirror. Wally falls back on to the bed and groans into the phone, the cord stretched taut across his chest.

He hears the priest say, "I told you that you were welcome to call me if you needed to talk."

He jumps up and crashes down the receiver.

It's suddenly very quiet in his room. Silent except for the yelps of the boys throwing the football in the street.

"Are you finished with that goddamn phone?" comes the voice of his father again. "I need to call the radio station. I know the answer to the prize question."

Wally just lies there. His cock curls up like a raw shrimp nesting in his wet kinky pubic hair.

"It was Edie Adams!" his father is shouting. "She was Our Miss Brooks. Did you hear me? Bring me the goddamn phone! We could win a hundred bucks here!"

Wally doesn't move, waiting for the phone to ring.

"Open this door! What are you doing in there? Jesus Christ, we could win a goddamn hundred—"

Wally just stares at the phone.

"Oh, forget it now," his father growls through the door. "Somebody just called in with the answer. Forget it now. Just forget it now."

At last Wally stands and cleans his mess off the mirror with Kleenex. He peels off his tight polyester pants and slips back into his jeans. He carries the phone out to his father.

"It was Eve Arden," he tells him.

His father glares at him. "Don't you think I know that? They just said it. Get outside and finish mowing the grass. Don't you think I know it was Eve Arden?"

Wally doesn't go outside. He just sits and waits for the phone to ring all day. But it never does.

12

WAITING FOR THE VAMPIRE

"There is a very good reason I have not allowed myself to die, not for more than a hundred years," says old Mr. Samuel Horowitz, the oldest man at the Hebrew Home.

"And what's that, Mr. Horowitz?"

"When I was a young boy in Russia, back in the days of the tsars, I was bitten by a vampire, and now I am afraid to die." He opens his eyes wide. "I am afraid that when I die, I will rise from my grave as one of the undead."

Regina Gunderson, new to her job as an aide at the Hebrew Home, wasn't expecting this. Nobody warned her about vampires.

"You don't believe me." The old man shifts in his chair and looks out the window. It's a bright January day. Samuel Horowitz's old black eyes blink against the day.

"The light hurts my eyes, you know," he tells Regina. "Has, ever since."

Regina offers a small laugh. "There aren't such things as vampires."

"You think not? You are wrong. In Russia, there were vampires. And one of them came to my home. Invited by my father, in fact. They must be invited, you know. They cannot enter a place unbidden."

"Oh, I see."

"His name was Count Alexei Petrovich Guchkov. He was a most charming man. Tall and handsome and dark. I was just sixteen. My father had money. They all hated my father because he was a Jew, but he had money, so they tolerated him. At least for a little while. Count Guchkov would come to our house and my mother would offer him wine, but he would always refuse. I found him mesmerizing. I could not take my eyes off him."

"Mr. Horowitz, here, have some tea—"

"You think it was merely a schoolboy fancy? You are wrong. One night, a cold black winter night, with the moon in the sky and the snow anxious to fall, he put his warm lips on mine and kissed me, with my parents just a few feet away . . ."

"Oh, please, Mr. Horowitz . . ."

"He kissed me, Miss Gunderson, and I liked it. He awoke in me passions I had forgotten from another life, passions that I have never felt since. His lips were warm but his hands were cold, but that was all right by me, especially when he moved his hands down my neck and over my shoulders, down between my legs . . ."

"Oh . . ."

"And then he pulled me into him, his strong arms wrapped around me, and I surrendered, willingly, eagerly, as he sunk his teeth into my throat and drank my young virgin blood."

Mr. Horowitz is quiet. He lets out a deep, long, labored breath and resumes looking out the window. Regina says nothing. She just sits there, breathing. Finally, with trembling fingers, she lifts Mr. Horowitz's cup of tea to her own lips, and drinks.

"I want to have my hair cut short and dyed black, like Elizabeth Taylor's," Rocky says, admiring herself in the mirror. She's blond, with tiny, delicate features. "Chase just adores Elizabeth Taylor. More than Sophia Loren now. Remember, Gina, how all he could talk about was Sophia Loren?"

"Yes," Regina says, sitting behind her on the bed.

"We're going away." Rocky looks at her sister through the mirror. "Chase is taking me on a little getaway trip."

"Oh, no, Rocky, please. I hate it when you go away."

"Now don't start with me, Regina. You'd think you were a child. Now relax. We'll only be gone for three days."

"*Three days?* Oh, Rocky, you shouldn't—"

She turns around to glare at Regina. "Now don't start. I'm twenty-one years old, Gina. I've wasted enough time."

Regina knows better than to debate her sister. She tries to quiet the terror that's surging even now up into her throat, that's constricting her arms from moving, that's popping out as sweat on her palms and cheeks. She watches her sister move over to the window and pull on her hose, not caring if the neighbors can see.

"So where are you going?" Regina asks finally.

"We're going on an *airplane!*" Rocky tells her, wide-eyed and big-mouthed, and for a moment Regina wants to slap her—slap her right across the face—but then pushes the thought away.

"We're going to St. Croix! It's in the Virgin Islands. We own it. The United States, I mean."

Regina says nothing.

"Can you imagine, Gina? White sandy beaches and a big sun overhead. And the water's so crystal blue and clear you can see the brightly colored tropical fish." She pauses, as if expecting her sister to voice disbelief. "It says so, in the brochure."

Regina gives her a small smile.

"Isn't it just too divine? It was Chase's idea. He's paying for the whole thing! His father's given him some time off from the bank. Of course he doesn't know Chase is taking a girl, but Chase has got him fooled good." Rocky flops down on the bed next to her sister, clutching the pillow to her chest and squeezing it. "Wasn't I lucky to find him?"

Regina stands and walks over to the mirror. She discovers her eyes. They stare back at her, big blue orbs, like the balls on the pool table Papa used to shoot.

"Rocky," she asks, not turning around. "Do you believe in vampires?"

But her sister has left the room.

"It was the year 1868," Mr. Horowitz tells her the next day. "I was a boy of eleven. Ever since then, I have been determined to stay alive. But it has been a life of fear. It has gripped me every night, the fear that I will not wake, that instead one cold night I will open my eyes to find myself in a coffin, the lust for blood overpowering me!"

"Please, Mr. Horowitz, please don't start talking that way again."

He eyes her. "Are you Christian, Miss Gunderson?"

"Yes."

"And you work here, as an aide in the Hebrew Home?"

"Yes."

"Ah, that is why I noticed the difference, why I thought you might believe. The Jews have stopped believing in such things. We have seen too much horror at the hands of men to believe in such things as vampires anymore. But we believed once. Have you ever heard the story of the Golem, Miss Gunderson?"

"No, Mr. Horowitz, and please, don't tell me. You'll frighten me more."

The old man moves his head against his pillow. His hair is still thick and white, loose around his face, a face of old bark, of a thousand crevices, of years of pain and anguish and scattered moments of joy, but mostly of fear.

"What kind of Christian are you?"

"What kind?"

"Yes. Are you Anglican? Catholic?"

"Lutheran."

"Ah. The German Protestant." Mr. Horowitz closes his eyes. "They hunted us down, but that was many years later. I was living with my sister and her husband then. I had never married, of course. Who would want me? I had been defiled. We had been driven from Russia by the Communists, but Germany wasn't far enough away to save me from a vampire. He still haunted my dreams. He could have found me, come to me, drank my blood again, if he had so chosen."

"Mr. Horowitz . . ."

"So leave if you don't want to hear! Why do you stand there, if what I tell you so disturbs you?"

"I'm concerned that you may be upsetting yourself."

"Upsetting myself!" The old man turns his head away from Regina. "I have felt this way for ninety years, as I hid not only from the Russians and the Germans but also from a creature of the night who was even more loathsome. I have feared death because of what it could mean to me. When the Germans forced us out, when in the black of night my brother-in-law huddled us under blankets and drove us to a waiting train so we could escape to America, I rejoiced. For so long I had wanted to come here, for only here, across the ocean, across the moving waters, would I be safe." He pauses. "You see, a vampire cannot cross moving water."

Regina has taken a seat beside the old man's bed. "Yet you are still afraid," she says, caught now by his tale.

The old man closes his eyes. "Yes. There is no escape. He could not get to me here, but in my blood his taint remains. I can't go on living forever! It has been an act of sheer will to live this long. I have kept death at arm's length for nearly a century. I have refused to open the door when he came courting, and he has come many times, Miss Gunderson. But I grow tired. I cannot hold out much longer. And when I die . . ."

"Yes?" Regina can stand it no longer. "What will happen when you die?"

"On the night of the third day, I will arise, out of my grave, a vampire myself, returned to feast on the blood of the living."

Regina Gunderson has placed her hands over her mouth. She cannot speak.

"Hey, stop that!"

Rocky is standing in front of the mirror again, wearing nothing but her black bra and red panties. Chase, her boyfriend, is on his hands and knees on the bed behind her. He's snapped the back of her bra strap so that it makes a sharp sound slapping against her flesh.

Regina pauses in the doorway. "Are you all right, Rocky?" she asks.

"I will be, if this lecherous monster leaves me alone."

Chase growls, making bear claws with his hands.

Rocky giggles. Regina turns to walk away.

"Hey, Gina," her sister calls after her. "Maybe you ought to go stay with Aunt Selma and Uncle Axel while we're away."

Regina pauses. Perhaps. Perhaps that might be best.

Chase laughs. "Oh, don't be ridiculous, Rocky. You act like Gina's the baby sister, instead of the other way around. She'll be fine. Won't ya now, Gina?"

Regina looks at him. A broad, dimpled grin stretches across Chase's face. All at once he bounces off the bed and lands in front of Regina. She makes a little yelp in surprise. Chase places his hands on her hips, drawing her in to give her a quick kiss on the nose.

Regina hates it when Chase does things like this. But she doesn't pull away from his grip. She just stands in front of him, not an inch separating their lips. She can smell his breath. Sweet, like candy.

"You just need to remember a few things," Rocky is saying, pulling on her lacy white blouse and buttoning it down the front, her black bra showing through. "Dicky, the paper boy, needs to be paid on Thursday. I've left the money in an envelope. And Mr. Otfinowski, the milkman, gets paid on Friday morning. Make sure you leave his money in the crate on Thursday night, because otherwise he comes so early you'll never catch him. We'll be coming back Friday afternoon, but by the time we get a cab from the airport and get dinner, it'll be late, so don't wait up."

"Okay," Regina says softly, nose-to-nose with Chase.

"Gosh," he says, studying her, "you've got pretty eyes."

She yanks away all at once and hurries down the hall to her room. She can hear her sister shushing Chase, saying he shouldn't have said that, that he knows Gina is shy around men.

"But I never noticed how *blue* her eyes were before," Chase is saying. That's when Regina turns on her radio very loud, singing along in her head to Pat Boone's "Ain't That a Shame."

The Gunderson sisters live in a four-room flat in an old building on Pleasant Street, just off Main. It's one of the grand old buildings of Brown's Mill, with the elegant moldings and filigrees of the nineteenth century. From her window Regina can see the top of the next building, and just beyond that the steeple of St. John the Baptist. Up the hill toward the orchards, she can just make out the corner of the cemetery, where Mama and Mormor and Rocky's baby are buried.

She gets into bed but can't fall asleep. She tosses and turns, thinking about Mr. Horowitz's stories. She tries to think of something else, but she can't.

"Oh, Rocky, Rocky, Rocky . . ."

Chase's voice seeps through the darkness from the other room.

Regina doesn't want to hear it. Even thinking about vampires is preferable to listening to that.

"Oh, *yesss*."

Now her sister's low, hushed voice comes through the wall.

Regina pulls her blankets up to her chin as she lies there in the dark.

I can still feel the warmth of his mouth and the coldness of his hands, here.

Tomorrow her sister will be gone. Three days and even worse: three *nights*. And Chase with her.

"Oh, *God!*" Rocky's voice suddenly calls out, and Regina gasps.

"Yeah, that's it, baby," Chase says, and Regina isn't sure if she really hears him or if his words are inside her head, a memory still burning from other times like this.

She flings back the covers and places her bare feet against the cold hardwood floor. The flat is dark as she stands and pulls on her robe. In the winter, with the windows closed, their building is utterly quiet. From two floors above, one might hear the soft chime of Mr. Goldstein's pendulum clock striking the hour. Or maybe the tinkling of Miss Wright's piano, or the radiators clattering with heat, or the buzz of electricity that one only notices when it's dark and still.

Regina scuffs her way down the hallway through the darkness. Flickering candlelight shines from the crack of her sister's door. It's enough to let Regina see the heaving of Chase's strong muscular back, Rocky's red-tipped hands laced around his neck. For several moments she watches soundlessly as Chase's back rises and falls, the bedsprings squeaking. Then she turns away.

In the dark bathroom, the tiles of the floor are even colder than the wood. Regina's feet react, wanting to run. But she stands beside the toilet, effortlessly finding the handle in the dark. She flushes.

The sound of the water rushing through the pipes in the great old building echoes among the rooms, as surely as they must have in each of the flats in the building. Somewhere above them perhaps Mr. Goldstein sits up in his bed and wonders who is awake at this hour. Below them maybe old Miss Wright opens her eyes and shakes her head in dismay.

When Regina leaves the bathroom, she knows the sliver of light from her sister's room will be gone, and the sounds will have stopped.

But still she cannot fall asleep.

Mr. Horowitz dies the morning Rocky and Chase get on their airplane and fly to St. Croix.

"Oh, no," Regina says, arriving at the Hebrew Home.

Mrs. Newberg nods. "Poor old warhorse. He didn't want to go. He fought like a tiger right to the end. It was before the sun was up. That was why he was fighting so, trying to hold back."

"I don't understand."

"He said he wanted to see the sun, one last time," Mrs. Newberg tells her.

"Oh."

"Very sad, really. But he'd lived a long time. A very long time. You were close to him, weren't you, Regina?"

But Regina isn't listening. Somewhere overhead, an airplane passes, and it seems as if the building shakes.

The movie is *Son of Dracula*, and it is paired with *Son of Frankenstein*. Regina stares at the poster beneath the Palace marquee: a top-hatted vampire raising his cape and baring his fangs. As a child, Regina had loved coming to the Palace to see the latest Deanna Durbin picture, or Andy Hardy, or anything with Alice Faye. She and Rocky would walk to the theater together, two little blond girls with bright blue eyes, skipping and holding hands. Sometimes they'd stay at the theater all day, through newsreels, cartoons, trailers, and double features, waiting until they were sure Papa had passed out on the couch.

"Do you like vampire movies?"

Regina is startled by the voice. She looks up from the poster and sees a man standing next to her, an older, distinguished man with gray hair and mustache.

"Oh, I was simply—"

She feels her voice catch in her throat. The sun is setting. Rocky should have arrived in St. Croix by now.

"It's quite good," the man is saying. "But of course, no one can top Lugosi in the original. Have you seen that version?"

He has a slight British accent, or at least Regina thinks he does. "No," she says. "Well, I don't remember. It's possible."

"And here I thought you were a vampire fan."

"Oh, no," she says. "I'm not."

"The matinee is starting in a few minutes. Would you care to join me?"

"No," she says. "I'm going—going for lunch. I only have an hour."

"Well, as it happens, I'm quite hungry, too. May I walk you to Henry's Diner?"

Regina thinks it odd that the man would know Henry's was her destination. But, after all, how many other lunch places are there on Main Street? She says nothing, just falls into step beside him as they make their way down the block.

"Of course, there is the German version. *Nosferatu*. A silent picture. Have you seen that one, Miss—Miss—?"

"Gunderson. Regina Gunderson."

He opens the door to Henry's Diner. "After you, Miss Gunderson."

They sit at the counter. Regina prefers it to a booth. A booth would imply they're eating lunch together, when they're not. This man is a stranger to her.

"I'm Stanley Kowalski," he says, leaning in, then grinning. "No, not *that* Stanley Kowalski."

Regina keeps her eyes cast down as she gives Lois the waitress her order for a grilled cheese and cup of tea.

"You seem nervous," Mr. Kowalski offers.

"No, no, it's just that—" She pauses. "A man I knew just passed away. I'm a bit out of sorts."

"I'm so sorry. Was he a close friend?"

She looks over at him. She can't help herself. It just spills out. The whole story of Mr. Samuel Horowitz and the Russian vampire count. Stanley Kowalski listens with rapt interest, nodding his head, lifting his eyebrows. When she's finished, he takes a long sip of his coffee, considering everything she's said. "No," he announces. "It's not possible."

"Of course it's not," Regina agrees.

"I'll tell you why it's not possible," Mr. Kowalski says, setting his coffee cup back in its saucer. "For a vampire to create another in his image, he must first *kill* his victim. If what Mr. Horowitz says is true, this Russian count forgot about him, as vampires must do the majority of their victims, otherwise we'd be overrun with the creatures. The vampiric taint wears off, I assume. Think of the Dracula story, my dear. Mina Harker was not going to turn into a vampire when she died. Poor Miss Lucy, on the other hand—she became a creature of the night because the count sucked her dry, so to speak, and killed her."

Regina is shocked, and it shows on her face.

"I'm sorry," Mr. Kowalski says at once. "Have I offended you?"

"I suppose I brought it on myself," she says, taking a breath. "I brought the horrible subject up." She slides off her stool. "I've got to get back to work anyway."

"Let me pay for your lunch," Stanley Kowalski offers.

"No, no, absolutely not." She hands two dollar bills across the counter to Lois. "Keep the change," she says, anxious to be out of there. Lois waves without turning around from the cash register.

"Think no more about it, my dear," the man assures her. "I'm sure Mr. Horowitz is sleeping peacefully in his cold grave."

Regina rushes out the door.

She had considered sitting *shivah* for Mr. Horowitz at the Hebrew Home, but something didn't seem right about it. Not because she was a Christian, but because, deep down, she knew *Mr. Horowitz wasn't really dead.* The corpse they had placed into the mausoleum was just waiting, waiting to live again. Three nights from now, it would claw its way through the satin lining of the coffin and break free of its prison.

"Stop this nonsense," Regina tells herself, and she places both her hands on the Formica top of the kitchen table and closes her eyes tightly. "Stop this nonsense right now, Regina Christina Gunderson."

When she opens them, she suddenly hears music: strange tinny music, as if from an old phonograph, somewhere in the building. It disturbs her, but she isn't sure why. She's just on edge because Rocky isn't here.

Poor Miss Lucy—she became a creature of the night because the count sucked her dry.

The tinny music seems to be growing louder. Who could be playing it? It seems old, very old, as if it came from a Victrola—

Her mind flashes on an image: Mr. Horowitz as a young boy in Russia, with the great noble Count Alexei Petrovich Guchkov bent over, kissing his hand, a Victrola in the back, playing this very same music.

"Stop it!" she scolds herself.

She heads into Rocky's bedroom and sits down on her neatly made bed.

"Just three days," she whispers to herself, staring at her reflection in the mirror. "Just three nights," she hears another voice say, inside her. And in the glass, she sees old Mr. Horowitz, chalk white face and bloodred lips, rising up from behind her on the bed.

She screams. Even as she turns and sees nothing there, she can't stop screaming. She has to cover her mouth with both of her hands to stifle the sound.

The next day, Regina helps the other aides pack up the dead man's belongings. There is no family. Some of his personal items will be distributed among the other residents. The rest will be discarded.

"You look tired, Regina," says Mavis, a colored aide. "No sleep last night?"

She sighs, lifting a small icon of the Virgin Mary from Mr. Horowitz's jewelry box. How odd that Mr. Horowitz should have it. Beside it rests a silver Star of David. Regina pricks herself on one of its sharp points. "Ow," she says, instinctively drawing the wounded finger to her mouth.

"Let me have the Virgin," Mavis is saying, looking over her shoulder. "No one here will want it."

Regina isn't sure. "We should ask Mrs. Newberg."

Mavis makes a face. "She'll say no. Come on, Regina. Who'll care?"

She says nothing, just hands over the icon to Mavis. That leaves the Star of David. Regina stares down at it for a few moments. Then she slips it into her pocket. Who'll care?

The sun edges the horizon.

Two more nights.

She prays she'll sleep better tonight. It's quiet now, no music. Usually Regina likes the quiet, because it's so different from what she was used to when Papa was alive. Papa always played the radio very loud, ball games and big band music. After he died, Regina threw out his radio and they've never had one since. Out went all of Papa's cigar ashes and bottle tops, swept by Regina's furious broom. She turned the place into a tidy little home for herself and Rocky.

It was good at first. Regina made dinner, pot roast and boiled potatoes, or sometimes cheese rarebit, often lighting candles to make the flat look extra pretty. On Friday nights the sisters would sometimes walk to Main Street to see a picture, the way they had as children, or maybe they'd head down to Miss Wright's to watch her television set. Miss Wright had been the first in the building to buy one, and Regina would laugh at Milton Berle and Sid Caesar. Yes, it was a good couple of years. They didn't even talk about the city anymore, or what had happened there.

But the very week Rocky turned twenty-one she met Chase Worthington. Chase was a rich boy from one of the big white houses up on the hill. He came into the bowling alley where Rocky worked, hooting and hollering with his college friends, and Rocky had tried to toss him out. Instead, she ended up going on a date with him, and Chase has been an almost nightly presence ever since.

Once again Regina is sitting on her sister's bed. The stillness of the place seems to swallow her whole. She draws a pillow close to her—the one Chase had slept on just two nights before. She wants to push that pillow into her face and inhale, but she dares not.

Suddenly, the music again. The same tinny music, coming from somewhere— not above, not below. Then from *where*? What song does it play?

She flings the pillow to the floor and stands. She should go to sleep now. She has to be at the Hebrew Home by seven. Tomorrow is Thursday. Tomorrow she must pay the paper boy. And leave the money out for Mr. Otfinowski.

A bang. She jumps. Something scratches at the window.

"Oh!" Regina cries.

Three long scratches scar the frost, scratches like fingernails.

"A squirrel," she says. "A squirrel."

It can't be anything else. It can't be the vampire. It's only been two nights.

"And besides," Regina says out loud, "Mr. Kowalski said the taint must have disappeared from his blood long ago."

She hurries to her room and undresses in front of her mirror. Standing there only in her bra and slip, Regina touches her face. She's so fair that at first glance it would appear she has no eyebrows or eyelashes. Rocky darkens hers with a pencil and mascara, but Regina wears no makeup.

She crawls into bed.

The music keeps playing. She tries to pretend it's not there but she can't manage the charade for long. She lies there picturing the Jewish cemetery out near Devil's Hopyard, that strange field where scaly hops grow yellow in the summer, where the Indians first heard unaccountable noises centuries ago, where the early English settlers had pronounced the land the devil's own. The noises, scientists would later say, were merely the rumblings of a minor fault far beneath the surface of the earth: but might they not be coming from hell? Or from the stark Jewish cemetery, where Mr. Horowitz's body lies in the mausoleum, waiting to live again?

Regina begins to cry.

"I feel very foolish," Regina tells Stanley Kowalski.

"Please don't."

They're back at Henry's Diner. Regina had called him, having found his name in the phone book. Mr. Kowalski was only too happy to meet her for lunch. This time they got a booth. Regina ordered a grilled cheese. "The usual," Lois smiled, scribbling onto her pad. Mr. Kowalski ordered a steak burger with onions, very rare.

"I must get this out of my head," Regina tells him.

"After tonight, the fear will be gone."

"I certainly hope so. I didn't sleep at all last night."

"Even if Mr. Horowitz really *is* a vampire, and even if tonight he *does* rise," says Mr. Kowalski, "there's no reason to believe he would come for you. And even if he did, vampires must first be *invited* into a home before they can enter. You are perfectly safe, Miss Gunderson."

"There was something connecting us," Regina says. "He picked up on that. I was different, he said. I would *believe.*"

"And do you?"

She hesitates. Lois brings over the grilled cheese, burned around the edges and a thin wedge of pickle on the side. "Your steak burger will be out in a minute," she tells Mr. Kowalski.

"Thank you."

Regina takes a bite, then remembers it's impolite to eat before the other person is served.

"Go ahead," Mr. Kowalski offers, but she shakes her head no.

"I'm not sure what I believe," Regina says. "I just wish my sister wasn't away. This wouldn't be happening if she were here."

"Is your sister some sort of magic talisman?"

"My sister wouldn't let anything bad happen. She's very strong."

"And you?"

"Here's your steak burger," Lois interjects, thrusting the bloody flesh between them on a plate. "With extra onions. Will there be anything else?"

"No," Mr. Kowalski says, looking over at Regina. "There will be nothing else."

After lunch, Regina calls the Hebrew Home to say she has a headache, that she won't be back. She isn't lying.

"Come with me," Stanley Kowalski says. "My house is just over this way. I want to give you something."

She shouldn't go; she should just head home. Get this crazy notion out of her head. She shouldn't go to a strange man's house. But she follows.

Stanley Kowalski lives on Walnut Street, two blocks past Regina's own street. The Friendly Barber Shop is on the corner. As they pass, Stanley waves to the barber, who's inside sharpening his razors.

It's a cold day. The wind is whipping, and Regina's cheeks grow red and hard. She's misplaced her gloves, so she shoves her hands deep down into the pockets of her coat. The sky is dark gray. Snow beckons.

"Here it is," Stanley says, opening his door. "My humble abode."

His flat smells like bananas. A parakeet in a wire cage chirps a greeting. "Hello, Mrs. Tennyson," Stanley says.

Regina stands in his little foyer, unsure of whether she should proceed.

"Ah, Miss Gunderson, don't be afraid. Please. Sit down."

"I shouldn't stay."

"But I must give you what we came here for."

Stanley Kowalski disappears down the hall. Regina gazes around the room, at the newspapers on the floor, the plate full of crumbs and empty Coke bottles next to the frayed overstuffed chair. Mrs. Tennyson squawks a couple of times at her. On the wall hangs a calendar: Jayne Mansfield, her enormous breasts bared, in a tiny fur-trimmed skirt and boots, shivering atop the hood of a car.

"Here we are," Mr. Kowalski says, coming back down the hall. He holds something in his hand. "You take this, Miss Gunderson. Wear it around your neck. This will protect you."

It's a crucifix, a large wooden one on a silver chain.

"That will do no good," Regina protests.

"Buy why not?"

"He was Jewish," Regina says plainly.

"Ah," Mr. Kowalski says, nodding.

"But *this*," Regina says, eyes lighting at the thought as she reaches into her pocket, "this will work." She produces the Star of David. "May I take the chain?"

"But of course. Oh, this is splendid."

Regina feels better already. Why hadn't she thought of this before?

Mr. Kowalski pulls the chain off the crucifix and proceeds to thread it through the small ring at the top of the star. "This was meant to be worn," he says. "May I put it on you?"

"Yes, please," Regina says, turning her back to him.

Mr. Kowalski slips the star around Regina's neck. "There," he says, and without warning he drops his arms around Regina, pulling her in, nuzzling her neck with his lips.

"Mr. Kowalski!"

"Oh, come, my dear," he soothes. "You came willingly."

"No," she says, but Mr. Kowalski's arms only tighten around her. Regina can't see his face, only hear his words and feel his lips pressing against her ear.

"Foolish child, to think that vampires can be stopped by silly little trinkets, that they only walk about by night," Stanley Kowalski says, and now his hands, his cold hands, are inside Regina's coat, unbuttoning the front of her blouse.

"No," she says again, but more meekly this time. "No, please."

Stanley Kowalski's cold hands touch Regina's skin. "Such a dear girl," he purrs. "Such a sweet, innocent child—"

"No," Regina says dreamily. "Not innocent . . ."

Mr. Kowalski laughs.

"No man would want me . . . no man . . ."

"Hush, dear girl," Mr. Kowalski says. "There shall be no more men. Only me."

And with that, he bites Regina Gunderson upon her neck.

It's started to snow.

"It's true," Regina says, walking out onto the sidewalk, her voice calm and full of wonder as she watches the fragile flakes accumulate on the black wool of her coat. "No two snowflakes *are* exactly the same."

Back at the flat, in the last slanting golden rays of the day, she puts on a pot of tea and contemplates dinner. "Rocky will want stew," she says out loud. She opens the freezer and looks down into it. No stew meat.

"Oh, dear," she says to herself, and then the sunlight is gone.

Rocky's away, Regina remembers.

And it's the third night.

The Star of David still hangs around her neck. She clutches it and breathes.

"What should I do?" she whispers, pressing her nose up against the cold windowpane, looking out across the rooftops in the direction of Devil's Hop-yard, where she can see, in her mind, the great stone door of the mausoleum in the Jewish cemetery sliding back, the demons of the hopyard dancing in strange homage to the risen Samuel Horowitz . . .

The teakettle is whistling, a piercing sound. But more, too: the tinny music, the sound of a Victrola at the Russian Imperial Court, or the sound of the radio Papa used to play, over and over, as he sat there drinking, drinking until his face became purple, drinking until he forgot the two young girls in the other room were his daughters.

Leave her alone, Papa. Leave Regina alone!

A knock at the door.

Regina tenses. For a moment she thinks she should hide, but then decides against it. The knock comes again. She takes a deep breath and walks over to the door, peering through the peephole.

It's Dicky. The paper boy. She had forgotten.

"Good ev'nin', Miss Gunderson," the boy says. His face looks bloated and distorted through the peephole.

She opens the door, stepping aside to let him enter.

Dicky seems unsure, but he comes inside. He's a tall youth, with long legs and a blonde crew cut. He can't be more than fifteen.

"Now where *is* that envelope?" Regina asks. Her voice is different: lighter, higher. "I know my sister left it around here for you somewhere."

Dicky shifts his weight from his left foot to his right.

Regina suddenly stops her search and looks over at the boy, a broad smile crossing her face. "Dicky, would you like a cup of tea?"

The boy looks off toward the whistling kettle. "Um, no, thanks. I've got to finish my route."

"It's snowing outside. And so very cold. Are you *sure*?"

"No, thanks."

Regina smiles. "Of course not. How silly of me. Boys don't drink tea." She touches the boy's cold hard cheeks with each of her forefingers. "I could make some hot cocoa," she tempts.

"No, thank you, Miss Gunderson."

She watches him for several seconds. Then the place between her legs starts to hurt again, and she remembers what happened there. She thrusts the envelope at him. "*Go*," she. says hoarsely. "Get out of here. This place is not safe. He's coming for me. Run. Save yourself."

"Miss Gunderson, are you—"

"Go, Dicky! *Run!*" she shouts. The boy does. Regina bolts the door behind him.

She closes her eyes. The teakettle still whistles on the stove but it cannot obscure the music. It grows louder every second. Regina can see Samuel Horowitz dancing in the hopyard now, his white burial gown swaying around him, his thick white hair blowing in the darkness. He leaves no tracks in the newly fallen snow.

"Oh, please, no," Regina cries, sitting down at the kitchen table, pressing her fingers into her temples. "Oh, why did Rocky have to go away and leave me?"

The vampire is getting closer. He floats over the snow, so white, so pure, all the way into town from the hopyard—down from the orchards, through the swampy neighborhoods of Dogtown, past St. John the Baptist Church, all the way down Main Street, past the Hebrew Home, past Henry's Diner, past the Palace Theater, up the block toward Regina's building . . .

"Stop it!" she screams at herself, but the music grows louder, a scratchy old tune, one she knows, one of her father's favorites, one of the songs that was always playing on the radio when he came into her room, his breath smelling of whiskey, Rocky crying in the next bed.

Leave her alone! Leave Regina alone!

The music—yes, the same—louder and louder—

And then the scratching at the window again, and this time it's no squirrel, it's a hand, an old hand, long gnarled fingers scratching to get in . . .

A vampire must be invited into the home.

Regina backs up into the cupboard in the dark kitchen, staring at the scratch marks in the frost on the window over the sink. "No," she whispers. "Please don't."

The hand reappears at the window, scratching away more of the frost.

"You don't want me," Regina cries. "I'm not what you think."

But the music only gets louder. And when the face of old Samuel Horowitz appears at the window, grinning wide and baring his fangs, Regina screams with every last vestige of what she once was. She screams and screams, but when it's over and no one has come, she finally looks up at the window and says, "Yes. All right. You might as well come in."

And she tears the Star of David from around her neck, tossing it across the kitchen floor, where it clatters for several seconds before finally settling among the dust beneath the Kelvinator.

Then the window over the sink slides open, a screech of icy metal against wood, just as, somewhere off in the building, the Goldsteins' pendulum clock begins to chime.

"Miss Gunderson?"

"Yes."

"My name is Stanley Kowalski." He grins. "No, not *that* Stanley Kowalski."

But Rocky doesn't smile.

The man becomes serious. "I came inquiring about your sister."

"Are you a friend?"

"I'd only just met her. We had lunch together on Thursday at Henry's Diner."

Rocky's eyes are still puffy. "And how did she seem to you?"

"Oh, fine, my dear. Just fine."

"Then you have no clue as to what happened?"

"No, I'm afraid I don't, Miss Gunderson."

Rocky begins to cry. "I should never have left her."

"There, there, my dear," Stanley says, taking the young woman into his arms. He holds her in the doorway, stroking her hair.

Rocky looks up at him. "How did you know something happened?"

The man smiles uneasily. "I came by in the morning. I saw the ambulance . . ."

"Oh, please, don't mention it again. Mr. Otfinowski has already described what he found when he came here, just as the sun was coming up, to deliver the milk . . . Oh, I should have been here!"

"I'm sorry, dear. I didn't mean to upset you again." Mr. Kowalski's eyes bear down on her. "Might I see her? You'll let me see her, won't you?"

"All right," Rocky says, turning to walk back into the flat, leaving the door open for Mr. Kowalski to follow.

"My dear," he calls after her graciously. "First you must invite me in."

In her room, Regina has heard it all. She huddles under her blankets, her neck bandaged where Rocky said she had tried to slit her throat with the Star of David. Rocky talks nonsense. She babbles about sending Regina away somewhere. Aunt Selma and Uncle Axel were here, too, and they talked the same. But Regina paid them no mind. Whatever they talk about doesn't concern her anymore.

Oh, how the light burns her eyes now. Such will be the way from now on. That much she knows for certain. But for how long? Will old Samuel Horowitz come back for her tonight and kill her? Or will he, instead, make her wait, wait like he did, living only through sheer force of will, living only because she was afraid to die?

Regina Gunderson finally understands most everything else, but this is the one thing she still doesn't know.

13

JACKY TRICKY

The hospital's very bright, too much to bear. Wally squints his eyes under the hot white lights as they head down corridors that twist and turn like some Clive Barker nightmare journey. When he stops for water at the fountain, his mother wrings her hands.

"Oh, please, Walter," she says. "Don't dawdle."

"I'm not dawdling. I'm thirsty."

The doctor, hands clasped, is waiting for them outside Uncle Axel's door.

"He won't make the day," the doctor confides, shifting his knotty features into their sympathetic guise, something he probably does two, three times a week. Wally's mother nods, wrinkling her cheeks to feign sadness. Wally doesn't play their game.

Uncle Axel is ninety-seven years old. What's left of him is drying up in his hospital bed. The smell of the cleaning fluid overwhelms everything else, but underneath Wally can still smell urine. The odor hits him, an almost physical force, when they push open the door to the old man's room. They stand over his bed, saying nothing, just looking down at him.

"You never liked him either," Wally says. "Admit it."

His mother makes no reply. Uncle Axel's sheets are perfectly starched, crisp, white. Lying beneath them are his bones, wrapped loosely in yellow skin that looks like last year's maple leaves: flaking, with veins dried up in networks of brown. His ears are large, two withered leaves of cabbage stuck ungainly to the sides of his head. His eyes are closed; his mouth, a black hole, hangs open. His cheeks are sunken into his face, and his wispy hair is white, whiter even than the pillow behind his head.

They stand over him, looking down. The old man is a relic of a past Wally has done his best these last two decades to forget.

"He's all I have left," Wally's mother says.

He looks over at her with contempt. *All she has left.* Uncle Axel is Mom's mother's sister's husband, and a nastier old man Wally never met. He was cruel to Wally, and cruel to his mother, too. She's told him the stories. But in the car on the ride over here, his mother had said that no one should have to die alone.

Fuck that. Wally *wants* Uncle Axel to die alone and full of misery, like a beast caught in a trap in the woods. He wants the old man to open his eyes, look around, see that he's alone, that no one cares. And then he wants him to die.

"All right," Wally whispers, his lips nearly in his mother's ear. "We've seen him. We can leave. You can tell all the busybodies in town that you saw him on his deathbed."

"Walter," his mother says. "I know he wasn't a very pleasant man, but he's all the family I've got left. I just want to show him a little respect."

"Respect?" Wally asks loudly, turning all at once to see if anyone has heard him. He lowers his voice again. "Don't talk to me about respect, Mother. Not while we're standing over this pile of shit."

"Oh, Walter."

They look down at him. The old man's eyes are open now, staring crookedly at his nose. Wally's mother covers her mouth with her hand, but neither of them say a word. The only sound in the room is the gurgling from Uncle Axel's throat. Wally freezes. His testicles tighten. He has the same feeling he had all those years ago.

It's as if Jacky Tricky is in the window, watching.

Aunt Selma was making dinner. Wally was bored, driving one of his Matchbox toy cars across the kitchen table, making an engine sound by swishing the spit back and forth in his mouth. He drove the car across the wax paper Aunt Selma had laid out for her pie and then over the bowl of fruit in the center of the table, a mountain of boulders. Apples and pears tumbled out of the bowl and bounced onto the floor. "Avalanche!" Wally shouted.

Aunt Selma smiled wearily.

Uncle Axel barged in, rubbing his oil-blackened hands together. His hair was gray, his eyes dark brown and very round. His face was weathered sandpaper, his ears large and very red with long, floppy lobes. He was a farmer, and his hands showed it: nails and knuckles permanently outlined in black, indelible grass stains on his fingertips. Sometimes Uncle Axel didn't wash his hands before dinner, despite Aunt Selma's urgings, and he'd leave greasy handprints on the tablecloth. He usually smelled like hay, sometimes manure, but now he smelled like oil. He'd been fixing the tractor.

Wally stopped playing the moment Uncle Axel came through the door. He watched the old man rub his hands on his dirty dungarees and grab for the fallen fruit. His round eyes narrowed. "Why is this kid inside?"

"He's playing with his cars, Axel," Aunt Selma told him, her voice far away.

The old man's ears flushed. "Get that goddamn filthy car off the table!" He whacked the back of Wally's head with the palm of his hand, the smell of lubricating oil swirling around the boy's face. "You want to mess up your aunt's table? Why don't you play outside like other boys? You a sissy? Huh? You a sissy?"

Wally took his car and headed for the back door.

"Dinner will be ready in a few minutes," Aunt Selma called after him.

Uncle Axel was grumbling, "Look at this bruised fruit. These apples were perfect. Now look at 'em."

Wally pushed open the screen door, letting it bang—*whack!*—as Uncle Axel hollered, "And don't slam that goddamn door! Jesus, the kid don't have no manners."

Uncle Axel and Aunt Selma lived on the far outskirts of Brown's Mill, where the woods were deep and the houses few. They raised chickens and pigs and grew corn. Walking out into the backyard, past bales of hay and old rotting tires, Wally breathed the air, pungent and cool, and heard Aunt Selma's voice carrying out behind him. "You really shouldn't hit him, Axel," she was saying. "He isn't ours."

The stench of cow manure hung thick out here. Wally kept walking, way up past the fence that surrounded the field. He plopped down finally under an old maple tree, leaning his back against the trunk. It was late summer. Most of the crop was gone and the yard was a jumble of tools and crates. Hens ran squawking through the grass. Baskets of corn Uncle Axel tried to sell by the roadside were starting to rot.

Television barely came in out here. The antenna on the roof was crooked and rusty, and though Aunt Selma kept asking Uncle Axel to fix it, he never did. Wally hated not getting to watch *Land of the Lost* on Saturday mornings. He found the little general store out here boring and inadequate, with outdated comic books and candy that had gone stale in its wrappers. He missed his friends, especially Freddie Piatrowski. All Wally had to keep himself occupied were his Matchbox cars. He couldn't wait to get back to school.

The color of the leaves was just starting to change, ever so slightly. A year before, Wally's parents had taken him on a trip in their big blue Buick, a trip up north to look at the leaves. It was the only time Wally could remember the three of them being happy—really happy, like the families on television, the Cunninghams or the Waltons or the Ingalls. They spent the night in a little rustic cabin and in the morning Mom made blueberry pancakes, while Dad took Wally into the woods to show him how to look for color changes in the leaves.

"You look first for the veins," Dad said, pulling down a branch and holding a translucent leaf to the sun. "When they start to turn yellow, that means the blood of the tree is no longer flowing, and so the leaves begin to lose their color."

"If its blood isn't flowing," Wally surmised, "then it must be dead."

His father nodded. "People say the trees look beautiful in autumn. Next time you hear that, you can tell 'em what they're really seeing is the leaves starting to die."

Wally hadn't wanted to come here to Uncle Axel's farm. He'd begged and pleaded with his parents not to send him again, but he knew there was no choice. Even at eight, he realized Mom and Dad weren't very happy together. Dad was away so much of the time, and Mom would start to cry so easily. Then Wally's father would get angry, and sometimes he smashed things. That was when it was really bad, and Mom would call Aunt Selma and ask if Wally could stay with them for a few days. But a few days always turned into a few weeks, and now the summer was almost over.

"I don't want to go," Wally cried as his mother helped him pack his things. "He's mean to me. Uncle Axel."

"How is he mean to you?" his mother asked, folding a sweater into his suitcase.

"He tells me about Jacky Tricky."

She let out a long sigh. "Oh, Walter," she said, cupping his chin in her hand. "He used to tell me the same story. And it frightened me, too. I was lucky because I had my sister Rocky to tell me it wasn't real. Uncle Axel just likes to scare children. He always has. But Jacky Tricky isn't real. You're a big boy now, Walter. You won't be afraid of him anymore."

The sun was going down over the trees. Shadows crept longer, fuller, closing in on him. The old maple was melting from its dull green to a heavy, forbidding blue. Crickets were chattering now, and a few mosquitoes sang at the boy's ears. Wally lay on his back and rolled the toy car over my stomach.

"Dinnertime."

Uncle Axel's voice was suddenly behind him. Wally sat up quickly but didn't look around.

"We've set four plates," Uncle Axel said, his voice soft and sticky. Still Wally wouldn't look around. He just sat there waiting, feeling the old man's voice drip on the back of his neck like the maple syrup Aunt Selma collected from the trees. "*Four* plates," Uncle Axel was saying. "One for me, one for Aunt Selma, one for you, and one for . . . can you guess?"

"He's not real," Wally said with as much conviction as he could muster. But he could feel his heart starting to pound harder.

"Whattya mean, he's not real? He's here with me right now. He's standing right here, right behind you."

Wally's breath caught in his throat.

"Yep, he sure is. Your old pal Jacky Tricky."

"He is not."

"Turn around and see for yourself, chap. He's reaching out for you. He's smiling. He's got very white teeth, you know. So white I can see them in the dark. Turn around. Don'tcha want to see his white teeth? His white, *sharp* teeth?"

Wally wouldn't look. He was eight now, not five. Jacky Tricky wasn't real. He was just something Uncle Axel made up to scare little kids.

But just the same, Wally could picture him standing there behind him, just like Uncle Axel said he was.

"He wants to shake hands witcha," he heard Uncle Axel say. "Can you feel his hand? He's reaching out for you, chap."

No! He's not real!

"He's reaching out for you! His hand's almost on your neck. He's smilin', Walter! He's gettin' closer, and closer—"

No!

". . . and *there!* He's gotcha!"

Something brushed the back of Wally's neck. He cried out, jumping up, stumbling, not looking back. He could hear Uncle Axel guffawing, slapping his leg. Wally ran straight into the house, the screen door whacking behind him. Aunt Selma, apron around her waist and looking as if she hadn't slept in twenty-seven years, clasped her hands together and said, "My heavens!"

Wally looked down at the table, panting for breath. Three plates.

Uncle Axel came in behind him. "Smells good, Sel."

She looked from him over to Wally, then dismissed whatever she might have been going to say. "Wash your hands, Walter," she told him simply.

Wally obeyed, then settled into his seat. Aunt Selma poured him some milk, then moved back to the stove. Uncle Axel sat down without washing his hands. He rested a fist beside his plate. Wally wouldn't look at him.

"Said he couldn't make it," Uncle Axel whispered. "Said maybe he'd stop by and see you tonight."

The old man winked. He moved his fist, leaving a black, oily smudge on the white tablecloth.

"Do you think he heard you?" Mom asks after Uncle Axel's eyes close again.

Wally shrugs. "I hope he did. I hope that's the last thing he hears before he dies."

"Oh, Walter, you've got to respect the dead."

"He's not dead yet."

"But he will be soon."

They're talking normally now, from opposite sides of Uncle Axel's bed. He's still making that gurgling sound.

"I think we should sit here," Mom says, pulling over a pink Naugahyde chair with a puncture wound.

"Mom, I have other things to do. Other people to see."

She looks up at him. "Oh, Walter, please let me just sit here for a while."

"For what? To hold his hand? To tell him the Good Lord watches over him?"

Mom's eyes well up. "He's all I have left, Walter. The only family I have."

Her son laughs. "Right. You keep saying that. So I don't count."

"Walter, I didn't mean . . ." She looks at the old man in the bed. "It's just that he . . . he took us in when we had no one. When Rocky and I were just girls . . ."

Wally's furious. "Not because he wanted to. Not that he ever said one kind word to you in that entire time. You've told me, Mother, told me how he bullied you and your sister—"

"Walter, please, it's not right to speak ill when a man is dying."

"Well, you stay if you want, but I'm not about to sit here and comfort him, not when he's *this close* to burning in hell."

Uncle Axel makes a sound, a kind of burp. Somewhere down there among all the gurgling Wally thinks he recognizes his old voice, caught in his throat. They both watch the old man's face and his chest, to see if this is it. But he goes right on breathing, right on gurgling, eyes closed.

"Aunt Selma," Wally asked, "there's no such thing as Jacky Tricky, right?"

She was tucking him into bed. She stopped and made a face, a tired little smile. She sat down on the bed and looked at the boy with her dark-ringed eyes.

"Uncle Axel been telling you stories again?"

He nodded, suddenly embarrassed.

"Don't pay him any mind, Walter," she said. "Uncle Axel just likes to have fun with you." She paused. "See, he doesn't know how to be with children. I guess that's because I could never give him any."

"He's not real, right? Jacky Tricky?"

"Now hush," Aunt Selma said, seeming too tired to go on. "Just stop thinking about all that."

She stood up and bent over to turn off the lamp. In its soft light, Wally thought she looked beautiful. She might have been old and tired-looking but she was still beautiful. His mother had told him that Aunt Selma, when she was young, had traveled all over the country. Mom said that before Aunt Selma had married Uncle Axel, the family had called her a flapper. Her sister, Wally's grandmother, had gotten married and had children, but Aunt Selma just kept flapping around. Wally didn't know what "flapper" meant, and Mom didn't quite know, either. "That was many years ago," his mother told him. "Ladies can't be flappers anymore."

Aunt Selma switched off the light. "I hope you'll understand about Uncle Axel someday, Walter. He just doesn't know about children." She kissed him, unseen wet lips on his cheek. "Good night."

Her perfume lingered in the dark.

Wally was almost asleep when the door opened again, the light from the hallway slicing the darkness of his room in a white column. In the doorway stood the silhouette of Uncle Axel, his shadow falling across Wally's bed.

"'Night, chap."

"'Night." Wally's voice was tight. He pulled the sheet up to his chin and held it there. His toes curled up under his sheets.

"And Jacky Tricky says good night too. He's in the window, you know, waving to you. Turn around and say 'night, Jacky."

The window was behind the headboard of Wally's bed. The boy didn't budge.

"Aw, poor Jacky," Uncle Axel said. "Don't get him angry now, chap. He's just a little guy. He can fit right there on the window box. But he's got *very* sharp teeth."

Wally watched as the door closed, the column of white light on the floor narrowing then disappearing altogether.

For a long time he lay awake. The sheets were very hot, and he was sweating, but he didn't dare kick them off. Somehow he felt safer with them across his legs. Behind him, he knew the window was open a crack. He could hear the crickets. He lay waiting, listening for any sound.

And then he heard it: a slight scratching at the window. His muscles tensed. He told himself that he was eight years old now, a big boy, and that Jacky Tricky *was not real*. Aunt Selma said he wasn't, and Mom did, too. Uncle Axel was the only one who said he was, and Dad said Uncle Axel was a *bastard*. Wally wasn't any more sure of what a bastard was than he was a flapper, but Dad had said it with such force that *whatever* it meant, Uncle Axel was *it*, and Jacky Tricky just couldn't be real.

But the scratching kept on. Wally imagined long, childish fingers tapping the glass, agile little feet jostling for balance on the window box. He could see those long fingers slipping under the crack, trying to raise the window, a hideous grin on his baby face as he struggled. Wally knew that Jacky Tricky had a wide grin, with lots of saliva running over his long teeth. He saw him just as he was, and no matter what anyone said, Wally knew Jacky Tricky was real, and there in the dark he was even more real than Mom or Dad or Aunt Selma. Wally knew that the little imp was right there at the window behind him, that he wanted to get his claws on his throat and bite him with those long sharp teeth of his.

And then he'd laugh. Wally knew he'd laugh. Sometimes, early in the morning before he got up, when the sun was just starting to rise and the air was orange and pink, Wally could hear Jacky Tricky laughing out in the woods. A high, long laugh that reached a crescendo and then trailed off. It wasn't a bird. It was Jacky Tricky, and Wally was sure of it. It was Jacky Tricky, running wild through the woods.

Uncle Axel had told him that Jacky Tricky was a lost boy, abandoned by his parents when he was only two, left in the middle of the woods to be raised by the bears and the foxes and the rats and the hawks, and then the devil let him live forever. No one knew how long he'd been out there in the woods, but he was there. Uncle Axel knew him. He'd made friends with him. Trouble was, Jacky Tricky just didn't like little kids—except to *eat*.

"He's been known to have 'em for breakfast with a side of extra-crisp bacon," Uncle Axel had said, many times.

Wally figured Jacky didn't like kids because he was *jealous* of them. He hated kids who still had a house to live in, and good food, and a mother and a father. Sometimes, during the day, when Wally played with his Matchbox cars or read his comic books, he felt sorry for Jacky Tricky. Sometimes he thought if he could only talk to him, tell him that he'd be his friend, then he wouldn't hate him anymore. Wally would tell him that his own parents fought a lot, and that sometimes he thought they didn't want him around. Sometimes he thought they'd like nothing better than to lose *him* in the woods. He would tell Jacky Tricky that sometimes he wanted to run away. He'd tell Jack Tricky that he wished he had a brother, somebody to play with, somebody he could talk to about all this stuff. Maybe Jacky Tricky could be his brother, and then he wouldn't be scared of him anymore.

But those were his thoughts during the day.

At night, Wally's thoughts were very different.

He heard the scratching again, and he began to whimper. He didn't want to cry out because Uncle Axel would come in and call him a sissy. He didn't want to cry out because he was eight years old now, a big boy who didn't believe in Jacky Tricky anymore. But he couldn't help it: there was the scratching again. It was him. He *knew* it was him, standing there, smiling with his crazy eyes, saying, "Turn around, Wally. Turn around and see me. Turn around and see that I'm real."

Wally began to cry. He bolted upright, and with a hard thrust he spun around in bed. And there, at the window, was indeed the face of Jacky Tricky—sharp teeth, claws, scratching. Wally screamed, and felt a surge zap through him, like the time he'd stuck a pin into the electrical socket. He screamed again, and again, jumping on the bed, and the whole room went white.

Aunt Selma's arms were suddenly around him, pulling him down, but not before he saw the bushy tail of a squirrel wave good-bye as it jumped back out into the night from the window-box.

"Axel, you've frightened the boy terribly bad," Aunt Selma said, her voice shaky. Wally crushed his face into her soft bosom. She still smelled of that sweet perfume. His nose was in the opening of her robe, and it slipped down to the spot where her breasts parted. There he rested, heaving with sobs.

Uncle Axel stood over them, shirtless, lots of fuzz. He wore a silly polka-dotted nightcap on his head. He chuckled. "'Kay, chap, tell ya what. I'm gonna go get my shotgun."

Wally peered over Aunt Selma's shoulder. He watched as Uncle Axel went into his room, and then came back carrying his big hunting rifle. He held it up to the boy. "See?" He walked out through the kitchen. Wally heard the screen door bang behind him.

He wasn't crying now, just heaving. Aunt Selma gestured toward the window and Wally looked. Uncle Axel was out there, the moonlight bright upon him. He disappeared into the bushes.

In a few minutes they heard a bang, a loud shot, and Aunt Selma whispered in Wally's ear, "There." He suddenly felt very silly that this whole charade had been enacted for him, but the sense of relief was stronger. Aunt Selma tucked him back into bed, and suggested she leave the light on.

"No, Aunt Selma," Wally said. "I'm okay."

She left the door ajar. Wally heard the screen door slam as Uncle Axel came back inside, and then he heard the door to their room shut. He heard them whispering, a hard, intense sound, as if they were arguing. Then he heard their door open again and Uncle Axel stomp into the kitchen. Cabinet doors were opened and closed with bangs. Then it was quiet.

Wally's breathing began to relax. He stared at the soft blue light that slipped into his room from the half-opened door. A black shadow moved into it. Wally raised his eyes. Uncle Axel stood in the doorway.

"You awake, chap?"

"Yes," Wally whispered, not wanting Aunt Selma to hear.

"Got somethin' to tell ya." Uncle Axel's soft words seemed to echo in the dark. "I *missed*."

"Okay, Walter," his mother's saying. "I suppose we can go."

"Finally."

His mother stands, not looking down again at the old man. "They couldn't have children, you know. I think it was always an ache in Aunt Selma's heart."

Wally just grunts, holding the door open for his mother. He lets it clack shut behind him.

Outside in the hall the lights seem to have gotten even brighter. Wally blinks against them, not knowing why they hurt his eyes so much. His mother is looking around for the nurse's station, trying to find the doctor. Wally waits by the old man's door, looking back in through the little glass window.

Not yet, you bastard. Don't die yet. I still have one thing to tell you.

He waits until his mother is out of sight, then slips back into the room.

The odor hits him again. He'd gotten used to it before, but even just the few minutes away has left him unprepared again. It's the stench of death.

He looks down at Uncle Axel. The old man's eyes are open, staring down his nose. He's still gurgling. His head seems to tremble, as if he's trying to lift it, to see who it is that stands there. Wally watches the old man's feeble attempt at life, not wanting to feel sorry for him, to feel any compassion. Still, it's a strange shiver, a pitiful effort to summon energy that no longer exists. He doesn't want to be reminded of Ned in his last days, his final hours. There can be no recognition here, no familiarity: nothing about this monster could ever remind him of Ned. Not even these last flickers of his spirit, these final tremors of life.

"Hello, chap," Wally whispers. His voice sounds strange and unfamiliar.

Uncle Axel's head shakes against his pillow. His grotesque ear-lobes wiggle.

It's happening. Wally can feel it. He's about to die. He's about to walk into hell and right past the gate Jacky Tricky is waiting to greet him, his sharp teeth ready.

And Wally's going to make sure he knows it.

"Do you recognize me?" he asks. "It's *Walter*."

He thinks he sees the old man's shoulders stiffen. His black eyes try to make out the form looming over him.

I hope you'll understand about Uncle Axel someday, Walter.

Wally snorts. Here's what he understands: that the old bastard made an unhappy boy even unhappier. A tight smile stretches across his face. *You think Jacky Tricky was bad, Uncle Axel? Meet Wally Day.*

"Wa—"

The old man is trying to say something. Wally pauses, not sure what it is. He says it again.

"Wa—er . . ."

It sounds like his name.

"Yes, Uncle Axel. It's *Walter.*" He says his name with force, the way his father had said *bastard* all those years ago. "And I have something to tell you . . ."

"Wa—ter . . . ," the old man rasps.

"Yes, it's Walter."

"Wa—ter—"

The old man's lips are chapped, yellow, flaking like mildewed French pastry. His tongue, shriveled and gray, clicks against the back of his throat.

"Wa—ter—"

It's then that Wally realizes what the old man is trying to say. On a table to his side sits a blue plastic water pitcher and some orange paper cups. Wally looks at them, and then back at Uncle Axel.

He's asking for water.

Damn you, old man, I'm not here to give you water. I'm here to tell you that you're going to hell and that right inside the gate, Jacky Tricky will be waiting for you, fangs and claws sharpened and—

"Wa—," he croaks, and his eyes, rolling, catch Wally's for just the briefest of moments.

I hope you'll understand about Uncle Axel someday, Walter.

Wally stands there, unable to move. He opens his mouth to speak, then shuts it. He clenches his fists at his sides, then opens them again. "Damn it," he whispers, turning away abruptly. "*Goddamn* it!"

He heads toward the door.

"Wa—ter—," he hears, very softly, behind him.

Wally stops.

He turns around.

When does the cycle end, Wally?

He gazes down at the dying old man.

When does it finally end?

"Wa—ter—," pleads the old man, his dry, cracked lips barely moving.

Wally stares at him.

"Damn Jacky Tricky," he says finally to himself.

He bends down, cradles Uncle Axel's head in his arm, and gently, ever so gently, holds the cup of water to his lips.

14

RESPONSIBILITIES

"It will just be for a little while," Luz is saying as they sit at the kitchen table, their cups of orange tea between them. "Just for a little while, Mrs. Day, and then I'll be back."

Ever since she'd gotten home from the hospital from seeing Uncle Axel, Regina has had the feeling that something terrible would happen. And now it has. Luz is going to leave her. She's going to *go*. She took the money and now she was going to go.

The girl had found her at the shed, trying to pry off the boards with a hammer.

"Mrs. Day, what are you doing? You wanted me to board it up!"

He's got to be in there. I dragged his body from the living room through the kitchen then out through the back door. His head bumped against each step of the back porch. I remember. I can see his head hitting every step. It's so clear in my mind.

But Luz said there was nothing in the shed.

I'm afraid I might be losing my mind.

It's happened before, why not again?

It wasn't a spa that they sent her to. That's what Aunt Selma called it, but it was no spa. It was an asylum. An insane asylum. A madhouse. A funny farm.

"What is your name?"

"Regina Christina Gunderson."

"And why are you here?"

"My sister says I tried to kill myself."

"And did you?"

Did she? Regina's never been sure. She can't imagine it; she was always so scared of blood. It made her think of the bloody bundle they took away from Mama's room. It takes courage to kill yourself, Regina knew, and she never was that brave.

But Kyle's blood didn't bother me. It was all over the floor and I mopped it up without giving it a thought.

"Mrs. Day," Luz said. "Why are you so frightened of the shed? What do you think is inside?"

"The policeman . . ."

"The policeman? You think he's in the shed?"

Regina could see him standing there in his blue uniform, his bushy mustache twitching.

Any idea where he is? Do you have any idea?

Walter . . . He came looking for Walter.

Are you going to press charges against the pervert? We can have his sorry faggot ass thrown in jail, Captain Day, I promise you that . . .

"Mrs. Day?"

She found Luz's eyes.

No, not Walter.

The policeman came looking for Kyle.

Kyle, who's in the shed.

"Mrs. Day, you're trembling."

"It's cold," she told Luz. "I should fire up the wood furnace. That will help."

"Mrs. Day, come inside with me. We'll make some tea."

She looked into Luz's eyes. So pretty. How she loved the girl, loved her more in that moment than she'd ever loved anyone. Once, a long time ago, there was another girl who looked like Luz. Regina's thought about that girl many times over the years. She was her friend. Her name was Terry. They were going to go to the Dogtown Deli and eat corned beef on rye.

"Kyle," she said, gripping the girl's leather jacket. "Kyle's in the shed."

"Oh." A terribly sad look had passed across Luz's face. She seemed as if she might cry. "No, Mrs. Day. Kyle's not in the shed, Mrs. Day. Trust me, he's not."

"He's there, he must be there—"

"Kyle's gone. And he's not coming back. I won't let him."

"He's in the shed."

"I know Kyle was cruel to you," Luz told her. "I know he made your life hell. But he's *gone*, Mrs. Day. And I won't let him bother you ever again."

Regina looked into the girl's face. So pretty, so dainty—but so *strong*, too. Strong like Rocky. Yes, just like Rocky.

"Do you hear me, Mrs. Day?" Luz's face was in hers, and she gripped the old woman's hands. "*I won't let him come back*. You don't have to worry anymore. Kyle's gone and your nightmare is over. I promise you that, Mrs. Day. I promise."

But now Luz was leaving.

"Is it okay if I leave Jorge here?" she's asking. "I can't send him back to my father. He would be so cruel to Jorge without me there. It would just be for a couple days, maybe three. I need to go to the city, Mrs. Day. I need to get a job."

"Oh, but you don't need a job, Luz. You can live here—"

"I'm going to be a model, Mrs. Day. Just like you said."

Suddenly Luz starts to cry. She can't speak. She shakes her head and waves her hands, unable to stop crying.

Regina reaches across the table and takes the girl's hands. What can she do? What can she say to console her, to stop her tears—awful, terrible tears that are breaking Regina's heart?

"*Hush little baby*," Regina sings, "*don't you cry, Mama's gonna sing you a lullaby . . .*"

Luz looks up at her. A small smile tricks across her lips.

"Oh, good," Regina says. "I've made you smile."

The girl wipes her eyes. "I knew you still had a beautiful voice."

"Oh," Regina says, blushing.

Luz sniffles. "Sing some more for me, Mrs. Day. Please?"

Regina laughs. "Oh, dear. What would I sing?"

"What did you sing on the stage?"

"Old songs. Songs you wouldn't know . . ."

"Sing one of them. Please?"

"Oh, I don't know . . ."

"Please! It would make me happy."

There's nothing Regina wants more, so, sitting there in her kitchen, with the light fading into dusk, Regina sings.

"*Don't sit under the apple tree,*" she begins, unused to the sound of her voice. She pauses and starts again. "*Don't sit under the apple tree with anyone else but me . . .*"

Luz chimes in.

"*With anyone else but me . . .*"

Regina sings the whole song, with Luz joining in on the refrain. When she's done, Luz claps, and Regina laughs, covering her face with her hands.

"So long," she says. "So long since I've sung."

"Thank you for singing to me, Mrs. Day." Luz stands, gives Regina a kiss on the cheek, then heads to her room to pack. By the time the sun has set, she has driven off in Kyle's car.

The wood furnace needs to be fired up. That would take away some of the cold. It always did. There weren't many things Regina loved about this house, but the wood furnace was one of them. It was the only thing that could take the chill off cold winter nights, especially when Robert was home, lying beside her, snoring, a stranger in her bed. Regina never slept well when Robert was home. He was always pulling the blankets to his side. Sometimes, in the night, when she'd awaken, her teeth chattering, she'd be angry, angry enough to scream, to pound her fists against her husband's back, to shriek at him for doing this to her, all of this, all of this horrible life—

But she never did. She just tiptoed out of bed, snuck downstairs into the basement, and added some wood to the furnace. Then she slipped back into bed, gingerly prying part of the blanket from Robert's hands, always careful not to wake him.

"I don't know how you manage," Bernadette had said. "Why not divorce him, Regina? It was only after I kicked Albert out that my life truly became my own again."

Robert had forbidden her from seeing Bernadette after the divorce. But Robert was away on the ship; he'd never know if Regina disobeyed him. She'd consented to the visit so that the boys, Walter and Kyle, would have a chance to play together. It was good for cousins to stay close. The boys were in the living room, eating popcorn and watching that vampire soap opera on television. Regina stood at her ironing board in the kitchen. She had offered Bernadette a cup of tea and her ex-sister-in-law had accepted, taking out a flask from her denim jacket and pouring a shot of whatever it was into the cup. Bernie had turned into quite the hippie, Regina thought: she was always off protesting the war and the military. Her hair was tied up in a bandana, and on the back of her jacket she had sewn a peace sign with red, white, and blue thread.

"Do you think they should be watching such things?" Bernadette asked her.

"You mean that television show?" Regina asked.

"There's a severed head in there," Bernadette said. "I just walked through and saw it. It's been chopped off and put in a box. And that man with the fangs is always running around biting girls on the neck." She shivered.

"Well, Walter loves it," Regina told her.

"But is it *good* for him? I mean, I *worry* about our children, Regina. Their fathers are war nuts. Whenever Albert is with Kyle, all he talks about is guns and killing. That's why I've set some limits on how often they can see each other. I don't want Kyle growing up warped." She made a face as if she thought Regina didn't understand. "Come on, you *know* what it's like, Regina. Robert is the same way."

Regina just sighed, ironing a sleeve of Walter's school shirt.

"I worry about our children, and so should you, Regina. Every night on the news they see all those dead Vietnamese people."

Regina looked up at her, disturbed. "Please, Bernie—"

"All of this has an *impact*. I heard Dr. Spock talking about it on the *Mike Douglas Show* yesterday. I'm really worried, Regina. How will our children grow up?"

Regina had never really thought about all this before. "Wally has a very vivid imagination," she told Bernadette. "He's like my sister. He just likes to . . . *imagine* things."

"Well, when that imagination starts leading him to chop off girls' heads and put them in boxes, then you'll say I was right." Bernadette opens up her purse and withdraws the silver flask again, pouring another shot into her tea. "We're responsible for them. We brought these boys into the world. We have to take care of them."

No, that's wrong, Regina thinks.

I didn't bring Walter into the world.

His father did. It wasn't me.

Oh, but it *had* been her. The pain—the terrible agony of his birth. Walter had torn her apart, ripped right through her—

"Missa Day."

She looks up. Jorge stands in the doorway, rubbing his eyes. He wears

Batman Underoos that are too tight on him. A round little belly protrudes over the waistband.

"Where Luz?"

"You know she went away for a little while, Jorge."

"Luz wants to go."

"Oh," Regina says. "Come here to me, Jorge."

He climbs up onto her lap. She feels his little hands encircle her neck.

"She'll be back in a couple of days. And then we'll make it real nice for her, won't we? She'll never want to leave again."

The boy doesn't say anything. He just rests his head on Regina's shoulder.

"Have you been looking for the treasure, Jorge?"

She feels him nod.

"Did you look where I told you?'

He nods again.

"In the basement? In the crate?"

He nods.

"Out in the yard? Under the trees?"

He keeps on nodding. Regina sets him down on his feet and stares directly into his eyes.

"Well, we've got to keep looking, Jorge. Will you help me?"

"I hep you," he tells her.

Regina holds the little boy's gaze. Once there was another little boy in this house. Strange how she can't remember him very well. If not for the photograph on the wall, she might not be able to picture little Walter at all. He slept in the same room where Jorge now sleeps, sat in the same chair, ate his Lucky Charms out of the same bowl.

"I want to be an actor," Jorge tells her, looking up at her with his big brown eyes.

"An actor?" Regina responds. "What a lovely idea. What a good actor you'd be."

The boy stares up at her with uncomprehending eyes.

"You could become famous, like Rocky and I were in the city. Oh, yes, you will be such a wonderful actor. What can I do to help?"

We're responsible for them. We brought these boys into the world. We have to take care of them.

How long has it been? Just a day since Luz left? Or weeks? Months? Regina can only remember one night in between the time Luz drove off in Kyle's car and now—one long, horrible, terrible night, when she'd sat up and wailed in bed like a child, cried like she hadn't in years, howled so loudly that she was sure Grace Daley next door must have heard her. But there may have been many other nights since Luz left than just that one. She forgets so much these days.

So awful much.

But not so much that she doesn't know it's nearing lunch time. Jorge will need to eat. She had to make sure he had lunch. *I'm responsible for him now.*

She scuffs across the floor in her slippers to peer inside the cupboard. Suddenly she has a splendid idea: she'll make Jorge her goulash! She used to make it for Walter, and oh, how he had loved it! It was his favorite meal. She'd fry up some hamburger in a skillet and then mix it in with Franco-American spaghetti. *Swedish goulash*, she called it. Walter would cover it all with a thick frosting of ketchup. "Make it again tonight," he'd badger her, and so she would. It was so easy. Hardly any clean up at all.

The doorbell rings just as she begins to open the can.

"Luz!" Regina shouts, rushing, despite her arthritis, to the door.

But it's a man.

It's—

Robert.

In his navy uniform, all pressed and shiny.

"Mrs. Day?"

"Who—?"

"I'm Lieutenant Bryce Bennett," the man tells her. "I've come to ask you a few questions about your nephew, Kyle."

"Oh." Regina's heart is thudding in her chest. It's not Robert. How silly of her. It's a young man. A nice-looking young man with a kind, friendly face.

"May I come in?" he asks her.

A few maple leaves blow through the open door.

"Yes," Regina says, "of course."

She steps aside to let the man in.

"Is Kyle here?" he asks, walking into the living room without waiting for her.

"No," she tells him. "He's not here."

"Have you heard from him?"

Regina begins to twirl the top button on her sweater. "No. I haven't."

Lieutenant Bryce Bennett is looking around the room. "His car's not in the garage. I checked on my way in. I thought you told the Brown's Mill police that he'd left his car behind when he left."

"Yes, yes, he did, but Luz took—"

"Luz Vargas?"

"Yes, she took—"

"His girlfriend. Have they gone off together?"

"Oh, no! Luz wouldn't—"

"Mrs. Day, the navy doesn't believe your story."

Regina makes a little startled sound. She stares at the man. No, he's not nice. Not nice at all. He's mean. Cruel. She begins to tremble.

The man comes close to her. She can smell his breath. Listerine. "What are you keeping from us, Mrs. Day?"

"Oh, nothing—I—"

"Mind if I look around?"

She doesn't reply, just stands there trembling. She watches as Lieutenant Bryce

Bennett turns away from her and begins walking around the living room. He looks at her end tables. He looks at the bookcase, running his finger across the spines of her *Reader's Digest* condensed books. He looks down at her puzzle of the Taj Mahal. He looks at the couch where she smashed Kyle's head in with the shovel.

Or the hoe.

One of them.

"May I see his room?"

"Luz and Jorge are using it now," she says, but the lieutenant is already down the hall. She follows.

"Jorge is the girlfriend's brother," the man is saying, lifting Jorge's teddy bear and turning it upside down, looking between its furry little legs. "Retarded, yes?"

"He's outside playing—"

He drops the teddy bear on the bed and moves across the room to slide open the closet. He runs his hand across Luz's blouses that are hanging there. Several empty wire hangers clang together.

"Are all her things here?" he asks. "See anything that's missing?"

Regina looks. "Her blue blouse is gone. And her striped top. And—and I think her sweatshirt . . ."

"So she's gone, too? Where did she go?"

"I don't know. She's looking for a job. She wants to be a model. She's so pretty I'm sure that—"

"She just left the kid with you? No way to get in touch with her?"

"It's just for a couple days . . ."

The lieutenant has moved over to the bureau where he pulls open the top drawer. What does he hope to find? All of Kyle's things are gone. Regina had thrown them all out when Luz moved in. All of his ratty, holey underwear and soiled socks—and his uniform. His spiteful blue uniform with its gold buttons. She got rid of it all. She wanted Luz to have plenty of room. Now Luz's lacy, pretty panties and bras take the place of Kyle's dirty, ugly things.

Except—

"Seems she took quite a bit, wherever she went," the lieutenant says, his hand rummaging through the drawers. "Not much here."

"She doesn't *have* a lot."

He pulls out a black bra, studying it, letting it dangle from his fingers. Then he drops it back into the drawer.

"And Kyle's clothes? Where are *they*?"

"I threw them out."

He lifts an eyebrow at her. "That certain he wasn't coming back, huh?"

Regina says nothing.

The lieutenant continues looking around, lifting the bedspread to peer under the bed. Then he heads back into the hallway, opening the door to the linen closet and looking inside. He ducks into the bathroom to check behind the shower curtain. Regina keeps following him, twirling the top button on her sweater.

"I'm not sure what you're looking for—"

"May I see the basement?" he asks abruptly.

Regina begins to shake all over.

Where is he? Where did I put him?

The crate in the basement?

The shed?

Did I bury him in the yard?

Regina says nothing as Lieutenant Bryce Bennett pushes past her down the hallway and into the kitchen. He yanks open the cellar door and clomps down the wooden steps. Regina follows only as far as the top of the stairs, where she stands listening to him moving things around in the basement. She hears a stack of cardboard boxes topple over.

"He lookin' for tresha?"

She turns. Jorge has come inside and stands behind her.

"Shh, Jorge," Regina says, her finger to her lips.

The lieutenant is heading back up the wooden stairs. "Mrs. Day," he asks, shutting the door behind him, "did Kyle ever mention the name William Penny to you?"

She thinks. "No. No, he didn't."

"Never? Not once?"

"No, I don't believe he—"

"*Think*, Mrs. Day! William Penny!"

"No," she says in a tiny voice.

"Kyle never told you how he bludgeoned Ensign Penny with a baseball bat and left him for dead, his brains oozing out onto the pier?"

"Oh, dear. Oh, no, never."

He's close up in her face again. "Because that's what he did, Mrs. Day. Right before his last leave, he beat an ensign to nearly an inch of his life. His name was William Penny, Mrs. Day, an African-American kid, a new recruit, age just nineteen." His eyes burn holes into her face. "You *sure* Kyle never mentioned him to you?"

"No," Regina says. "He never mentioned him to me."

Why now does she hear the applause? The hoots and whistles of the soldiers, cheering her on, begging for another song?

What if she had become famous? What if she'd never come back, stayed in the city, become even more famous than Dinah Shore?

They'd be alive, she thinks. Kyle. And Robert. And Rocky.

And William Penny, too.

And me, Regina thinks. *There would be no Walter, but I'd be alive. I'd be so alive.*

Lieutenant Bryce Bennett is sneering. "He thought no one would ever know. He thought he'd messed the kid's brains up so bad he'd never be able to tell who did it. But he was *wrong*."

"Oh," Regina says, her hands over her mouth. Jorge grips her around the waist, holding her tightly.

"Is okay, Missa Day," the boy tells her.

The lieutenant leans in even closer. He lowers his voice. "If you're covering for him, you and this girlfriend of his, you would be interfering with a criminal investigation. You realize that, Mrs. Day, don't you?"

She nods.

"So you want to tell me where he is?"

"I—I don't know—"

The yard? The crate in the basement? The shed? The attic?

"I don't know where he is!" she sobs.

"We're going to find him," the lieutenant says. "And his girlfriend, too."

"Yes," Regina says, desperate suddenly. She grabs the lieutenant's hands. "Yes, you must! Find Luz. *Please* find Luz!"

15

THE WORLD ACCORDING TO ZANDY

"Someday," Zandy promises, "we won't have to hide. We won't have to pretend."

Every Sunday afternoon Wally hops on his bike and pedals all the way down Washington Avenue to Main Street, then hangs a left and crisscrosses through traffic to head out along River Road to Dogtown. There he spends the day with Zandy and his friends, who have their one day off from fixing cars and painting fences. Miss Aletha sings show tunes at the piano and Bertrand practices his magic act, trying (mostly without success) to pull parakeets out of a hat. They listen to records—mostly Bob Dylan, the Stones, Mama Cass—and watch old movies on television. They smoke a considerable amount of grass.

"Someday," Zandy tells him, leaning back in his beanbag chair and inhaling a long drag on his pipe, "I'll take you to a gay pride parade in the city."

Wally beams. "I've seen the pictures of them in the newspaper."

"Babe, it's fabulous." He lets the smoke out in rings above his head. "Lots of balloons and banners and great music to dance to. We'll go and we'll watch all the hundreds and hundreds of homosexuals walking right through the heart of the city. You'd never believe there were so many."

"I used to think I was the only one."

"Babe, that's one line that gets repeated every generation. But hopefully for not much longer. Things are changing, babe. You'll see."

Wally's practically jumping out of his seat. "What will we do in the city?"

Zandy laughs. "Oh, we'll stay out all night. We'll party until the sun comes up."

John Travolta and his friends in Brooklyn had nothing on the dreams Zandy promised him. "When can we go?" Wally badgered. "*When?*"

"Oh, you've got to be a little older, babe. Just a little bit."

Zandy passes him the pipe and Wally takes a long drag. He feels the buzz immediately, like a jolt of electricity.

"Alexander Reefy," Miss Aletha says, coming into the room, "you take him across state lines and you're going to jail."

"Same for you, Missy," Bertrand reminds her, "for supplying us with some exquisite weed."

Zandy's stretched out in his beanbag, ignoring both of them. He's got eyes only for Wally. "It's going to be so different for you, babe, when you get to be our age. It's getting better all the time. Out there in San Francisco it's like Sodom by the Sea. They even got a real live fairy elected to the city government. Harvey Milk is his name."

"Milk?"

"Yeah. Milk. Funny name for a fairy, huh? But he's showing all us queers that we got to stand up for who we are." Zandy takes the pipe back from Wally and inhales, leaning his head back so his long dark hair brushes against his naked, freckled shoulders. "You've got it made, Wally, babe, you and all the little ones to follow."

And he reaches over then and kisses him, his smoky breath on Wally's mouth. Wally smiles, taking Zandy's hands and placing them on his lips, kissing them and licking them, sucking each one of those knotty, twisted, *beautiful* fingers into his mouth.

Sleeping in Zandy's arms, there is nothing else. No menacing father. No impossible expectations. No taunts. No bullies. No doubts, no fears, no separation from the living. Once Wally had been alone, so completely and powerfully alone. But sleeping with one ear pressed against Zandy's furry chest, listening to his heart, there is nothing else. For the first time since he was little, in those long-ago, nearly forgotten days before his mother's abandonment, Wally is happy. Content. Safe.

The only reason they'd ever met in the first place was because Wally had *balls*. That's what Zandy says. Otherwise they'd still be strangers, Wally out in his quiet little subdivision off Washington Avenue, Zandy in his little shack in the swamps of Dogtown.

But Wally, hunched down and ready to spring, with the blinds of his windows pulled down tight, had begun making phone calls to Alexander Reefy.

"How would you like to suck my cock?"

"I might be interested."

That's what Zandy had said: *I might be interested.* Wally hadn't known what to say in response, so he just slammed the phone down. *I might be interested.* No one had ever said *that* to him before.

Even though Freddie Piatrowski had told him that Alexander Reefy was a homosexual, to hear it confirmed—to hear a man acknowledge that *he might be interested* in sucking his cock—was almost too much for Wally's senses.

That night, he couldn't sleep. He beat off three times remembering those four simple words: *I might be interested.*

"Do you remember that guy that Freddie told us about?" Wally asked David Schnur the next day at school.

"What guy?"

"You remember. The guy. The . . ." Wally paused. "The homo."

"Oh, the one that lives in Dogtown."

"Yeah. You remember his name?"

David made a face. "Why should I remember his name?"

"Alexander Reefy. Like reefer. Remember?"

"Who cares what his name is?"

Wally leaned in close to his friend. "How do you think Freddie *knew* he was a homo? How come he's so *sure*?"

"I don't know, Wally," David said, turning on him with supreme discomfort shining in his eyes. "Why are you asking *me*? Why don't you ask *him*?"

Wally looked straight into David's long, pinched face. He had to tell someone. He had to speak the words.

"He said he might be interested in sucking my cock."

"*Freddie?*"

"No! Alexander Reefy! The homo!"

David seemed appalled. "When did he say that?"

"We were goofing on him. We crank-called him."

"Who? You and who?"

Wally was already sorry he'd said anything. "Me and some guys. You don't know them."

"And he really said he wanted to suck your cock?"

Wally looked off, vaguely in the direction of the orchards. Somewhere behind those trees was Dogtown, and somewhere in Dogtown was Alexander Reefy.

"He said he might be interested," Wally said, lost in a dream. "He might be interested in sucking my cock."

"Wally, come over here."

He's getting ready to go home, walking his bicycle out of the backyard when Miss Aletha calls to him.

"I want to talk with you a moment," she says.

"What is it?"

Her hair is pulled back in a simple ponytail. Her low-hanging breasts, braless, make odd indentations in her Grateful Dead T-shirt.

"I want you to be careful," she says.

"I always am. I avoid Main Street, which has all the traffic."

Miss Aletha smiles. "Yes, of course, be careful riding your bike. But I want you to be careful in other ways, too."

"What ways?"

"How old are you, Wally?"

"You know how old I am. You gave me a birthday party two weeks ago."

"You've just turned fourteen."

Why is she telling him this? Like he doesn't know how old he is? Is she that high?

"You're fourteen and Zandy is thirty. More than double your age."

"I know."

She sighs. "He's lived a lot more in his life than you have, baby. We all have."

"I know that, too. That's why I like hanging out with you guys."

"Just be careful, baby. I worry that—"

"What's this little powwow?"

They look up. Zandy has come sauntering around from the backyard, still shirt-less, with that thick mat of black hair on his chest that excites Wally so much.

"Missy is just telling me to be careful."

Zandy exchanges a look with Miss Aletha, then turns back to Wally. "You better be getting home, babe," he tells him, "or else your parents are gonna start asking questions."

Wally smirks. "I'm out playing ball with Freddie Piatrowski."

"That's right." Zandy walks up to him and tousles his hair. "Such a little star athlete."

Wally feels the shudder zap through his body, the same shudder he feels every time Zandy touches him. His cock gets hard in his cutoff denim shorts again.

"Be careful riding back home," Zandy whispers in his ear.

Wally looks up. Miss Aletha has gone back into the house.

It was Wally who made the first move. Coiled up like a Slinky ready to shoot across the room, he had called Zandy again.

"Can I come over?" he breathed.

How he found the nerve, the appalling guts, to ask such a thing, he's never been able to fathom. Zandy explains it simply by saying he has *balls*—and that day they were filled up to the bursting point with boycum. It was a lazy Sunday in the early spring, when the buds on the trees were all starting to pop and the daffodils were opening in his mother's rock garden. Wally's father was snoring in his chair in front of the TV in the living room. He was home all the time now, working at Schaefer's Shoes, and on the weekends all he did was sleep. In the kitchen, Wally's mother was packing lunches for her husband and son to take with them the next day. Bologna and cheese sandwiches on Wonder bread, with a thick smear of mayonnaise.

Wally had pulled the phone down the hall into his bedroom, and cupped his hand around his mouth as he whispered into the phone.

"Please. Can I come over?"

"How old are you?" Alexander Reefy asked.

"Sixteen," Wally lied.

It was an age pulled from the air. Something told him it held some magic. He didn't know it was the age of consent in the state. But Zandy did, and he agreed. "All right," he said. "Come on over."

Wally can't remember much of that first bike ride over to Zandy's house. He assumes he came straight down Washington Avenue, dodging the traffic, then turned left on Main, scooted around the Lutheran church and South End News and then past the factories along River Road. He does remember that Zandy's front porch light was on. He parked his bike and marched up to the little red house and rapped on the door.

"Who are you?"

"I'm Wally. I called you."

Zandy eyed him from the crack in the door. "Yeah, like every day for two weeks. What do you want by coming over here?"

"I want to have sex with you."

Zandy seemed stunned by his precociousness. "No way you're sixteen," he said, checking him out.

"I can't wait that long."

The man behind the door laughed out loud. "You little ballbuster."

"Please."

"Please what?"

"Can I come in? Your light is on."

Zandy glanced up at his front porch light. "So it is. But what's that got to do with all the tea in China?"

"*Please.*"

Zandy sighed and held open the door.

They almost didn't have sex that day. Wally may have gotten inside but now he was at a loss. What did he do next? What did he say? Did he just take off his clothes right there in the foyer? Did he grab Alexander Reefy's bulge, so enticing in his faded Levis, covered in paint splatters and American flag patches and flower appliqués? What did homos *do* to start having sex?

For his part, Zandy seemed aloof and indifferent, sauntering over to the frayed overstuffed chair, sitting down next to his Lava lamp, sipping some tea and lighting up a cigarette. Wally sat opposite him on the musty-smelling couch.

"There's a whole world out there, kid, and when you're old enough you'll find it," Zandy told him. "We all do eventually. You've just got to be patient."

"I *can't* be patient. It's like I'm ready to explode. I think about it all the time."

"*Sex*, you mean. You think about sex."

"Yeah." Wally's throat was tight, his breathing hard.

"There's more to being gay than just having sex, babe. You'll find that out. It's about culture and music, dancing and friendship, all sorts of things. Not just sex."

Wally nodded. It was a perspective he would come to appreciate in the weeks and months to come, but sitting there that first day it meant nothing to him, just a phrase—a string of words to get past if he wanted to have sex.

Zandy thanked him for coming. He promised him that things would get better for him, that all he had to do was wait, and then he walked him to the door.

Now or never, Wally thought.

He grabbed the older man's crotch.

"You little hooligan," Alexander Reefy said, his voice deeper than before.

There was a moment of suspended time, of paralysis. Their eyes held.

Wally grabbed his crotch again. The cock inside was harder this time, fuller.

Zandy reached down and kissed the boy full on the lips.

* * *

That first day all Zandy had to do was touch Wally's dick. With those hands, those knotty hands. Hands that fixed cars, changed oil, rebuilt engines. Hand jobs—no sucking, no fucking. But it was enough. Wally came in ten seconds, flat. Then he was out of there, pedaling back home on his bike as fast as his frightened little feet would take him.

But the following Sunday he was back, and that's when Zandy gave him his very first blow job. He sat Wally down on the edge of his bed, kneeling in front of him and unzipping his fly. There was no expectation of reciprocation.

This time, Wally didn't run, but hung around for a while. Zandy gave him some apple juice and they sat in his living room, papered with posters of Karl Marx and Janis Joplin and Barbra Streisand. With Zandy sitting next to him on the couch, his arm draped around his shoulders, Wally started to cry. Fear? Shame? Gratitude? He had no idea. Zandy sat there holding him. "Yeah," he said softly, stroking Wally's hair. "I know."

Wally couldn't remember ever being touched like that. The hand in his hair, the soft caress of his face, felt nothing like what he was used to. His mother had never touched him like that, even when he was little and things were good between them. And the only time his father ever touched him was to smack him against the back of the head. The same place Zandy caressed while Wally cried.

That was the real epiphany. Zandy's hand, full of softness and gentleness and love. Wally closed his eyes, allowing the sensations that spread through him to fill him up, to send waves of energy through his body that were more shattering than anything he had ever known before. Zandy's hand—stroking his hair, running down his back, tickling his arms. *This* was the revelation, far more even than the orgasm he had just experienced.

The next time, Wally met Zandy's friends. A tall man-woman everyone called Miss Aletha, who wore a blond wig and purple mascara. Bertrand, her (his?) boyfriend, a thin, shy man with tattoos on his arms, who was learning to be a magician. They all worked together as handymen, mechanics, odd-jobbers—a slow-paced existence, a leisurely stroll through life. There were others, too, who'd wander variously through Zandy's house, strange-looking types with mustaches and flannel shirts and very tight jeans, using female pronouns to refer to each other and popping Donna Summer and the Bee Gees into the eight-track. Wally has come to love the music that fills Zandy's house. Even more, he loves that he can tell these guys that he jacked off to John Travolta in *Saturday Night Fever*. They all had, too. And unlike David Schnur, they *admitted* it.

Nowadays, Wally and Zandy often make love in the orchards, one a smooth pink boy, the other a dark furry man. The whole experience has been shattering for Wally. That's the only way he can describe it: *shattering*. Everything he used to think about—even the *way* he used to think about things—has been shattered into a million pieces. It was as if he'd been living with a hard clay shell around him, and he'd finally burst through it, breaking free.

"Do you want to feel me inside you?" Zandy whispers in his ear.

"Yes," Wally pants.

It hurts bad. Wally wants him to stop but doesn't dare ask him to—because he knows he wants this. He wants to feel every bit of it.

"Oh," his mother says, lifting his dirty underwear out of the hamper. "Oh," she says, and Wally knows immediately what she's found.

She looks over at Wally with terrified eyes.

"Are you . . . is everything . . . all right, Walter?"

Why had he put his bloody Fruit of the Looms in the hamper? Why not toss them in the Dumpster behind the Dairy Queen? Why had he put them in the hamper for his mother to find?

"I'm fine," he says defiantly.

She says nothing more, just gathers up the clothes into a basket and lugs it downstairs to the washing machine.

"You need your mother's help," Miss Aletha tells him. "She could be an ally."

Wally laughs. "No. She can't help me. I've given up on her."

"Well, you can't let your father decide your life. He'll have you marching off to World War III. When you graduate you should go to a college of your choice."

"I want to go to acting school. I want to be an actor."

"A regular Montgomery Clift," Zandy says, smirking, settling down into his beanbag and lighting a joint.

Bertrand is at the dining room table practicing his magic act. A green parakeet is perched on his finger and Bertrand is trying to entice him to dive into a top hat filled with birdseed. "I'm hoping to land a job," Bertrand says, "with Ringling Brothers."

"That might be the best thing for you, too, babe," Zandy says, winking over at Wally. "Run off and join the circus."

"I will," Wally tells him, "if you come with me."

He catches the gleam in Zandy's eye. No, Zandy's not handsome. His face is craggy, scarred with pocks. His beard isn't trimmed very well and his eyebrows are starting to grow a little wild. But when he smiles, his eyes light with such fire, and they dazzle Wally. When they share that look between them, Wally doesn't feel fourteen years old. He feels grown-up, ageless, a wise old man. His cock stirs in his jeans.

Later, they make love, in the orchards again, kissing each other so hard that their teeth clink against each other. Zandy runs his tongue down over Wally's chin to the hollow of his throat and all the way down his goose-pimply, concave chest to his belly button. Wally's cock is aiming at the moon. Zandy swallows it with one noisy gulp. The boy shoots hard, sending tremors all through his body. Zandy swallows every drop.

Zandy's cock isn't always as hard as Wally's. In fact, it's often soft, a fat brown stub. When he wants to fuck Wally he has to tug at it for a long time in his hand, greased up with Vaseline. Then he sticks it in Wally fast, as if he's afraid it will go soft again. Wally knows if he put his mouth on Zandy's cock it might stay harder longer, but it's the one thing he hasn't been able to bring himself to do, and he wonders why.

"Are you in love with him?" Missy asked one night, after Zandy had fallen asleep, snoring like a bear in his chair.

"Yes," Wally answered.

She smiled indulgently. "Do you know what that even means?"

Wally bristled. "Of course I do. Aren't you in love with Bertrand?"

"We've been together sixteen years. Do you think you and Zandy will be together that long?"

"Why not?"

She sighed, running her hand through his hair. "You're right. Why not indeed?"

Am I in love with him?

Do I even know what that means?

Of course he does.

"Someday," Zandy's telling him, holding his hand as they walk through the orchard, the june bugs chirping all around them on this late summer night, "someday the world is going to be very different."

"You keep saying that."

"Because it's true. Someday, babe, we'll be able to hold hands anywhere, not just here, hidden in the woods."

That doesn't seem to matter to Wally. Before he met Zandy he'd felt so alone. Now he can't imagine things any better than this. He *likes* being in the orchards with Zandy. If they *never* leave these sweet-smelling trees he wouldn't mind. Not one bit.

Except, he thinks, the city *does* sound exciting. And in the city he can be an actor. Like Montgomery Clift. Zandy told him Clift was gay, just like they are. *Gay*—Wally repeats the word in his head—*just like they are.*

"We're going to be a free people someday, Wally," Zandy is saying. "They got a dyke elected up in Boston. And we kicked Anita Bryant's ass down in Florida. It's our time, babe. You just watch.

It's gonna be *grand*."

Wally smiles. "When can you take me to the city?"

"One of these days. I promise."

"And we can stay out all night and dance until dawn?"

Zandy kisses the top of Wally's head. "Yeah. We can do that."

"It's gonna be *grand*," Wally echoes, and he rests his head against Zandy's shoulder as they walk through the trees.

16

REGINA, FROM FOUR TO SIX

It's 4:00 on Friday afternoon, and Regina Christina Gunderson realizes she's alone.

She's typing a letter for Mayor Winslow to the federal government regarding Social Security. The mayor doesn't understand what it's all about. Neither does Regina.

She listens to the girls in the office talking. "Whatcha making for supper tonight, Betty?"

"Leftover corned beef," Betty answers. "What about you?"

"Oh, I don't know," Ruth says. "Maybe chicken. I just don't know. Elmer's always so picky."

It's 4:01 and Regina, slowly nodding her head over her typewriter, realizes she's alone.

"Regina," comes the voice of Mayor Winslow from his inner office. "Any letters that need to be signed before I leave?"

"Yes, sir," she says, getting up from her desk, pushing back her chair on its little wheels. She shakes the letter free from its carbon, watching transfixed as it's caught by a draft and hangs suspended in the air for a moment before fluttering aimlessly to the floor.

"There's just this one, sir," Regina says.

She walks into his office and hands him the letter over his enormous mahogany desk. His eyes drop down the page and he scrawls his signature. Regina notices his pink scalp through his thin white hair as he leans over to sign his name. Mayor Winslow is a very pink man.

It's been three weeks since he'd hired her. Regina had stood meekly in front of his desk, hoping for a job, holding a note from her high school typing teacher, who was a second cousin of his. All around them that day had been dozens of girls, all of them knocking on office doors at City Hall. So many birds, Mayor Winslow had observed with a grin—with no guarantee that the doves would be picked out from the pigeons.

"My cousin says here that you just got out of the hospital," he said, looking up at her from the note.

"It was a spa. A health spa."

The mayor glances back down at the note. "The Valley Institute." He returns his gaze to Regina. "And how long were you there for?"

Regina felt her face burn. "About a year."

"Did you go there after your sister died, Regina?"

Everyone in Brown's Mill knew about Rocky and how she died. The accident had happened up on Eagle Hill and there had been a large photograph on the *Reminder*'s front page. Lots of mangled metal and broken glass. Rocky's car had plunged down an embankment, bursting into flames.

"No, sir," Regina says. "She died while I was there."

"I see. But you're better now?"

"Oh, yes, much better. The spa did wonders for me."

Mayor Winslow set down the note and looked up at her. "And so pretty too," he said, smiling, his face glowing very pink.

He gave her the job.

Now he's holding the letter he's just signed between two pudgy fingers, one with a shiny gold wedding band contrasting against the pink. For a moment Regina is still, intent on counting the little white hairs that grow from his knuckles. And then she smiles, blushing, taking the letter and wishing the mayor a good night.

"You have a good night too, Regina. And a lovely weekend." He plays with his wedding band as he speaks. "Do you need a ride home, Regina? I'm happy to drive you."

"Oh, thank you, but I'm meeting a girlfriend. We're having dinner."

He smiles. "Some other time then."

Regina just smiles. "Yes. Some other time."

Aunt Selma had found her a place to live in Dogtown. Mormor would have been appalled had she still been alive—Dogtown was filled with Eye-talians and blacks—but it was the cheapest place Aunt Selma could find. "We can't keep supporting you forever," Aunt Selma said. "You're going to have to get a job."

Regina sits back down at her desk.

"Frank wants me to do a pot roast," Ruth is saying. "As if I want to work all day and then come home to make a pot roast!"

"Tell him if he wants pot roast, *he* should make it," Betty says.

"It would taste like shoe leather."

"So he'd learn."

The girls laugh.

Regina stares at her typewriter. She's been meaning to clean the keys all week. All her *o*'s and *p*'s keep getting filled in with ink. It's an old Royal typewriter, heavy and black, not unlike the one she'd learned on back in high school. Her typing teacher, Mayor Winslow's cousin, was an old woman with orange hair named Miss Hemm. She was the first person Regina went to see when she got out of the spa, because she remembered Miss Hemm fondly and there was no one else to go see now that Rocky was dead. Regina had lovely memories of Miss Hemm, sitting in her typing classroom in the late afternoons, when the sun slanted its rays through the tall windows and spilled out across the old hardwood floors in sharp, diagonal lines. Miss Hemm would allow Regina to come into the school and practice on the typewriter.

"Want to do mine when you're done?"

Regina looks up. Betty's standing over her, watching Regina pick at the caked ink in her typewriter keys with a straight pin.

"Sure," Regina says. "I'd be happy—"

"I'm only kidding, sweetie," Betty says, covering her typewriter. "I'm heading out of here early. Got to stop at the market and get something to go with the corned beef."

Ruth is putting on her coat. "Any plans for the weekend?"

Betty nods. "Heading into the city to see Elmer's sister and her kids."

"Oh, that'll be nice."

Regina's listening with one ear, still picking at her keys, feeling a sense of revenge as she pops out the offending soot. Soon her o's will be clean, her p's sharp.

"I remember during the war," Betty's saying, pulling on her coat, "we were stuck here in Brown's Mill all the time. No chance for holiday weekends. Funny how quiet things are now that the boys are home. Thought it'd be just the opposite."

Regina dabs the cleaning fluid over her keys and watches it soak into the black grime.

"Well, I'm off," Betty says. She walks around to the front of Regina's desk. "Your letters all finished?"

Regina nods.

"Stick around until he's through, okay? Don't leave until he's gone."

"Okay," Regina agrees. "Have a nice weekend."

Betty starts to say, "You too," but Ruth runs up to her with one last item of business.

It's 4:30 and Regina tries not to think about being alone.

Last Saturday she took a walk past the house where she'd lived as a little girl. Someone had painted it green and put a fence around it. But Mama's cherry tree was still out in front, bigger now than Regina remembered it. From the sidewalk she could still see the initials she'd carved there when she was eight, the year Mama died. She'd used a nail file to carve her initials in a heart with those of Dennis Appleby, a boy one grade ahead of her. Dennis parted his hair down the middle, and Regina thought he was very sophisticated. She never told Dennis that she liked him, didn't so much as even give him a clue, not even when they were in high school and they sat next to each other in the cafeteria and Dennis sometimes carried her books for her.

And then she heard he'd been killed over the North Atlantic early in the war.

Better that than to live without arms like—what was his name? The soldier who took her out in the city. Who sat there applauding her when she sang—what song was it? There are so many things Regina can no longer remember. But she remembers Dennis Appleby and her mother's cherry tree.

"They really aren't cherries," Regina reminded herself, standing in front of the house that used to be hers and now was painted green.

"No, Gina, you can't eat them," her mother told her, long ago, when she was five, maybe six. "They're not cherries. I just *call* it my cherry tree. They're crab apples. And you can't eat them."

Regina remembered her mother's fingers, softly probing inside her mouth, gently removing the bits of bitter crab apple. She'd put four into her mouth, picking them up from the grass where they lay scattered prettily under the tree. Regina had made a face, maybe a sound, and her mother, kneeling in the dirt planting geraniums, had come running.

They went into the house and Mama had poured her some milk.

"Here, Gina, drink. That'll get rid of the taste."

"Mama," she said after she'd drained the glass, white foam on her upper lip, "they really aren't cherries?"

"No, honey," her mother said, with a sudden sadness, putting her arms around her. "They really aren't cherries."

A pink hand is suddenly splayed on her desk. Regina looks up to see the mayor smiling at her. She makes a little gasp.

"Regina, the very best of weekends to you."

She shifts uncomfortably.

"And to you, sir."

"Are you sure I can't offer you a ride?"

"Yes, thank you. I'm meeting a girlfriend."

"All right, then."

He strides out into the hall. Regina can hear his footsteps echoing down the long, deep corridor for a full minute. Then he reaches the stairwell and is gone.

"We can close up shop now," Ruth says.

Regina covers her typewriter.

"It looks like rain," Ruth's saying, looking out the window. "Did you bring an umbrella?"

"No. It was sunny this morning."

"Yes, I know. What strange weather we've been having."

Ruth slips into the mayor's office and comes back carrying a large black umbrella. "Here," she says, thrusting it at Regina. "Use his."

"Oh, no. I couldn't."

"Why not?"

"What if I lost it?"

"Regina, you're very responsible."

"No. I couldn't take that chance."

Ruth's eyebrows fuzz together. "All right. But don't blame me if the heavens open and you end up looking like a sick alley cat."

Outside, a heavy gray rain shadow looms over Main Street. Regina says good-bye to Ruth and sits on a bench waiting for the bus, breathing in the cool, damp air. Passersby walk quickly, glancing up at the gathering clouds.

Regina studies her hands. She's bitten the nail of her right index finger down to the quick. It helped in typing, but it hurts her now.

The bus pulls up and throws open its doors to her. Regina steps inside, depositing her coins and sitting up front. Her feet hurt. She'll soak them tonight. That'll be nice.

At least she'll make it back in time for dinner. Often she missed the meal Mrs. Unwin, her landlady, served, and she'd have to eat it cold in the kitchen. "I serve a hot meal in the dining room promptly at 5:30," Mrs. Unwin had told her on the day she moved in. "I can't keep cooking all night. If you're going to be late, you might want to eat out. Or else have the meal cold in the kitchen."

Regina can't wait to get to her room. It's small, but she's glad it's small. It's nicer that way. It reminded her of her room at the spa, which she had come to love. She'd covered the walls with photos clipped out of magazines: sailboats and flowers, kittens and angels, movie stars and goldfish. All the other people at the spa knew she collected pretty pictures, and sometimes they'd give her ones they found. Even Howard Greer gave her a picture once: Grace Kelly in a white dress and pearls. Regina pasted that one directly over her bed.

Of course, at Mrs. Unwin's house, she couldn't paste anything on the walls, but she liked her room just the same. She had a firm mattress on her twin bed, a chair, a table, and a two-drawer bureau. It was in the rear of the house, where she had a view of the backyards of the houses on the other side of the block.

At night sometimes she'd sit and watch from her window as an old black man played his flute on the porch of a second-floor apartment. His music was always so soothing to Regina. He played for hours at a time, rarely stopping for breath, his eyes always closed. The sound of the flute lilted gently across the quiet neighborhood. It seemed to touch everything, to give life even to inanimate objects, like a clothesline pole or a rusted old wheelbarrow. Against the night sky the trees danced, waving their arms against the face of the moon. The curtains at her window swayed gently in time with the old man's music. Regina sat there transfixed, blissful, at peace. And then the old man would stop, tired, letting out a long breath and running his hand over the white bristles on his head. Regina would be drifting off to sleep, her forehead pressed against the windowpane.

But some nights he didn't play. Sometimes Regina waited for him by her window for hours, staring at the stillness of his back porch. Sometimes she fell asleep waiting for him, and she'd wake up in the middle of the night, her neck hurting as she slept against the wall.

The bus screeches and jolts her. Regina stands, taking her transfer and hurrying off at Buckeye Street, where she waits for the bus to Dogtown. She could walk home from here, she knows, but it looks like rain.

She sits down on the bench. She's alone. Regina closes her eyes and pushes her hands deep down into her pockets. It's getting cold.

Then she hears a fluttering beside her. She opens her eyes, just a bit, and realizes she's *not* alone. A woman sits next to her on the bench, reading a newspaper. Where did she come from? Regina could have sworn there was no one on the bench when she sat down. How long has she been there? Regina can't see the woman's face hidden behind the newspaper. But her nails are neon pink.

Regina quickly glances up at the sky. The rainclouds are heavier now, and the air is thick and damp. It's dark, darker than usual for just a little after five.

She jumps a little at the sound of newspaper rustling. The woman's eyes meet hers over the paper. Regina nods, and she thinks the woman smiles, although she can't see her mouth. Just her eyes.

She remembers Rocky's eyes, how you could tell she was smiling even if you couldn't see her lips.

"She was driving," Aunt Selma told Regina. "She must have skidded in the rain. That's all they can figure. But she was killed instantly, they say. She and Chase both."

"Excuse me, but are you going into Dogtown?"

"Yes," Regina says, her eyes still caught by the woman beside her. "I am."

"I was worried I'd missed the bus."

"Yes, I was wondering too."

The woman shivers. "Well, another comes in a half hour, but it looks like rain."

"Yes, it does."

The woman looks back down at her paper. Out of the corner of her eye, Regina studies her. She likes the woman's clothes. She wears a brown dress suit, the jacket with broad, padded shoulders. Her shoes have high heels and an ankle strap. She has red hair, hinting at blond, done up in a sweep in front and long in back. A strand of hair has fallen in front of her eyes, and she absently pushes it away. Regina follows the woman's pink nails as they cross her face and come to rest in her lap. *She's no typist*, Regina thinks.

A soft mist kisses her cheek. Regina looks up quickly, but the rain is teasing her. The woman does not move.

She smells like Rocky, too. Her perfume is the same. Lilacs.

"She was drunk behind the wheel," Uncle Axel snarled, seeming to delight in giving her the gory details of her sister's death. "She was drunk when she wrapped her car around that tree."

"She was not!"

"Oh, yes, she was. She was wild. I always knew that girl would come to no good."

"You're wrong! Rocky wasn't wild. She was—"

"And he was going to leave her, that college boy. That's why she was drunk. They were fighting. She knew his rich daddy didn't want him hanging out with some floozy who—"

Regina covers her ears, as if that will block out the memory. It was the slick roads. That's why Rocky's car went down the embankment. That's why—

She realizes the woman next to her is staring at her. Regina smiles awkwardly, dropping her hands from her ears.

The woman folds her newspaper in her lap. "Do you live in Dogtown?" she asks.

"Yes, I do."

"Funny name for a neighborhood, isn't it? But that's what everyone calls it."

"Yes, everyone does."

"I just moved up from the city. I'm staying with a friend until I can find a place. How long have you lived in Dogtown?"

"Oh, just a little while."

"Where are you from?"

Regina hesitates. "Well, I was born here. Brown's Mill. But I—I only just moved to Dogtown."

The woman lights up a cigarette. Regina watches her every move: striking the match, inhaling the smoke, letting it out through her nose.

"I'm originally from the city. Lived there all my life. I moved here to start over." The woman sighs, crossing her legs. "Everyone starts over at least once in their lives, don't you agree?"

"I suppose so."

"It's not a bad place, except when the swamps get a little rank."

"I lived in the city for a while," Regina tells her.

"Oh, really? When was this?"

"During the war."

"What did you do there?"

"I was a singer. I—well, my sister and I—we sang at a nightclub."

"That's swell," the woman says, exhaling smoke. "But you came back to Brown's Mill?"

Regina looks up at the sky. "It does look as if it's going to rain."

"I'm Theresa Santacroce," her companion says, green eyes looking over at Regina from under long lashes. "Call me Terry."

"I'm Regina Gunderson. My sister used to call me Gina, but nobody ever does anymore."

"Well, I'll call you Gina. How about that?"

Regina laughs as she shakes the other woman's hand. Terry's face is tanned, an Indian summer tan, and Regina pictures her walking through the city, taxi-cabs honking, people scurrying by, her eyes closed and her face lifted to the sun.

"I like your shoes," Regina ventures.

"Do you? Oh, thanks. I was in the city last week and got them. Do you ever go into the city anymore?"

"No."

"Oh, we must go sometime. My friend doesn't like to go shopping, and she never leaves Brown's Mill. Can you *imagine*?"

"Oh, no!" Regina laughs. She hardly notices the light tickle of raindrops all at once on her face.

"Ooops, here comes the rain," Terry says, and pops open her umbrella. It makes a little *poosh*. Regina shrugs helplessly.

"Here, share mine," Terry offers, patting the spot next to her. Regina slides over on the bench, finding dry protection under Terry's umbrella.

"It was sunny this morning," Regina says, smiling so hard her face feels funny.

"Such strange weather we've been having," Terry says, and they both giggle.

"I think the heavens are going to open up," Regina says. "What do you think?"

"I think they just might," Terry agrees. There's a moment of silence between them, the warmth of their thighs pressing against each other. "So what do you do?"

"I work for the mayor."

"Oh, that must be exciting."

"Not really." Regina shrugs. "I'm just a typist."

Terry throws down her cigarette butt and stubs it out on the sidewalk with the toe of her high-heeled shoe. Still holding the umbrella with one hand, she shakes another cigarette from the package. "Smoke?" she asks Regina.

"Oh, no, thanks."

Terry lights up, inhaling deeply and closing her eyes, then letting out her smoke slow and deliberately, savoring it.

"So," she says.

"So!" Regina laughs ridiculously.

Terry smiles. "Do you like being a typist?"

"Well, it's all I know how to do."

"Oh, come on. I don't believe that."

"No, really. I didn't go to college or anything." She can feel her outside leg getting wet, so she pulls in farther, closer to Terry.

"But you're a singer. You know how to sing."

"Oh, yes, but—well—"

"You must have been good if you sang at a nightclub."

Regina just looks at her. "Oh, well, I guess I . . ." Her words trail off. "What do *you* do for work?"

Terry takes another drag on her cigarette. "I knock on doors, honey."

"You're a traveling saleswoman?"

Terry laughs. "I'm a searcher. That's what I am. I knock on doors and see what's behind them."

"That's an unusual job," Regina says.

"You think? It's all about believing in yourself, Regina. I knock and knock and knock. My philosophy is sooner or later someone's got to answer."

Regina laughs. "I guess I'm just not that good at knocking on doors."

"Give it a try sometime, Regina."

A gust of wind sweeps rain under their umbrella and wets their legs. They both yelp, pulling even closer together.

"Well," Terry exclaims, raising her voice, "I think you're right. The heavens have officially opened!"

Laughter again. Regina can feel the warmth of Terry's leg pressing against hers.

The rain pounds hard against the pavement now, splashing onto their feet, making a steady beat on top of their umbrella.

"Tell you what, sister," Terry says, "if we make it through this alive, what say we stop off for a corned beef on rye at the Dogtown Deli?"

"That'd be swell," Regina says. She's missed Mrs. Unwin's hot meal by now anyway. Going to the deli would be fun. She would tell Betty and Ruth all about it on Monday morning, just as they'd tell her stories about their weekends. She would tell them how she and Terry ate corned beef sandwiches and maybe a caramel sundae and how they talked all night, laughing and joking—

She feels Terry's hand softly on her knee. She looks down. Neon pink nails on Regina's white knee.

"Real nylons," Terry's saying softly. "Remember how hard these were to get during the war?"

Regina feels her heart quicken. Terry's hand slides down, around to the top of Regina's calf.

"These feel like *silk*," Terry says, and she turns her face toward Regina. "Are they?"

"No," Regina answers quietly.

She hears the scream of the bus as it approaches, its brakes shrieking in the rain.

Terry's still looking at Regina, smiling. "Ahh," she purrs. "Salvation has arrived."

Regina stands up abruptly, knocking the umbrella. Terry's hand falls from her leg, thrown to the bench. The rain dances on Regina's head.

"I just remembered," Regina blurts. "I've got to go back to Town Hall. I've got to wait for *that* bus instead."

"Back? But why?"

"Because I forgot something. The mayor—I was supposed to—"

"Supposed to what?"

Regina can't speak.

Terry starts to smile, her lips curling to say something, but then she stops, as if she'd changed her mind.

Regina stares down at her wet shoes. The rain pounds at her. The bus splatters through the puddles, coming to a stop in front of them. Its doors are flung open with a squeal of metal, inviting them into the dry comfort within.

Terry looks at her with silent eyes. "Are you coming, Gina?"

"No," Regina says, her lacquered hair slowly beginning to melt around her face. "I told you. I have to go back."

Terry nods slowly. Then she turns, almost as if in slow motion, like they do in the movies sometimes, and she leaps like a ballet dancer across the deep dark puddle that separates the bench from the bus.

And yet it's the strangest thing: Regina doesn't see her go inside. It's as if Terry just leapt over the puddle and disappeared. No coins rattle in the money collector. The driver never looks up to see anyone go by. He just stares at Regina as if she's crazy.

"Whatsa matter?" he grunts. "Aren't ya gettin' in?"

"No," she says. "I'm—I'm waiting for another bus."

The door retreats as it had opened. There's a hiss of black smoke, and the bus screeches off again through the puddles. Regina watches it splash down the watery canal that once was a street. It turns at a far block, heading for Dogtown. She sits back down on the bench, no umbrella this time, and the rain drenches her.

She wipes her watchface on her sleeve. It's 5:45. She sits in the rain and watches without moving when the bus to Main Street comes by, and finally, closer to six, she boards the last bus to Dogtown.

The bus driver, a different one this time, arches a furry eyebrow at her. "Sure is raining cats and dogs, ain't it?"

The bus is almost empty. An old black woman way in back, a teenaged white boy with freckles up near the front. Regina stumbles to a seat in the middle, the wetness of her clothes squishing against her skin, the backs of her legs sticking to the fake leather seats. She puts her head against the window and stares out into the dark. She watches as the rain hits the glass, exploding into thousands of crystal drops, much as it must have against the car windows the night Rocky died. The wipers would have struggled across the windshield in a vain attempt to keep the torrential rain from blocking her sister's vision. And then her wheels had slipped on a curve, and she plummeted into the gorge—or else Rocky had turned to Chase and said, white teeth in the dark, "Here is the place we die."

Regina watches the streetlights bob through the watery, distorted glass. She'll go to her room and put on a dry robe and eat a cold dinner in the kitchen, and then she'll go to bed. There's nothing else. It's much too miserable a night for the old man to play his flute.

17

MAKING LOVE

"What if Zandy dies before you get to see him?"

"What if I threw you out into traffic before anyone could stop me?"

Dee smirks, sitting beside him in the front seat of the car. "You do brittle real good, man, but I know you like me."

Wally sighs. "I'm just not ready to go over to see Zandy yet. I've been too caught up with my mother's bullshit. But that's ending today." He pulls into the parking lot beside the CVS drugstore. "You want anything?"

"What I want they don't sell at CVS." He grins. "But I'll take an Almond Joy."

Wally smiles. He's going in for a newspaper. A *real* newspaper, not the *Brown's Mill Reminder*. He needs to read something *real*. Something about what's going on outside this little river valley town, how *real* people are living their lives. He's tried calling Cheri three times this morning but got her voice mail. He's craving some connection to the city.

"Hey," Dee says as Wally slides out from behind the wheel. "Look who's over there. Talk about your mother's bullshit."

Wally's eyes follow the direction in which Dee's pointing. Idling in a No Parking zone in front of the drugstore is Kyle's Trans Am, and leaning against the passenger side door is Luz, smoking a cigarette.

Dee hurries out of the car himself, following Wally as he walks up to the girl.

"Hey," Wally calls.

Luz turns to look at him. She immediately becomes agitated, throwing down her cigarette and stubbing it out with her toe.

"What's up?" Wally asks.

"Nothing," the girl replies.

"Looks like you're waiting for somebody."

"No," she says, but Wally doesn't believe her. "I'm not waiting for anybody."

"So how come you're standing there?" Dee interjects aggressively.

She looks at him with utter disdain. "Like I don't have a right to stand where I want?"

"You're in a No Parking zone with the car running," Wally observes.

Luz gives him a face. "Who are you, the cops?"

"Well, it just looks like you're waiting for someone," Wally offers. "And I was just wondering if it might just so happen to be my cousin Kyle."

She glares at him. "I told you. I don't know where Kyle is."

"So," Wally says, getting in close, "if I go into that store right now, I won't see him? I won't find him in there?"

Luz pulls away from him and walks around to the driver's side of the car. "I don't know who the fuck you'll find in there. I don't know where Kyle is. How many times do I have to tell people that?"

Wally peers into the car. On the back seat there are three suitcases.

"Going somewhere?" he asks.

"Yeah," she says, looking off toward the drugstore, then back at Wally. "I'm going out of town. Got a problem with that?"

"You and Kyle?"

"Fuck off," she says. She's trembling; Wally can see that quite clearly. "Why do you have to harass me?" she's asking. "I've never done anything to you."

"I'm just making sure you're being straight with my mother," Wally says.

Luz laughs. "Me being straight with your mother? Why don't *you* try it, Walter Day? Why don't *you* try being straight with her?"

"Hey," Dee pipes in, "is that a slur against being gay?"

Luz looks over at him as if he were some annoying insect, then returns her ire to Wally. "Why don't you just try being a good son to her for a change? Maybe actually *talk* with her, *listen* to her. Maybe stop judging her, yelling at her. I've *seen* you. I've seen how you talk to her."

"You don't know what you're saying," Wally says.

"I know your mother one whole hell of a lot better than you do. She's a good woman, a good person. If you're worried about how somebody's treating her, you oughta take a good long look in the mirror first before you start giving shit to others."

She looks up at the drugstore once more, then makes a sound in frustration. She whips open the car door, slides in, gunning the motor and screeching off. Smoke and skid marks are left behind.

"What a cunt," Dee says.

But Wally's already hurrying into the drugstore. *He's got to be in here*, he's thinking. *She was waiting for him, and now she's taken off.* Up one aisle he runs, then down the next. Kyle's *got* to be in here. He's got to be!

"Did you see a man in here?" he asks the woman at the counter, out of breath. "A man about my age, short-cropped hair, blond, kind of looks like me, my height?" The woman just looks at him strangely, shudders, then turns her attention without answering him to the customers waiting in line.

Dee's been up and down the aisles too. "There's nobody like that in here," he tells Wally. "He probably snuck out while we were talking to Luz and she sped off to pick him up around the corner."

"Fuck," Wally says.

"That's probably what happened," Dee says, "don't you think?"

Wally forgets about his newspaper. He just pushes back out through the door into the morning, heading down Main Street. Dee follows.

Why don't you try it, Walter Day? Why don't you try to be a good son to her for a change?

Across the street stands St. John the Baptist Church, its brownstone steeple slicing into the blue sky. It's one of the few things that haven't changed about downtown. Wally crosses the street without thinking, heading down the alley between the church and its adjacent school, a squat brownstone structure that also hasn't changed very much.

"Where are you going?" Dee asks, jogging up behind him.

"It's got to be around here somewhere," Wally says, suddenly consumed.

"What is?"

"It's here," Wally says. "It's got to be here."

"Man, are you losing it?" Dee complains. "You're acting very weird. Let's just go see Zandy and get it over with."

Wally doesn't reply. He starts running his hands along the side of the school building, examining the exterior, stone by stone. "This was my eighth grade classroom," he says. "Right here through this window."

"Dude, you are freaking me out," Dee says.

"Eighth grade," Wally murmurs. "Before my whole fucking world crumbled in on itself."

"What are you *looking for*?" Dee demands.

"I know it's here," Wally says. "Right under the window. I know it's here."

In eighth grade, he still had friends. Things weren't as bad then. His father hadn't yet come home for good, and *Saturday Night Fever* was still a year in the future. His life hadn't yet changed, taken that fork in the road that led him to Zandy and all the shit that came afterward. But even in eighth grade Wally had a sense of what was to come. He was a smart boy, after all. The smartest in his class. He knew what lie ahead.

"*Jewboy*," Freddie Piatrowski spit.

David Schnur stood his ground.

"What are you doing in a Catholic school anyway? Why are you here?"

David said nothing.

"I'll tell you why you're here," Freddie said, grinning, "Because you kept getting the shit kicked outta you in public school."

The other boys hoot.

"Well, I can only promise you one thing, *Jewboy*." Freddie slammed his fist in his palm. "More of the same."

Freddie Piatrowski was the boy Wally had wanted to marry. He'd announced it to his kindergarten class, said right out loud that he loved Freddie and wanted to marry him when he grew up. And in some ways that had never really changed, not even after Wally came to understand that boys could only marry girls. Freddie had been his best friend all these years. They had slept at each other's houses, sometimes in the same bed, and they'd done all sorts of boy stuff together, like telling scary stories and playing with trucks and catching frogs. *I still want to marry you*, Wally would think, looking straight into Freddie's green eyes, though he knew he could never again say the words out loud.

Freddie was very handsome. Not handsome like Wally, who was *girly* handsome, handsome in the perfect, symmetrical way that made mothers gush when they looked at their child's class photo. "Oh, there's a good-looking boy," they'd say. "Is that Wally Day? He sure is a handsome one, don't you think?"

No, Freddie's kind of handsome was nothing like that. Freddie was handsome in a boy way. His face was tilted, not perfect, no symmetry at all. His mouth was wide and crooked in a manner that the girls seemed to love: big smile, big lips, big teeth. By eighth grade, the girls weren't paying attention to Wally's kind of handsome anymore. Freddie had replaced him as the most desirable boy in the class. Freddie—with the thin white scar between his upper lip and nose, the result of an accident with a jackknife, the very same he'd brought to school once and received a detention for. Freddie—with his crooked face and big mouth and wiry arms that could shoot a basketball straight into its net from across the playground. That was the kind of handsome that mattered by eighth grade.

Freddie Piatrowski is why I fell in love with Ned, Wally would come to realize, years later. The two had a lot in common. Scars. Jackknives. A lack of symmetry to their faces, their bodies, their lives. So much in common. Except—

"Kick his ass!" Freddie had ordered his troops. "Kick that Jewboy ass!"

Except Ned would never have done what Freddie did.

If Ned had been there, he would've stopped it. He would have saved David from the beating he got. But Ned wasn't a classmate of theirs at St. John the Baptist school. Ned was far, far away, in a place Wally had yet to even hear of. In eighth grade, Wally had no idea that Ned even existed—so there was no one he could have imagined, no one to conjure up in his thoughts, to rush in and rescue poor David Schnur.

Least of all himself.

They ganged up on him. All the boys from the eighth grade class of St. John the Baptist surrounded the new boy, the Jewboy, David Schnur, and they attacked. Freddie led the way, but they all got in their licks. Even Wally.

Dear God, even me.

Had he punched him? Maybe kicked him in the ribs when he was down? Wally can't remember what he did, and doesn't want to, but he knows he did something. In high school—a year and a whole world away from that incident outside the grammar school—David would become Wally's friend. His only friend really. Never did they mention the incident to each other. Maybe David didn't know Wally had been a part of it. So many boys had participated that maybe David hadn't realized Wally was there.

He knew. Of course he knew.

"Take that, you Jew faggot!" Freddie shrilled, kneeing David right in the balls. The boy crumpled and fell to the ground screaming. The boys moved in, kicking

David between them like a soccer ball. David let out a hideous scream, a sound like a train whistle, or the screeching brakes of a bus. That's when Father Carson bolted out of the rectory and the boys ran like hell in a dozen different directions.

Wally ran, too, taking refuge on the side of the school building. From there he could watch as the priest knelt beside David. Father Carson, so young, so handsome. He was so kind to David, so gentle. He helped the boy to his feet, his arm around his back, leading him into the rectory. Wally's heart was racing in his chest. He would remember looking up at the sky and being surprised by how bright and blue it was, how beautiful was the day, indifferent to the horror that had just taken place. Pigeons were cooing on the window sills. A bluejay squawked from a telephone wire. Wally stood there, panting. He wondered if David would die, if they'd kicked a hole in his head, or ruptured a lung, or tore open his stomach.

Jew faggot.

Wally began to cry. He was a smart boy. He knew what was coming.

From his pocket he produced a coin. A quarter probably, or maybe a dime, one with a rough edge. He began to scratch at the mortar between the brownstones of the school building. He scratched carefully and diligently, intent at his task, forming each letter with deliberate strokes.

"Here," he says finally, turning to Dee. "Here it is."

The boy leans in.

Etched into the stone, faded by time but still plain to see, are two simple words:

HELP ME.

"So," Dee asks him, "did you ever get beaten up like that yourself?"

"Not like that. And not at school. Just by my father."

They're sitting out on Missy's back steps, smoking a joint, a tiny hangnail of a moon riding high in the sky. Wally feels a hand slide into the pocket of his coat. It's chilly out here. They can actually see their breath in front of their faces. Dee pushes his shoulder into Wally's, nestling in close to him for warmth. He shoves his hand down deep into Wally's pocket and looks up into his eyes.

"I got beaten up even worse that that," the boy tells him. "One time a bunch of kids in sixth grade threw me out the second-floor window of my school. And then down on the ground there was another group of assholes waiting to wipe the playground with my sorry faggot ass."

Wally looks over at him. The moonlight plays with his face, making him seem at turns both younger and older than he is.

"How did they know you were gay in sixth grade?"

"I was always playing Mariah Carey on my Walkman. I had photos from *Saved by the Bell* all over my locker. On my math book cover I drew a big red heart and wrote I LOVE JOEY LAWRENCE."

Wally smiles. "Okay, so maybe there were a few clues."

"It was all *so* mid-nineties." Dee shudders, snuggling in closer against Wally. "Of course, that was before my mother went crazy and married Leo."

Wally can smell the boy's hair. It's freshly washed and all of the usual spiking gel is gone. Still orange, but it's soft. And sweet.

"Has your mother tried to contact you at all?"

"Nope. In court she said she was praying for me."

"And she's still with the bastard?"

Dee nods. "Of course she is. She doesn't believe in divorce."

"But kicking her kid out of the house is okay."

"Hey, I was the one to leave. The day they took me to see that faith healer freak—man, I knew it was time to go. And my caseworker knew just the place for me." He grins, rubbing his head against Wally's arm like a cat.

Wally thinks about standing up. It would break the contact between them. It would get Dee's hand out of his pocket. It would end the buzz he's feeling, the stirring in his crotch. But he doesn't. He just takes in a long breath and lets it out slowly.

He looks across the yard and sees himself, fifteen years ago, sneaking over Miss Aletha's back fence. Across town, Dee would have been in his crib, teething. Wally's mouth was sore then, too. Bleeding even. His father had punched out a tooth.

"There was nothing official about it when I came here," Wally says. "Missy just took me in. There had been so much scandal that my father didn't want anymore, so when I refused to come home, he just said, 'Fine, let him stay there.' He disowned me as his son, said a faggot belongs with a freak anyway."

They're quiet. Wally feels whatever's buzzing between them ratchet up another level. He can't let it go on any longer. So he stands. Dee's hand falls out of his pocket.

"I'm going to bed, buddy," Wally says thickly. "It's getting too cold out here."

The boy looks up at him. "Even with all that shit, look how good you still turned out. Famous actor and everything."

"Sarcastic brat," Wally says, grinning down at him.

"Maybe a little." Dee stands. "But actually you *did* end up okay. You didn't kill yourself or become a drug addict or a hustler."

Wally smirks. "Some would say *unemployed actor* is only a step away from drug addict or hustler."

"Oh come on. You did that movie with Susan Lucci."

"My big claim to fame."

"And that other one, with Judith Light."

Wally laughs in disbelief. "I played a taxicab driver in that one. I had *one line*. How'd you know about it?"

"You're on the Internet Movie Database. I checked you out when Missy said you were coming. I rented whatever I could find."

Wally looks into the boy's eyes. He's adorable. He's goddamn fucking adorable. "I've got to go to bed," he says softly.

"Tell me the truth, Wally. Do you think what Zandy did with you was wrong?"

Wally says nothing in response. He just keeps looking into Dee's eyes. The night is so still, seeming to have dropped over them like a heavy blanket. Wally can hear his heart beating in his ears.

"I mean, you said he taught you stuff," Dee says. "Told you that you'd change the world."

"He said *we* would change the world. Gays. Homos."

"And we *have*, haven't we?"

Wally smiles weakly. "I suppose we have."

Equal rights, TV shows, civil unions, even honest-to-goodness marriage in some places. Ned might be dead, and Zandy might be dying, and Wally might be here tonight alone—but still, we did it. We changed the world.

"I wouldn't ever be straight," Dee's saying, "even if it meant things would be easier for me. I know that much anyway."

Wally keeps looking at him. The orange hair, the piercings, the defiant little jut to his chin, the adolescent, self-defensive sarcasm. And yet, he's already as wise as Wally. There's nothing left to teach him.

Except . . .

"Guess I'll see you in the morning then," Dee says, turning away from Wally's silence.

"Donald," Wally says, and his voice comes out like a croak.

The boy looks back.

Wally approaches him. He places his hands on his shoulders.

"What is it?" Dee asks. "What's up with you?"

Wally leans down and kisses him, full on the lips.

Hard candy and licorice. That's what the boy's skin tastes like. They're in Wally's bed, and Wally is running his tongue over Dee's face, around his neck, across his smooth chest. Beneath him the boy is writhing, his cock standing up hard and straight, so incongruous to his slim body. It's a big, proud nine-incher, blood engorged, putting Wally's to shame.

"Oh, man," Dee says, "Oh, fucking man."

Wally's tongue circles first one nipple, then the next. He flicks the little pink buds. Dee nearly jumps through the ceiling. "Oh, man! Oh, fucking *man*!"

What did I taste like? What did my skin remind him of? Maybe milk and Sugar Pops. Orange soda. Nestlé's *Quik.*

"This feels so good," Dee says, grabbing Wally by the shoulders.

"Yeah," he tells him. "Yeah, it does."

"You're great, Wally, you know that? You're great."

The boy's eyes shine. Wally won't let himself think. He just pushes down and kisses Dee hard, their tongues dueling for supremacy inside their mouths. They wrestle each other, rolling back and forth on the bed. Dee's cock is dripping precum. Wally licks it like a melting ice cream cone, one big swipe of his tongue up the shaft. Dee moans.

"Hey," the boy says suddenly, grabbing Wally's wrists.

Wally looks up at him. Dee's eyes bear down at him across his chest, still glistening from Wally's saliva.

"What did your boyfriend die of?"

"AIDS," Wally says, and he can taste Dee's precum as it slides down his throat.

The boy sits up on his elbows. "Do you have it, too?"

Wally sits back against the wall, feeling his cock soften even as Dee's remains stiff and hard, pointing at the ceiling.

This is it: the source of his pain.

This is why he wakes every morning alone.

This is what burns at him, keeps him from living, from breathing, from looking up at the sky. This is what sent him into that depression all those months ago, sent him to those drugs, those doctors, to that place Cheri found for him. A little rest home, she called it. A retreat. Yeah, *right*. It was a funny farm. A nuthouse. A fucking insane asylum. And Wally had been there for almost six months, lost in his grief.

"I don't have it, Dee," he tells the boy finally. "I don't know why or how but I don't. I *should* have it. I should be dead."

Wally closes his eyes. He feels his cock shrink, curl inward, take refuge in his pubic hair.

Dee slides over to sit beside him. "I don't think I have it either," he says, "but I was only tested once, and that was last year."

Wally opens his eyes and studies the boy's face. How serious he is. How sincere. How brilliant his blue eyes, only an inch now from Wally's own.

"Can I ask a question, Wally?" the boy asks.

Wally nods.

"How many times have you done this?"

Wally blinks. "Done what?"

"This."

"You mean . . . had *sex*?"

"Yeah. With a guy."

"Christ, Dee, I don't know. You mean in my whole *life*?"

"Yeah," Dee says.

Wally laughs. "I can't count. I mean—*hundreds*. Ned and I—we played around a lot. Together and separately. It was okay, we understood it. It was the way we lived."

"I've done it three times," Dee tells him.

"Three times," Wally echoes.

They look at each other, not saying anything for several seconds.

Then Dee falls back into the pillows. "Come on, Wally, fuck me."

Wally lies down on top of him. They start to kiss but Wally's dick stays soft. He licks the boy's neck, nibbles his ears. He tries to taste again the candy of his skin, but he's becoming self-conscious now, aware of how stubbornly soft his dick remains.

"Here," Dee says, pushing him up and going down on him. Wally's not prepared. The warmth of the boy's mouth takes him by surprise. He tries to will himself a boner but it's just not working. Even with Dee's lips sliding up and down, Wally can't get hard. Meanwhile, the boy's cock remains so effortlessly engorged.

"I want you to fuck me," Dee says, looking up from Wally's crotch.

"There's more to sex than fucking," Wally says, gently guiding the boy by the shoulders back up to the pillows. He pushes Dee's legs up into the air and aims his tongue toward his anus. The boy shudders when Wally makes contact, shouting out, gripping the sheets with his hands. Dee's insides are more tart than his skin, tangy and a little gritty. Wally inhales deeply the boy's spunkiness, and massages his silky tissues with his tongue.

"Oh, man, Wally, oh, fucking man," Dee moans.

Wally's cock is lengthening. He reaches over the side of the bed, finding his backpack on the floor, all without breaking contact between his mouth and Dee's anus. He unzips the backpack, fumbling inside for a condom. He finds one, tears it open without looking, and begins manipulating it over the tip of his cock.

"Aw, yeah, Wally, fuck me."

But as soon as the latex begins to unroll, Wally loses his erection again, and rolls over onto his back in frustration.

"What's the matter?" Dee asks.

"I . . . I'm too tired, I guess."

"It's okay. Just do what you were doing."

Wally sighs, returning his tongue to the boy's butt. Dee spits into his hand and begins masturbating his enormous cock. In moments he shoots, sending gallons of semen across the bed, several globs landing in Wally's hair.

"Impressive," Wally says, smiling.

Dee just closes his eyes.

Wally stands, searching for something to clean up the mess. He settles on a dirty sock, wiping off the boy's chest first, then trying without much luck to get the jizz out of his hair. Dee still lies there with his eyes closed. Wally tosses the sock into the corner of the room and settles back in beside the boy, putting his arm around him.

"You are so adorable," Wally tells him.

"Thanks," Dee says.

Then he stands. It takes Wally by surprise. Dee stands, his softening cock still impressive, swinging between his legs. He's looking around at the floor. Finally he spots his underwear and pulls it on, then does the same with his jeans.

"What's going on?" Wally asks.

"Nothing," Dee says. His voice is even. "I sleep better by myself."

"Oh." Wally doesn't know what to say. "Okay."

Dee's pulling on his shirt. "You didn't expect me to sleep with you, did you?"

Wally tries to find the boy's eyes but they're averted. "Not if you don't want to."

"I'm sure you don't want some kid getting attached," Dee says.

"Come here," Wally says, patting the spot on the bed beside him.

"Look, man, I got what I wanted. It's cool."

"What do you mean?"

The boy shrugs. "I got my rocks off. I told my friends I'd get you into bed and I did." He laughs. "You old guys are all the same. All a kid like me has to do is smile and we've got you. So it's cool. We both got what we wanted, right?"

"Dee, it wasn't like that—"

"Dude, come *on*. I'm telling you it's cool. You've done this hundreds of times. You told me so. You don't have to start the whole 'It was really meaningful' thing with me. I'm not attached. It's cool." He places his hand on the doorknob. "So it was fun. Thanks. See you around."

Wally says nothing, just stares at him. Dee gives him a quick little smile. Then he's gone.

What does a gay kid want most of all? Does he want platitudes and theory? Wise words and sage counsel? Deep and meaningful relationships with horny older men? Fuck that. What had *Wally* wanted, that first day he'd ridden his bike over to see Zandy?

He'd wanted *to get his rocks off*.

But more than that: he'd wanted his sexuality affirmed. He'd wanted proof that it was real, that it could happen, that he was an attractive person, that he was as gay as much as anyone else, that an adult might actually take him seriously.

Seriously enough to want to have sex with him.

Seriously enough to love him.

For that's what it came down to: Zandy had loved him. Maybe it was wrong what he did. Maybe he didn't always do right by Wally. But Zandy had loved him, in a way no one had ever loved him before.

And no one would, ever again.

Except for Ned. But Ned's love had been different. It was the love of an equal. The love of a peer. They had been boys, wild with possibilities, tumbling over each other in bed and in life. Together they were a whirlwind of energy, of adventure, of exploration. Zandy had been grounded, rooted to the earth.

He met Ned toward the end of his freshman year in college. Ned was born in the city, a plumber in his family's business, a big bruiser with lots of "dezes" and "dozes" in his speech. Who would have thought this would be Wally's great love? They met when Ned had come with his uncle to fix some pipes in Wally's dorm. Enough meaningful glances had been exchanged between the boys for Ned to sneak back into the dorm that night, making love to Wally in his upper bunk as his clueless roommate slept soundly. From then on, Ned and Wally were inseparable.

Ned loved the fact that Wally was an actor. Opening night, no matter where it was—Dubuque or Dayton or Tallahassee—there was Ned, front row and center, leading the applause. "I'd'a been an actor, too," Ned would say, "if I'd been handsome like Wally."

But Ned *was* handsome. So what if he had a gut from too much beer and started losing his hair at twenty-three? He had the most amazing eyes, ice blue like a Siberian husky's, and the cutest nose, almost like a girl's, turned up and perky. Wally was a regular at the gym, keeping his body fit and toned: he *had* to, if he wanted to land parts. But Ned got squishy over the course of their decade together, and sometimes he'd forget to trim his nose hairs unless Wally reminded him.

And Wally loved him for it.

"Have you given any thought to what it will be like when he's gone?"

Wally lifts his eyes. He's no longer in bed in Miss Aletha's house. He's in the hospital cafeteria, drinking coffee to stay awake, sitting opposite Cheri. Even here the lights are so bright that they make Wally nauseous. Eight floors up Ned is in his last days of PCP.

"No," he tells her. "I have not given any thought to that at all."

She takes his hands in hers. "Sweetie, I worry about you. You're down to skin and bones yourself. The reality is that Ned isn't coming home this time."

Wally pulls out of her grip and runs his hand through his hair. He watches as little flakes of skin drift down to land in his coffee. "He's rallied before," he manages to say.

"Wally, he has *AIDS*." Cheri reaches over to place her hand on top of his again. "He can only rally so many times."

How can she understand? Cheri's never had a boyfriend who lasted longer than a few months, and he's been with Ned for a *decade*! Ten whole goddamn years! He's been with Ned since he was *eighteen*, a scared, confused little boy still shamed by his family, his teachers, his town for what had happened with Zandy. Ned *saved* him. Ned is his *life*. Ned is as much a part of Wally as his blood vessels, his muscle tissue, his brain.

And she has the nerve to ask him if he'd given any thought to what it would be like when Ned was gone.

He'll never be able to think about that. Never.

He can't sleep. He throws aside his sheets and heads downstairs, where he sits at the kitchen table, eating the last slice of ginger cake with his hands. He hears a sound and looks up. Miss Aletha comes in, a kerchief around her head.

"Did we wake you?" Wally asks, an eyebrow arched.

She pours herself a glass of orange juice and sits down beside him. "I heard a few bedsprings."

"You wanted it to happen, didn't you?"

She shrugs. "I just wanted fate to take its course."

"I'm an old man, Missy." He breaks off another piece of the cake. "An old man who couldn't get it up."

"Oh."

"It doesn't matter. He was just in it to get sex. I know how boys that age are. Their dicks rule them. I was the same way."

"Not really."

"No, I was. So I made sure he got off. I gave him what he wanted."

She's just looking at him.

"I don't know why it's bothering me so much. I mean, he's just a kid. It's not like I have . . . *feelings* for him or anything. He's a kid and I had sex with him. That's all it was."

"Okay. That's all it was."

"That's all it was."

You're great, Wally, you know that? You're great.

There's more to being gay than just having sex, babe.

Why does it sting so much? The boy's attitude? The way he left, the way he hadn't spent the night, sleeping beside him, his ear pressed up against Wally's chest, listening to his heart? He can't stop remembering how sweet Dee tasted, how fresh his hair smelled as they sat outside, looking up at the moon, the boy's hand in his pocket.

"I shouldn't have done it," Wally says.

"Why not?"

"Because . . . because now I feel like shit. Like I'm out of the game. A joke. An old man who can't get an erection. Meanwhile, he's sleeping like a baby up there, not giving the whole thing a second thought."

"So it's all about you." Miss Aletha leans back in her chair, cocking her head as she looks over at him. "All about your own perceptions. That's always the way with you, Wally. Isn't Donald entitled to his own set of emotions? He thinks it didn't mean anything to you so he's acting like it didn't mean anything to him."

"Maybe it didn't."

"In case you've forgotten, Wally Day, any time a sixteen-year-old has sex, it *means something.*"

"Oh, Missy, it doesn't matter. I'm all sidetracked here." He pushes the plate, bare except for crumbs, away from him. "Taking my mother to see goddamn Uncle Axel. Hauling bags of dirt around her yard. And today, I was on my way to see Zandy and I wussed out."

"You apparently had other things to tend to."

"I need to do what I came here for and then get the hell back to the city."

"Then do it. Why are you stalling?"

Wally can't answer.

"Maybe you *don't* want to leave Brown's Mill. Maybe that's it. If you do see Zandy, after all—*finally* see him, *finally* make your peace—then there's nothing left to keep you here. Nothing left to keep you hung up on your past, nothing to bitch about, nothing to feel sorry for yourself about."

"I'm not feeling sorry for myself," Wally says, annoyed. "I'm just pissed off at all the bullshit in my life."

She folds her arms across her chest and looks at him intently. "So would you like me to hand you a deck of cards so *you can deal with it?*"

He sticks his tongue out at her.

"Wally, it's been almost *seven years* since Ned died."

"He was the love of my life!" Wally bangs his fist against the table, startling himself as much as her by the suddenness of his emotion. "I'm sorry," he says, calming down a little, "but seven years isn't long enough to make the pain go away."

"So how long is long enough? Nearly *twenty years* have passed since you left your mother's home, with all those issues unresolved. And it's been longer than that since what happened with Zandy. Is that how you're going to live your life? Never dealing with anything, never putting anything to rest?"

He stares at her, his lips tightening.

Missy sighs. "I thought after the breakdown, after spending time at the institute, you'd come back with a better take on life. I thought you'd try to see things differently. But it's always about *you*, Wally. Always about how *cheated* you've been, having parents who failed you and a lover who died on you. Life's been so unfair to you. But what about everyone else? Do you ever stop to think about the *other* person's experience, what it's like for them?"

"Of course I do."

"No, you don't. You're too busy wallowing in a puddle of self-pity. You retreat from life. You lose touch with friends. You let your career slide." She stands suddenly, looking down at him, arms akimbo. "When I've spoken to you, when I've asked if you've met anyone new, the answer has always been the same. For seven years now you've chosen to live as a hermit. You act as if life has dealt you such a blow that you can never get up again. Well, people *die*, Wally! And people *go on living!*"

He's angry now himself. "You can't understand," he tells her.

"Why not? I had a lover die on me, too. I had parents fail me, too. Jesus *Christ*, Wally! Ned *loved* you. Hell, *Zandy* loved you! You said that yourself! Zandy loved you and I loved you! God *knows* I've loved you! You've had all *sorts* of love to make up for where your parents failed you!"

Wally just sits there, looking up at her.

She sighs again. "Do you know what today is?"

"No," Wally says.

"It's the day Bertrand disappeared, eight years ago."

"Why do you always say he disappeared? Bertrand *died*, Missy."

"He *disappeared*." She wraps her arms around herself. "He was here one day, gone the next. That's how it went, for a whole generation of queens. They just faded away."

She reaches up, undoing the knot of her kerchief. She slips it off her head, exposing her baldness. Wally is startled. Miss Aletha rarely allows anyone a glimpse of herself without her wig.

"When the sun comes up tomorrow morning," she says, "I want *life* in this house. Do you hear me? I want laughter, happiness and the promise of youth. No more despondency, Wally. No more self-pity."

"Missy," Wally says, "I'm sorry if I've come at a bad time . . ."

"Eh? I can't hear you, dear."

He raises his voice. "I'll go back to the city tomorrow."

"I can't hear you," Miss Aletha says, heading out of the kitchen. "I'm a deaf old lady. If you're going to talk to me, you'll have to speak up."

Wally follows her. She's being obstinate.

"A whole generation," Miss Aletha is saying, lighting a candle. She places it on a table and stands back to admire the flame. "They just disappeared. Here one day, gone the next. But we haven't forgotten them. They didn't live in vain."

She opens a drawer, withdraws a photograph of Bertrand. He's wearing a tuxedo and top hat, and on his shoulder is perched a white dove. She sets the photo beside the flame and looks down at it.

Wally comes up beside her. He places an arm around her waist.

"No, we won't forget them," he tells her.

They're quiet, watching the candlelight flicker on the glass of Bertrand's photograph.

"You're right," Wally says. "Zandy loved me And I loved him. That's what I need to tell him."

Miss Aletha makes a soft sound in her throat as way of reply.

"That's why I came back," Wally whispers. "To tell him that I loved him."

They stand that way for a long time, just watching the flame.

18

SUSPICIOUS MINDS

"I've come to say good-bye, Mother."

"Oh, Walter. So soon you're leaving."

Regina looks up at her son. How tall he is. How good-looking. Such broad shoulders. His blond hair is starting to recede slightly at the edges of his forehead. It's a face, a body, she doesn't know, doesn't remember. He's been saying he's Walter these last few days, but he could be a stranger, anyone really, someone just pretending to be her son. Walter, to her, isn't nearly so tall. He has no unshaven whiskers on his cheeks. He's just a boy, seven, maybe eight, in a baseball cap and Converse sneakers. This is who she sees standing in the doorway in front of her. A boy, not a man. But the expression on the face is the same: distant, fretting, eyes cast downward.

"Please don't make me go," he's saying. "Don't make me go stay with Aunt Selma and Uncle Axel. Please don't make me."

"Walter," Regina says, "I wish you didn't have to go"—but to whom does she speak? This man, here? Or the little boy in her mind?

Walter sighs. "I have a couple things still to do, but I'm getting on the road by this afternoon. Now, Mother, remember to take the pills the doctor gave you. They'll help your mind. You won't be as anxious or forgetful."

"Yes, Luz made a chart for me—"

Jorge suddenly appears in the doorway to the living room. Walter spots him and steps inside. He glares at the boy, who runs off, suddenly frightened.

"The girl took off but she left her brother here?" Walter asks, outraged.

"Yes. It's fine, Walter. Jorge's a good boy. Just like you were, Wal—"

"Mother, you can't take care of him on your own!"

"Why can't I?"

He leans in close to her. "Mother, he's *retarded*."

"He's a good boy," she insists.

Regina feels strangely emphatic about the point. She can feel her chin lift, her shoulders stiffen.

"Mother, you can't—" But Walter's voice trails off. "Fine. Okay, fine. Do what you want. Keep him here. It's your problem. Yours and his sister's. If she wants to waltz off with Kyle and leave you stuck with her retarded brother—"

"She's not off with Kyle," Regina says, still feeling defiant. "She'll be back. She said she was coming back."

Walter's shaking his head. "I *saw* her yesterday, Mother. She was clearly going off with someone."

"And what makes you so sure it was Kyle?"

Walter sighs.

"Kyle is *not* with her," Regina says. "Luz is a good girl. She's free now of Kyle. I made sure of that."

Walter looks at her, his eyebrows lowered. "What do you mean you made sure of it?"

"I just mean—" Regina put her hand to her forehead. "Oh, I don't know what I mean. I get so confused."

"Well, I've had as much of this as I can take. I'm leaving now, Mother. I'm going to do what I came back to Brown's Mill to do, and then I'm getting the hell out of here."

He turns to leave. That's when they spot the police car pull into the driveway.

"We'll need the boy to make a statement and press charges," Officer Garafolo told them.

He had sat in her living room, right there on her couch, and his boots had tracked grime all across her gold shag carpet. He wore a blue uniform, tight around his bulging belly and overweight thighs, and Regina remembers how shiny his badge was. His boots, too: as shiny as Robert's had been, before he left the navy and went to work at Schaefer's Shoes.

"Of *course* we'll press charges," Robert had replied, his lips thin and white. "The man's a pervert. A danger to every child in Brown's Mill."

Regina watched her husband closely. His face looked different than she'd ever seen it before. Pulled and pinched, white and tense. His fingers were clawed inward. He paced back and forth like a dog in a pen, looking over his shoulder constantly. He let his breath out in short tiny wheezes.

Officer Garafolo nodded. "If you press charges against him, we can have his sorry ass thrown in jail, Captain Day. I promise you that."

"I want him *put away*," Robert shrilled, and for a moment Regina didn't know who he meant—the pervert or Walter—because his eyes had darted ferociously over at their son.

Walter was sitting on a chair opposite the policeman. Unlike his father, he was completely still. He stared at the floor, his hands clasped and dropped between his legs. He looked so small, even though he was fifteen now.

"May I make you some tea?" Regina asked Officer Garafolo.

"No, thank you, ma'am."

Her husband glanced at her with annoyance, then turned his attention back to the policeman. "I want you to go over there now and get him. Get that pervert before he can molest any other children."

"I'd like the boy to come down to the station first and give his statement. Can he do that?"

"Of course he can."

Walter didn't stir.

"Tell him you can, Wally!" Robert shouted.

The boy's eyes flickered up from the floor. He met his father's gaze. "I can do it," he said, and it was a voice Regina didn't recognize.

"Let's go then," Robert said.

The policeman stood. Walter stood, too, though his eyes were back to the floor. He walked slowly behind his father and Officer Garafolo, passing his mother without saying a word. She reached out to touch his shoulder but pulled her hand back at the last moment. No one said anything else as they went through the door. Regina watched as the light came on as the police car backed out of the driveway, carrying her husband and her son.

Then she got out the vacuum to clean up the dirt the policeman had left behind.

"Mrs. Day?" Officer Garafolo is coming up the walk. "May I speak with you, please?"

Walter looks from her to the policeman.

"Of course," Regina says, and hurries to let him in. Garafolo enters, and his eyes come to rest on Walter. They all stand awkwardly in the foyer. "You remember my son, Walter?" Regina asks.

The policeman nods. "Sure. How you doin'?"

"Is this about my cousin again?" Walter asks.

The policeman nods. "Just following up." He turns to Regina. "I understand a navy investigator was here?"

Walter looks sharply at Regina. "You didn't tell me about this, Mother."

"No, I—" Regina begins twiddling a button on her blouse. "He was a very nice young man. He said he was going to find Luz for me."

"Luz?" Garafolo asks. "You mean Luz Vargas, the girlfriend?"

"She was staying here," Walter says. "But she's taken off, leaving her brother behind."

"Interesting," says Garafolo.

"What have you found out about Kyle?" Walter asks impatiently.

"Can we sit down?"

"Of course," Regina says. "May I make you some tea, Officer?"

"No, thank you, ma'am."

She watches as he strides into the living room and settles down on the couch. No grime, no mud, this time. The shag carpet is long gone, replaced by a brown-sugar berber. The man from Grant's who'd installed it told her that the nylon-olefin construction promised long-lasting stain resistance and exceptional durability. So far it's held up very well, and it's been, what? Twelve years? It's outlasted Grant's, in fact, which went out of business.

Walter sits opposite the policeman. "Look," he says, "you keep coming by here asking my mother about Kyle. What more can she tell you? She's told you everything she knows."

"Well, I've got Uncle Sam asking lots of questions." He looks over at Regina, who sits in the rocking chair. "This Lieutenant Bennett seems to think Kyle blew out of town to avoid being charged with assault."

"That sounds like Kyle," Walter says.

"Well," Garafolo acknowledges, "he *does* have a record of assault right here in Brown's Mill. And I've suspected all along that the girlfriend knows more than she's saying."

"So go after her," Wally says. "I saw her yesterday at CVS. She had suitcases in the backseat of Kyle's car. She was clearly heading out of town."

"Do you know where she was going, Mrs. Day?"

"To the city. She's going to become a model."

"Isn't it the navy's job to find out what happened to one of their guys?" Walter stands suddenly, looking over at Officer Garafolo in a very strange way, as if he's challenging him. Regina watches her son in fascination. He has exactly the same glint in his eye Robert would sometimes get, when he was angry and was going to show someone he meant business. "I *mean*," Walter is saying, "it's one of their boys who's gone missing. Isn't it up to *them* to find him?"

"Maybe he's not missing," Garafolo says, holding Walter's gaze. "Maybe he's dead. And if somebody killed him here in Brown's Mill, well, then it's *my* job to find out who."

"*Dead*?" Walter seems outraged, infuriated. "You think he's *dead*?"

The policeman shrugs, looking over at Regina. "What do you think, Mrs. Day?" She twiddles the button at her throat but doesn't speak.

He was lying right there on the couch. Right where you're sitting. I came in from the garden and picked up the hoe and smashed it down into his head. The hoe or the shovel. Or maybe the rake. I smashed it down into his head once, then again, then I think a third time as he tried to get up. He staggered into the coffee table. He died right there and there was a lot of blood.

"He had a lot of enemies in this town," Garafolo says when Regina doesn't answer. "I suspect he was dealing drugs. There are a lot of scenarios I could come up with."

And then I dragged his body out of the living room and down to the basement where I put him in a crate—no, not a crate—in the shed—I dragged him out the door and put him in the shed—no, no, no, the shed is empty. The shed is empty. The shed is empty . . .

Garafolo lets out a sigh and stands. "Well, if you remember anything, or if you hear from the girlfriend, please let me know." He trains his eye on Regina. "Do you mind if I just look around a bit, Mrs. Day?"

Walter moves up behind him quickly. "You have a search warrant?"

The policeman smiles pleasantly. "I just wanted to look around. If the lady says no, I'll leave."

"I'm not sure what you're looking for," Regina says. "You've already looked around several times before."

"Yeah," Walter says. "I think enough is enough. You ought to go."

The policeman levels his eyes with her son's. "Okay, whatever you say." He pauses, still holding Walter's gaze. "So, buddy. You ever get your life straightened out?"

Walter frowns. "What do you mean by that?"

Regina is watching them, but her mind is somewhere else.

Where is he? Where is Kyle?

"Just that I remember all that drama from way back . . ."

Why must I always be so fearful of phantoms hiding somewhere in my house?

"Yeah, well, thanks for asking," Walter is saying, "I got it straightened out just fine."

I dragged him downstairs and—

Dear God! I dragged him downstairs—I did! I dragged him downstairs!

Walter has gotten so close to the policeman that it looks as if he might punch him. "And you know what, Garafolo?" he's saying. "I'm still a big, flaming, cocksucking homo."

"Dear God," Regina says, and she faints, dead away, onto the floor.

When Regina was a girl, living with Papa, there was a man who lived in the attic apartment of their building on Pleasant Street. His name was John Neumann. He was about fifty years old and had never married. Papa called him an old Jew fairy, but whenever Papa would go out it was to Mr. Neumann that he'd send Regina and Rocky to stay. Papa said that Mr. Neumann was the one man in Brown's Mill he could trust with his two sweet, pretty, young daughters. He'd wink when he told friends that. Regina never understood what that wink meant, but she knew she liked Mr. Neumann very much.

"Are you all right, Regina?" he would ask her, every time they stayed with him. "Are you sure?"

"Yes," she'd insist. "I'm fine."

It was early one Saturday morning and they'd been there all night. Papa hadn't come home. He was supposed to have been gone just an hour but he never showed up to collect them. So Mr. Neumann had fixed them each a bed of blankets and pillows on his living room floor. In the morning he made them corn flakes and rye toast with raspberry jam.

"She's *not* all right," Rocky told Mr. Neumann.

All night Regina had been crying. She wasn't sure why. She'd just started to cry around 2:00 a.m. and had kept on crying straight until dawn.

"What troubles you, Regina?" Mr. Neumann asked her.

"I was just afraid I was alone."

"But Rocky was right there next to you. And I was in the other room."

"I know."

Mr. Neumann had looked so sad sitting there across the table from her. "Maybe you should talk to one of your teachers."

"*Tell him*," Rocky urged, kicking her sister under the table.

"I'm *fine*," Regina insisted.

"She's not fine," Rocky said.

Mr. Neumann just continued looking sadly at her.

It was around that time that the people came and took them away from Papa for a while, sending them to stay with Aunt Selma and Uncle Axel. Regina can't remember how old she was then. Ten, eleven, twelve. Maybe thirteen. So much of their time with Papa is a vague blur to her. But she knows they didn't stay long with Aunt Selma. It was a problem of school districts, she thinks: Aunt Selma and Uncle Axel lived too far outside town and there was no way of getting them to school. So they went back to live with Papa, and there they stayed until they ran away to the city to become famous.

"And we would have been, too—"

"Would have been what, Mrs. Day?"

Regina blinks. Officer Garafolo's big bushy mustache is twitching in her face. She's on the couch. Walter sits beside her.

"Are you all right, Mother?"

"Did I faint? Oh, dear, how silly of me."

Walter's looking down at her. She can't tell what he's thinking. He seems annoyed. Or concerned. Or maybe a little guilty. Then he moves his eyes over to the policeman.

"She's on some new medications," he says.

Regina watches as her son stands and walks with Garafolo toward the door. They're whispering about something, hard, angry whispers, but she can't hear what they're saying. Still, she can tell that Walter is defending her, coming to her defense, standing between her and that fat, smelly policeman and his unending questions, questions that have made her feel as if she was losing her mind.

That's why I called him. That's why I called Walter and asked him to come home. Because he's my son. Because sons take care of their mothers.

That is, if mothers take care of them.

Did she take care of her son?

He was my responsibility. Did I take care of him?

Of course she had. She made him Swedish goulash for dinner. She bought him school clothes and comic books. She made him that witch's costume, even though Robert was so opposed to the idea. She washed Walter's underwear, even when it was fouled with blood and other things she could barely allow herself to imagine. She let him watch that vampire soap opera even though Bernadette insisted it could warp his mind. She let Walter do whatever he wanted, and every night before he went to bed, she always made sure he brushed his teeth.

Of *course* she took care of him.

"Mother," Walter says, sitting back down beside her again once the policeman is gone. "Maybe it's time you told me about Kyle."

She blinks. "Kyle?"

"Yes. Kyle."

They say nothing for a moment, just holding each other's gaze.

"When was the last time you saw him?" Walter asks.

"I—I'm not sure . . ."

"*Think*, Mother!"

Her son's voice frightens her. It's cold and hard. Like Robert's.

It was graduation day, wasn't it? The last time she saw Kyle? Eighth grade graduation from St. John the Baptist, and Walter was receiving an award from Sister Angela. Oh, how handsome Walter had looked in his beige corduroy suit and green tie. Regina had been right there, snapping the camera, because Robert would want to see the pictures. He'd pass them around the ship, saying, "Here's my son. My son, the future admiral."

But there was commotion in the back of the auditorium. It was Kyle and his friends—and they were drunk! Drunk, at age twelve! And they were urinating— urinating! Right there, in front of the whole school. All over the floor of the auditorium. Sister Angela had screamed and Father Carson had run down the aisle, but it was too late. The children had all seen, and Walter's award ceremony was ruined. Kyle was expelled after that. Poor Bernadette was a wreck by then, drunk all the time herself. Regina can't remember if that's when Albert shipped Kyle off to the military academy, but that was it. The end of Kyle. They didn't have to see him again after that.

Except he came back. Kyle came back . . .

"Mother, you've got to concentrate."

She blinks, looking into Walter's eyes.

"When was the last time you saw Kyle?"

She puts a hand to her head. "I—don't remember—"

He turns away from her, swearing under his breath.

He hates me, she thinks. *My son hates me.*

"Mommy," he's asking as he sits with her in the dirt of her rock garden, "who do you love more, me or Daddy?"

Neither one of you, a queer little voice in her head says all at once. But she pushes it away. "Oh, Walter," she says instead, "what a thing to ask."

Of course she loved her son. That was nonsense.

That night, the night after he'd asked her that question, she had looked at herself in the mirror, studying the lines around her eyes. The house was so quiet. She liked it when it was quiet like this. Walter was asleep and Robert was on the ship. It would be months before he returned. She could sleep late, she could sing as she washed the dishes, she could start watching her afternoon soaps again. Funny how even after weeks away she could tune in to them and still under- stand everything. *Not like life*, Regina thought, studying her eyes—but that's what made the soaps so much fun to watch.

On *The Guiding Light*, for example, the last time she'd tuned in, Bill Bauer had been cheating on his wife, Bertha. Poor Bert had found a lady's hat on the couch, with a veil and a flower in it, and she knew *very well* what was happening inside the other room.

Has Robert ever cheated on me? Regina asked herself, stretching the skin on her forehead, making it taut, the way it had been when she was young. She'd never really considered the idea before. It was silly. There was no one to cheat with on the ship. It was all men. And when Robert was home, he was here, in this house, every single night.

Every single night.

Regina laughed a little, looking at herself. *It might be nice if he cheated*, she thought, scandalizing herself for being so naughty. *It would get him out of the house.* She covered her mouth as she laughed some more.

Why had there been no other children? No little girl? Robert had wanted another child. He would look at Walter playing jump rope with the girls instead of tag with the boys and he'd say, "Let's get it right next time." Robert wanted a different kind of boy, when of course what Regina wanted was a girl.

He ruined it for me, Regina thought, her hands dropping to her abdomen. *He tore me open and the doctor said that was it, no more children.*

Of course, that hadn't stopped Robert from trying; he never believed what doctors said anyhow. But Regina knew it would be impossible. She'd have no girls. Only the boy.

She suddenly felt very sad for Walter, the little boy she hardly knew sleeping in the next room, his poster of H. R. Pufinstuf on the wall. She got up from her mirror and tiptoed down the corridor. Slipping into the boy's room, she stood over his bed, looking down. The sheet across his tiny chest rose and fell with every short breath he took.

"I don't know about boys," Regina whispered in the dark. "I don't know what you're supposed to be or what I'm supposed to do. If you were a girl, I'd know. I'd dress you up real pretty, the way Mama dressed Rocky and me. I'd take you for ballet lessons and teach you how to sew. If you had been a girl, everything would have been so much better for everybody."

He cooed in his sleep, turning over onto his side.

"You would have been your father's little princess and I would have tied beautiful ribbons in your hair." She paused, looking down at him. "But you're a boy, and I don't know about boys."

His mother reached down to touch his soft little face. "But still. You're a good boy, Walter. You're a good boy."

And with that, she tiptoed out of his room.

He's not leaving, her son. Not yet.

She spoons some Swedish goulash onto a plate for him. She'd made it special for him. He sits at the kitchen table, not saying very much.

"Ketchup," she says. "You'll want ketchup." She turns to Jorge. "Will you bring out the ketchup? Walter likes ketchup on his goulash."

Jorge eyes Walter with a little jealousy. He's not sure about this strange man who barked at him, who's sitting now slumped in a chair at the table, eating the meal Missa usually made for him. But he obeys Regina, who smiles as she watches the boy.

"I'm so glad you decided to stay and have supper with us, Walter," she says, as she sits down at the table herself. "Eat up now. I know this is your favorite."

Walter takes a bite. He can't help but offer a little smile.

"You see?" Regina beams. "You remember now how good it tastes. Do you ever make it for yourself in the city?"

"No," he says. "I've never made it for myself."

"Do you remember, Walter, how we would sit eating my goulash on TV trays in the living room, watching *Match Game PM?* How we used to laugh, you and I, when Brett Somers and Charles Nelson Reilly started carrying on?"

He laughs, almost despite himself. "Yes, I remember."

They're quiet. Walter seems to consider saying something, stops, then finally goes ahead. "I've worked with him, you know," he says. "Charles Nelson Reilly. He's a brilliant acting teacher."

Regina can't speak for a moment. "You've worked with *Charles Nelson Reilly?* Oh, Walter! *Really?*"

He doesn't answer. He seems embarrassed, as if he wished he hadn't told her. He just brings another forkful of goulash to his mouth, then puts his head back and closes his eyes as he chews.

Jorge is standing at Regina's side, looking up at her with his big brown eyes, feeling forgotten. She pats her lap, and he gratefully climbs up.

"I can't get over it," Luz had told her. "How he's taken to you. He's usually so afraid of people."

Regina looks down into the little boy's face.

"Push him down if he gets too heavy," Luz would add. "He can be like a dog, just sleeping in your lap all night if you let him."

"You're not too heavy, are you, Jorge?" Regina asks.

She looks up. Walter is staring at her cradling the boy.

"Thank you for supper, Mother," he says abruptly, standing up, "but I've got to go."

"Oh, Walter, you're not going for good, are you?" She tries to stand, but Jorge remains insistent in her lap. He is indeed too heavy for her to budge.

Walter stands over her. "I don't know. Let me just say good-bye now in case I'm not able to stop back—"

Regina feels terribly desolate all of a sudden. "Are you still going to see—*him?*"

Her son's face tightens. "You mean Alexander Reefy?"

Regina nods.

"Yes, I'm still going to see *him*, Mother. That's why I came back to Brown's Mill."

"It wasn't because I called you?"

"Goddamn it, Mother!" Walter seems to snap, the way Robert used to snap, his emotions suddenly shooting across the room and ricocheting against the wall. "No, not because you called me! What—do you think you can just call me and then make me some Swedish goulash and I'll just forget all about the past? You think you can just suck me into your life and your dramas and make me *care*?"

"Walter, I—"

"Why *should* I care? Why should I care what some goddamn homophobic cop thinks about you? Why should I care what happened to that asshole Kyle? Why should I give a damn when you never did? Not once, Mother! Not once did you care about what. happened to me when I was growing up! Not *once!*"

"Oh, Walter, please, you were always such a good boy—"

But he's paying no attention to her. He rushes out of the kitchen. Regina can hear the front door slam as he leaves.

She starts to cry.

She sits there, crying almost as hard as she had the night Luz left. She forgets all about the little boy sitting in her lap.

A little boy who eventually reaches up with his sticky hands and places them against Regina's cheeks.

She looks down at him.

"You're a good boy," she says, between her tears, "aren't you, Jorge?"

He smiles a gap-toothed grin up at her.

Regina pulls him close.

"I had a little boy once," she says, rocking him in her arms. "He was a good boy. Just like you. He was a very good boy."

19

IT'S GOING TO BE GRAND

The day after Schaefer's Shoes closed its doors for the last time, Wally let the world find out what he'd been doing with Alexander Reefy in the orchards.

The little shoe store just couldn't compete with the brand new Shoe Town that had opened up on North Washington, next to the new Burger King with the giant playground. "There's a big parking lot out there," Wally's mother would say, by way of explanation, as if parking lots could explain the entire world. His father, meanwhile, blamed Jimmy Carter and the A-rabs.

Standing in front of his house, Wally dreads going inside. He just stands there on the sidewalk looking at the front door, his bookbag slung over his shoulder. What will his father be like today? What will he do? Yesterday had been very bad. The store was gone, he was out of work, they were all going to end up on the street. Wally hopes his father has gotten so drunk that he's fallen asleep in his La-Z-Boy.

Finally he works up the courage to go inside. His father is sitting wide awake on the couch, not moving, not speaking, just staring into the air.

"Don't say anything to him," Wally's mother whispers. "Just go to your room and pray, Walter. Just pray."

Pray for what? For Shoe Town to get struck by lightning? For Jimmy Carter to resign? For the A-rabs to give us free oil? Wally closes his door and lights up a cigarette. Newports. His parents have begun to suspect he smokes in his room but can never prove it. He keeps the window cracked and aims the smoke outside, an incense stick burning at all times to cover up the smell.

It's raining. Or maybe that's just how Wally will come to remember it, because his life is about to become a drizzly blur, a damp mist shrouding everything he does.

"You're going to end up like your cousin Kyle if you don't change your ways," his guidance counselor had scolded him.

"What am I doing that's so wrong?" he'd challenged back at him.

"Wally, you once were the most promising student in Brown's Mill. You could have had your pick of colleges. But you're barely passing chemistry and sure to fail trigonometry. The only class you've got decent grades for is art history. Face it, Wally, you can't make much of a career as an art historian."

And why not? So Wally breezed through his classes, sometimes stoned from a morning joint, pilfered from Missy's house when she wasn't looking. School *sucked*. He had no friends left at all: David Schnur had transferred over to Mayville after a particularly savage beating by a group of seniors outside the gymnasium. They claimed he was spying on them in their jockstraps in the locker room. Some of the teachers actually acted as if they thought David deserved what he got.

"David Schnur was a cocksucking faggot," Freddie Piatrowski told him. "I *know*. I caught him once with some kid out behind the bleachers."

"No way," Wally said. "You really saw him with another guy?"

"Oh, yeah. Sitting real close together. Him and some guy. Talking like they were little faggot girlfriends." Freddie had scowled. "You ought to be glad he's gone, Wally. Hanging around with him only made *you* a faggot, too."

Might he have stood a chance at that moment? Might there have been a opportunity for redemption? Later, Wally would remember that conversation with Freddie: did he miss his last shot at a normal life? With David gone, might he have regained his old friends, been accepted back into his old world?

No, not so long as Zandy remained in the picture.

For the moment, however, Wally remained too obsessed about the identity of the boy David had been making out with to really ponder anything else. So there was *another* gay kid in Brown's Mill? Fucking David Schnur. He'd never admitted that he was gay. Sure, Wally had kept his secret from David, too. But David—clueless David—keeping a secret from *him*?

It was good he was gone. What kind of a friend was he? Lying, sneaking around? What kind of a world had Wally fallen into for the last few years? They were all sneaks and liars, every single one of them—including Zandy. In a world of shadows and half-truths Wally had chosen to live, forfeiting his place among his peers.

Once upon a time, Wally had liked school. But now he hates it, hates the snide remarks of his classmates as he stands at his locker, hates the mocking in the cafeteria, hates the fact that he's a dreg, an outsider, a faggot. He dreads every morning that his mother comes in to wake him for school, raising the shades and calling out her cheery "Good morning, Walter!" as if she's fucking Carol Brady. *That's where any resemblance to the perfect mother ends*, Wally thinks bitterly. *That stupid "Good morning." It ends right there.*

"I want to go to the city *now*," he told Zandy a couple of weeks ago. "I gotta get out of school."

"Like you could make it in the city as a high school dropout."

Zandy sounded like his goddamn father. Wally exploded. "I'm going to be an *actor*! I don't need a diploma! I have *talent*! I did *Look Back in Anger* last spring!"

"Listen to you, James Dean."

"James Dean was gay, too," Wally said.

"Like that has anything to do with all the tea in China."

Wally stood before him, defiant. "So what happened to all your great promises, huh? They all *talk*? Everything was gonna be grand, you said."

"Babe, you've got to have a little patience. You've only just turned *fifteen*."

Wally fumed. "My drama teacher told me she'd never seen a student with so much talent. To do Osborne at my age and make it convincing—"

But Zandy wasn't really listening. He was too intent on filling up his pipe with grass. Fucking zone head. Space cadet.

When had it changed?

The very last completely happy time Wally could remember with Zandy was a night shortly after Halloween, when they'd hiked up into the orchards and filled two baskets with the picked-over apples.

"Miss Aletha taught me a secret a long time ago, when I first came to Brown's Mill," Zandy said—and it struck Wally that he hadn't known that Zandy came from anyplace else. Why anyone would *choose* to come to Brown's Mill was beyond his grasp, but Zandy seemed happy enough.

"What secret?" Wally asked.

"The secret is in these apples." Zandy was picking off the misshapen fruit from the branches. "Everybody leaves them behind. But they're the sweetest of the bunch, and they're free."

He was right: they *were* sweet. They picked as many as they could find, stumbling in the dark, shivering and laughing and biting into the hard sweet fruit, oblivious to the threat of worms or the chance of being discovered. They went back to Zandy's house and baked Miss Aletha a pie and Wally still remembers how she cried, the mascara running down her cheeks, and that was the last completely happy time he ever had with Zandy and his friends.

He exhales his cigarette smoke in rings, watching them float out the window. His mother thinks he's praying in here.

His mother is a fool.

"Why aren't you in any sports?" his father would shout at him. "Why don't you have any girlfriends? Why are you always hanging around with the riffraff in Dogtown?"

His father knew the answers to those questions. Wally could see it in his eyes. And his mother's face simply went tight, abandoning Wally to anything his father wanted to imagine.

"Sometimes I want to forget it," he told Miss Aletha.

"Forget what?"

"Being gay. Just forget all about it."

She laughed. "Do you think that's possible?"

"Why not? I'm an actor. I can be anything I want to be."

"I suppose you could." She gave him a look that said he was being foolish but that she loved him anyway. "You could act anything but sooner or later you'd get tired of acting, I suspect."

"No, I wouldn't. I never get tired of acting."

"You're in high school," she said, leaning in across the table at him. "I understand what's going on for you, Wally. I went through it myself. Figured what the hell, I've got a penis—or what's left of it—so I might as well *try* to live as a boy. I figured it was easier to do that than to keep squawking about it, trying to get the damn thing cut off, getting my parents all riled up and the kids in school all in a dither, picking on me, beating me up." She sat back in her chair. "You're tired of being an outsider. You want to fit in. Who doesn't, Wally? Who doesn't?"

He stares out the window. When the flamers get picked on or pushed around in school, he never says a word. He hates those kids; he isn't like them; they really *do* deserve what they get. Even David Schnur, out there snuggling under the bleachers with some boy—*who? Fucking who?* Wally really wants to know. It's just as well now that he hadn't intervened during David's beating. Why implicate himself? He's glad David is gone. Being friends with David had ruined him in the eyes of his old friends. Once he'd had *lots* of friends. He remembers how it used to be: sleeping over Freddie's, hanging out with him and Michael and Philip, sneaking peeks at slimy old issues of *Penthouse* in the abandoned factories. This gay stuff had cost him everything. And David—duplicitous David—was hardly a friend worth defending. So Wally's glad he did nothing. Instead, he'd just leaned against the gym in his tattered denim jacket, smoking his cigarettes, watching the jocks kick his former friend around as if he were a soccer ball.

"He deserved it for being such a flamer," Wally says now, peering out the crack of his window and watching it rain.

A pouring, driving rain.

At least, that's the way he'll always remember it.

"I knew my father would follow," Wally would tell Miss Aletha, years later. "It's like I wanted to blow up my whole world—my parents, Zandy, myself."

On the day after his father lost his job, Wally finally can't stand being pent up in his room any longer and strides out of the house into the rain. When he passes his father in the living room, the older man stirs from his position on the couch, like a bear awakening from hibernation. He follows his son outside, watching as he heads down the road. Wally watches him out of the corner of his eye. He sees his father get into his car and back it out of the driveway. His father drives very slowly and deliberately, because Wally *walks* all the way to Zandy's house—bikes were for faggots, after all—and yes, it definitely *is* raining, because Wally will always remember how cold and damp he is when he finally arrives.

Without knocking he walks into the little red brick house. Zandy comes into the room wearing just his boxer shorts. He's freshly showered, the hair on his chest all alive and shiny and not at all matted.

"Hey, babe, what's up?"

That's when Wally hears his father behind him. He's shouting, "We're going to have you arrested, you pervert!"

"What the—"

"You filthy pervert! You filthy stinking pervert!"

Wally's father grabs his son by the back of the shirt. Wally doesn't try to break free.

"Hey man, let him go!" Zandy cries. "Don't hurt him—"

"Don't *you* tell me what I can and can't do with my own goddamn son!" His father drags Wally out of the house, pushing him down Zandy's front steps. He looms over him, thrusting his finger into his face. "Tell me the truth! Have you been having sex with that pervert?"

Wally feels curiously detached, as if this is all a movie, a fantasy in his head. "Yes," he says, "I've had sex with him."

His father smacks him then, right across the face, right there in front of Zandy's house, in front of a gathering group of kids. Zandy tries to stop him, but then Wally's father hits Zandy too, and Wally will always remember Zandy's mouth bleeding and Bertrand running out of the house and down the street, his hands fluttering, his parakeet escaping. Wally's father grabs his son by the hair and shoves him into the car. Wally is unemotional as his nose begins to bleed and his father starts the ignition.

"Don't hurt him!" Zandy shouts, running after the car. "Don't you dare fucking hurt him!"

And that's the last glimpse Wally has of him: running after the car shirtless, in his polka-dotted boxer underwear, with a bleeding mouth and wide-open eyes.

He doesn't have to face Zandy in court, because he's just fifteen and isn't required to testify in person. All he has to do is go down to the police station and tell Officer Garafolo the whole story, watching him eat his egg salad sandwich as he writes it all down. Then, when they get home, his father makes him repeat the story for his mother. Wally throws in a few extra details just for her, like how his ass bled when Zandy fucked him the first time and how she'd seen the blood in his Fruit of the Looms. Her face turns green, then white, and finally she passes out on the floor. Wally's actually glad about that, that he'd managed to get that much of a reaction out of her.

"Are you smoking in there?"

"So what if I am?"

"Open this goddamn door!"

"Fuck *you*. Bust through it if you're so goddamn strong!"

It feels amazing, taunting his father. Talking back, not being afraid. The other night his father had tried to smack him and Wally had caught his arm. Held it tight and twisted it a bit. He was nearly as tall as his old man now. He'd forced his father to back down.

"What's the matter?" Wally had spit at him, making Dad's knees buckle as he twisted his arm. "You only hit people weaker than you? You only pick fights with little boys and women? If a guy's too big, you back down. Is that why they kicked you out of the fucking navy? That why, big man?"

His father had made a lunge for him, breaking free, but Wally had slipped past him, getting to the safety of his room and sliding the lock into place, laughing all the while.

He clamps his earphones over his head and cranks up Zeppelin. Of course there'd been a scandal. The *Brown's Mill Reminder* wrote a huge story using Zandy's name and picture, and although Wally's identity wasn't revealed, everyone knew it was him. "You *are* a fucking fag," Freddie had said, cornering him in the cafeteria at school with a bunch of his friends from the track team. "You really *are* a fag, Wally Day!"

"Fuck you, Freddie."

Fuck 'em all, Wally thinks.

In my thoughts . . . I have seen . . . rings of smoke through the trees

And the voices of those who stand looking . . .

When things with his father got too bad, when they had a knock-down fight where Wally smashed his father's nose and his father knocked out a couple of Wally's teeth, Wally finally took off. He headed to Miss Aletha's. She was the only one Wally could go to. She accepted him in, no matter what he'd done, and somehow she got Wally's father to agree that he could stay with her for awhile, even though having his son staying with a transsexual probably only made things worse for him around town. But it was clear his father had had enough of his faggot son. Faggots belonged with freaks, he said. His father even started insisting that Wally wasn't his, that his real father must have been some guy named Sully, apparently a figure from Wally's mother's past that he had never heard her speak about. Then again, his mother had never spoken about much.

As for Zandy, he went to jail.

You little ballbuster, you.

Over the years Zandy would come and go from Wally's thoughts. A zoned-out hippie with a big furry chest and gnarled hands. *It was wrong what he did,* Wally would think, making love to Ned, his body so smooth, so young, so much like his own. *I didn't know what I was consenting to. I was too young. I was so fucked up. I didn't know who the fuck I was. It was wrong what he did.*

Long stretches of time would pass when Wally never thought of Zandy at all. After all, things happened so fast after he left home: he got accepted at drama school, his father hanged himself, Wally left Brown's Mill at long last for the city. The first day he arrived, he *did* think of Zandy, stepping out of the train station and looking around at all the people and the tall buildings and the flashing lights. *You'll see, babe. It's gonna be so different. It's gonna be like nothing you've ever seen before.*

And he thought of Zandy again the first time he and Ned went out to a gay bar and stayed out all night, dancing and fucking with strangers in the back room, smoking way too much dope and even snorting his first line of coke. He thought of Zandy then, wondering if he was still in prison or if he'd gotten out by now, trying to imagine for just the briefest of seconds what he looked like now, and if he'd gone back to live in the little red brick house.

Yet most of the time he never thought of Zandy at all. Wally was living his life. There was too much to do—too much to see, taste, and feel—to waste time sitting around, thinking about the past.

But Zandy had been right.

It sure as hell was grand.

20

COLIC

The baby is crying on the living room floor. Regina's trying to make a phone call but she keeps dropping the phone. Her hands go to her hair and she starts to whimper. She bends down and once more picks up the phone.

She's trying to call Bernadette.

"Operator. May I help you?"

Yes, help me. Help me please!

"May I help you please?"

"Yes," Regina manages to say. "Diamond. Diamond 64352."

The baby is screaming. He hasn't stopped crying since Robert went away.

Bernadette will know what to do. Bernadette has a baby the same age and he's a good baby. He never cries. He's a perfect child.

Why can't Walter be more like Kyle?

"I'm sorry. There's no answer."

Regina drops the phone again.

Oh, dear God—*why won't he stop crying???*

"Excuse me, might I have this dance?"

Regina looked up into the dark eyes of a handsome man in a blue navy uniform. His gold buttons were shining. Was he asking *her*? She blushed. No, not possible. He was so much younger than she was, and so handsome he could have any woman in the room. She looked over her shoulder, but there was no one behind her.

"He means you, Regina," Sully said to her.

"Me?"

"Yes," said the man in the navy uniform, smiling such a pearly smile of straight, even teeth. "I'm asking you."

"Oh, but—" Regina was caught by his eyes. "I'm here with Sully."

"Go ahead, Regina," Sully told her. "It's okay."

"Are you sure?" Regina asked. But the question wasn't posed to Sully. It was posed to the man in the navy uniform who was asking her to dance.

Sully was Betty's brother—Betty, her coworker from the mayor's office. Betty, who'd been trying to get her hitched forever. Betty, who was certain she and Sully would make a splendid pair. And they might have, Regina supposed, many years later, remembering the earnest fellow with the rosy cheeks and full lips. Nearly three hundred pounds Sully weighed, but he had a certain grace all his own.

"Sure, go on ahead," Sully had urged Regina, even giving her a smile. "Dance with him. It's okay by me."

Why does he cry so?

I've fed him. I've fed him and burped him and laid him down in his crib. But all he does is cry.

She's so weary. If only she could talk with Bernadette. Bernadette is very smart. She knows about babies.

"Bernadette has *no trouble* getting Kyle to sleep," Mother Day told her. "You just have to be *regular* with Walter, Regina. Feed him at the same time every day and put him down at the same time. Get him on a *schedule*."

The baby is crying where she left him, in the middle of the living room floor.

Regina looks around the room. Empty boxes are stacked against the wall and soiled diapers are piled in a heap, waiting for the washer. The Christmas tree still stands in the corner. It's beginning to slump.

Dear God. What time is it?

"Now, don't forget," Mother Day said when she called on the phone. "The ladies from the church will be at your house at noon sharp. Be a dear and tidy up a bit, will you? Do you have enough tea bags?"

Regina had been holding Walter then, jostling him in her right arm, cradling the phone between her ear and shoulder. "How many will there be?" she asked her mother-in-law.

"Oh, I don't know, dear. Lillian Mayberry, Jeanette McCarthy, Jetta Coughlin, myself . . . Three, four, I suppose, no more than five."

"No more than five," she repeated.

"The ladies are so looking forward to seeing little Walter. Of course, they've all seen Kyle several times now, but never Walter. Bernadette has had them over for tea *three times* now. You'll have him up and dressed?"

The baby was getting fussy and Regina felt a headache coming on. "I've got to go, Mother Day."

"Of course, Regina dear. You won't forget to tidy up, will you? I hate to be such an old nag, but you know Lillian Mayberry as well as I—and really, dear, it's not good to leave trash lying about. Attracts flies."

"Is he your boyfriend?"

"Sully? Oh, he's—no, he's—he's the brother of a lady I work with."

"Ah, yes." The navy man smiled. "That's where I've seen you. At the mayor's office."

"Yes." Regina smiled. "I work for Mayor Winslow."

"Good man. An old friend of my family." The navy man smiled. "I'm sorry. How rude I am. My name is Robert Day. Lieutenant Commander Robert Day, United States Navy."

"Oh." She couldn't stop blushing. "I'm Regina Gunderson."

"What a beautiful name. Is it Danish?"

"Swedish."

Lieutenant Day flashed that pearly grin at her. "I knew you were Scandinavian the moment I glanced across the room and saw you sitting there. You're so fair, you hardly have any eyebrows."

Regina stumbled awkwardly, nearly tripping over the man's feet.

"I'm sorry," she said. "I'm a terrible dancer."

"Not at all," he said. "It was completely my fault."

What was the music they were dancing to? Sinatra? Tony Bennett? She could never remember, but then something fast by the Four Seasons came on, so Lieutenant Day had escorted her off the dance floor, his hand on the small of her back. They headed over to the bar and he bought her a glass of wine. She drank it quickly. He ordered her another.

"So what do you do for Mayor Winslow?" Lieutenant Commander Day asked.

"I'm just a secretary."

"I'm sure it's exciting working for a politician."

She laughed. "Oh, not so . . . I just—"

His eyes were twinkling at her. "I imagine you get to see all his secret political papers and the like."

Regina had to look away he was so handsome. "Oh, no, I just type letters."

"Come now. Working for a big politician like Mayor Winslow must be very glamorous."

She laughed again. "Oh, no. It's just a job. I've been there almost eight years now."

They returned to the dance floor when something slow came back on. Regina was feeling heady from the wine. Lieutenant Day pulled her close to him and whirled her around.

"What were you saying about not being a good dancer? You're a regular Cyd Charisse."

"Oh!" Regina's face burned. "No, really, I'm not—"

He gave her a quick dip then pulled her back up to him and kissed her lightly on the nose. She was too stunned to say anything.

"Cyd Charisse, Leslie Caron, Ginger Rogers—baby, you've got 'em all beat."

"Really?"

"You could've been a Broadway dancer."

She laughed. "Well, I was a singer once—"

"Well," said Robert Day, "that settles it. I've got to see you again." He lowered his face very close to hers. "Because, baby, I want to hear you sing."

How was Regina to know then what she'd find out later? That the Days weren't old friends of Mayor Winslow. That they were Republicans, and the mayor was a Democrat, and they weren't friends at all, that they hated each other. How was Regina to know that the books she showed Robert would contain evidence of the mayor's embezzlement schemes? How was she to know that taking those books home with her would ultimately lead to the mayor's resignation?

That's why he asked me to dance. That's why.

"I've got to focus," she says. "The church ladies. It's almost noon."

They're Catholics. Oh, how Mormor had *hated* Catholics. *Papists*, she'd called them. *Roman idol worshippers.* As a girl, Regina had always been a little afraid of Catholics, with their statues and incense and all that muttering in Latin. But now she was one of them—at least on paper, because Mother Day had said it was the only way Robert could marry her. And Robert *had* to marry her, Mother Day insisted. After all, Regina was having his baby.

The same baby who keeps screaming now, who thrashes its little arms and legs in the middle of the living room floor. Regina picks at dried egg yolk on the kitchen table. It's getting under her fingernails. She sits down on a metal folding chair and pulls her bare feet up to look at the soles. They're black.

"Really, my dear, you need to keep the floor clean. It's unsanitary. When I was your age I already had two little babies and they could *eat off* my kitchen floor."

Regina closes her eyes.

"It's my duty, Regina. There's a war on. I've got to go."

She had gripped the lapels on his blue navy jacket. "But what about when I have the baby, Robert? I'll be all alone."

"I can't do it *for* you, Regina," he said. He was smiling. A joke. Of course he couldn't do it for her. Her body was swelling up. She was sick every morning. Soon the baby inside her would be forcing its way down through her insides. It would spread her open, rip her apart, so it could make its way into the world. Robert was right. No one could do this for her. She had to do it all by herself.

This is what happened when men touched you.

She hears Rocky screaming in agony. She had sat outside the room at Aunt Selma's house where her sister had had her baby. She remembers how Rocky screamed and screamed and screamed, until finally the doctor had to knock her out. Even still, after all that, Rocky's baby had been born dead.

But not Regina's.

Walter is very much alive. He lies there crying his heart out in the middle of the floor.

"You've got to be brave now," Robert said as he left her. "Can you do it? Can you be brave, Regina?"

She puts her hands to her ears to block out the crying.

What does he want from me?

"Isn't he precious?" Mother Day had said after he was born. "He looks just like my Robert. Don't you think so, Regina dear?"

Regina stands, moving into the archway between the kitchen and living room. She looks down at her crying baby. She wants to tell Mother Day that he isn't so precious. He's hateful. He cries to spite her. To spite all the agony she went through bringing him into this world. This goddamned world that sends fathers off to fight Communists and makes mothers take care of babies all by themselves.

Why had she let him touch her?

"Would you come back to my room with me," he had breathed in her ear, "before I head off to face certain death in the jungles of the Mekong?"

And then they'd had to get married. Mother Day was adamant about it. Insisted that Regina quit her job, leave her little apartment in Dogtown, abandon the church Mama had loved so much.

Little Walter continues to cry on the living room floor.

"*Stop it!*" Regina screams, but the noise only worsens.

He's all red now, Mother Day. He's shat his pants, too. Does he look like Robert now?

Lillian Mayberry had had a grandson who drowned in the backyard well. Bernadette had told Regina the whole tragic story. "Oh, it made everyone cry when it happened," Bernie said, bouncing her boy Kyle on her knee, Kyle who never cried, who smiled and hiccupped and went to sleep whenever she lay him down. "Don't you remember it, Regina?"

"No."

"Oh, maybe it happened while you were away in the hospital."

"It was a spa."

"Well, whatever. The story of the poor little Mayberry boy was all over town. The poor child had fallen down there one afternoon while he was playing. His mother was only a few yards away, hanging clothes on the line. The whole town came out for that funeral. All the ladies were crying."

Regina can see them, hear them.

"Such a sweet little boy."

"A darling."

"An angel."

Regina's not so sure.

Maybe Teddy Mayberry was a monster. Maybe his mother pushed him.

Regina's looking at little Walter, but she's thinking of Lillian Mayberry's grandson down there in the well, his face all blue and puffy.

"You should feed him at the same time every day, Regina, and get him on a regular schedule. Otherwise, the crying will never stop."

The crying will never stop.

"Wait, don't."

"What's the matter, Regina? Don't you like it?"

"Don't," she said.

Robert just laughed.

"I'm—I'm not what you think—"

He laughed again. "So it's not your first time? As if it's mine. Just lie back, Regina. Just lie back."

"No, don't—"

"I said lie back!"

Her baby's little fists are clenching the air. Regina's fists are pounding her temples. Her eyes are closed and she's leaning against the refrigerator listening to him cry in the other room.

I can't do it for you, Regina.

"I—I'm so tired," she had said to Mother Day last week.

Her mother-in-law was fretting over the crib. "We never had colic in our family. Were you like this as a child, Regina dear?"

Little Walter begins shrieking, the loudest cries yet. How can so much noise come from so little a creature? Regina suddenly pounces on the radio and turns it up full blast. She sings along with Martha and the Vandellas. *"There'll be music swaying and records playing—"*

Her baby screams higher to compete with her. She sings as loudly as she can. *"Dancin' in the street! Oh—wohhhh!"*

"Oh, my dear, one other thing. The Christmas tree. You know it really should have come down by the Feast of the Epiphany. You know how the ladies from the church can be."

Regina's trying to remember what time Mother Day and her church ladies are supposed to be here. She can't see the clock. The crying is getting in the way.

"Robert," she'd begged, "let me go stay with Bernadette."

"My brother and his wife have their own baby, Regina. You can't keep running to them."

"Or—then—someone—"

Aunt Selma? No, Aunt Selma and Uncle Axel were angry at her for marrying a Catholic. Uncle Axel had called her a Papist whore. Betty? No, Betty had never forgiven her for what happened to Mayor Winslow.

"Now, Regina, stay right here," Robert had said to her. "My mother can help you out, but you've got to start learning how to take care of yourself. You have a child now, Regina. You're just going to have to learn to be responsible for the first time in your life."

She's back to standing in the doorway of the living room. The Christmas tree slouches in the corner. It's brown and almost bare, its needles covering the floor. Boxes lie scattered underneath its branches, brightly colored paper crumpled in heaps. The baby screams as he writhes among the needles.

"I'll be home as soon as I can, Regina. Take care of my son. Tell him all about me. Tell him I'm making our country safe for him to grow up in, that I'm off making sure he can grow up proud and free."

Regina walks over to the baby in the middle of the living room. He screams at her feet. She looks down. For a moment the child opens his tiny blue eyes and stares up at her. She stares back, silent.

"Regina, dear, you cannot allow that child to sit in a soiled diaper. That can cause severe irritation. Imagine what it would be like to sit in your own bowel movement for hours at a time."

Can you do it? Can you be brave, Regina?

Otherwise the crying will never stop.

She starts to inhale and exhale very fast, pushing herself over to the window, where she looks out and sees nothing: no day, no night. There is only whiteness, a cold whiteness, like snow gusted up against the window. There is nothing outside. And in here: there is only the crying.

Why won't he stop?

She staggers back to the tree, brushing against a lifeless branch. Dry brown needles scatter to the floor.

"Concentrate on the task at hand," she tells herself, remembering what they had taught her at the spa. "First thing. Take down the tree . . ."

The baby cries in uncompleted, tearless gasps. His face is purple.

Regina removes one, then two, ornaments from the tree. She wraps them carefully in newspaper and places them in a box. But then she drops the third ornament, a silver angel, the only one left from the ones Mama used to hang. She'd brought them over from Sweden. It smashes on the floor.

"No," Regina says.

There's a moment of stillness so deep, so terrible, even the crying cannot penetrate.

And then she turns, swinging her arms, whipping off icicles and stars and hurling them across the room like a firestorm in the night sky. She stomps on top of old red balls, delighting in their fragility, the ease with which they crumble into dust under her bare feet. She ignores the pain, the sharp glass piercing into the soles of her feet. She lunges at the tree, pushing it over. It falls on top of her baby. He screams.

"Let *me* cry, too!" she shouts at him. "*Let me cry, too!*"

She stares down at her baby writhing between the bare brown branches of the tree, his purple face scratched and bleeding.

"Oh, he's so small," she says softly, almost a whisper.

So small.

She looks over at the couch.

And the pillows so big . . .

Her hands are in her hair again. She's screaming. Mother Day is pushing her, shoving her hard, screaming back at her. The church ladies are picking up the baby. Now they're handing him to Mother Day.

Go ahead! Take him! Raise him! Turn him into another Robert!

Mother Day jostles the screaming baby in one arm and dials the phone frantically with the other. Regina flops down onto the couch and puts her hands over her face. She sits that way, not moving, not speaking, not thinking, until the crying has finally stopped.

It's left to Lillian Mayberry to sweep up the broken glass.

21

THE SECRET

"*You* act as if you think she killed him."

Wally wants to punch the son of a bitch. Has for *years*. Wants to haul off and smack him, right here, right at his desk, right in his big, fat, foul-smelling face.

"What I think doesn't matter," Sergeant Garafolo tells him, shrugging, and goddamn it if he isn't eating again, this time a jelly donut, with powdered sugar all over his mustache. "The navy thinks he skipped town to beat an assault charge. Can't argue with Uncle Sam."

"But still you'd like to search my mother's house." Garafolo stares up at him from his desk. "Yeah. I would." "Okay." Wally's seething, and it shows. "Let me get this straight. Despite the fact that my cousin nearly bludgeoned some guy to death, despite the fact that he has a long history of disciplinary problems in the navy, despite the fact that he could be facing a long stretch in jail, you still think his disappearance is totally unconnected to all that. You think, instead, that his senile old aunt who can barely lift a bag of groceries killed him and stuffed his body in a closet."

A small, tight smile dares to move across Garafolo's face. "All I said, *Walter*, is that I'd like to do a search of her house. That's all."

"Why haven't you gone after the girlfriend? I tell you, she was—"

"We *did* go after her. And indeed there was a report from her father that she was seen driving off with somebody who fit the description of Kyle. The father couldn't *swear* it was Kyle in the car, but it might have been." He shrugs. "Probably was."

"So there. You've got it."

"But when the girl was questioned in the city, she claimed it was her cousin she was with. Some cousin who's helping her get a job as a model." Garafolo sighs. A glob of jelly drops from his donut onto whatever official form he'd been reading at his desk. "Fuck," he says, dabbing at the jelly with a napkin.

"Look," Wally says, "I've been in my mother's house several times over the last few days. If he was there, dead or alive, I'd have *seen* something." A terrible memory shoots through his head. "*Smelled* something, if he was dead."

"I've signed off on the case," Garafolo tells him irritably, not looking up at him, still wiping jelly off the document on his desk. "I've turned it all over to Uncle Sam. If I had my way, sure, we'd be doing a search of your mother's house. But the navy thinks they know the answer."

"Well," Wally says, "in this case, they do."

There's nothing more to say. He stands there watching Garafolo make the stain on the paper even worse.

Why had he come here? What was the point?

Stalling again, that's why. Stalling, when he had other business to attend to. Much more important business—which he would do, *finally*, and then hightail it out of Brown's Mill. He'd stayed in this goddamn hellhole far too long.

So why had he wasted even more time coming to the police station?

Because of his mother. That's why.

It's always my mother, deep down.

She was the reason he'd come back to Brown's Mill in the first place. He'd told her she wasn't, but she was. He came back because his mother had called him. She'd been upset. This fucking asshole right here, stinkface Garafolo, was upsetting her.

I think I may be losing my mind.

Wally heads out of the police station without any further word to the fat smelly cop. He hurries down the hallway toward the front door, his footsteps echoing curiously above him in the high, vaulted ceiling of the station.

Just as they had that day.

"Tell your story, the whole story, you little pervert," his father had said.

That's why I came here. I'm retracing my steps, only backward. Miss Aletha's house. The police station.

And now Zandy.

Wally steps outside into the overcast day. The people of Brown's Mill are milling about, walking up and down the sidewalk, their faces as gray as the sky. They bump into him, brush his shoulders as they pass, but never make contact with his eyes.

Wally stands still, unable to walk any further.

This morning Dee had given him a hearty wave and salute, as if nothing had happened. He was off to school, he announced to Missy, and afterward he'd be at the arcade downtown, hanging with his "peeps." No sign of conflict, no sign of turmoil in his young, unlined, carefree face. Wally had watched as the boy bounded down the steps and hopped astride his bike, pedaling off into the morning.

"Wally Day?"

He moves his eyes to the man suddenly standing beside him. A bald, paunchy man reeking of bacon grease and burned coffee, a stained, tattered apron beneath his overcoat.

"Freddie?" Wally asks. "Freddie Piatrowski?"

"Yeah," the man says, and they shake hands.

But what do they say? No words are needed. Wally knows it all without Freddie having to offer a syllable: he's getting off the breakfast shift at the Big Boy, where he's worked as a cook for the past ten, eleven, maybe twelve years. He has a wife—no, he's divorced by now—with several kids, one of whom Wally is certain is retarded, just like Freddie's sister Helen. He knows all this just by looking at Freddie, and he believes every bit of it's true.

"Visiting your mother, Wally?" Freddie asks. 'That why you're here?"

"Yeah," Wally says. "That's why I'm here."

Freddie nods. "You still an actor, Wally? I've seen you on TV, you know. That movie with the gal from the soap operas. What's her name? You know who I mean."

"Yeah," Wally tells him. "I know who you mean."

"So you still doing that? Acting?"

"Yeah," Wally says. "I'm still acting."

Freddie smiles awkwardly. That's all. That's all they'll say.

I wanted to marry him. Told everyone in my kindergarten class that he was the person I would marry someday.

"Well, good to see ya, Wally," Freddie says.

"Yeah," Wally tells him. "Good to see you, too."

Freddie hurries on past him, glancing up at the sky to see if it's going to rain.

Wally stands riveted to the spot. He turns toward the corner of Main and Washington, where poor Dicky Trout staggers down the street, drunk as a skunk at ten in the morning. A few yards past him cadaverous old Mr. Smoke leans against a parking meter, a cigarette dangling from his thin blue lips, still not dead from lung cancer after all these years. A bit of commotion in the crosswalk makes Wally look: a woman is scolding an overweight teenage boy. Could it really be Ann Marie Adorno, she of the big pimply tits and tight sweaters in high school, now devolved into a shrill, pop-eyed mother of a fat, belligerent son?

Wally stands there, caught by the scenes around him. The people of Brown's Mill go about their day, glancing up at the sky now and then to check for rain. But they never look at each other, and the lost, bewildered man who lingers on the sidewalk never even gets a glance.

Had there ever been anything good about this place?

The Palace Theater. It had been good, Wally thinks. So much more majestic than that little Cine 1 and 2. The Palace had closed when Wally was nine, but he remembers sitting in the cobwebby old balcony eating popcorn and watching *Beneath the Planet of the Apes*. That was good. That was a good memory.

And the factories. They were the ruins of Mordor for him, and Wally was Aragorn, or sometimes the elf princess Arwen. Or else they were an abandoned abbey and Wally was the vampire Barnabas Collins, with his coffin hidden in the basement . . .

And South End News, that was a *very* good memory. Every Thursday afternoon after school, Wally would head there to buy his comic books. There was a smell to the place: newsprint, bubble gum, tobacco, all mixed together into a wondrous fragrance that would hit him as soon as he pushed open the door. He feels an ache in his chest to be able to inhale that aroma once again, but South End News is gone. Long, long gone.

And, finally, the orchards. Here is the best memory of all. Wally stops his car in the same place he had on his first day back in Brown's Mill, hoping once again to spy some lovers among the trees. But the orchards are still today, quiet. The leaves are mostly gone now, bare branches scratching against the gray, overcast sky.

Here is the place I first knew love.

But what about Mother?

Again his thoughts turn to her, even here.

What love has she ever known?

He's surprised by the question. It gnaws at him.

What love has his mother ever known?

Did she ever love Wally's father? It seems unlikely. Who, then? Wally knows so little. Who were his mother's friends? There was a man named Sully . . . but who was he? Had he mattered? Or had he been just a name his father liked to throw at her—his father, who probably knew as little about her as Wally did?

Who else? Who else was there in his mother's life? Her sister . . . Wally certainly knows his mother had loved her sister. She always talked about Aunt Rochelle. *Rocky,* she called her. Oh, yes, it was clear she had loved Rocky. But who had loved *Mother*? Who had loved Regina Gunderson?

He's suddenly terrified by the answer, by the realization that it's possible *no one* has ever loved his mother. Oh, maybe Rocky had, but Wally sensed that the aunt he'd never known had always been so busy leading her own life that she'd had little time left over for her sister. Of his grandparents, he knew next to nothing. His grandmother had died when Wally's mother was just a little girl. His grandfather had been a drunk, and certainly there had been no love coming from the sadistic Uncle Axel or the coiled, repressed Aunt Selma.

No one's loved her.

"No one," Wally repeats to himself, as the first scattering of raindrops dances upon the windshield.

And who had loved Zandy?

"Who's he?" Wally had asked, all those years ago, holding up a photograph of a red-haired man in a sleeveless sweater, oxford shirt, and checkered bow tie.

"That's Lance," Zandy told him, sitting in his beanbag, smoking a joint. "My first love."

Wally felt a momentary stab of jealousy. "Where is he now?" he asked.

"San Francisco, last I heard."

Wally beamed. "You're going to take me there someday, right?"

"Sure, kid. I'll show it all to you."

"And can I meet Lance?"

Zandy laughed. "Oh, I don't know. I broke his heart."

"You did?"

"Afraid so. I wasn't much older than you at the time, and he was a college man." Zandy folded his hands over his chest and smiled. "You can tell he's a college man, can't you? From the way he looks? You can always tell college men from their pictures."

Wally settled down beside him in the beanbag, his chin resting on Zandy's chest as he looked up into his eyes. "So how did you break Lance's heart?"

The older man let out a slow ring of smoke over his head. He seemed to be considering his answer. "I grew up, I suppose. I had other things to do, other places to see. I just stopped returning his calls. Oh, I'm sure he got over it." He took another drag off the pipe. "He probably doesn't even remember me anymore. But I remember him. I may have broken his heart but still, I've carried him around in mine all these years."

That's the image Wally will keep of Alexander Reefy: sitting in his beanbag chair, his face ringed with smoke, his gnarled, beautiful hands folded over his chest.

And this is where Alexander Reefy ends up: a squat, gray, two-floor apartment building, the old Hebrew Home converted into public housing. Here there is no front porch light to flick on and off as his libido wills. Only a stoop covered with hardened mounds of chewing gum, littered with cigarette butts, graffiti spray-painted on the concrete.

Wally gets out of the car.

He hadn't brought an umbrella. He hurries across the sidewalk as the rain pounds the pavement, stepping up quickly to the buzzer. He sees the name. A. REEFY.

He doesn't hesitate. He presses the button beside the name. He hears the shrill electronic sound it makes somewhere inside the building.

And then he waits.

And waits.

There's no answer, no crackling voice coming over the intercom to ask, "Who is it?" Wally wonders for a moment if he's gone out, but Zandy's too sick to go out, Miss Aletha had told him. Maybe he's too sick to even open the door.

A young woman is suddenly behind him. She smiles shyly as Wally steps aside, allowing her to slip her key into the lock. In her arms she juggles a bag of groceries, so Wally gallantly holds open the door for her. "Thank you," she says, stepping inside.

Wally nods, following her. She doesn't appear to be uncomfortable with him doing so, nor with his presence behind her up a flight of stairs. At the landing, however, she turns quickly and unlocks the door to the first apartment on the right. Once she is inside, Wally hears a chain lock slide into place.

He looks down the hallway. Zandy's apartment is 211.

Taking a deep breath, he begins to walk. The building smells of mold and mildew. The gray carpeting is marred by large brown stains. At the far end of the corridor, a window is imprinted with grimy fingerprints, letting in shards of dull gray light.

On his left, he finds 211.

If it were me, I sure as hell wouldn't want to go all by myself to face somebody who's life I ruined.

He gathers his thoughts and knocks. Raps once, then twice. Not too loudly but not just a tap either.

He listens. He hears nothing. He decides Zandy's gone, perhaps in the hospital. His whole trip here has been in vain.

But then he senses something from inside: a shudder, an animal stirring back to life after a long hibernation. There's a sound, a noiseless kind of sound, as if from under something: a pile of blankets, maybe, or a mound of pine needles and soil.

"Zandy?" Wally whispers through the door.

There's the sound of air, a strange quiver, like the flurry of wind in the eaves. Then it's quiet again.

"Zandy? It's Wally Day."

He swallows hard. Why should Zandy want to see him? Who's to say he doesn't hate him? And who would blame him? Miss Aletha was right: this has been all about Wally, all about *his* needs—his need to see Zandy, his need to make peace. He'd given no thought to whether Zandy would want to see him. He should go—get out of here—turn and run back down this filthy hallway—

Then he hears the scuffing. Footsteps approaching the door. And finally a voice, softly entreating:

"Go ahead," it says. "You're welcome to come in."

"It's the one myth about homos that I hate the most," Ned had said. "I can take the nelly jokes and the opera queen stories but when they start in on saying we're out to recruit little kids, that's when I get mad."

He had been clipping his toenails as they sat watching TV. One of the Pats—Robertson or Buchanan—was on the news going on about how America needed to protect its kids from predatory homos. Ned was getting angrier with each toenail clipped. One flew up from his foot and actually pinged against the glass of the television set.

"Will you be careful with those?" Wally grumbled. "I'm going to have to get out the vacuum if you don't clean up."

"Like the perv you sent to jail," Ned said, not listening.

"Oh, come on, Ned. Not the same thing at all."

"How was it different?"

"I was fifteen. I *wanted* it."

"He started you at *thirteen.*"

"I rode my bike over there. I rang his doorbell. I grabbed his crotch."

"It's gross. What was he? Forty?"

"No." Wally stood from his spot beside Ned on the couch and walked over to the closet to retrieve the handheld vac. He switched it on and began sucking up the little crusts of toenails scattered across the carpet. "Besides," he said, shouting over the noise, "he was good to me. He taught me a lot."

"So is he still in jail?"

Wally switched off the vacuum and sat cross-legged on the floor. "I don't know," he said, staring.

"Missy not tell you?"

"We never talk about Zandy."

"What could he have possibly taught you, Wally? He was a zoned-out hippie. What did he even do for a living? Collected welfare, right?" Ned looked down at his hands, his nails and fingerprints permanently outlined in black from all the pipes he had cleaned. "I can't stand freeloaders."

"He was a handyman," Wally said, his voice distracted and far away. "A jack of all trades . . ."

"So what did he teach you? How to fix a leaky faucet? How to spackle walls? How to put a hinge on a door?"

"No," Wally told his lover. "He never taught me any of that."

"Wally Day," comes the voice from the darkness of the shuttered room behind the door.

Wally can't see him clearly. The figure behind the door is vague and imprecise. It steps aside to let Wally in.

The apartment is dark, cast with a strange blue glow. Venetian blinds are pulled tightly against the windows. The smell is foul: cigarettes, urine, bad milk. And something else, too . . .

Wally turns to look at the man standing beside him, his eyes struggling to adjust to the dimness. He can discern that Zandy is wearing a long untucked flannel shirt, way too big for him, though it probably fit him when he was healthy. On his legs are gray sweat pants, stained and torn. He's barefoot.

"Wally Day," he says again.

He stands there in the dark, grinning. It's difficult to recognize him. Zandy's face has the skeletal look Wally has come to recognize as a last sign of the plague: deep hollow cheeks, wide eyes, protruding teeth. His breath is rancid, as if all his organs were decaying inside of him, the stench making its way up through his mouth. He's unshaven. Poking out of the flannel shirt Wally can see his chest hair. What he'd once so eroticized is now a straggly tuft of gray.

"Zandy . . ." he says, and his voice breaks.

"Wally."

"I . . . I wanted to come and see you."

"Well," he says, "here I am."

Wally reaches over to touch him, to shake his hand, something. But Zandy just folds his arms over his chest. His hands—those wonderful, magnificent hands—brush against Wally's as he does so, and the sensation causes Wally to pull back. At the moment of contact he felt nothing. It's as if his hand swept through smoke, not flesh.

"Zandy," he tries again, "I want you to know—"

The other man laughs. "How sorry you are? Is that it, babe? Is that why you've come?"

Wally feels as if he'll start crying. "Yes. I suppose that's part of it."

For a flash he sees the old Zandy: the face hidden behind the death mask. He's transported nearly two decades back into time, and feels a strange stirring in his loins.

"And what should I tell you now?" Zandy asks. "What is it that you've come back to hear me say?"

"I don't know."

"How about 'I exonerate you?'" Zandy asks suddenly, his eyes lighting up, filled with a strange light incongruous to the dark. "Isn't that why you came back? To receive absolution from a dying man?"

"Zandy—"

"Well, you're too late. I'm already dead."

He moves away from Wally abruptly, heading over to his ratty couch, where he sits—where he's probably been sitting for days at a time.

"Look, Zandy," Wally says, following him. "I can understand your anger. And I don't need you to forgive me. I've had to do that for myself."

He stops. Looking down at the frail, tiny man on the couch, it's as if he can see right through him: lungs and heart and ribcage, and then the fabric of the upholstery beyond.

Wally goes on, desperate to find the right words. "I just wanted to say that I was a fucked-up kid who nonetheless loved you very much." His voice cracks again. "And still does. And always will."

Zandy gives him a small smile. "You little ballbuster, you."

"There was so much, so very much you taught me. I am who I am because of you. Everything I know about being gay, about our history, our traditions—you taught me. You taught me not to be ashamed. You taught me that what I felt wasn't wrong. That I could love and be loved. I owe you enough to at least come back here and tell you that—"

"You don't owe me anything." Zandy puts his hands over his face. They're as knotty as Wally remembers, but thinner, so much thinner. "Nothing. Not a thing."

"But I do."

He removes his hands to look back at Wally. "All you owe me is a good life. Have you had one, Wally? Has your life been good?"

Wally's not sure how to answer.

"Have you had love, Wally? Did you find love out there in the world?"

"Yes," he tells him. "I found love."

"Then that's all you owe me. To tell me that."

Wally moves in closer to him. "What about you, Zandy? Have you had love?"

The frail little man on the couch grins. "Finally he asks." His eyes sparkle again with that strange glow. "Tell me, Wally. What do you know about me?"

Wally's not sure what he should say.

"How old am I, Wally? What did I want to be when I was a kid? Were my hopes realized, my dreams accomplished? Is that what I wanted to be, a Brown's Mill handyman?"

Wally tries to say something, but can't.

"Was it all worth it to me? You? Going to prison? My whole life?"

"I don't know," Wally admits, and he starts to cry.

Zandy shrugs. "And now it's too late to find out. Because I'm gone."

Wally crouches down in front of him. He touches Zandy's knees. Once again he's struck by their incredible lightness, their lack of solidity. It's as if he's touching air.

"Zandy, I'm sorry—"

"Sorry doesn't matter. The only thing that matters is what you do now."

"I don't understand," Wally says.

"You think your time here is finished? You think you can just go back to the city now and forget all about Brown's Mill, when there's so much you still don't know, so much you've never bothered to find out?"

He looks at Wally with those wide, distended eyes.

"It's *still* going to be grand, Wally. It's still going to be oh-so-fucking grand."

Wally just kneels there, saying nothing, staring into Zandy's eyes.

The older man smiles. "Do you remember, Wally, the secret Miss Aletha taught me?"

Wally hesitates for just a second. "You mean . . . about the apples?"

"Yes," Zandy says. "How sweet are the twisted apples that they leave behind."

They hold each other's gaze, and Wally can see through his eyes.

He knows what he means.

"Don't worry," Zandy says. "You can't get infected by a dead man."

Wally nods. He's not frightened, being here with the ghost of a man who loved him, who he loved in return, the ghost of a man he could have been, and still might be. They hold each other's gaze for several seconds. Then Wally runs his hands up the length of Zandy's bony thighs, gently pulling down his sweat pants. His fingers caress cold, cold flesh. He finds Zandy's dick, shriveled and blue, and for the first time takes the icy shaft into his mouth. Zandy moans, and for a second Wally remembers that voice: the soft cooing in his ear, the gentle assurances of self, the promises of a world yet to be explored. And when his lover shoots, Wally takes his semen down his throat, drinking every last drop of that sweet freezing liquid. It burns all the way down, purifying him.

"He's dead," he tells Miss Aletha when he returns to her house.

She's outside, clipping the purple roses from their vine. "Some warm water," she says. "That'll keep these for a few more days."

The sun is setting in a watery mix of reds and purples.

Wally just stands there, looking at her. "You're not surprised."

"No," she says, putting aside the roses and peeling off her gloves. "I knew it was a matter of days. But I also knew you'd get there in time."

"But I didn't," he tells her.

She smiles, reaching up to touch his face with her old spotted hands. He covers them with his own. "Yes, you did," she assures him. "You told him what you needed to tell him. And he knows. He's always known."

Inside, he climbs the stairs to his bedroom, the place he'd first found peace. He looks out over the factories, over the tops of the buildings along Main Street, over the cold brownstone steeple of St. John the Baptist church. He can see the orchards, too, and if he tries hard enough, he can even see—at least in his mind—his mother's house on the quiet little cul-de-sac where he grew up.

And there, in the wind, underneath the honking of horns and the sounds of children at play, he can hear something else. He's sure of it.

He can hear Helen Piatrowski scream.

22

AND I DETEST OF ALL MY SINS

The night is cold. This afternoon the man came by and brought the wood, piling it up beside the house out back. Regina is grateful for that. She can't wait to fire up the wood stove. She'll be warm then. Everything will be okay once she has the stove aflame.

"Luz home?"

"No, not yet, Jorge," Regina says, tucking the boy into bed, pressing his teddy bear in beside him. She kisses the child on the forehead. "But I'm sure she'll call soon. In the meantime, I'm here, so don't worry about anything. I'm here and I'll keep you safe, Jorge. I promise you that."

She thinks she really ought to have given him a bath, but she can do it tomorrow. Yes, tomorrow she'll give him a bath.

"He'll need to go back to school, too," Regina says to herself, walking back down the hallway into her dimly lit living room. "He was going to school when they lived with their father. I know that much. Now, what school was it? A special school. It was a special school for special children . . ."

She hauls out the yellow pages from the cabinet, setting it down on a table and switching on a lamp. Dull yellow light illuminates the book. She flips through the pages until she finds SCHOOLS, but she finds none that are special.

Outside the wind whips against the house. Regina shivers.

"I'll need to haul the wood down into the basement," she says. "But I can't possibly. I'm not strong enough. My arthritis—"

But I dragged his body down. I was strong enough to do that.

She presses her fingers into her temples.

"I need to call Walter," she mutters. "He can bring the wood in for me."

But how can she call him? He has one of those new portable phones. She's seen it clipped to his belt. But she doesn't know the number.

She'll have to call him at Howard Greer's house.

She has *that* number. She's had it for a long time in her address book, ever since Walter first went over there to live. She disguised the number, writing "Lillian Mayberry" next to it, so that if Robert ever went through the book he wouldn't find it and get angry with her. She never called the number, of course, not once during that whole time Walter was there, but at least she'd had it. She'd felt better having the number.

She gets out her address book and flips to the M's.

There it is. *Lillian Mayberry.* Except Lillian Mayberry is long dead, buried out at Eagle Hill with her poor little grandson who drowned in the well. Regina reads the number out loud and then dials. It takes a while, as she doesn't have push buttons on her phone. She has to wait until each number has completed its rotation across the face of the phone before she can dial the next.

Finally, there is ringing at the other end of the line.

"Why are you here?"

Howard Greer was wearing a white smock and purple eyeshadow. The day was bright, and they were all in the garden. One man was having a fit over by the rose of Sharon, with the nurses eventually needing to tie him down in his chair. But most everyone else was behaving well, enjoying the sunshine. Regina was sitting on a bench reading a magazine—*Confidential,* she thinks, that scandalous one—when Howard Greer had stood over her, his arms akimbo.

"I see you all the time," he said, his chin held high, "just sitting here, with your nose in a magazine or a book. So why are you here?"

It wasn't a question Regina had an answer for. "I—I just needed a rest," she said. That's what Aunt Selma had told her. That she just needed a rest. Sometimes people laughed at Regina when she told them that, but it seemed to be good enough for Howard Greer, who smiled and sat down next to her, crossing his legs like a woman.

The first time Regina had seen him, in the day room, she had screamed. But she'd grown used to seeing him by now. Howard Greer would have been a handsome young man if not for the eyeshadow. Oh, Regina had to admit it was a pretty color, and it set off his violet eyes, which looked like Elizabeth Taylor's, she thought. But men weren't supposed to wear makeup. Looking at him closely, Regina could see he plucked his eyebrows as well, and there may have been some foundation and rogue on his cheeks, too.

"You've cut a photograph out of that magazine," he observed.

Regina smiled. "Oh, yes. Ava Gardner. I paste pictures on my walls."

"They *let* you?"

"Oh, yes. They said I could decorate my room any way I like."

Howard Greer shrugged. "I suppose it's like the eyeshadow. They indulge us a little bit so they can get our trust. Then zap!" He pounds his right fist into his left palm. "They get you!"

"What do you mean?"

He disregarded her question, studying her face as closely as she'd studied his. "Oh, you *are* a pretty girl. So fair."

Regina blushed. "Thank you."

"Even your eyelashes. I can barely see them." He smiled broadly. "Would you like some mascara?"

She watched as he withdrew a small pink vial from his pocket. He unscrewed the top to reveal a clotted black mascara brush.

"Just a little?" he tempted. "Just enough to bring out those baby blues?"

"Well, all right," Regina said.

Howard Greer's hand came toward her, brandishing the mascara brush. She drew in her breath and tensed her body tight, trying to hold her eyelids still. He gently coated her lashes, first the tops, then the bottoms. It felt good, tickly. Regina smiled.

"Voilà!" Howard pulled back to look at her, evidently pleased with his work. He dug back into his pocket and this time produced a small compact mirror, which he held up so that Regina could see herself.

"My," Regina said. Her eyes jumped out at her, big and bold, outlined in black. "How different I look."

"Now, a little pencil to your brows," Howard murmured, artfully coloring her eyebrows. "And then a little rouge—"

"Okay, faggot, time to go inside," a male nurse said, coming up behind them.

"Oh, but I haven't finished her face."

"You heard me."

"Oh, poo." Howard frowned. He began replacing his cosmetics in the pocket of his smock, one by one. The nurse tapped his foot impatiently but Howard ignored him, keeping his focus on Regina. "Tell me, young lady, do you like Grace Kelly?"

"Do I!" Regina clapped her hands. "Oh, she's more beautiful even than Elizabeth Taylor!"

The nurse began tugging at Howard's arm. "Okay, okay," he barked. "Don't damage the merchandise!"

Regina watched as he was led down the path back toward the building. The nurse and another aide, both men, were pushing him along, laughing at him, calling him "faggot." Howard's hands were all fluttery in the air. Finally they disappeared inside, and that was the last time Regina ever saw Howard Greer, until one time, many years later, when she spotted him in the A&P, wearing a wig and a dress.

But that night, when she went back to her room, on her pillow was a glossy black-and-white photograph of Grace Kelly, in a white dress and pearls. There was no note, but Regina knew who it was from. She pasted it over her bed, and when she left the spa she took it with her. She has it still, somewhere, in one of the boxes in the basement.

"'Lo?"

"Hello."

"Who's this?"

Regina clears her throat. "I'm looking for Walter Day."

"Okay, but *who is this?*"

"His mother," Regina says.

"Whoa, okay," the person on the other end of the phone says. "This is Dee. *Donald.* I met you the other day when we were putting dirt down in your yard."

"Oh, yes, of course," Regina says. Donald. A nice boy. He had orange hair but he had been awfully nice to help Walter with the dirt.

"Wally's not here," Donald tells her.

She hears someone come up behind the boy. There's some mumbling, then the young man comes back to the phone.

"Missy wants to talk to you."

"Missy?"

"Hello?" comes a new voice over the phone. Deep, a little raspy. "Who is this?"

"This is Regina Day."

"Mrs. Day." There's a short pause on the other line. "How are you?"

"I'm fine." Regina thinks about that statement. Yes, she supposes she *is* fine. Better than she thought she'd be, actually, with Luz gone for so long. "I'm doing *fine*," she says again, determinedly.

"Well, Wally will be back soon. Would you like me to have him call you?"

"Yes," Regina says. "I'd like him to call me."

"Is everything all right, Mrs. Day?"

"Oh, everything's fine. Jorge's sound asleep, and I had the wood delivered. The wood for the stove."

"I see . . ."

"Oh, forgive me," Regina says, laughing. "That's why I was calling, you see. I need Walter to help me. With the wood."

"Okay. I'll have him call you."

"Thank you ever so much." She pauses. "Oh, and by the way. I never had a chance to thank you."

"Oh, it was a long time ago, Mrs. Day." Howard Greer's voice sounds compassionate, the way it had that day at the spa. "I did what I had to do."

"Oh, but you didn't *have* to."

"Well, I wanted to. Wally needed help. I was glad I could—"

"No, I meant for the photo of Grace Kelly. I've treasured it ever since."

There's another pause, longer this time. "Grace Kelly . . ."

"Yes, thank you. It was so very thoughtful."

"Yes, Grace Kelly," Howard Greer says, almost as if he was just remembering it himself. "In a white dress and pearls . . ."

"It meant the world that someone would be so nice."

Howard Greer's voice has grown thick. "You just sit tight, Mrs. Day. I'll have Wally call you as soon as he gets back."

Regina's still smiling as she hangs up the phone. She closes her eyes and she's back at the spa, surrounded by all her pretty pictures.

Sometimes it's difficult to figure out where the dream ends and life begins. The other night, Regina dreamt she was back with Rocky in the apartment on Pleasant Street, listening to Miss Wright play the piano somewhere far off in the building. It was such a nice tinkly sound and it stayed with Regina even after she woke up. She was so confused when she looked around her bedroom, because it wasn't hers. There were no pretty pictures pasted to the walls. It was *Robert's* room, and what was she doing in *Robert's* house?

And the time, a few days ago, when she must have fallen asleep over her jigsaw puzzle, because round about three o'clock in the afternoon she woke up to see Walter come in, home from school, heading into the kitchen to make himself a peanut butter and marshmallow fluff sandwich. It *was* Walter. She was sure of it. She would recognize her own son, wouldn't she? Short blond hair with a cowlick sticking up in back, wearing his St. John the Baptist uniform of navy blue pants, white shirt, and blue crested tie. Later, she even found the knife in the sink with the fluff still on it. She was sure she did.

"Mrs. Day, are you all right?"

It's Kyle's girlfriend, that pretty Luz. So polite this one is, so unlike the other girls he's brought here, with their hard eyes and raspy cigarette voices.

"Oh, I'm just a bit in a fog, I suppose, Luz. But I'm all right."

"You seem a little shaky. Do you want me to call a doctor?"

Regina feels terribly sad all of a sudden, thinking about Doctor Fitzgerald. "Oh, I don't have a doctor anymore. My doctor died."

"But we can call another one, Mrs. Day."

They hear the automatic garage door rattle open and Kyle's car, music blaring, glides into the garage.

"Kyle's home," Regina says. And she sees the small, tense smile cross Luz's face.

Dreams. When she was a girl, she used to dream of the circus. "Remember the time Mama took us to see the elephants and the acrobats?" she'd ask Rocky.

"You're a goon, Regina. We never went to the circus."

"We *did*. I remember it so clearly. The big blue and yellow tents. The girls in their pink costumes on the white horses. And the clowns—"

"We *never went to the circus*, Regina!"

Why did Rocky get so angry with her whenever she mentioned the circus? Regina couldn't understand why her sister insisted they'd never been there, never seen the tents and the girls and the horses and the clowns. Regina still dreamed of the circus, almost every night, still saw all its marvels in her mind. How could she dream it if she'd never been there? How could the images be so vivid, so full of color and life?

"It's a *movie*, Regina! You're remembering a movie!"

Regina was near tears. "I am *not*! We went to the circus with Mama! Mama took us and we had such a good time! We laughed and we laughed and we—"

She pauses.

"Oh, look! Here come the elephants! Look, Mama! Look at their floppy ears! And their trunks! Look, that one's raising his trunk at us! He's going to sneeze! Oh, Mama, cover your face!"

Regina laughs at the memory, standing there giggling in the living room.

"And what's so goddamn funny, old woman?"

Her eyes meet Kyle's.

"Look," her nephew growls, "I'm in a hurry here. I need some food. What you got in the icebox?"

"I've got—oh, I'm not sure—fish sticks, I think."

"Make 'em up with some beans, okay?"

"All right, Kyle."

"Luz!" he shouts. "Where the fuck are you?"

What I did, I did for Luz.

He was a bad boy, Kyle. Always was. She knew that, even when she let him come live with her. But he had no place to go. His mother was dead and he stood there crying in Regina's living room. "You're all I have, Aunt Regina. All I have!"

So she said yes. He'd promised to do little jobs for her around the house—fix the garage door, paint the ceilings—but he never did. He would just sit there holding belching contests with his friends around the dinner table, insisting that a good belch was a compliment to the chef. But Regina never found it complimentary. She would just open the window because the smell would get so bad.

Then out would come the cases of beer and the loud, pounding music on the stereo. What was that band called? Leonard Skinner, Regina thinks. Something like that. It wasn't the type of music she liked, but she tried to put up with it, because it would be nice to have voices in the house once again, young voices, laughing and carrying on. Maybe having Kyle wouldn't be so bad, if it meant young people and laughter.

But then Kyle had started taking money, and calling her names, and he bullied poor Luz so much that it made Regina cry. She'd sit up in her bed at night, listening to them having sex in the other room, Luz crying out—not in pleasure, Regina was certain, but in terrible, hideous, unbearable agony. Even getting up and flushing the toilet did no good. They just kept going at it, the bed squeaking, Luz crying, Kyle making horrible sounds like a dog.

When was the last time you saw him, Mother? When was the last time you saw Kyle?

It was the night Luz picked him up at the train station in Mayville. He came in there instead of the naval airport where she usually got him. And he wasn't wearing his uniform when he came into the house. He tossed his duffel bag full of dirty clothes onto the couch, immediately dialing numbers on the phone and whispering angrily to whoever picked up on the other end.

She can hear him now, the whispering that went on into the night.

She turns, following the phone cord. It's stretched down the hall into Kyle's room, pulled under the crack in his door—the same way Walter used to pull it all those years ago, when he'd take the phone down there and talk for hours. How angry Walter would get if she knocked on his door. How very angry. How much anger there's always been in this house.

"—*I don't give a shit, Luz will do what I say—*"

Regina stops outside Kyle's door. His words, whispered but fierce, come at her through the night. *Luz.* He's talking about Luz.

Sometimes, when Walter was in his room, Regina would quietly approach, pressing her ear against the door. It was naughty of her, she knew that, but she did it anyway. And what she heard was terrible. Terrible, awful things her son was saying. Dirty, sexual things. But she listened anyway. She listened and would remember them at night, lying beside her husband, snoring and smelling of whiskey. Her husband—that man she lived with for almost twenty years, who bellowed at her and cursed at her and breathed fire when he was angry, that man she never knew, never liked, and has never missed.

She presses her ear up against the door the way she used to do.

"She speaks Spanish, so she'll be perfect," Kyle is saying.

A pause.

"Fuck that, man. I'll just tell her she *has* to come."

Another pause.

"Look, fucker, that isn't even your concern. I'll handle Luz. You just get me the tickets. Two one-ways to Mexico, preferably nonstop."

Mexico?

"As soon as you *can*, fucker! Tomorrow, the next day. I don't have a lot of time. I'm supposed to be back on the ship in three days. They'll come looking for me after that. Hold on a second, all right?"

Regina gasps. Is he coming toward the door? Will he open it and find her here? What will he do? She starts to bolt but then she hears him strike a match. The pungent aroma of marijuana wafts through the door.

"Stop worrying about *Luz*, you asshole. She'll do what I tell her. If I tell her I need her to come along, she will."

Regina's heart is thudding in her chest. She turns, heading back to her room, but she's hurrying too fast. She steps on a creaking board, and it sings out into the night.

"Hold on a minute," she hears Kyle say.

By the time he flings open his door she's back inside her room, her door shut behind her. She leans up against it, breathing heavily. She never knew she could move so fast.

What else, she thinks, might she be able to do?

"What did you call me for?"

Her son's voice is cold, unforgiving.

"Walter?"

"Missy said you called. What's going on?"

"Oh. Walter." She presses a hand to head. What was she thinking? Why had she called him?

"I need to find a school for Jorge," she says. "A special school."

"That's not your responsibility, Mother. You need to call his father—"

"No, no, no, it *is* my responsibility! It *is*!"

She hears her son sigh on the other end of the line. "You called about the wood, Missy said. You wanted me to bring some wood in for you."

"Oh, yes, the *wood*, Walter. For the stove in the basement."

"Fine. I'll do it tomorrow. On my way out of town."

"Oh, thank you, Walter. Thank you."

He's a good boy, her son is. Always has been. She hangs up the phone, remembering how good he always was, how she would look down at him sleeping and think: *You're a good boy, Walter. You're a very good boy.*

Regina didn't know about boys, of course, but still, Walter was good, there was no doubt about that—and there were times, she had to admit, she truly enjoyed being with her son. Watching *Match Game* and eating goulash. Planting marigolds in the rock garden. Shopping at Grant's, playing peekaboo between the ladies' dress racks, giggling when the sales clerk placed a frilly hat on the boy's head and he paraded around the store.

And how Regina had *loved* listening to Walter read. He would do *so well* whenever one of his teachers or Father Carson would ask him to read a passage from the Bible up at the pulpit during Sunday Mass. Regina never liked going to Mass, but when Walter read it was worth it. It was like *music* listening to Walter read, it really was.

He had gone on to become an actor. Yes, Regina had seen him. She'd catch him on a commercial or on the Lifetime channel late at night when she couldn't sleep—like in that film where he frightened poor Susan Lucci so bad. Regina hoped maybe he'd turn out good in the end, not really be a psycho killer at all. Maybe he and Susan would even get married at the end, but no such luck. Still, it was fun to watch her son on television, remembering those years he'd walk around the backyard, talking to himself, acting out scenes.

He had gone to the city, just as Regina had once, but Walter hadn't come back the way she had, riding in Uncle Axel's bumpy truck, leaving the tall buildings and flashing lights behind. Regina still remembers how she cried when they passed the sign on the south road that read ENTERING BROWN'S MILL. That was before they built the highway, and the only way into town from the city had been through the orchards. Regina was grateful for the darkness offered by the trees, so Rocky wouldn't see her cry.

"We had a dream we might become famous," she had told Aunt Selma, who'd scoffed at her.

"Please, Mother, help me," Walter had said to her. "It's my dream!"

Dreams. What's real and what are dreams? Maybe dreams *are* real. Maybe she really *did* go to the circus. Only she didn't go during the day, and she didn't go while Mama was still alive, but rather at night, while she slept, and Mama had come down from heaven and scooped her up and taken her to the circus, because she'd always wanted to take her when she was alive but had never had the chance, not until now.

And so that's how she killed Kyle. She'd always wanted to do it, always wanted to take the hoe or the shovel or the iron rake and smash it down into his head—into Robert's head, into Papa's. And so she had finally done it, brought that rake or shovel or hoe right down into Kyle's head as he slept there on the couch, and thereby saved Luz from Mexico, from everything Kyle had planned for her, from the whole horrible life he was getting ready to force upon her.

And then she'd mopped up the blood and made herself a cup of tea.

"Hello?"

Regina's voice cut through the morning.

"Is this the Brown's Mill police department?"

A pause.

"Yes, this is Regina Day. May I speak with Officer Garafolo? Oh, yes, hello, how are you? I'm fine. No, no, it's not anything like that. I want to report a missing person."

Another pause.

"My nephew. Kyle Francis Day. He was in the navy. I think he's gone AWOL."

She looks up as she settles the phone back into its cradle. Walter is coming down the hall from his room.

"He's gone?"

"Yes. He's gone. You can be sure of that."

Walter pulls out a chair and sits down with her at the table.

"So can I be an actor, Mom? Is that okay?"

"Of *course* it's okay, Walter."

"Really?"

"Yes. *Really*. Maybe you'll become famous."

"Like you were."

She smiles a little sadly. "Almost. I was almost famous." She starts to cry.

"What is it, Mom? Why are you crying?"

He reaches over and takes her hand.

"Oh, Walter," she says, "I don't know what's happening to me."

On the other end of the phone she hears him take in a breath of air and hold it there: "Are you still seeing Doctor Fitzgerald?" he asks finally.

"No, no, no, he died, Walter. Years ago."

"Then you need to find a new doctor, Mom. I can't do anything for you."

She feels a surge of feeling in her chest, a desperate, silent scream. "Would you come home, Walter?" she asks all of a sudden. "Please? I don't know what else to do."

There's no answer.

"Please, Walter. Please?"

Still there's silence.

"Oh, Walter. I—I think I may be losing my mind."

* * *

The wind whips against the side of the house.

The wood. She needs to fire up the woodstove. She can't wait until tomorrow. She must do it tonight. She'll do it herself, if she has to. Only then—only when the woodstove is blazing—will everything finally be okay.

She braves the cold in her pink nightgown, heading down the back steps. There's a large moon in the sky, offering a milky white light. The trees are bare, their limbs silhouetted against the sky. Assaulted by the wind, she makes her way across the lawn. Then, deep inside it, she hears a voice.

"Mrs. Day! Mrs. Day!"

Regina looks up and squints.

"Luz!"

The girl approaches from the other side of the fence that lines Regina's backyard. Kyle's car is behind her, parked in the driveway.

"Mrs. Day, I'm sorry I've been gone so long," she says.

A frisky wind catches Luz's black hair, blowing it around her lovely face.

Regina grips the top of the fence, staring into the girl's eyes. "Oh, Luz, I'm so happy to see you!"

The girl starts to cry. "Oh, Mrs. Day," she says. "I need to ask your forgiveness."

"Forgiveness for what, dear?"

"For what I did." Luz's tears fall against her cheeks in the moonlight.

"What did you do?"

"I took some money from you, Mrs. Day. I'm so sorry. So very, very sorry . . ."

Regina just wraps her arms around herself.

"Two hundred dollars." Luz composes herself. "I spent it. But here—" She thrusts a fifty-dollar bill over the fence at Regina. "I'm going to pay you back! Every cent."

Regina looks at the money but doesn't accept it. "Why did you take the money, Luz?"

"I needed it." She's crying harder, not looking Regina in the eyes.

"So you could go to the city and become a model. Isn't that right?"

The girl lifts her eyes to Regina's. Mascara runs down her cheeks.

"You keep that money," Regina says. "*Use it*. It's *time*, Luz. Time for you to *go*."

Luz says nothing at first. She just keeps standing there holding the money across the fence. Finally she withdraws her hand, crumbling the fifty back into her palm.

"You can't stay here in Brown's Mill," Regina tells her. "I know what's that like, how a girl with dreams needs to get out of here. That's why I did what I did. I did it for *you*, Luz. And as much as I will miss you, it would be selfish to want you to stay. You have to *go*."

The girl wipes her eyes. "You're right. I *can't* stay here. I've never been happy here. You know that."

"And in the city, you *can* be happy."

Luz starts to tear up again. "Oh, I don't know about that, Mrs. Day..."

"Of *course* you can. You're going to be a famous model."

Luz just starts to cry harder. Regina reaches across the fence and rests her knotty, spotted hand on Luz's shiny black hair.

The girl looks into her eyes. "I had to come back and ask your forgiveness. I carried such guilt here, in my heart, for the last few days. I went to the priest, Mrs. Day, and told him of the horrible thing I had done to you. He said I must return the money, but I told him that I couldn't, that I'd spent it. So he said that I had to tell you, and I had to pay you back." Luz shudders with leftover tears. "And then I said the Act of Contrition with him."

Regina is still stroking the girl's hair. "I remember the Act of Contrition from when I was a Catholic." She smiles, a little wryly. "They would make you say it to show you were truly sorry for something."

The girl nods.

"Then let's say it together, Luz."

Luz looks at her. "Say it...?"

"Yes," Regina says. "Together. How does it begin again?"

Luz hesitates a moment, then says, "*My God, I am heartily sorry for having offended thee...*"

Regina joins in. "*And I detest of all my sins—*"

Luz follows along.

"*—because of thine just punishments,*" they both intone, "*but most of all because I have offended thee, my God, who are all good and deserving of all my love.*"

Again Luz falls silent.

"*I firmly resolve...,*" Regina prompts.

"*...with the help of thy grace,*" Luz says.

"*—to sin no more—*"

"*—and to avoid the near occasion of sin.*"

"Amen," Regina says.

"Amen," Luz echoes.

"Now go, Luz."

The girl looks up at her. "But I've come for Jorge..."

"No. Not Jorge. Not yet. It would be too much for the boy. He's happy here. When you're settled, then you can come for him."

"Oh, but Mrs. Day, I couldn't possibly impose on you—"

"He's a good boy, Luz," Regina says. "And you will be doing all sorts of new things now. Like all those beautiful girls I see on TV and the covers of magazines. You can do it, Luz. I know you can."

"I'll send you money," Luz promises.

"No," Regina says. "I don't want it."

"But I must—"

"All you must do is *go.*"

Luz starts to cry again. "Oh, Mrs. Day, you are a *saint*. A saint on earth."

Regina just touches the girl's face. How beautiful she is. How lovely.

"As soon as I can I'll come for Jorge," Luz says, between tears. "I'm going back to the city, and I'm going to make everything right! Maybe I really *will* be a model!"

They clasp hands in the moonlight.

"Thank you, Mrs. Day," Luz exclaims, turning to hurry back to Kyle's car. "You won't be disappointed in me! I promise!"

Regina just beams.

"I owe it all to you, Mrs. Day," Luz calls, sliding in behind the wheel and starting the engine. "All to you!"

The Trans Am roars into life. Its headlights momentarily blind Regina, who turns her face and squints her eyes as she watches Luz back out of the driveway then turn the car's wheels to screech off down the street.

"Go, Luz, go," Regina says softly.

The wind seems to have died down. She no longer feels so cold.

The wood can wait until tomorrow.

23

A GOOD BOY

"Will you give this to Donald Kyrwinski, please?"

The woman standing in front of him is holding a blue parka with synthetic fur around the edge of the hood.

"It's getting colder now," she says. "He's going to need it."

"He's inside," Wally says, accepting the coat. "Do you want me to get him?"

"No," the woman says, hurrying back down the steps into the night. She's thin, blond, very fair and very frightened. "Just give him the coat, please. Thank you."

Closing the front door, Wally turns to see Dee standing behind him.

"Yours, I take it."

The boy looks at the coat in Wally's hands. "Like I'd wear such an ugly thing."

"Why didn't you come out and see her?"

"She didn't want to see me." Dee shrugs. "Just throw the coat on the rack."

Wally does, then follows Dee into the living room.

"It says something that she came over with it," he suggests.

"Oh, yeah? What does it say?" Dee flops down into a chair and hits the remote, turning on the TV. It's the Shopping Channel. Suzanne Somers, or somebody who looks likes her, is selling jewelry.

Wally decides not to pursue the subject of the boy's mother. What indeed *did* it say that she had brought over a winter coat for her son to wear, but chose not to see him?

"I hear you're heading back to the city in the morning," Dee says.

"You hear right."

"So you finally got over there to see Zandy and he was dead, huh?" Dee starts flicking through the channels with the remote control, a kaleidoscope of images, a cacophony of sound. "Talk about ironic."

Wally says nothing.

"I thought you wanted me to go with you," Dee says, settling on the Game Show Network. A rerun of an old *Match Game* episode. Brett Somers is hitting Charles Nelson Reilly over the head with her card.

"You were at school," Wally tells him.

"I'd have skipped out if you asked me."

Wally holds up his hands. "Far from me to contribute to juvenile delinquency."

Dee raises his eyebrows as he turns for the first time to look at Wally directly. "A little late for that, don't you think?"

Wally narrows his eyes at him. "You're no delinquent, Dee."

"So you gonna take me with you? To the city?"

Wally hadn't planned on engaging with the kid. He hadn't even wanted to *see* him again. He'd just wanted to go to bed, avoid him, then blow out of town in the morning without saying goodbye. Would teach the little prick right for being so aloof.

But he sits down in the chair opposite Dee and looks over into his eyes.

"I can skip school tomorrow," the boy is saying. "Then it's the weekend." His eyes are big and pleading. "I can take the train back Sunday night. So can I go with you? *Please*?"

"Dee—"

"Oh, come *on*, you know what it's like. How *horrible* this place is."

"It's not horrible," Wally tells him. "You can *make* it horrible. Just like there are many people for whom the city becomes a horrible place to live."

Dee just makes a face and turns back to the television. He's disgusted, apparently giving up on Wally once again.

"Come on," Wally challenges him. "Tell me something good about Brown's Mill."

"There *is* nothing good."

"Hot fudge brownie sundaes at the Big Boy."

Dee snorts. "You can get 'em anywhere."

"There's got to be one thing, Dee." Wally's not sure why he's being so insistent, why it matters so much, why the boy intrigues him the way he does, why ever since they'd had sex he hasn't been able to get Dee off his mind. "Tell me one good memory of being a kid in Brown's Mill and then I'll consider taking you with me to the city."

Dee looks at him as if he's insane.

"I'm serious," Wally says.

"Since when did you sign onto the Brown's Mill Chamber of Commerce?"

"Come on, one thing."

Dee scrunches up his face, shaking his head. But he's thinking. Wally can tell he's thinking.

"Okay," the boy finally says. "Being in *Peter Pan* in grade school. I loved that play. It was awesome. They rigged it up so we could fly on wires and everything."

Wally smiles. "Were you Peter?"

Dee laughs. "I *wish*. I was just one of the Lost Boys. Mr. All-American-Boy Dean Dalrymple got to play Peter."

Wally pauses a moment. "All American Boy?"

"Yeah." Dee rolls his eyes. "Some freak who got all the teachers gushing over him because the American Legion named him their All American Boy. I mean, who gives a fuck? How geeky is that?"

Wally laughs. "Yeah," he admits. "It's pretty geeky."

"So I can go with you? To the city?"

"I said I'd *consider* it."

"I'll start packing." Dee leaps up out of the chair. "You going to say good-bye to your mother? Any more jobs for you to do?"

"I have to carry some wood down into her basement," Wally says.

"I'll help you," the boy says, bounding up the stairs to pack.

"I said I'd *consider* taking you!" Wally shouts after him. "Not that I definitely *would*." But Dee is already upstairs.

Wally stands and walks over to the window. The stench from the swamps is heavy tonight. He looks out onto the way the moonlight reflects on the rusted roofs of the old factories next door. It makes them look like medieval castles. Or a vampire's lair.

You going to say good-bye to your mother? Any more jobs for you to do?

Wally lets out a long sigh. "What else, Mother? What else is there for me to do?"

Once, twenty years ago, he'd gone to her house to say goodbye, and he'd ended up staying a week. It was right before he left for college, right before he left Brown's Mill for good. His father had been dead for a few months by then, and Miss Aletha had encouraged Wally to go over to his mother's house, to make some kind of overture to her. And Wally had gone, he'd actually *gone*—because somewhere, deep down, something was still twisting, still living, still *feeling* for his mother. What it was, he wasn't sure. Love? Probably not. Obligation? He owed her nothing. But something. There was something.

"Maybe you'll find out by going there," Missy said. "Maybe she'll surprise you."

"Oh, she surprises me all right," Wally whispers, looking out into the dark. "She never ceases to surprise me."

He closes his eyes and leans his head against the glass.

She doesn't have any eyebrows. When she was young it hadn't mattered. She was blond and blue-eyed, with eyebrows so fair they practically disappeared against her soft pale skin. She had the face of an angel then, and Wally knows that face. As a boy, he would turn the pages of her yearbook, Brown's Mill High School, Class of 1944, and gaze down at his mother, so young and pretty, with her blond hair and dark red lipstick, smiling demurely into the photographer's lens. Wally remembers the inscriptions of the fellas who'd soon be marching off to war. "Dear Sweetie." "Dear Angel." When he was a boy, Wally had concurred with the sentiments: his mother *was* an angel, a vision of light and loveliness. But as he got older, the face in the yearbook and the inscriptions of the fellas could only be appreciated as expressions of camp.

She'd started penciling her eyebrows after she got married, when her hair had gotten darker and her face began to get old. She was older than most of the other mothers; kids would always ask Wally if she was his grandmother. But when she did her face she made herself look as beautiful as a movie star. Wally remembers sitting entranced, watching his mother at her vanity table. She'd open her eyes wide and arch her eyebrows high, carefully tracing them with her pencil. She'd follow that with applications of rouge, powder, and lipstick. Wally would watch her face come to life, come into its true beauty. He'd watch her transform from a tired old mother into the angel of Brown's Mill High.

Once, when he was six, Wally had snatched his mother's eyebrow pencil and drew an entire carnival of black, smudgy creatures. His mother had laughed and taped the picture up on the refrigerator. When he was sixteen, Wally had taken her pencil again—to darken his first moustache, the hairs of which, like her eyebrows, were too blond to see.

Wally's looking at his mother now as she stands in the hallway of their house, and he feels endlessly sad that she has no eyebrows. He'd come to say good-bye, one last attempt at some kind of relationship. He was on his way to the city, to college, to a new life far away from all the horrors of the past few years. But he had found her ill. She's been in bed for days, she said, coughing and wheezing. She stands in the doorway of her room, Kleenex tucked up inside her sleeve. Her robe is held together at her throat by a giant safety pin.

How can he leave? How can he leave her now?

"I'm going to make you some soup for lunch," he says.

"No, Walter, that's not necess—" And she begins to cough—hard, wracking, dog-like sounds.

He ignores her and lights the old burner with a match, lowering the burst of blue flame to a simmer. "Please, Mother. Just go back to bed."

He had come to say good-bye, to just spend a half an hour—but he wouldn't leave for a week. He'd call Miss Aletha later and tell her he was staying the night. And the next, and the one after that.

"I'm going to call Dr. Fitzgerald," Wally calls down to his mother.

"Oh, no, there's no need—"

"I'm calling the doctor, Mother."

He gets his secretary on the phone. The doctor doesn't make house calls anymore, she says, but when she hears it's Regina Day she says she's certain he'll make an exception—given how much the poor lady's been through. Wally thanks her and hangs up the phone.

"The doctor is coming tomorrow at four," he tells her.

"Oh, thank you, Walter."

He looks back at her. How drawn she looks. How old.

"You might want to do your face," he says.

"Yes," she says, nodding. "I'll do my face."

How many years had it been since it was just the two of them in the house? When Wally was a boy, his father had simply been an unwelcome visitor, an intruder who needed to be tolerated for the duration of his stays but who never, thank God, was a permanent fixture. It wasn't until Wally was thirteen that his father had come home for good, never returning to his ship. It was only then that Dad started drinking his days into oblivion, becoming increasingly nasty and sullen and bitter, only then that hell had burst up through their floorboards, destroying their home and their way of life as completely as if their furnace had exploded and the place had burned to cinders.

It was quiet now. Wally walks through the house marveling at the stillness. But echoes of the past can still surprise him around any corner.

You little pervert! Do you have any idea how you have shamed the name of Day?

She found him in the basement. His father.

Hanging by his own belt, Wally knows. *She found him hanging from a rafter. He was probably all blue or black or green—whatever color hanging corpses turn.*

Have you any idea how you have shamed the name of Day?

He hears his mother hacking in her room.

Why did I come back here? Wally feels trapped, tricked, bewildered. *What was I hoping to find?*

"I'm going out for a bit," he tells his mother, standing in the doorway to her room.

"All right, Walter."

"You'll be okay there for now?"

"Yes. I'm fine." She looks over at him. "Walter?"

"Yes?"

She fumbles for words. "I want—I want to be able to tell you to have a good time, wherever you're going. I *want* to say it, but I can't. Because ever since you left, Walter, I don't know what it is that you *do*."

He laughs, a little bitterly. "You never have."

"No. I suppose I never have." She looks at him, as if looking at him for the first time. "And I never asked."

The Nyquil she's taking must be making her loopy. She's never been this inquisitive before.

"Mother," he tells her, "you can rest assured I'm not doing anything wrong."

"It doesn't have to be *wrong*," she says weakly, looking up at him with her sunken blue eyes. "I just don't understand. It's something I just don't understand, Walter."

She covers her face with her shriveled old hands, the veins on the back making a network of blue.

"Your life outside this house has always been mysterious," she says from behind her hands. "I've never understood what it is that you do."

In that moment, in that moment when she sat there so weak, so frail, so desperate, covering her old face with her old hands in her bed, he wanted to stay with her forever. He wanted to call Missy and tell her he was never coming back, that he wasn't going away to school, that he was going to forget all about the city and acting and being gay and just stay home with his mother. Stay home with her and watch game shows and eat goulash and plant marigolds in the rock garden, forever and ever. *We could be happy again, Mother. Just you and I. The way it was, a long time ago.*

He walks over to her, putting his arm around her shoulders and kissing her cheek. When was the last time he had kissed her? Years ago. An eighth grade play, perhaps? The day Sister Angela presented him with his certificate for perfect attendance?

He feels her hand press his, slipping something inside his fist. Wally looks down. A five-dollar bill rolled up tightly, still moist from her palm.

"Mom, I don't need—"

"Take it. It's not much. It'll make me feel better if I know you have it."

He stuffs it down into the front pocket of his jeans. He imagines her lying there, nervously rolling it tighter and tighter, as she waited for him.

He had no place to go. He just needed to get out of the house. So he walks down Washington Avenue to Josephine's old house. No one's bought the place since she died. People think it's haunted. Wally imagines it might be. He looks through the window into the empty rooms inside. Then he sits on the steps with his face in his hands.

It doesn't have to be wrong. I just don't understand.

And it wasn't all her fault for not understanding, for not wanting to know. It was *his* fault, too, for not wanting to tell her. "And why don't you want to tell her about your life?" his therapist had asked, before Wally decided that therapy wasn't working, that he was just wasting Miss Aletha's money. "After all, your father's gone now. Why not try telling your mother a little about who you are?"

"I don't know," Wally replied, defensive, on edge, coy. "What is it that you *want* me to say? That maybe some place deep down I still want her to love me, and I think that if I tell her about who I really am, she *won't?*"

"Maybe that's some of it."

"*Some of it?* Isn't that enough?"

But more. The goddamn therapist had wanted *more.*

When he gets home, he finds her vomiting, deep wracking spasms that threaten to split her frail little body in two, just the way it had happened when Wally was born.

"I wish you'd consider coming back for Zandy's memorial."

Miss Aletha stands in the doorway watching as Wally tosses his few belongings into his backpack. His razor, his toothbrush, the sweatshirts and underwear he'd bought over in Mayville when this little trip home turned out to last longer than he expected.

Funny how that has a way of happening.

Wally looks over at her. "Is that really a good idea?"

"Why not? He'd want you to be there."

"Do you think?"

She nods.

Wally zips up his backpack and sets it against the wall. There. He's all set to get on the road first thing in the morning. All set to blow out of here.

"And him?" Missy nods toward the other room. "Are you taking Dee with you?"

"Yeah," Wally says. "I'm taking him with me."

He likes how that sounds. As silly as it might be to feel that way, he likes how that sounds. *He's taking Dee with him.*

Missy sits down on the bed and arches an eyebrow up at Wally. "But I thought he was just using you. Just trying to get a job. Concerned only about getting his rocks off."

"Yeah," he says, smiling, sitting down next to her. "At this point, I take what I can get." He rubs noses with her. "I'll make sure he's back for school on Monday."

"I'd appreciate that. Don't want the state calling me an unfit guardian."

Wally kisses her cheek. "You're the best, Missy. You know that?"

She grins. "So I've been told. A few times in this long, long life." She looks over at him. "So any news about finding the boy?"

"What boy?"

"Your cousin. The one who's gone missing."

Wally smirks. "He's *not* a boy, Missy. Kyle is my age."

"You're all boys to me. Well, I hope he's okay, wherever he is."

Wally stands up. "Kyle was a monster."

"He was a *boy*, just like you."

"No. He was *born* wrong. The wiring in his head wasn't right."

"You don't know that."

"The things he did, Missy. I had fucked-up parents, too, but I didn't beat people up. I didn't steal and do drugs and piss all over the school."

"Oh, that's right, you were a good boy."

Wally just laughs.

"Who's to explain why we do the things we do?" Missy asks. "Why one of us chooses one form of rebellion and another does something else? Who's to say why and how we settle on our own particular method of survival?"

"But Kyle was *cruel*," Wally says.

He'd come here to make peace, Wally supposes, but he can never make peace with Kyle. Kyle was bad. Kyle was cruel. He can't make peace with that.

"He was my evil twin, my doppelganger, my foil, my Bizarro double," Wally had once described Kyle for Ned. He remembers a time when both were eight, when they got into a knockdown, rolling-on-the-grass kind of fight. Kyle had whupped Wally's butt, leaving him with a shiny black eye.

His mother held an ice pack to his face.

"What did you fight about, Walter?"

"You."

"Me?"

"Kyle said you were crazy."

He remembers his mother's face when he said that. He saw the little lines indent across her brow, the sudden whiteness that came to her lips.

"And why did he say that?" she asked.

Wally was so angry, so filled with outrage. "He said that Aunt Bernadette told him you were sent to live in a funny farm."

His mother said nothing, just removed the ice pack to inspect his eye.

"What's a funny farm?" Wally asked her.

She replaced the ice pack. "Just a place where people go."

"And the people there are funny?"

She smiled, even laughed a little. "Yes. I suppose they are." She paused. "Not always, though. Sometimes they're very sad."

Later, when Wally would go to the institute after Ned's death, they asked him if depression ran in his family. "I think my mother was institutionalized once," he told them, "but I don't know any of the details."

Not a one. As a boy with a shiny black eye, he had looked up at her and asked, "How come you never told me about it? The funny farm?"

His mother looked as if she might cry. "I suppose there are many things I've never told you, Walter."

"Like what?"

"Like . . . oh, I don't know." Her eyes moved past him to look out the window. "Like how when I was a little girl I used to love to dress in pretty clothes and tie ribbons in my hair. Like how I used to pick the crab apples from the tree because I thought they were cherries." She looked down into Wally's face. "Like how, when you were born, I didn't know if I could do it right, be a mother to a little boy. How could I understand what boys go through?"

She removed the ice pack again and sat there with it in her hands. And then she started to cry. It made Wally very uncomfortable. He watched her, not knowing what to do or say, just wanting her to stop crying, just wanting her to smile. Mothers weren't supposed to cry. They were supposed to be strong. Strong and pretty and smiling.

"You can't be going around getting into fights, Walter," she said at last. "Especially without your father here. He'd know how to handle it, but I don't. I've gotten through a lot, Walter. I got through my Mama dying and Rocky dying and I even got through going to the funny farm. But I don't know if I can get through this."

He didn't know what she meant by "this."

"Oh, Walter," his mother said, "I want to do what's right. I want to be a good mother. But sometimes I just don't know what to do. Sometimes I just don't understand."

"What don't you understand?" Wally asked, reaching over and taking the ice pack from her hands to place it against his eye. It was starting to throb again.

"About *you*, Walter. What makes you so different."

She wiped her tears then, holding out her arms. Her son fell into them, dropping the ice pack, heedless about his eye, just grateful beyond words that she had stopped crying and that she was taking him into her arms.

"I'm going to try, Walter," his mother said, her lips at his ear. "I'm going to try to be a good mother, to do the right things. But you'll have to help me, okay?"

He nodded against her breasts. "How?"

She held him tighter. "Just be a good boy. Can you do that? Always be a good boy?"

He nodded again. It was a big thing to ask, to *always* be a good boy, especially since he didn't always know what a good boy was supposed to do.

Still, he decided, if she was going to try, he would too.

Standing in the hallway outside her bedroom that last week before going away to school, he listens to her retch, spewing up into a plastic bag the last of the tomato soup he had made for her.

Stop doing this to me! You're the mother! You're supposed to be taking care of me! You were supposed to take care of me all along—and you never did! You broke your part of the bargain! You didn't try! You didn't even fucking try!

She's quiet now. "Are you all right?" Wally calls into her.

"Yes," she says in a voice that pops with phlegm.

He pokes his head into her room. "You sure?"

She nods, turning on her side, away from him.

Wally hears a car in the driveway. "Dr. Fitzgerald's here, Mom. I'll send him down."

She doesn't reply.

Wally heads back into the kitchen and sees the kitchen is a mess: unwashed pans in the sink, old newspapers in a pile, and he hadn't had a chance to empty the garbage. Coffee grounds are seeping through the paper bag onto the floor. He pushes the bag under the sink just as the doctor rings the bell.

"Thanks for coming," Wally says, letting him in.

"No problem." Dr. Fitzgerald is an old man. He takes off his hat and sets it on the couch. His face holds a thousand creases when he smiles. "I've gotten out of the habit of making home visits, but I've known that old gal in there for years. In fact, I brought *you* into this world, Walter."

They head down the hallway. His mother looks up and smiles when they enter. Wally realizes she hadn't been able to fix her face. The doctor will see she doesn't have any eyebrows. Her face is gray, her wrinkles deep. "Dear Angel," the fellas had written. Wally spots the plastic bag filled with vomit sitting by the side of the bed. He picks it up.

"I'll leave you alone," he says, shutting the door behind him. He carries the bag of vomit to the garbage and sets it on top. He covers it with the newspapers and lifts the whole pail, intending to take it out and dump it in the can outside.

But the garbage falls. Coffee grounds, eggshells, crumpled Kleenex tumble across the kitchen floor. The plastic bag opens and Wally watches as his mother's vomit oozes out, orange and pink, Campbell's Tomato Soup with Phlegm and Bile.

He starts to cry.

Always be a good boy, Walter. Can you do that?

By the time Dr. Fitzgerald comes out of the room, most of the garbage is cleaned up. Wally stands with his arms folded over his chest as the old man walks down the hall.

"Well," the doctor says, one side of his mouth crooked in a grin, "I guess the old gal will pull through."

"She's okay?"

"She does have a mild case of pneumonia. But I don't think she needs the hospital." The old man smiles. "Looks like she's got a pretty good nurse right here."

"So," Wally presses, wanting to be sure, "she's okay?"

"Yes, son," the doctor says, folding his stethoscope into his case, "she's okay." He snaps the case shut. "I think you were so worried because you just didn't know what it was. We always imagine the worst."

Wally nods.

They walk to the front door and shake hands. "I've given her a shot of penicillin," the doctor says. "I'll stop back in a few days. By then she'll be up and around. She's a tough old bird. She's survived a lot worse than this."

The doctor knows of what he speaks. He knows how she found her husband swinging from a beam in the basement. He knows how her son scandalized the town. He knows even more, too—much more, in fact, than Wally.

"She's stronger than she thinks," the doctor tells him again. "I do believe she can handle anything."

Yes, Wally's thinking, as he looks into the man's wise old eyes, *I believe she can. The question, doctor, is can I?*

24

GOING HOME

"Hold still, you little monkey."

Regina smiles as she runs the comb through Jorge's thick black hair. He's sitting facing her on a kitchen stool.

"You see," she says, "I know a thing or two about raising little boys. I had one myself once. I know that you've got to keep their hair combed because they're always messing it up."

She hits a snarl, and the boy lets out a yelp.

"Oh, I'm so sorry, Jorge!" Regina feels terrible. "I'll be more careful."

He looks up at her with those big brown eyes. She cups her hands against his cheeks.

"If we're careful," she tells him, "we'll be just fine."

He giggles, burying his face in the folds of her yellow polka-dotted dress.

Gosh, it's been so long since she's worn this dress. It's her favorite. It makes her feel so gay. So much like Rocky.

"The *second* thing I know about little boys," Regina says, resuming her work with the comb, "is that you can't let them get behind in their schoolwork." She glances down at Jorge with one eye. "That's why I'm so glad you remembered the name of your special school."

"Gee Stwee," Jorge chirps.

"Yes. Green Street. You remembered the name! Of course you did. You're a smart boy, Jorge. A very smart boy!"

He throws back his head and lets out a long, jittery laugh.

"Your teacher is *so* excited that you'll be back with the class," Regina tells him. "She said you haven't missed too much that you can't make up."

He beams.

Regina smiles back at him. "How about, after school, we take a walk over to the playground? Would you like that?"

Jorge jumps up and down on the stool. "Yes, Missa! Yes, Missa!"

"You can play on the swings and the teeter-totter. Oh, how Walter used to love the teeter-totter. We'd sit on it all morning, he and I, up and down, up and down . . ."

She leans back to look at the boy's hair.

"Oh, you *do* look so nice with your hair combed. Of course, if we go to the playground, you'll just get it all mussed up again. But that's all right. Boys will be boys!"

She looks across the room toward the window. The trees have all lost their leaves. Winter is closing in fast, but come spring, she knows, the leaves will be back, just as the bulbs she planted along the walk will push through the dirt and sprout yellow flowers. The winter will be cold and probably long—very long, she fears—but Regina's prepared for that. And the spring, she's certain, will be so beautiful, so warm, that everything will prove to have been worth the while.

"What 'bout tresha?"

She looks back down at the boy. "Now, no more thinking about the treasure, Jorge. You're all the treasure I need."

"But tresha!"

"Hush, now, Jorge. I know where the treasure is." She leans back once again to make sure his hair looks neat. It does. She did a splendid job. "There's no need to be looking for the treasure anymore."

She pulls the boy to her bosom again and hugs him tight.

Now if Walter will only remember about the wood.

Wally opens his eyes. Dee's looking up at him, his chin resting on Wally's chest.

"'Morning," the boy says.

"'Morning," Wally echoes, his voice raspy.

"I was wondering when you were going to wake up."

Wally grins. "You've been lying there watching me sleep?"

"Yep." Dee pulls forward to kiss Wally on the mouth.

"Hey," Wally cautions, "morning breath."

But they kiss anyway.

They'd spent the night together. The whole night. The boy came rapping at Wally's door, that big boner of his poking through his pajama pants.

"So," he said, "you wanta do it again?"

Wally eyed him. "Sure."

The boy had started to climb up onto the bed, but Wally stopped him midway, holding his arm. "On one condition," he said.

"What?"

"You stay all night. After we both come, you let me hold you. You fall asleep in my arms."

Dee tried very hard to show no particular emotion in his face. "Okay. Whatever."

So that's what they did. They made love not once but twice, the first time hard and fast and passionate, with Wally penetrating the boy, Dee hooking his fingernails into Wally's back. The second time had been slower, gentler, ending with Dee falling asleep in Wally's arms, just as Wally had wanted.

"Do you think," Dee asks now, sitting up, straddling Wally across his chest, "there might be any auditions in the city this weekend?" His orange hair tumbles down into his face. "I mean, since I'll be there, maybe I can try out for something. Anything."

"Maybe," Wally says. "I'll see what's going on."

The boy grins. "Wouldn't it be cool to be in a show together?"

Wally laughs. "Yeah. That would be cool."

Dee swings his leg over the bed and hops to the floor, his big floppy penis swaying between his legs. He grabs a towel and heads toward the door. "I'm going to shower really quickly," he says. "Let's not hang around for long, okay? Let's get on the road soon."

Wally rolls over in bed. "Remember I have to stop by my mother's."

"Oh, right. The wood."

"Yeah," Wally says. "The wood."

Wally watches as the boy wraps the towel around his middle and saunters out the door. No question he's adorable. In another few years that body is going to make an awful lot of men pretty desirous. He's going to fill out nicely, lean muscle on a strong frame. Not to mention the cock. Dee will be quite the catch, and that's probably when Wally will lose him.

Last night, making love with Dee, he had kissed the tautness of the boy's stomach, running his fingers along the soles of his smooth, unwrinkled feet. There had been no problem keeping an erection last night. Wally had felt something he hadn't in a long time. Not just lust, not just desire. But—dare he think it, without sounding goopy or sentimental—*hope*. Not hope for anything specific, not for anything absolute, certainly not with Dee. Just hope. The opposite of despair. The antidote to apathy.

He places his feet against the floor. And so it's time to go. Time to hit the road, return to the city.

And, for a couple of days anyway, Dee will be with him.

He likes how that sounds.

"I wish you'd really think about the memorial service."

Wally looks up. Miss Aletha leans in the door frame, her arms crossed against her chest.

"When you bring Donald back on Sunday, you could stay over until Monday. It'll just be a small affair. Just a few of us."

Wally stands, approaching her. "You really think that's a good idea?"

Missy nods. "I do."

"I told him, you know," he says, taking into his arms the old woman who saved his life, who, once again, has put him on his path, set him right. "I told him what he'd meant to me, how everything he taught had stayed with me all these years." He looks down into Miss Aletha's old eyes. "I'm sure somehow he heard me."

"I'm sure he did, too."

Wally's eyes move to look out the window, over the hills. The orchards are nearly all bare now, stark fingers against the cold sky. But the leaves will return, as they do every year, and so will the lovers to the woods.

No time for breakfast; Dee is too anxious to get on the road. Missy unzips his backpack and thrusts inside a couple pieces of cornbread wrapped in aluminum foil. "Don't start in about too many carbs," she scolds. "You need to eat *something*."

Wally showers quickly. It's a cold morning, with his feet shivering against the tiles of the bathroom, but there's abundant sunshine, not a cloud in the sky. He hurries down the stairs, shouting back over his shoulder to Dee that he'll be out at the car.

He tosses his backpack into the trunk, Miss Aletha following close behind him. "I don't have to tell you to take care of him," she says.

Wally can't resist a grin. "I promise I won't let him do anything that I didn't do myself when I was his age."

"Oh, good God," she says, shuddering. "I should haul him back inside right now."

Wally laughs. "Come *on!*" he shouts back into the house. "Bus is leaving!"

Dee makes a mad dash down the front steps, the screen door slamming behind him, and tosses his suitcase into the backseat.

"Whoa!" Wally says. "What's up with that head?"

The boy grins over at him. He's shaved off all his hair. All that orange spikiness is gone, replaced by a near-military buzzcut. He looks . . . so much older.

"I figured orange hair was *so* Brown's Mill," he says. "A big deal here but probably pretty lame in the city."

Wally smiles. "Maybe I'll do the same."

"You should. You're starting to lose it up front, you know." Dee suddenly stops. "Fuck! My MP3 player!" He bolts back into the house.

"He won't want to come back," Miss Aletha says, a little emotional.

"Oh, he will." Wally smiles. "He knows what's here for him."

Dee bolts past them, with not only his MP3 but his pillow tucked under his arm.

"Why are you bringing that?" Wally asks. "You don't think I have pillows in my apartment?"

"I like my own," he says. "It's the same one I've had since I was ten."

Wally watches as Dee slides into the front seat, his pillow beside him, the tiny sound of Avril Lavigne sneaking out from his headphones.

"You know," Wally says, turning to Miss Aletha, "I might get used to having him around. Maybe I *won't* send him back."

Miss Aletha shakes a crooked finger at him. "You'll send him back, and he'll finish school, and *then*, if he chooses, he can come back to you."

How old her eyes look. How filled with everything: life, history, love, sadness, grief, wisdom. Everything but regret. How wonderful that must be, to live a life without regret.

Dee honks the horn.

"Okay, okay," Wally shouts.

"But there's one more thing," Miss Aletha says.

Wally looks at her.

"Your mother."

Wally sighs. "Yeah, yeah. I'm going over to deal with the wood for her."

"But did you ever find it, Wally? What you came here looking for?"

He doesn't respond. He looks from her over the orchards, in the direction of his mother's house, somewhere on the other side of the trees.

"It's there, Wally. I'm sure of it. You'll find it if you just look for it."

"Will you come *on*?" Dee calls from the car. "If we wait any longer everything's going to be *closed* when we get to the city."

"Nothing *closes* in the city," Wally shoots back.

He turns his eyes back to Miss Aletha.

"I love you, Missy."

"I'm so glad you came home, Wally," she says, her arms encircling his neck.

In the backyard, in the hour he has before they need to set out for school, Jorge is playing his games. He's running in circles, talking to himself. So let Grace Daley from next door call and suggest the boy needs to see a psychiatrist. She said it about Walter, when he'd be out there playing *his* games, and even though she's now deaf and nearly blind, she might well say it about Jorge. But Regina doesn't care what anyone thinks. Jorge's having a good time out there, and that's all that matters.

He wants Swedish goulash for breakfast, so Regina's frying up some ground meat in the pan. He likes a little pepper in his. Luz always made his food a little spicy, so he's used to it that way. Walter never liked too much pepper. Every boy is different. That's something else she knows about boys. Regina adds the pepper and sautés the meat. They'll have breakfast, then she'll walk him to school, and afterward they'll head over to the playground. There will be lots of children there. It will be so nice to watch them all play.

A sound distracts her. A car in the driveway. She turns off the burner on the stove and walks over to the window to peer out from behind the curtain. Her heart begins to thump a little harder; she's always a little nervous it will be that policeman again. Or that mean young man in the navy uniform.

But it's not.

It's Walter!

"Hello, Mother," he says, getting out of the car. That young man, Donald, the one who helped with the dirt, gets out of the other side. His hair is different, Regina notices. Actually it's *gone*.

"Well, hello, Walter," Regina calls, opening the screen door to greet her son. "You remembered about the wood!"

"Yes, I remembered." He pauses. "Of course I remembered."

Jorge has come running around to the front yard, having heard the car. He stands in front of Walter, looking up at him.

"You remember Jorge, don't you, Walter?"

"Yeah, sure," Walter says, tousling the boy's hair. "How ya doin', kid?"

Jorge eyes him with some suspicion still.

"I'm making him Swedish goulash for breakfast," Regina says.

"For *breakfast*?"

"It's what he wanted," she tells him. "Maybe you'd like to stay for some."

"Um, no, thank you, Mother. We've got to get on the road."

"Yeah," Donald says, "Wally's showing me the city. I've never been."

"Oh, never?" Regina welcomes them all into the house, taking Donald's hands in her own. "Oh, you'll love it. You will *love* the city. There is so much to see, so much to do . . ."

"Yeah," the boy says, grinning. "I can't wait to get out of this town."

Regina looks at the three of them. Jorge so small, so dark. Donald so wiry, so wide-eyed. And Walter . . . so tall and fair today, not so much like Robert, who was, after all, very dark. No, today Walter looks more like—well, more like the way she suspects Mama's baby would've looked like, had he lived to grow up. Or *Rocky's* baby, for that matter.

"Or my own baby," she says, before even realizing she's saying it.

Wally looks at her. "What's that, Mother?"

She's lost in another one of her reveries. Wally realizes he can't just leave without making sure she's okay. A week ago, he wouldn't have cared, or at least he'd have acted as if he didn't care. And he's still not sure how he really feels, but he knows he can't just leave, can't just go back to the city without some sense of where she is, how she's getting by. She had called him, after all, and he had come.

"Are you taking your pills regularly?" he asks her.

"Oh, yes, I still have the chart Luz made up for me."

"Has she come back?"

"No. She's going to stay in the city." His mother clasps her hands together and looks up at him earnestly. "She couldn't stay here, Walter. There was nothing in Brown's Mill for her. She's going to become a famous model in the city. You saw how pretty she was."

Wally looks down at the boy at his mother's side, clinging to her dress. "But him . . ."

Regina stiffens a little, her hand clutching Jorge around his tiny shoulder. "It's just for a little while."

"But, Mother, you know you get confused at times . . ."

"No, not about Jorge. We do fine together, don't we, Jorge?"

The boy nods, looking up at Wally with wide, insistent eyes.

Regina's adamant about this. She won't let her son think that Jorge is too much trouble for her. "Jorge takes care of me as much as I take care of him," she tells Walter. "Every morning he says, 'Take your pills, Missa!' He calls me 'Missa.' He can't say 'Mrs.' So he calls me 'Missa.'" She smiles and tousles the boy's hair. "It's a good name."

Wally's surprised by how touched he is by Jorge's attachment to his mother, how moved he is by his mother's hand in the boy's hair.

"Missa," he says, thinking of another old woman with a similar sobriquet. "Yes," he agrees, "it's a good name."

"Oh, by the way, Walter," Regina says, as she returns to the kitchen to resume frying the ground beef. "The hospital called this morning. Uncle Axel died during the night."

He raises an eyebrow and sighs. "Well, Mother, if you want to go to the funeral, I'll . . . I'll take you. I'm coming back Sunday night to bring Dee home . . ."

"Oh, no." She's thought about this. She's made her decision. "I've no intention of going. I'm not even sure there will be a funeral. *I'm* certainly not going to arrange one. I did my part. For many, *many* years, I did my part. More than I *should* have, I suppose." She sighs. "He wasn't very nice to me, or to you, either."

Wally approaches her. She's dumping in a can of Franco-American into the skillet. "Mother," he says tentatively, "before I go back to the city, I want to—I want to make sure that you're okay."

She smiles. "I'm fine, Walter."

"I'm just worried that—" Wally stops, looking back over at Jorge and Dee, then returning his gaze to his mother. "I don't think anybody will be bothering you anymore about Kyle, but if they do—"

"If they do . . ." she echoes, holding his eyes.

"Mother," Wally asks, "do you have any idea where Kyle might have gone to?"

Her eyes flicker away.

"Mother, do you?"

Why shouldn't she tell him? He's her son. She can't keep hiding it.

"Jorge," she says, "why don't you take Donald outside and show him the magic castles you told me about? The ones in the air that only you can see?"

"Kay Missa!"

She smiles. "Maybe Donald will be able to see them, too, because he's still young, and I think only young people can see magic castles in the air."

Dee looks oddly at Wally, but accepts the little boy's hand when it is offered, and follows him out the back door into the yard.

"Walter," Regina says, turning back to her son when they are alone, "I *do* know what happened to Kyle."

"For God's sake, tell me."

"I killed him, Walter."

"Mother!"

"I did." She stirs the goulash once more, then turns off the flame. She doesn't tremble. She holds her chin steady and takes a deep breath.

"I killed him in there," she says, pointing toward the living room. "On the couch, while he slept. I came in with the hoe and crashed it down into his head."

"Mother!"

"If they find out, I only hope it's after Jorge is gone. After he's joined Luz in the city. Because I wouldn't want—"

"Mother, stop it."

Regina looks up into her son's face.

"You didn't kill him, Mother."

"Oh, but I did . . ."

"No, you *didn't*, Mother. You're confused. This is why you need to take your pills."

"Oh, but I do take them. And I *did* kill him, Walter, I did . . ."

Her son is leaning in close to her now. "Mother, listen to me. Don't you see? Luz has gone off with him. You can't believe her story that she just went off to the city to become a model. She's with Kyle. They planned this together. She's off with him now—"

"No," Regina says. The thought is monstrous. "Luz wouldn't—she wouldn't do that—she didn't want to go with him—she took the money from me so she could go to the city and become famous . . ."

"She took money from you?"

Regina looks up into her son's eyes.

"I *did* kill Kyle, Walter," she says, getting more agitated now, losing her calm. "I came in with the hoe and smashed it down into his head. Then I dragged his body—"

Wally can feel sweat breaking out all over his body. "Mother, it's a physical impossibility. Look at you. Your arthritis, the way it pains you. You could never have lifted that hoe over your head, let alone dragged his body."

"But I did. I lifted the hoe—or maybe it was the shovel—"

"You see, Mother, how confused you are?"

She fights to keep the thoughts and images clear, the words from getting all tangled up in her mind. "I dragged him down to—to the *basement*, Walter, and I put his body in that crate—"

"Mother, I *looked* in the crate. There was no body."

Now she trembles. Now her whole body is beginning to shudder, her heart pounding in her ears.

"No, I mean in the shed—no, I buried him—"

"Mother, stop this."

"I *did* kill him! I did!"

She begins to cry. Wally takes his mother by the shoulders.

"Mother, you did *not* kill Kyle. You just *wanted* to kill him. And God knows, with reason. But you didn't. You've imagined it. This is just another trick of your mind. Look at me, Mother. Our minds play tricks on us. Yours has played tricks before, hasn't it? You were committed to a mental hospital . . ."

"It was a spa . . ."

"Mother, you can't afford to indulge your fantasies. Not anymore. Not with that asshole Garafolo prowling around. You're only guilty of being highly susceptible to the power of suggestion."

"No, Walter, you don't know—"

"I *do* know, Mother. I'm just like you! I had my own delusions, my own fantasies, after Ned died. They had to put me away, too, Mother. I had my own time at the funny farm."

She looks at her son. "Walter . . ." she says, reaching out to take his hand.

He hadn't meant to tell her that. But it was out there now.

"So we've got to keep our heads clear, Mother," he tells her. "You did *not* kill Kyle. You only imagined you did. Kyle was on the run. He thought he'd beaten a kid to death. He was looking to escape. *You did not kill him!*"

Suddenly she pulls herself away from him. It's a violent move, fierce, furious.

"Don't take this away from me, Walter!" she hisses. "Don't you *dare* take it away from me!"

Wally backs away, stunned.

Regina moves across the kitchen, a tigress, a seething, rageful she-devil, like nothing her son ever remembers seeing before.

She raises herself to her full height, her chin in the air, her jaws clenched tightly. "Don't stand there trying to take it away from me! The way every man in my life has taken everything! Taken everything that ever mattered to me!"

"Mother—"

She pushes away his hands. "Like Papa—what he took—what he did—"

The memories rush into her head like a pack of mad dogs.

"Like Robert—taking everything—*everything* away from me! Like all the others! All the *men!*"

She claps her hands over her ears.

"All the men," she repeats, crying now.

Wally can't speak for a moment. Then he reaches out his hand.

"Not this man," he tries, softly.

"It's the only thing I ever did!" She flares up again and her eyes flash at him. "*The only thing!* Don't take that away from me, Walter! It's the only time I ever stood up and said *no!* The only time I ever made anything *right!*"

She strides once more across the room, then turns to look back at Walter.

"If I hadn't killed him, he'd have taken Luz to Mexico. She would never have made it to the city! Never become famous! I saved her, Walter! I did it for her! She would have been trapped here otherwise. Trapped like I was, Walter, all those years!"

Wally tries to make sense of what his mother is saying. "What are you talking about, Mother? What do you mean by Mexico? Is that where Kyle is?"

"He's in *hell,* Walter! *Burning in hell* with all the rest of them!"

Wally looks over at his mother, at this wild-eyed creature who stands in front of him. He doesn't know her. But then, he never has.

"Don't take it away from me, Walter," she says, her voice breaking, her posture softening.

He touches her face with his hand. "All right," he says. "I won't take it away from you."

"Thank you," she says, softly now.

Wally stares into her blue eyes. They're quiet for several moments, just looking at each other.

"Who are you, Regina?" Wally finally asks, his hand gently touching the gray hair that's pulled back from her face. "Who lives inside there? Where have you been? What have you seen?"

She just blinks.

"I've never known," he says. "Never known."

No, he hasn't, Regina supposes. For seventeen years they had shared one bathroom in this little house, one toilet, one bathtub. They ate their meals together. They slept in beds separated by only the flimsiest of plywood walls. But never had he known who she was, and she had never known him.

Regina lifts her hand to press against the one her son has placed upon her cheek.

"Perhaps," he's saying, "perhaps I can come back . . . and begin to find out?"

"Yes, Wally," Regina says, tightening her grip on her son's hand. "Maybe we can both . . . find out."

Dee's tooting the car horn from the driveway.

Wally turns to his mother as he stands with her in the doorway. "Are you sure you're going to be all right? Taking care of the boy?"

She smiles up at him. "I like having him here. I can do it, Wally. I raised you, didn't I? And look how wonderful and successful you turned out."

There's nothing ironic about her words. Wally just sighs. "I'll stop by on Monday, Mother," he tells her.

"But the wood, Walter. You promised you'd bring the wood down to the basement."

"Oh, of course."

She smiles. "You're a good boy, Walter."

He holds her gaze.

Outside the wind smacks him hard against the face, a chill wiggling down the back of his shirt. He gives Dee a sign just to wait one more minute and hurries out to the backyard, where, against the fence, the firewood is stacked in a neat pile. Wally bends down and lifts several pieces under his arm. He grips the door of the bulkhead with his free hand, yanking it open. The wind almost immediately blows the door shut again; Wally has to hang on tight to keep the door in his grip. It sure *is* getting cold. But in a few moments, he knows, his mother will have the woodstove blazing, and it will pump warmth throughout her house. She'll snuggle up with her orange tea and graham crackers and she'll be warm. It makes Wally happy to know this.

He makes nine trips in all, hauling armfuls of wood down into the basement. He drops them in front of the stove, like offerings to some beneficent fire god. It's a big, squatting iron monster, the stove—twenty years old or more, with a large hatch on its side leading to its oven.

"Walter." His mother's voice calls down the cellar steps. It's a calm, cool voice, so unlike the shrillness of just a few moments before.

He looks up. She stands silhouetted at the top of the stairs.

"Yes, Mother?" Wally calls back.

"Will you get the fire going for me? Save me a trip down the stairs?"

"Sure."

"Thank you, Walter."

Upstairs he can hear her teakettle starting to shriek.

He bends over, feeling a twinge of—what?—arthritis, this early?—in his hip. But he disregards the pain, taking hold of several pieces of firewood. He pulls down the iron handle of the stove, and with a hiss and a screech, opens the door, throwing in the wood.

It's a flash of color that he sees.

A flash of—something.

But whatever he saw in the stove before he threw in the wood, it's covered now.

He stares into the gaping hatch.

What *was* it?

What did he think he saw in there?

Nothing. It was nothing.

A sneaker.

No, it wasn't a sneaker. That's ridiculous. It wasn't a sneaker, and it certainly wasn't a *foot*—protruding from the ashes and woodchips and crumpled newspaper.

Now whose mind is playing tricks?

Now who's being susceptible to the power of suggestion?

Upstairs the teakettle is still shrieking on the stove.

So move the wood, he tells himself, *if you want to be sure. Move the wood aside and see what's underneath.*

"Will you fire it up, Walter?" his mother calls again from the top of the stairs. Her voice is calm, careful, deliberate.

So move the wood.

He can't budge from where he stands, can't even lift an arm.

"Yes, Mother," he finally manages to call back. "I'll fire it up."

But he just keeps staring at the stove, listening to the teakettle whistling upstairs.

Then, one by one, he loads the furnace with the rest of the wood, and sets it ablaze.

"All ready?" Dee asks.

"Yeah," Wally says, sliding in behind the wheel. "All ready."

Regina has come out onto the front porch.

"Wave to my mother," Wally says.

"See ya later, Mrs. Day!" Dee calls from the window.

Regina waves back. Even blows them a kiss.

Above her, the chimney is beginning to puff dark gray smoke. The smoke drifts over the neighborhood, out from their little cul-de-sac toward Washington Avenue, down to Main Street, over the orchards, and into the swamps of Dogtown. Wally had loaded the furnace with enough wood to keep the fire burning, hot and ferocious, all day long, maybe well into the night. All that will be left when it's done will be soot and ashes. And Monday night, when he stops by again to talk with his mother, to have maybe the first real talk they've ever had in their lives, he'll load it up again, get that stove blazing hot once more. His mother's house will be warm and toasty when they sit down, with orange tea and graham crackers, and begin finding out who each other really are.

"So how long does it take to get to the city?" Dee asks, leaning up next to Wally's ear, startling him just a little.

"Oh, not long. It's a world away but not very far."

Dee slides back over to the window, watching the buildings of Brown's Mill pass by. "Good-bye Dogtown! Good-bye Main Street! Good-bye, good-bye, good-bye!"

They pull onto the highway, leading up over the hill.

"So what are we going to do first when we get there?" Dee asks.

"Anything you want, babe. Anything at all. Sky's the limit." Wally smiles, looking over at him. "This is going to be everything I've told you it'll be."

He returns his eyes to the road heading out of town.

"It's going to be grand."

ACKNOWLEDGMENTS

As always, thanks to my indulgent and thoughtful editor, John Scognamiglio; my industrious agent, Malaga Baldi; my partner, soulmate, and husband, Timothy Huber; and—especially—my loyal readers. You can reach me at www.williamjmann.com.

ABOUT THE AUTHOR

William J. Mann is best known for his studies of Hollywood and the American film industry, especially *Kate: The Woman Who Was Hepburn*, named a Notable Book of 2006 by the *New York Times*, and *Hello Gorgeous: Becoming Barbra Streisand*. He is also the author of *Wisecracker: The Life and Times of William Haines*, for which he won the Lambda Literary Award, *Behind the Screen: How Gays and Lesbians Shaped Hollywood*, *Edge of Midnight: The Life of John Schlesinger*, and *How to Be a Movie Star: Elizabeth Taylor in Hollywood*, which *Publishers Weekly* described as "like gorging on a chocolate sundae."

WILLIAM MANN

FROM OPEN ROAD MEDIA

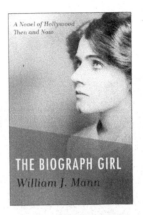

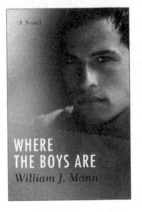

OPEN ROAD

INTEGRATED MEDIA

INTEGRATED MEDIA